Coloring Whiteness

THEATER: THEORY/TEXT/PERFORMANCE
Series Editors: David Krasner and Rebecca Schneider
Founding Editor: Enoch Brater

Recent Titles:

Cutting Performances: Collage Events, Feminist Artists, and the American Avant-Garde
  by James M. Harding

Illusive Utopia: Theater, Film, and Everyday Performance in North Korea
  by Suk-Young Kim

Embodying Black Experience: Stillness, Critical Memory, and the Black Body
  by Harvey Young

No Safe Spaces: Re-casting Race, Ethnicity, and Nationality in American Theater
  by Angela C. Pao

Artaud and His Doubles by Kimberly Jannarone

The Problem of the Color[blind]: Racial Transgression and the Politics of Black Performance by Brandi Wilkins Catanese

The Sarah Siddons Audio Files: Romanticism and the Lost Voice
  by Judith Pascoe

Paul Robeson and the Cold War Performance Complex: Race, Madness, Activism
  by Tony Perucci

Passionate Amateurs: Theatre, Communism, and Love
  by Nicholas Ridout

Dark Matter: Invisibility in Drama, Theater, and Performance
  by Andrew Sofer

Simming: Participatory Performance and the Making of Meaning
  by Scott Magelssen

Acts: Theater, Philosophy, and the Performing Self
  by Tzachi Zamir

The Captive Stage: Performance and the Proslavery Imagination of the Antebellum North
  by Douglas A. Jones, Jr.

Coloring Whiteness: Acts of Critique in Black Performance
  by Faedra Chatard Carpenter

Coloring Whiteness

ACTS OF CRITIQUE IN
BLACK PERFORMANCE

Faedra Chatard Carpenter

The University of Michigan Press
Ann Arbor

Copyright © by Faedra Chatard Carpenter 2014
All rights reserved

This book may not be reproduced, in whole or in part, including illustrations, in any form (beyond that copying permitted by Sections 107 and 108 of the U.S. Copyright Law and except by reviewers for the public press), without written permission from the publisher.

Published in the United States of America by
The University of Michigan Press
Manufactured in the United States of America
♾ Printed on acid-free paper

2017   2016   2015   2014   4   3   2   1

A CIP catalog record for this book is available from the British Library.

ISBN 978-0-472-07236-1 (hardcover)
ISBN 978-0-472-05236-3 (paperback)
ISBN 978-0-472-12065-9 (e-book)

For my parents,
Dr. Patricia Myrl White Chatard
and
Dr. Peter Ralph Noel Chatard Jr.

Acknowledgments

If I had the space to thank all those who made the journey toward this book possible, my acknowledgments section would rival the length of a chapter. While I hope to thank every person who has touched my process in some way, I would like to take this opportunity to recognize those whose impact has been most direct.

I am among a staggering number of academics and artists who have flourished under the astute and infinitely generous direction of Harry J. Elam Jr. I diligently strive to perform with the same strength and compassion that Professor Elam always exhibits. I have also been blessed with a small but dynamic cadre of mentors whose expertise and long-standing support have been vital to my growth as a dramaturg, teacher, and scholar. To Sydné Mahone, Carlton and Barbara Molette, and Caleen Sinnette Jennings I extend my heartfelt gratitude.

I have gained invaluable insight from countless collegial exchanges, beginning with my professors and fellow students at Stanford University. I am especially grateful to my cohort members, Jisha Menon (whose theoretical mind never ceases to amaze me) and the luminous Brandi Wilkins Catanese (my conference buddy, sounding board, and nerve calmer for over a decade). I am thankful and glad for the goodwill and good works of Tori Bailey, Miya Gray, Nicole Fleetwood, Lawrence Neeley, Lisa Thompson, and Tim'm West. Beyond Stanford's campus, E. Patrick Johnson, David Krasner, Sandra G. Shannon, and Sandra L. Richards have served as beacons of inspiration, and I have been further fortified by the genuine warmth and thought-provoking scholarship of colleagues such as Adrienne Braconi, Monica Ndounou, and the ever-impressive Harvey Young.

On arriving at the University of Maryland, College Park, I was welcomed into a community of dynamic faculty, staff, and students. Frank Hildy, Heather Nathans, Catherine Schuler, and Dan Wagner all led different legs of my course through UMD. Special thanks go to Stephanie Bergwall, Bonnie Thornton Dill, Laurie Frederik, Sandra Jackson, Esther Kim Lee, Sheri Parks, Rita Phelps, Scot Reese, Korey Rothman, Camilla Schlegel, Leigh Smiley, and Nancy Struna. To my Sister Scholars (aka Hilary Jones, Michelle Rowley, and Psyche Williams-Forson), please know what an honor it has been for me to sit at the table with you. And to Jeffrey McCune, thank-you for all our café conferencing (and for the title of this book)! I also celebrate the ingenious students at the University of Maryland. The queries, affirmations, and thoughtful contestations offered by my students have served to make me a better thinker, teacher, and communicator. In terms of institutional support for this manuscript, I am indebted to the funding I received from several University of Maryland programs. A Research and Scholarship Award (RASA) from The University of Maryland's Graduate School; a Faculty Seed Grant from The Consortium on Race, Gender, and Ethnicity (CGRE) and the Maryland Population Research Center (MPRC); and a DRIF Subvention Award from the College of Arts and Humanities offered me the time and fiscal support to complete this project.

Another community that has shaped my artistic and scholarly endeavors is the professional theatre community within and beyond the DC Metro region. Kwame Kwei-Armah, Karen Evans, Gregg Henry, Kim Peter Kovac, Deirdre Lavrakas, Irene Lewis, Jennifer Nelson, Ari Roth, and my treasured friend and colleague, Gavin Witt, have granted me immeasurable opportunities to work as a professional dramaturg in their esteemed institutions and programs, and I am exceedingly appreciative of these experiences. Buoyed by my membership in Literary Managers and Dramaturgs of the Americas (LMDA), I offer special thanks to Cindy SoRelle and Geoffrey Proehl for their leadership and guidance.

Understanding the inextricable connection between practice and theory is at the heart of this book, but at the very center are the artists themselves. To the practitioners who generously allowed me to interview them and share their words (Rayme Cornell, Walter Dallas, Lydia Diamond, Timothy Douglas, Nancy Giles, Jefferson Pinder, Carlos Russell, Daniel Tisdale, and Douglas Turner Ward), I hope you find this work to stand as due tribute to your rich contributions.

Of course, despite inspiration, ideas, and intentions, this book might never have been actualized without the enthusiasm and consistent encouragement of my lead editor, LeAnn Fields. From our very first meeting, LeAnn granted me a level of attention and consideration that writers dream of receiving. Further facilitating this process has been the gracious assistance of Alexa Ducsay and Marcia Labrenz, and the efficacious efforts of the appointed committees and editorial staff members at the University of Michigan Press. My appreciation extends to yet another publishing house, the Cambridge University Press, for allowing sections of my 2012 article "Spectacles of Whiteness from Adrienne Kennedy to Suzan-Lori Parks" to be reprinted with permission. I also thank Anita Grisales for editing several chapters of this book in its earlier form.

Finally, I relish the chance to thank the most important people in my life: my closest friends and family. Over the years I have learned that it takes a village to raise a child *and* it takes a village to birth a book. I am beholden to my local villagers—particularly the Jones family, the Brown family, and Laura Wilson Townsend—for helping me do both. Shona Jackson is unique among my compatriots, for she has been actively invested in my professional growth while also offering unconditional friendship. And for over twenty-five years, Laura Morse has cast the light I needed to engage with difficult introspection, entertain new possibilities, and erupt with outrageous laughter. As far as my family is concerned, I could not be more blessed. I have been embraced by my Carpenter family with unbridled affection, expressed most potently in the words and deeds of Carole Carpenter and Toni Primas. There is also great comfort in knowing that my sisters, Andrea and Tahra Chatard, are always there if I need them. My parents, Peter and Patricia Chatard, are models for parental and personal achievement; they simultaneously exemplify abiding love and support *and* an unrelenting drive for excellence.

But it is to my husband, Don, and my children, Trey and Kendall, to whom I must express the most profound gratitude. Ironically, you are among those who may never find a need for this project, yet your lives were affected the most by its production. Admittedly, I have spent an inordinate amount of time in front of the computer screen these past few years, but you have always been there to remind me of what is most precious. So I thank you for all the times you exercised thoughtful, measured patience—and all the times you forced me to break away, breathe, and play.

Contents

INTRODUCTION: Dramaturgies of Whiteness in Contemporary African American Performance — 1

CHAPTER ONE Douglas Turner Ward's Play on Whiteness: *Day of Absence* on America's Public Stages — 30

CHAPTER TWO Staging Hegemonic Whiteness: *The Bluest Eye* and the Performative Paradoxes of (In)visibility — 80

CHAPTER THREE Whiteness as "Becoming": The Corporeal Crossovers of Daniel Tisdale and Michael Jackson — 117

CHAPTER FOUR "Mixing It Up": Enacting Whiteness in the Comedic World of Dave Chappelle — 161

CHAPTER FIVE "Sounding Off on Sounding White": Aural Whiteness, Linguistic Whiteface, and the Economics of Opportunity — 194

CODA: Whiteface to Postrace? The Artful Interrogations of Jefferson Pinder — 225

Notes — 239

Bibliography — 279

Index — 293

Introduction
Dramaturgies of Whiteness in Contemporary African American Performance

A few years ago, while preparing a lecture on political theatre in the 1960s, I turned to my bookshelf to find *The Civil Rights Movement: A Photographic History, 1954–68*.[1] As I flipped through its pages, I was struck by a particularly powerful image that I had largely overlooked earlier. The photograph features several young black men on the historic, suffrage-driven march across Alabama in 1965. Among them, downstage, is a figure ostensibly in "whiteface"; coating the marcher's brown face is what appears to be a thick layer of opaque white cream. Using his face as a canvas and the cream as paint, the word *VOTE* is written on his forehead.

This picture—and the other photographs taken of the young man during that particular march—are stunning whiteface performances that animate the subject of this book: portrayals of whiteness in contemporary African American art and performance. Art scholar Cherise Smith, writing about one of the photos, aptly observes how the contrast "makes the youth appear ghostly," while the "imaging of 'whiteface' dramatizes the racial politics of the march."[2] These images serve as rich symbols of a specific moment in American history and as metaphors for the civil inequities that still trouble us today.

Smith's observations concisely describe the power and meaning conveyed by these riveting images. On the most obvious level, the young man's use of white cream serves as a symbol of the civil rights era and the struggle for black suffrage by vividly animating the all too common, white against

USA, Alabama. Selma March 1965. (Bruce Davidson, Magnum Photos, USA.)

black, day-to-day racial dynamics of the 1960s. Smith's reference to the figure's ghostly appearance resonates in another way, reminding viewers of the epic violence and brutalities civil rights workers faced, as well as of the injustices that still haunt our present. Most potent is that the striking contrast between the ultrawhite substance and the youth's brown skin capitalizes on our awareness—and perpetuation—of racial binaries, underscoring persistent perceptions of difference and disparity.

The picture's content and context capture this dissonance: the marchers are fighting against institutionalized and systematic oppression. After all, those outside of America's privileged communities had long been denied the ability to vote, and this denial was often perniciously linked to the issue of literacy. Thus, this photograph captures an extraordinarily poetic performance: the whiteness that covers this young man is literally—and through the "literary"—curtailed, written on, and revised by his act of intervention and resistance. The young man's corporeal blackness is seen underneath the "VOTE" scrawl; his insistent black presence is breaking through a whiteness that previously obscured black political visibility.

And finally, in this photo the youth's eyes are actually directed *away* from his most obvious audience member—the photographer. This instant catches the young man in a moment of expressive action. With his mouth parted as if in the midst of a song, conversational response, or aural charge, he wears the whiteface with a spirited, politicized, and activated intention. His whitened veneer does not seek to gain a black audience's approval or appreciation, nor does it aim to taunt a white audience by creating discomfort or disregard. Within this political performance, whiteface is not used as a reductive condemnation of white people, nor is it simply a recontextualized, reactive response to the use of blackface minstrelsy. Rather, the marcher's strategic, utilitarian use of whiteness is a call for humanity, equity, and justice for both blacks and whites. The visual potency of symbolic whiteness is used proactively to reenvision racial dynamics and resonates as a signal on both sides of the racial divide. In fact, the very ability to visualize and translate the "VOTE" message to a viewing audience is contingent on a relationship between black and white. Like the Civil Rights Movement itself, in order for the young advocate's message to be observed, black and white must work together on a corporeal canvas to translate intentions and achieve results.

From the political impulse that inspired the young marcher's presentation to the metaphoric resonance found in his display of whiteface to the style and nature of the picture's embedded signs, the photograph's portrayal of whiteness parallels several understudied expressions found throughout African American performance. *Coloring Whiteness: Acts of Critique in Black Performance* aims to bring critical attention to these types of expression by examining how African American playwrights, performers, and visual artists use conceits of whiteness to comment on racialized conditions, circumstances, and identities rather than making rigid determinations about raced bodies. Exploring a variety of artistic genres and forms, this book investigates enactments of whiteness, ranging from the use of white makeup and suggestive masks to literary motifs and cultural narratives regarding "white" characteristics and qualities. A shared component of the texts studied here is their use of dramaturgical strategies to make whiteness "strange," thereby revealing it as a social, political, and economic construct. Thus, the critical analysis throughout *Coloring Whiteness* explores how African American artists resist the presentation of whiteness as normative and, in the process, expose the fallacies associated with racial designations.

Reading an eclectic mix of images and texts against and through each other, *Coloring Whiteness* examines presentations and perceptions of whiteness in plays, TV journalism, comedy sketches, street theatre, visual art, videos, and voice-over work from 1964 to 2008. The year 1964 offers a useful starting point for this project. In terms of theatre, it marks the national debut of Adrienne Kennedy's *Funnyhouse of a Negro*—an important text to consider when investigating portrayals of whiteness in African American performance. Of course, *Funnyhouse* was not the first African American play to theatricalize whiteness, but it does stand as a definitive work within the canon of such texts. Kennedy's *Funnyhouse* is a paradigmatic play, notable for its innovative structure and well-documented influence and—most relevant to this study—pioneering in its cutting-edge consideration of racial identity (aspects I discuss at greater length later in this introduction). Through its troubled protagonist, *Funnyhouse of a Negro* interrogates the complexities of identity formation, thereby standing in opposition to the popular, yet far less nuanced, sentiments of its era. Broadly speaking, the culture of 1960s America emphasized the bifurcated duality of black and white, categorical divisions that were underscored by the politically charged events of the Civil Rights Movement, as well as Black Power and the Black Arts Movement. These real-life happenings—enacted and scripted on the national stage—stood in contradistinction to the atypical considerations revealed in Kennedy's canonical play.

Just as *Funnyhouse of a Negro* offered evidence of ideological shifts within America's expressive culture, 1964 also marked discernible shifts within America's political landscape. The Civil Rights Act of 1964 was a monumental piece of legislation in the interest of racial equality and tolerance. Moreover, it helped to propel and inspire other sociopolitical interventions and movements. For example, both the Feminist Movement (second and third waves) and the Gay Liberation Movement of the 1960s and 1970s benefited from the momentum and gains garnered by earlier civil rights activism. Recognizing that these intersecting energies inform the evolution of identity politics in America, *Coloring Whiteness* also considers how readings of gender and sexuality influence our racial constructs. Consequently, while perceptions of race delineate the conceptual parameters of *Coloring Whiteness*, I advance my analyses of whiteface and whiteness through the acknowledgment of these other historicized struggles and their complementary explorations of class, gender, and sexuality.

The proliferation of both legal and popular positions regarding human difference underscores the fact that people often possess—and seek to claim—a syncretic or fluid sense of identity. This reality challenges America's antiquated allegiance to singular identificatory markers, a fact that is resolutely signified by the ever-increasing interest in multiraciality and "mixedness." With respect to this, *Coloring Whiteness* directly wrestles with notions of mixedness as well as "postrace" ideologies. Unsurprisingly, the attention paid to multiracial identities and postracial sensibilities increased exponentially due to the historic presidential campaign and eventual election of President Barack Obama in 2008. Thus, by critiquing select performances of whiteface and whiteness from 1964 to 2008, my study explores artistic texts that were created shortly after the legal (though not necessarily actualized) demise of racial segregation through a time in which racial discourse regarding mixedness and postraciality dominated the public imagination. Accordingly, my significant bookend dates of 1964–2008 (from the Civil Rights Movement to the election of President Obama) offer *Coloring Whiteness* a prolific yet focused frame in which to consider the tensions and theories within American identity politics.

Notably, *Coloring Whiteness* investigates both familiar dramatizations of whiteness and underinterrogated enactments, contributing to ongoing dialogues regarding the role of performance in the construction of racial projects.[3] While encouraging both scholars and practitioners to reconsider and redirect the various ways in which racialized identities are constituted in contemporary art and everyday life, this project aims to disrupt easy assumptions regarding cultural productions that employ signatures of whiteness and/or racialized iconography. As exemplars of creative expression and social critique, the works featured here challenge both academics and artists to reimagine how the practice of theories and the theories of practice can revise antiquated and/or erroneous racial narratives.

BLACKNESS THROUGH WHITENESS: CRITICAL EXPLORATIONS

Despite the inherent significance of black performance within scholarly discourse, forging due space at the academic table for the study of black performance has been a long-standing endeavor. Addressing the academy's initial reticence to embrace this line of inquiry, E. Patrick Johnson writes:

> While black performance has been a sustaining and galvanizing force of black culture and a contributor to world culture at large, it has not always been recognized as a site of theorization in the academy. Similarly

marginalized as the black bodies with which it is associated, black performance, while always already embedded within institutionally sanctioned and privileged forms of performance, has often been neglected as a intellectual site of inquiry.[4]

This book contributes to the remediation of this institutionalized neglect and, in doing so, is beholden to countless scholars whose pioneering efforts and innovative conjectures inspire my own interest and methodological approaches in the study of African American performance. With a recent groundswell of texts addressing black performance, *Coloring Whiteness* is buoyed by an integrated wave of critical race theory and performance scholarship. As a beneficiary of these ever-proliferating areas of study, I am indebted to the work to which this book corresponds and responds.

Among the ideas with which *Coloring Whiteness* engages is E. Patrick Johnson's treatment of "appropriation" in relation to the performance of racialized identities. In his oft-referenced text *Appropriating Blackness: Performance and the Politics of Authenticity*, Johnson asserts that "'blackness' does not belong to any one individual or group. Rather, individuals or groups appropriate this complex and nuanced racial signifier in order to circumscribe its boundaries or to exclude other individuals or groups."[5] In signifyin(g) on Johnson (i.e., repeating his assertion with a signal difference), I would suggest that the same observation can be made in regard to whiteness.[6] Like blackness, whiteness—also a complex and nuanced racial signifier—can be appropriated in order to demarcate racial and cultural differences. For example, this book project explores how African American artists appropriate signs of whiteness in order to interrogate and disturb the boundaries and circumscriptions that have historically privileged whiteness over blackness. The fruit of this artistic labor animates Johnson's declaration that performance is not only "useful in deconstructing essential notions of selfhood" but it "must also provide a space for meaningful resistance to oppressive systems."[7]

In a similar vein, the work of Harvey Young also recognizes the constructed nature of racial identification, as well as how embodied presentations can verify or trouble oppressive ideologies within the world of theatre and everyday life. In *Embodying Black Experience: Stillness, Critical Memory, and the Black Body*, Young reminds us of Pierre Bourdieu's employment of habitus, noting that "social expectations are incorporated into the individual, and the individual projects those expectations back upon society (and other individuals)."[8] As Young explains, when someone claims (or is cast into) a particular social category, society teaches that individual how to behave, and the resulting performances are deemed either befitting or unbefitting by one's social network. A dynamic process, habitus is dependent on rearticulations of behavior—"habit" versus conscious reenactments. In order for this process to be effective and actualized, we cannot be conscious of our performances; we must forget that we are "performing."

Through his own careful rearticulation of Bourdieu's habitus, Young employs the idea of "black habitus" to reference how the black body is "socially constructed and continually constructing its own self."[9] Recognizing the way in which Young's black habitus works, one could extend the concept to the various expressions of whiteface and whiteness featured in this book, thereby expanding the notion to encompass other racialized presentations. In the select case studies presented here, projections of whiteness—particularly as they are devised and disseminated in contrast to blackness—ultimately reveal how society has historically read and understood racial difference while also suggesting how black people should understand and see themselves. The spectacles and manifestations of whiteness discussed in this book animate DuBoisian doubleness in a highly expressive way. With a playful consciousness, deliberate and popularized constructions of whiteness exploit and resist the "regulated improvisation" of racial habitus as embodied within staged performances or experienced in our day-to-day lives.[10]

While Young's work suggests how the awareness of racial habitus can destabilize assumptions, Brandi Wilkins Catanese calls for a similar contravening cognizance through an appeal for "racial transgression." In explicating her notion of racial transgression, Catanese examines how casting and roleplaying "expose the limits placed on racial discourse in order to violate them and force the possibility of progressive action."[11] In a similar vein, I take a turn toward the issue of casting to further consider how casting decisions can disrupt familiar expectations regarding racialized performance. While I do this by drawing attention to the understudied possibilities created by audible (rather than embodied) performances, Catanese's interrogation of casting practices inexorably enriches my own thinking. Case in point: among Catanese's many astute assertions is that *nonconforming casting* is a more nuanced turn of phrase than "nontraditional casting." In complete agreement, I follow her lead and adopt the term *nonconforming* in constructing my own understanding of *nonconforming whiteface*.

Although clearly situated within a genealogy of studies related to black performance culture and critical race theory, *Coloring Whiteness* is distinguished by its focus on whiteness. An important point to make, however, is that while all the performative texts in this book wrestle with whiteness, *Coloring Whiteness* is, unequivocally, not a book about white folk. On the contrary, it has relatively little to say about white people or the experiences of those who claim a self-appointed or socially sanctioned white identification. Rather, *Coloring Whiteness* is about contemporary African American cultural expression. It explores how self-identified African American artists and individuals express the intricacies of their own racial and cultural identities through (in relation to, and often because of) the social scripts and common tropes associated with whiteness. The case studies in this volume are concerned with understanding how abstract perceptions of whiteness affect the lives and experiences of black Americans, experiences that are documented through and by African American performance.

The performance texts in *Coloring Whiteness* explore expressions of whiteness in relation to blackness (and vice versa) while also interrogating *intraracial* dynamics within contemporary African American communities. Their enactments of whiteness, both conceptual and visual, create opportunities for audiences to consider the increasingly complicated ways in which racial and cultural identity is configured *within* the social networks of self-identified African Americans. Borrowing the words of E. Patrick Johnson, not only do the performances detailed here disclose how "blacks have used performance as epistemology and resistance,"[12] but these enactments of whiteness are prime examples of how "black performance provides a space for black culture to reveal itself to itself—to come to *know* itself, in the process of *doing*."[13] This knowing of self is, in part, propelled by a *consciousness* of double consciousness—an expressed understanding of the relationship and tensions between black and white, self and other.

While relatively few scholars have focused on the study of whiteness in American performance, there are innumerable theorists, scholars, and writers who have addressed themes of whiteness within the broader sphere of the American imagination. Among these cultural curators are oft-noted names such as W. E. B. DuBois, James Baldwin, Toni Morrison, bell hooks, Ruth Frankenberg, David R. Roediger, Tim Wise, and Matthew Wray. Writing with the spirit of advocacy and intervention, these philosophers, academics, and artist-activists are among those whose works have helped found and foster critical whiteness studies. As an academic field, critical whiteness studies is relatively new, but the critical study *of* whiteness has been in practice for as long as concepts of whiteness have shaped and impacted the material lives of nonwhites.[14]

The observations and questions raised through critical whiteness studies help to propel my readings of whiteness throughout this book. As a conceptual touchstone among many possibilities, my focus on whiteness within black performance culture reflects the fact that studying whiteness demands the recognition that whiteness is in constant negotiation with racialized perceptions of blackness. Likewise, the investigation that follows also pays due attention to the axes of gender, sexuality, and class—all of which are inextricably informed by notions of race. In terms of identifying the parameters of my critical turn to whiteness, *Coloring Whiteness* examines the social scripts and tropes that are frequently—but not always consciously—associated with whiteness. These include, but are not limited to, the ways in which whiteness is aligned with absence, normativity, supremacy, privilege, beauty, purity, terror, and death.

Reading tropes of whiteness within and through African American cultural expressions, this project understands whiteness as a fluctuating abstraction that fosters ideologies with both discursive and material consequences. Leaning on the words of critical whiteness theorist Ruth Frankenberg, *Coloring Whiteness* knows whiteness as "a location of structural advantage in societies structured in racial dominance."[15] As an ever-shifting descriptive, public understandings of whiteness are not static or void of contestation (they are influenced by the particulars of time and place), but what remains consistent is whiteness's nature of relativity. Whiteness is perceived to occupy the ultimate position of authority or dominance within Eurocentric, western societies. These societies, and often their representatives, exercise dominance rooted in and perpetuated by the fiscal inequities and economic exploitation inordinately confronted by non-European, raced bodies.

Whiteness, as a self-perpetuating, tautological dynamic of advantage and privilege, sustains itself through hegemonic sensibilities. Commonly understood as normative, whiteness has historically reigned as paradigmatic, presumably bearing or exuding model characteristics to which all humanity should ascribe. Accordingly, the identification of whiteness is often not racialized, but rather others are raced in relation to whiteness. This common, subliminal tendency equates whiteness with a standardized humanness (others are raced, but white people are just people). Subsequently, whiteness *is* by being what it *is not*.

In analyzing what whiteness is/is not, *Coloring Whiteness* examines both textual tropes and embodied enactments of whiteness, and a number of these latter expressions are conveyed through the use of theatrical whiteface. Whiteface, in common parlance, is hastily—and often erroneously—

identified as a simple inversion of blackface minstrelsy. While the 1990s witnessed a proliferation of scholars who addressed how blackface minstrelsy influenced the formation of racial, cultural, and national identities in America,[16] noticeably fewer scholars have addressed the equally provocative phenomenon of whiteface. Among the notable exceptions, however, are scholars such as Susan Gubar, David Krasner, Nadine George-Graves, Helene Gilbert, Mary Brewer, and Marvin McAllister.[17]

Of these, the book-length works of Mary Brewer and Marvin McAllister have been most significant in terms of addressing whiteness and whiteface in American performances. Brewer's *Staging Whiteness* (2005), to my knowledge, is the first book-length study of whiteness in contemporary drama.[18] Through her concise textual analyses of twenty-six plays, Brewer addresses how whiteness is portrayed in the work of twentieth-century American and British playwrights, exploring how the play texts reinforce and/or critically analyze representations of white power and privilege. The breadth of Brewer's study embraces manifold manifestations of whiteness, thereby highlighting its "historic malleability"—efforts that serve her aim to complicate perceptions of whiteness and reveal the mechanisms that perpetuate racist ideologies and structures. Similar to Brewer's work, *Coloring Whiteness* reveals varied and divergent enactments of whiteness. While my own study focuses on the expressions and advocacy of African American artists, I share Brewer's interest in complicating notions of race and disrupting racist belief systems.

A particularly impressive treatment of whiteface is Marvin McAllister's *Whiting Up: Whiteface Minstrels and Stage Europeans in African American Performance* (2011). Published shortly before I completed *Coloring Whiteness*, McAllister's *Whiting Up* is a fundamental contribution to the study of whiteface performance. *Whiting Up* continues McAllister's earlier explorations of nineteenth-century "whiteface minstrels" and "stage Europeans,"[19] and his expanded discussion of whiteface minstrelsy and stage Europeans from nineteenth-century black social performance to present-day art and entertainment is formative and illuminating. However, within the context of *Coloring Whiteness*, neither of McAllister's terms—*whiteface minstrelsy* and *stage European*—are appropriate descriptors for how I choose to distinguish between the whiteface enactments featured in this book.[20]

To that end, readers may notice that throughout *Coloring Whiteness* I avoid using the term *minstrelsy* in relation to whiteface performance, opting instead to use phrases such as "enactments of whiteness," "theatrical whiteface," and "presumed whiteness." My resolve is motivated by the concern that the term *minstrelsy* may too readily prompt readers to make assumptions or analogous associations between the histories and impulses of blackface minstrelsy and whiteface—a linkage that *Coloring Whiteness* aims to trouble. In addition, I recognize that the highly theatrical roots of the term *minstrelsy* may also, inadvertently, bring to mind the colloquial and stigmatizing description of "acting white"—an erroneous association that McAllister also cautions against in *Whiting Up*.[21] As I address in chapter 4, the notion of acting white has a complex idiomatic history. As a phrase that is bound to sentiments of rejection and accusation from both sides of the racial divide, the premise of acting white is based on the debilitating fallacy that class-related expressions of cultural capital are a consequence of one's racial identity. My attempt to circumvent undue correlations between the performances and portrayals in this study and acting white is yet another reason why I choose not to use the term *minstrelsy* in relation to the enactments featured here.[22]

Building on the innovative scholarship that precedes me, as well as the ever-increasing interest in transracial performance, *Coloring Whiteness* offers critical observations and asks significant questions in order to reimagine and reinscribe the ways we talk about these dramatic presentations. In doing so, another aim of this book is to detach transracial performance from unexamined assumptions regarding its insidious reputation. The long shadow of blackface minstrelsy should not make audiences instantly deem all transracial mimicry foul—transracial performances are not, in themselves, inherently problematic. Rather, much depends on the style of their execution, the content of their messages, and the realized intentions of their creators. While the scope of this project does not allow for a widespread examination of texts that recuperate transracial performance strategies for progressive or anti-inflammatory commentary,[23] it does focus on instances in which embodied presentations of whiteness work to counter, rather than affirm essentializing racial narratives.

This is not to say that the irresponsible vacuity of traditional blackface minstrelsy cannot also be located in whiteface expressions (such performances would, according to my logic, then qualify as "whiteface minstrelsy"), but I argue throughout the breadth of *Coloring Whiteness* that the nature and impetus of the whiteface performances explored in this book are decidedly different. While blackface minstrelsy was often deployed to comment on the quality and value of differing bodies, the texts I study comment on the contrasting *experiences* of bodies due to racial designations.

Historically, blackface presentations enacted by white performers were utilized to circumscribe both black and white identities, thereby fixing public understandings of both blackness and whiteness. The satirical/critical use of contemporary whiteface, however, consciously interrogates *imagined* whiteness and institutionalized privilege rather than circumscribing a desired racialized image. So, while the whiteface performances discussed in this volume may "reverse" the performative principles of blackface, they do so in order to also *invert* the politicized intentions that helped motivate early blackface minstrelsy. Theatrical whiteface may embody a cultural critique of blackface minstrelsy (and, correspondingly, America's history of racism), but this signifyin(g) act is not analogous to a true reversal. Rather, theatrical whiteface consciously highlights and troubles abstractions of whiteness, thereby underscoring the constructed nature of *all* racial identities.

In other words, it is often the *idea* of whiteness as a social construct that is "put on trial" with the use of whiteface—a far different dynamic than the historic renditions of white blackface minstrels who mocked, parodied, and questioned black intellect and humanity. And, while scholars such as Eric Lott and W. T. Lhamon have revealed to us the ways in which blackface was used by white performers to wrestle with their own identificatory markers (e.g., class, masculinity, and nationalism), these expressions reflected deeply ingrained sentiments; they lacked the level of self-consciousness and self-reflexivity that seem ever present in contemporary whiteface performances. In fact, it is this self-reflexivity that is evidenced by a common characteristic of many whiteface enactments: they frequently offer purposeful deliberations regarding both *inter-* and *intracultural* dynamics. Thus, ironically, enactments of whiteness create opportunities for audiences to consider the increasingly complicated ways in which racial and cultural identity is configured within, as well as beyond, the social networks of black Americans.

DRAMATURGING WHITENESS: A METHODOLOGICAL ASIDE

Over the past nineteen years, I have had the good fortune to serve as a professional production dramaturg and/or professional play development dramaturg for a number of theatre organizations and companies.[24] *Coloring Whiteness* draws on these experiences just as much as it draws on my insight and training as an academic and educator. My practical involvement with embodied performance, audience reception, and the creative process inevitably shapes my research and scholarly writing. Moreover, my intimate experience with dramaturgical approaches and methodologies is particularly useful when it comes to analyzing whiteness as both a product and process of our social imaginations.

Synthesizing the scholarly and the artistic, a dramaturg strives to understand—and communicate—how creative expressions "work" in terms of both theory and practice. A key charge of the dramaturg is to recognize the various elements of a theatrical story (its unfolding narratives; its use of repetition, metaphor, and patterns; its use of sign and spectacle; its rules, according to the world of the play, etc.), as well as how these various elements work "from imagination to embodiment."[25] Moreover, as a bridge builder, a dramaturg facilitates productive exchanges between various individuals and working clusters to strengthen both the theatrical and metatheatrical event(s) in question. Fostering dialogue within and between groups (members of the creative team, the witnessing audience, the producing institution, and the community at large), the dramaturg facilitates activities that engender a deeper understanding of our culture, society, and communities.[26]

Many of the considerations that guide my analyses in *Coloring Whiteness* are the same types of queries and concerns that demand my attention when I serve as a dramaturg for theatrical productions. Among these provisional dramaturgical undertakings are (1) an acknowledgment of the time and context of the work's development or production; (2) textual analysis; (3) a concern for the embodied and enacted text, beyond its literary form; (4) a consideration of audience reception and the impact of artistic framing; (5) an awareness of interpretive possibilities versus interpretive absolutes; and (6) a consideration of the goals and intentions of the featured performers and art makers.[27]

The elastic aims described above give credence to the belief that acts of dramaturgy are often best illustrated through anecdotes and examples. Nevertheless, a collective understanding of dramaturgy is grounded in a basic, albeit pliable, concept: the practice of dramaturgy requires serious considerations regarding the creation, development, production, and reception of a performance text. Whiteness, on the other hand, alludes to the perceived possession of a European lineage and the ways in which Eurocentric markers secure and perpetuate racialized privilege. Bringing the practice of dramaturgy and the study of whiteness together, *Coloring Whiteness* "dramaturgs whiteness" by exploring the methodologies associated with the writing, development, production, and reception of performances that wrestle with whiteness as a social force and construct.

Less concrete, yet still worth noting, is what the theatre scholar Geoffrey S. Proehl would refer to as my critical engagement with a "dramaturgical sensibility."[28] Proehl uses the term *dramaturgical sensibility* to "talk about a kind of awareness that is as much felt as thought."[29] In my case, working directly with artists has fortified my predilection to resist offering prescriptions and declarative assertions over suggestions and impressions. While I share my readings of performance texts in *Coloring Whiteness*, I fully recognize that a number of factors inform my analyses, including my own politics of location and the time and context of a text's production, as well as my decision to analyze these particular texts alongside one another in this book. I offer my thoughts as contributions to a critical archive of analysis and inquiry while also trusting that this work will inspire other "producible interpretations." Propelled by my dramaturgical sensibility, I hope these explorations will subsidize the approaches and reception of practitioners and audiences, inspiring new ways for their creative experiences to be shaped and received.

My work as a dramaturg has also sensitized me to the great benefit of talking directly with the producing artists whenever possible. To that end, *Coloring Whiteness* is informed by original interviews with playwrights, directors, performers, and cultural critics. The inclusion of artists' voices is a valuable element in this study and, moreover, their perspectives help keep us mindful of the importance in acknowledging artistic intention when analyzing audience reception or formulating scholarly opinions. Well known is the fact that creators cannot ensure how audience members will receive any single, intended message. This, in part, is the wonder and frustration of art: the impact and meaning of its reception is shaped by its audience as well as its devisers. Quite often, however, our focus is placed on a spectator's judgment with relatively little attention paid to the art maker's vision. This is not always by design or choice—the opportunity to glean insight directly from art makers is often unavoidably inhibited by the parameters of time, place, and circumstance (as indicated by my fervent attempt, but eventual inability, to interview Dave Chappelle). Nevertheless, many of the artists featured in this book have generously shared their thoughts and visions, and I have tried to use these opportunities to strengthen this study as much as the circumstances of access have allowed.

ENACTING WHITENESS IN ADRIENNE KENNEDY'S
FUNNYHOUSE OF A NEGRO

When considering the nature and temporal span of my study, there is no performance text more exemplary of the whiteface enactments of which I speak than Adrienne Kennedy's *Funnyhouse of a Negro* (1964). Written in the midst of the Civil Rights Movement and the Black Arts Movement, *Funnyhouse of a Negro* erupted on the American stage at a time when ideas of blackness and whiteness were often treated as conceptual polarities in everyday life, as well as in our cultural productions. Kennedy's play, however, used motifs of whiteness to deconstruct the notion of racial binaries, and in doing so it forcefully demanded that audiences and critics alike reimagine the possibilities of black art *and* black identity. Thus, by including a dramaturgical reading of *Funnyhouse of a Negro* in this introduction, I hope to set the stage for this book's conceptual trajectory while also framing *Funnyhouse of a Negro* as a prime example of the multilayered ways that whiteness is expressed and analyzed throughout the pages of *Coloring Whiteness*.

A striking piece of contemporary African American theatre, *Funnyhouse of a Negro* dramatizes a world of fragmentation and confusion. Sarah, the play's protagonist, wrestles with her liminality—a sense of identity that straddles unyielding perceptions of black versus white. Obsessed with superficial and erroneous signifiers of whiteness (straight hair and "white" skin, a glorified British lineage, a university education), Sarah fears the things she associates with blackness (hairlessness and dark skin, stereotypes of an uncivilized ancestry, African masks) with equal fervor. Troubled by her inability to possess (or acquire) the requisite credentials to fit neatly within the parameters of whiteness, Sarah's beleaguered mental state is expressed through a pastiche of repeated narratives and grotesque imagery—all akin to the frenetic energy of a circus-styled "funnyhouse."[30]

Although Adrienne Kennedy's play won an Obie Award, the debut of *Funnyhouse* was, like the mental state of its protagonist, markedly uneven, and it garnered mixed reviews. Some black critics condemned the self-hatred expressed by the character of Sarah, while other audience members found the form of Kennedy's play—a dramatic structure that reflected the play's themes of fragmentation—too unconventional for their taste. Nevertheless, still other audience members found both the content and the form of *Funnyhouse of a Negro* fascinating—if not completely comprehensible. White critics were among those who overwhelmingly applauded Kennedy's work. An advertisement for the play in the January 17, 1964, edition of the *The New York Times* boasts a number of accolades for *Funnyhouse of a Negro*, calling Kennedy "a new playwright with a somberly original imagination" and "an author who has a mind of her own and a gift for burning eloquence."[31] However, a review by Howard Taubman of *The New York Times* reveals the ambivalences exposed by such praise.

> [A] relatively unknown territory is explored and exposed. Miss Kennedy, herself a Negro, digs unsparingly into Sarah's aching psyche—and by extension into the tortured mind of a Negro who cannot bear the burden of being a Negro and who is too proud to accept the patronage of the white world.
>
> Sarah, of course, is in extremis in her suffering, and it may even be suggested that her visions are those of one who is deranged. But one cannot doubt that in her intensity she reflects what it is to be a sensitive Negro.[32]

Expressing his intrigue with Sarah's turmoil, Taubman's commentary also reveals the distance of a white critic who is accustomed to viewing the Negro as other. Surmising that Sarah is "too proud to accept the patronage of the white world," Taubman implicitly offers two erroneous, but related, suggestions: (1) that the "white world" is actually offering Sarah some type of patronage, and (2) that it is Sarah's debilitating hubris—rather than her damaged self-esteem—that deters her from alleviating her own pain. And finally, the conjecture that Sarah is a "sensitive Negro" subtly suggests that her sensitivity—whether we are to interpret it as evidence of her humanity or her intellectual prowess—is atypical of most Negroes. Taubman's review, primarily descriptive, reflects a clumsy naïveté that justifies African American concerns regarding the reception of Kennedy's play.

For Adrienne Kennedy, however, the ultimate commercial and critical success of *Funnyhouse of a Negro* was tempered by the derision the play received from other African American artists and critics. Kennedy's own reflections, offered almost forty years later, reveal how deeply affected she was by the play's detractors. Despite garnering critical acclaim, Kennedy estimated that more than two thirds of her audience found *Funnyhouse of a Negro* detestable: "And I was torn apart by the people that hated it. They didn't like Sarah (the lead character in the play). They thought she was a disgraceful character, and they didn't like me. They thought I was just like

Sarah."[33] The fact that *Funnyhouse of a Negro* hit the stage just as the Black Arts Movement was gaining momentum certainly contributed to the harsh scrutiny it received. Produced in a time when slogans such as "Black Power" and "Black Is Beautiful" were fashioning the ideology of black American pop culture, some feared that Kennedy's play directly challenged the ideology of the Black Arts Movement by disclosing painful rifts within the African American community. Writes Robert Scanlan:

> The idea of accepting and embracing one's blackness, of celebrating it and elevating it to a place of pride and respect, might well suggest itself as a cure for the "state of mind" expressed in Kennedy's play, but she was not the one to suggest it. "Black is beautiful" was the new slogan emerging in the mid-sixties, and Kennedy's brutally frank expression of a black heroine's resentment of her black bloodlines in *Funnyhouse of a Negro* was out of sync with the emerging black politics of the time.[34]

Reinforcing the firsthand observations made by the original director of *Funnyhouse of a Negro*, Michael Kahn ("I think Adrienne was severely ostracized. Her plays were considered neurotic and ... not supportive of the black movement,"),[35] Scanlan's comments characterize how Kennedy's plays are habitually distinguished from the work typically associated with the Black Arts Movement.

What has come to light with time and retrospection, however, is that many critics may have failed to recognize the ways in which Kennedy's play followed the tenets of America's burgeoning black nationalism. Afrocentric critiques of Kennedy's play targeted the depiction of its protagonist's psychological exile from her African American identity. Sarah—a victim of societal racism and her own self-hatred—finds refuge through the creation of her alter egos: the Duchess of Hapsburg, Queen Victoria Regina, Jesus, and Patrice Lumumba.[36] This complex of character(s) certainly represents the protagonist's splintered psyche, but it also suggests the unavoidable disparities that exist within any self-defined community.

While the dramatic portrayal of self-hatred in *Funnyhouse of a Negro* was met with understandable resistance by nationalistic activists, artists, and citizens, Kennedy's work was far more aligned with the professed goals of the Black Arts Movement than is often credited. As Lotta M. Löfgren illustrates in her intertextual reading of LeRoi Jones's *Dutchman* and Kennedy's *The Owl Answers*, Kennedy's dramaturgy actualizes many of the tenets famously articulated in Jones's "The Revolutionary Theatre" and Larry Neal's "The Black Arts Movement."[37] During the era of the Black Arts Movement, both Jones (aka Amiri Baraka) and Neal critiqued notions of white cultural and spiritual superiority, with Neal famously asserting, "The motive behind the Black aesthetic is the destruction of the white thing, the destruction of white ideas, and white ways of looking at the world."[38] While the protagonist of *Funnyhouse of a Negro* clearly denigrates her blackness and idolizes whiteness, the play itself is equally rich with references that counter this sentiment. Throughout *Funnyhouse of a Negro*, Kennedy pointedly deconstructs and disempowers "the white thing" by staging both haunting and perverse images of whiteness.

One of the most visceral and immediate methods Kennedy uses to interrogate perceptions of whiteness in *Funnyhouse of a Negro* is through the play's use of what I refer to as "tinted whiteface" ("tinted" because, as noted in the stage directions, the whiteface is styled, in the words of Homi Bhabha, as "not quite white").[39] In describing the characters of Queen Victoria and the Duchess of Hapsburg, Kennedy writes:

> BOTH WOMEN *are dressed in royal gowns of white, a white similar to the white of the Curtain, the material of cheap satin. Their headpieces are white and of a net that falls over their faces. From beneath both their headpieces springs a headful of wild kinky hair. Although in this scene we do not see their faces, I will describe them now. They look exactly alike and will wear masks or be made up to appear a whitish yellow. It is an alabaster face, the skin drawn tightly over the high cheekbones, great dark eyes that seem gouged out of the head, a high forehead, a full red mouth and a head of frizzy hair. If the characters do not wear a mask then the face must be highly powdered and possess a hard expressionless quality and a stillness as in the face of death.*[40]

As described, Kennedy's portrayals of Queen Victoria and the Duchess of Hapsburg fully animate a number of tropes employed in critical whiteness studies: whiteness is not only presented as a constructed identity, but it is made hypervisible, strange, and even terrifying. Yet the playwright also deliberately notes that Victoria and the duchess "look exactly alike," thereby suggesting that whiteness, as a process and system of power, works in recurring and habitual ways.

Kennedy also offers potential producers two ways to connote the whiteness of these characters: through the masking properties of makeup or through the use of tangible masks. In both instances, the characters' highly visible "wild, kinky hair" becomes highlighted rather than visually suppressed. By offering audiences a persistent sign of the real body beneath the mask, Kennedy reminds us of the inescapably integrated (and miscegenated) reality of blacks and whites. These masking techniques bring attention to their own construction, thereby also emphasizing the fabricated nature of our racial identities.[41] To this end, Deborah Thompson observes the signifyin(g) strategy of Kennedy's whiteface, that is, the way in which Kennedy's whiteface *references* blackface minstrelsy by adopting its use of transracial mimicry while simultaneously *revising* its meanings through enactments of white, rather than black, representation.

> Adrienne Kennedy's *Funnyhouse of a Negro*, "Signifyin(g) upon" racism's master trope of minstrelsy, asks fundamental social, philosophical, and ontological questions about what "race" "is," how it comes to be reified, and how the impossible absolutes of "black" and "white" come to be internalized and even naturalized onto our skins and into our bodies.[42]

Affectively conveying the impossibility of racial absolutes, Kennedy posits her tinted whiteface as resistant to strict delineations. Rather than actually being white in hue, her whiteface is envisioned as a "whitish yellow" or "alabaster." This tinted whiteface further underscores the possibility of racial miscegenation and the impossibility of racial purity. Kennedy's use of tinted whiteface not only illustrates the fact that pure whiteness is a mythic notion (for both black and white bodies), but she also stages Richard Dyer's assertion that "We need to recognise white [is] a colour too."[43]

Moreover, Kennedy does not simply stage generic references to white people; her parodic dramatizations are focused on iconic, Eurocentric figures. Thus, her garish spectacles of whiteness continue to animate tropes of whiteness, the chosen subjects of her whiteface offering us compelling considerations. As referenced earlier, Queen Victoria and the Duchess of Hapsburg are loaded images when it comes to symbols of power. In the words of Jacqueline Wood, these characters "merge as loci of power informed by contemporary global experiences of patriarchal imperialism and racism. They are dominant white figures, superimposed upon blackness, symbolizing the political imposition of European power."[44] While the queen and duchess serve as symbols of colonialism and white domination, it should be noted that Kennedy's chosen characterizations are also commenting on the specific, personal narratives of these historical figures and, in doing so, further dismantle idealized perceptions of whiteness.

In the case of Queen Victoria, Kennedy's dramaturgical strategy is emboldened by the ways in which the queen exemplifies the height of Britain's colonial rule, while simultaneously representing the tenuous life of a royal figure.[45] A significant character in the annals of British history, Victoria represents the politically astute and influential historical period known as "The Victorian Age." Yet Victoria was also a woman who suffered from familial distress and bouts of debilitating depression during her reign. Relying heavily on the counsel of her prime ministers, Queen Victoria may have ensured the continuation of the monarchy despite its diminishing power; however, the fact remains that she was a symbolic, rather than political, leader. Thus, her life symbolizes yet another form of masking: a mask of power that obscured the virtual impotence of a constitutional monarchy.

Similarly, the Duchess of Hapsburg may represent the prestige and power associated with nobility, but her personal history echoes the precarious mental condition of Kennedy's protagonist. The duchess (also known as Carlotta) was first cousin to Queen Victoria. In 1864 Napoleon III appointed her and her husband, the Austrian archduke Maximilian, to the Mexican throne, leaving them penniless and powerless against Mexican revolutionaries.[46] Although the Duchess of Hapsburg began to display signs of mental illness, she traveled to Europe to request aid from Napoleon III and Pope Pius IX and eventually descended into full-blown schizophrenia.[47] While her husband was eventually tried for treason and executed by a Mexican military tribunal, Carlotta was diagnosed as incurably insane and spent her remaining years banished to her family's castle.[48] Carlotta's tragic story was dramatized in the 1939 motion picture *Juarez*, a film that so intrigued Adrienne Kennedy that she created the Duchess of Hapsburg character for *Funnyhouse of a Negro*.

Thus, rather than simply championing characters from the British monarchy, we can read Kennedy's dramatization of Victoria and the duchess as further evidence of the playwright's revisionist strategies. These royal representatives in *Funnyhouse of a Negro* symbolize British power, but they also symbolize the arbitrary and precarious nature of social status—befitting characters with which to question the assumed authority and idealized status of whiteness.

Just as Kennedy uses the queen and duchess to deromanticize idealized perceptions of whiteness, so does her inclusion of *"a hunchback, yellow-skinned"* Jesus. Described further as a *"dwarf, dressed in white rags and sandals,"*[49] Kennedy's Jesus, marked by tinted whiteface and disfigurement, rebukes modern representations of a white, beatified Jesus while also challenging notions regarding Christianity's inviolability. The misshapen and racially ambiguous Jesus violates the insistence on binary constructs such as good-evil, white-black, and normal-abnormal.[50] In addition, Jesus's embodiment—an amalgamation of various dichotomies—also speaks to the precarious and problematic role Christianity has played in the lives of enslaved and colonized people; he symbolizes Christianity as a comfort and form of liberation as well as a source of persecution and oppression. Subsequently, Kennedy's physical depiction of Jesus, with its antihegemonic hints of discord and resistance, signifies the potential for both racial and religious transgression.

While Kennedy's use of tinted whiteface is visibly articulated through her unconventional representations of Queen Victoria, the Duchess of Hapsburg, and Jesus, masks are also used throughout the play to interrogate and destabilize traditional notions of racial identity.[51] Even the various material possessions collected by Kennedy's protagonist can be seen as an attempt to mask evidence of her blackness. Desperate to acquire privileges associated with whiteness, Sarah adorns her small New York apartment with miscellany—photographs of castles and plaster statues—with hopes of obscuring the ways her raced body is perceived. Thus, the play's set—as representative of Sarah's troubled existence—exhibits its own form of masking. According to the stage directions, the setting of *Funnyhouse* simultaneously exalts and perverts whiteness. Kennedy describes the milieu as having *"unreal and ugly"* white light and *"ghastly white"* curtains like *"the interior of a cheap casket,"* all of which accentuates the *"unnatural BLACKNESS"* that swaths the stage space.[52]

Despite Sarah's maddening idealizations of whiteness, *Funnyhouse of a Negro* presents both whiteness and blackness as fabricated and affected. Although the accounts of Sarah and her various selves are framed as repeated and reenacted memories, their manifold contradictions purposefully emphasize the mutable nature of perception and reflection, most potently aggravating assumptions regarding racial absolutes. To that end, the various components of Kennedy's dramaturgical arsenal—including her conflicting plot line(s) and stage spectacles—all serve to deconstruct the notion of discrete and finite racial categories. In fact, as Claudia Barnett contends, Kennedy's dramaturgy actually challenges the significance of "the narrative" itself:

"[N]arratives are not the focus of [Kennedy's] plays.... She focuses instead on state of mind and of being—womanhood, fragmentation, longing—and thereby problematizes the very nature of narrative, diminishing its power by undermining its authority."[53] By undermining the authoritative status of the narrative, Kennedy underscores the uncertainty of her protagonist and deprivileges the problematic status of any singular accounts, including those related to the prioritization of whiteness and identity formation.[54]

My focused treatment of *Funnyhouse of a Negro* addresses a number of the thematic refrains analyzed in *Coloring Whiteness*. Tackling several tropes that arise within critical whiteness studies, Kennedy's dramatic narrative artfully animates the (anti)normativity of whiteness, the (de)privileging of whiteness, the (im)purity of whiteness, whiteness as terror, and even whiteness as death. It is, after all, the inevitability of Sarah's death that is finally vocalized when she asserts, "I want not to be. I ask nothing except anonymity."[55] This utterance not only foreshadows Sarah's suicide but also simultaneously alludes to her schizophrenic delusion that "to be" is to be other, to be noticeably marked—to be black. By enveloping herself in a fantastical world of whiteness (she dreams of possessing white friends and "rooms with European antiques and my Queen Victoria"), Sarah hopes to acquire an identity that is no longer marked as other.[56] Her hope to "not be" is a desire for an inconspicuous presence that promises to engender, rather than limit, her transgressive existence.

In wanting "not to be," the character of Sarah also gives credence to the so-called invisibility of whiteness. This invisibility, as Richard Dyer notes, is not a matter of *not* being present or seen but rather the experience of unconditional acceptance and ubiquity: "[I]n Western representation whites are overwhelmingly and disproportionately predominant, have the central and elaborated roles and above all are placed as the norm, the ordinary, the standard."[57] In addition, Dyer reminds us of the associations made between whiteness and *disembodiedness,* a conceptual link that resonates with both Sarah's desire and her eventual suicide: "To be without properties also suggests not being at all. This may be thought of as pure spirit, but it also hints at non-existence, or death."[58] This haunting allusion is reinforced by the *Funnyhouse*'s grotesque images, all of which perpetuate disconcerting associations with whiteness.

The play's continual parade of whiteface, embellished spaces, and ornate objects creates a visual interplay that reveals how *racial* identities (like costumes, set pieces, and props), can be embraced or discarded by their proprietors. Correspondingly, the whiteface countenances of Jesus, Queen Victoria, and the Duchess of Hapsburg—visceral evidence of the imprisoning nature of racial signatures—open the possibility for the play's audience to recognize how real physical cues represent, and misrepresent, *cultural* identities.

An ideal text with which to ground my study, *Funnyhouse of a Negro* employs theatrical whiteface, in tandem with thematic refrains and semiotic codes of whiteness, to interrogate America's racial binaries and historic privileging of white over black. Equally important is the fact that Kennedy uses these motifs of whiteness to ultimately complicate readings of blackness and black identity (and she did this in 1964—a time when such complex representations of African Americans were neither popular nor embraced). Kennedy's *Funnyhouse of a Negro* exemplifies the nuanced readings and critical narratives that all the texts in *Coloring Whiteness* invite. Moreover, in recognizing how the play was originally received in relation to how it might be received if it debuted today, *Funnyhouse* serves as an intriguing text with which to consider the role and development of identity politics within African American art and theatre.

THE MANY FACES OF WHITEFACE: PARSING OUT TERMS

My investment in both performance analysis and praxis leads to an interest in determining how whiteness may be translated or activated on and through black bodies, in art and real life. Accordingly, I use the foundational concept of "whiteface" and its inherent allusions to racialized performance to help formulate descriptors for some of the ways whiteness can be presented, interpreted, and applied in African American cultural productions. Through my employment of terms such as *tinted whiteface, optic whiteface, nonconforming whiteface, naturalized whiteface, linguistic whiteface,* and *presumed aural whiteness*, this project particularizes phenomena in our lived experiences while also offering translatable, producible interpretations for staged work.

Significant, however, is that the terms I offer should not be framed as wholly discrete—they are often concurrent and interrelated. In addition, the following terms are best understood through artistic purpose *and* audience reception, thereby highlighting the role of intentionality in performance practice and theorizing.

Tinted whiteface: As addressed in my analysis of *Funnyhouse of a Negro*, *tinted whiteface* describes a visage that is intentionally "tinted" rather than appearing as ultrawhite or flesh toned. The unnatural aspect of tinted whiteface underscores the constructed nature of imagined whiteness, thereby suggesting the possibility of racial mixture and/or the impossibility of racial purity.

Optic whiteface: The construct of imagined whiteness is similarly interrogated by optic whiteface, but it is expressed by the absence of color. Paying homage to the "optic white" metaphor in Ralph Ellison's *The Invisible Man*, *optic whiteface* describes whiteface that is opaque, paintlike, and bright white.

Nonconforming whiteface: Recognizing that whiteface is already perceived as a "nontraditional" form of racialized performance, nonconforming whiteface violates expectations even further by employing tangible items *beyond* an actor's body in order to signify whiteness. Void of face paint, makeup, or facial masking altogether, *nonconforming whiteface* refers to the intimation of a character's corporeal whiteness solely through the use of theatrical props, symbolic attire, or similar material accoutrements associated with the actor's body.

Naturalized whiteface: Naturalized whiteface is the intentional process of "whitening up" through artistic intervention, elaborate makeup, plastic surgery, or medical technology. These transformations may not result in a realistic or aesthetically pleasing countenance, but they suggest a deliberate effort to acquire the phenotypical markers and cultural capital frequently associated with whiteness.

Linguistic whiteface: Linguistic whiteface is intentionally deployed by performers (storytellers, comedians, actors, etc.) for the sake of deliberately portraying a persona of "whiteness." It is the self-conscious and often exaggerated manipulation of one's vocal qualities (including variables such as word choice, grammar, and timbre) for the sake of suggesting that the speaker is white or "white identified."

Presumed aural whiteness: Referencing a speech style of everyday life, presumed aural whiteness is based on an audience member's assessment rather than a speaker's intention. Characterized as speech that is assumed to emanate from white (versus nonwhite) bodies, presumed aural whiteness is typified by its association with "sounding white."

I employ these user-friendly terms in the interest of practical translations and critical specificity. Nevertheless, I recognize that activated performance engenders countless connotations through the process of reception and, regardless of one's objective or motivation, alternative readings are inevitable. Yet and still, I believe that creating a more complex vocabulary in relation to racial mimicry and racialized perceptions can enrich our interpretations and embolden our artistic choices with a greater sense of awareness and purpose.

OVERVIEW OF CHAPTERS

As modeled by my reading of *Funnyhouse of a Negro*, this book addresses specific forms of whiteface while simultaneously considering other strategies used to connote and examine perceptions of whiteness. Informed by a dramaturgical approach, each chapter offers close textual readings through interdisciplinary means and methods.

Readers may readily recognize that the following chapters are ordered, for all intents and purposes, chronologically. While they follow what is essentially a temporal progression, the methodological styles exhibited in each chapter suitably differ, thereby reflecting the specifics of the various genres in question as well as the distinctive lines of inquiry that propel each chapter's investigation. Aided by the luxury of retrospection, I would concede that my analyses of theatre texts (represented by literary scripts as well as staged productions) are greatly informed by textual readings—evidence, no doubt, of my interest in dramatic literature and my professional training as a play development and production dramaturg. To that end, my theatre-oriented chapters were scribed with the hope to offer theatre makers and educators practical, applicable, and accessible ways of animating, interpreting, and teaching the featured texts. The chapters that wrestle with other performative mediums are not as explicitly bound to this imperative and, accordingly, may strike readers as engaging more directly with theoretical ruminations. While the style of my critical engagement is modified from chapter to chapter, each chapter aims to analyze the complex, dynamic, and nuanced readings of whiteness in and through black performance.

Venturing from my discussion of *Funnyhouse of a Negro* (1964) to the artwork of Jefferson Pinder (2008), *Coloring Whiteness* follows a conceptual trajectory that begins during the Civil Rights Movement—an era in which formulaic ideas of race often focused on the binarism of black and white. It closes with the consideration of artwork that was created in a time in which America's racialized imaginings were propelled by thoughts of a so-called postracial moment, as signified by the presidential election of Barack Obama. Selecting work that spans five decades, the temporal frame of *Coloring Whiteness* grants me a range of materials and sociopolitical topos with which to explore the meanings and messages of whiteness in the work of African American artists.

Chapter 1 continues to explore the civil rights era by turning its attention to another canonical play of the 1960s, *Day of Absence* (1965). Written by Douglas Turner Ward, *Day of Absence* is a brief one-act play that chronicles the sudden absence of blacks within a small southern town. Reading the early history and critical reception of *Day of Absence*, this extensive chapter is divided into two parts. The first half focuses on the artistic efficacy of Ward's thematic use of whiteness and his strategic use of optic whiteface. Buoyed by whiteness's paradoxical associations with both absence and presence, this chapter also demonstrates how Ward used these conceptual links to offer a pronounced critique of America's race relations.

The second half of chapter 1 highlights the underexamined television debut of *Day of Absence* in 1967 when it was adapted for the small screen and presented as part of the premier episode of the Public Broadcast Laboratory (PBL). This investigation not only reveals how Ward's metacritique of whiteness was packaged and framed for consumption on the national stage, but it continues to activate the tropes of absence and presence by revealing how *Day of Absence* subsequently inspired blacks and Latinos to "take a day of absence" from civic life in order to protest social inequities and/or commit to racial solidarity. By addressing the metaperformances inherent in these demonstrations, chapter 1 highlights the long-lasting cultural impact of *Day of Absence* while simultaneously considering the current efficacy of the play's artistic premise.

Similarly inspired by the absence-presence dyad traced throughout chapter 1, the next chapter of *Coloring Whiteness* studies Lydia Diamond's stage adaptation of Toni Morrison's *The Bluest Eye* and the way the play animates contesting notions of white (in)visibility. Introducing a different type of adaptation process (from a novel to a stage play), chapter 2 advances an analysis of absence-presence and (in)visibility to consider how *The Bluest Eye*'s transition from literature to embodied performance necessarily demanded dramaturgical negotiations of omission and addition.

Integrating these practical dramaturgical issues while dramatizing the psychological demise of its central character, Pecola, *The Bluest Eye* beckons back to *Funnyhouse of a Negro* by affectively embodying the pervasive and devastating consequences of white, hegemonic thought. My study of *The Bluest Eye* focuses on how the play stages the prioritization of whiteness through the tragic character of Pecola, a young black girl who dreams incessantly of having blue eyes. In doing so, this chapter further discloses how tropes of whiteness can create opportunities for inter- *and* intraracial examinations of blackness.

As chapter 2 reveals, the character of Pecola yearned to acquire blue eyes because she believed that if she looked "whiter" she would better adhere to America's paradigm of ideal beauty, and, correspondingly, she would be more valued and esteemed. By the end of *The Bluest Eye*, Pecola does experience a major metamorphosis: she transitions from a state of troubled sanity to a state of undeniable madness, tortured by crushing betrayals and the impossibility of being truly loved. But what *if* Pecola's wish for a physical transition—brown eyes to blue—were possible? Would becoming "whiter looking" really promise the possibility of greater happiness and success?

Chapter 3 takes up these rhetorical queries through the work of the visual artist Danny Tisdale and the well-documented physical machinations of pop artist Michael Jackson. Both artists illustrate the instability and malleability of racial signatures and create performances that address the cultural and economic capital to be gained by "looking whiter." In addition, Tisdale's fictional racial transitions (as represented by his guerrilla performance *Transitions, Inc.*) and Michael Jackson's well-publicized physical metamorphoses speak to the manner in which markers of whiteness are packaged and marketed for public consumption. Casting a light on naturalized whiteface, this chapter entertains the conceit that naturalized whiteface—like naturalized citizenship—is utilized with the hope that it will qualify one for accessibility, acceptance, and membership among those who are white identified.

While the reality of medical science and technological advancements offers us the opportunity to imagine black bodies transitioning into seemingly whiter ones, chapter 4 reminds us that "whitening up" (and "blackening up," for that matter) has always been a factual—if not always acknowledged—aspect of American culture. This chapter examines the multiple ways in which the television series *Chappelle's Show* interrogates whiteness and racial belonging by centralizing themes of "mixedness." Although scholars such as W. T. Lhamon have argued that blackface minstrelsy was a way for white performers to embody and *imagine* the possibilities of miscegenation, I argue that Dave Chappelle's use of tinted whiteface and nonconforming whiteface help to highlight the *reality* of interracial liaisons and multiracial identities in the twenty-first century.

This chapter enters new conceptual terrain by exploring mixed-raced identities and television comedy; however, it also continues my dramaturgical reflections on audience access and reception. It was, after all, the fear of reinforcing—rather than subverting—racist ideologies that prompted Dave Chappelle to eventually walk away from his groundbreaking series. The circumstances of this departure bring me back to the very questions that are raised by Chappelle's comedic skits: who has the position or authority to police racial membership, boundaries, or representations; and what is lost or gained for those who choose to transgress racial demarcations related to perceived audiences or cultural authorities?

Befittingly, chapter 5 wrestles with some of these same questions as well. Rather than focusing on how judgments regarding racial and cultural authenticity are made in terms of visible signs or biological notions of race, however, this chapter offers readers the opportunity to think about how *audible* signs of racial membership are equally impactful—and erroneous—when it comes to such subjective discernments. Differentiating between the practice of linguistic whiteface and the phenomenon of presumed aural whiteness, chapter 5 addresses how audiences imagine whiteness in the aural performances of African Americans.

While this exploration considers "real-life" presentations (as exemplified by Barack Obama's style-shifting speech), it primarily focuses on voice-over work to think about the personal losses and gains at play when it comes to actors who "sound white"—or are deemed *not* to "sound black." This chapter's turn to advertising prompts me to wrestle with a number of new queries. For example, how does our vocal quality or the way we speak "sell" a particular vantage point or message about identity? And how does an awareness of our auditory assumptions encourage us to consider the ways nonconforming casting may move beyond visual representations to include diverse, unexpected, and nonstereotypical audible presentations?

I conclude *Coloring Whiteness* with a coda that activates my last query about moving "beyond visual representations" by challenging audiences to reimagine and redirect their visual vocabulary when it comes to whiteface expressions in African American art. Through a brief discussion of Jefferson Pinder's short Butoh-inspired film *Afro-Cosmonaut (White Noise)* (2008), I argue that Pinder illustrates the ways in which whiteness can be used to comment on access and transcendence above *and beyond* issues of race. My closing ruminations about Pinder address the current trajectory of African American artistic expressions, disclosing how our work increasingly challenges unilateral readings of both whiteness and blackness. Using Pinder's art as my template, I argue *against* the idea that we are in a postracial era, asserting that we are (and have been) entering an increasingly multiplicitous era, one that acknowledges and gives voice to the claiming of complex identities.

Although each chapter functions as a self-contained investigation, together they create a constellation of creative and critical considerations that explicitly inform and respond to one another. Grounded in dramaturgical analysis, the texts in *Coloring Whiteness: Acts of Critique in Black Performance* illustrate how contemporary African American performance uses motifs of whiteness to (1) "color" whiteness; (2) deconstruct notions of white superiority, privilege, entitlement, and purity; and (3) complicate perceptions of blackness. In the process, these enactments of whiteness do much more than simply invert racial representations and/or reify revised racial hierarchies. As revisionist—and revisioning—tactics, these artistic expressions complicate how we perceive others as well as how we perceive ourselves.

CHAPTER ONE

Douglas Turner Ward's Play on Whiteness
Day of Absence on America's Public Stages

DRAMATIC RIFFS ON WHITENESS

On November 15, 1965, Douglas Turner Ward's *Day of Absence*, a "reverse minstrel show done in white-face," debuted at the St. Marks Playhouse. The commercial success of the stage play led to a remarkable event in November 1967: the play was filmed and presented as part of the premiere episode of the Ford Foundation's "television experiment" known as the Public Broadcast Laboratory (PBL)—predecessor to today's Public Broadcasting System (PBS). The debut episode of PBL hoped to address the need for racial dialogue, and to that end the program featured several segments that focused on the issue of race, including Douglas Turner Ward's stage-to-screen presentation of *Day of Absence*. While *Day of Absence* was, thematically, an appropriate fit for the evening's program, its inclusion proved to be disastrous for PBL: 29 out of 119 stations dropped the television program before it even aired, citing *Day of Absence* as their reason.[1]

This chapter uses Douglas Turner Ward's *Day of Absence* to examine how tropes and theatrical strategies of whiteness are used to foster explorations of African American identity in contemporary performance. By examining the early history and critical reception of the play, it considers how Ward's dramatic presentation of whiteness was originally received on the stage and the small screen, thereby indicating how artistic interrogations of whiteness were interpreted by racially diverse audience members in the

1960s. This exploration highlights a key issue: the significance of "institutional dramaturgy." In this context, *institutional dramaturgy* refers to the way a producing institution strategically frames and brands its work—a dynamic that inevitably affects how the meaning of a performance text is transmitted and received by potential audiences.

In using *Day of Absence* as a case study, this chapter not only underscores the ways institutions of theatre and television contextualize their productions, and thereby influence audience perceptions, but it also reveals how the power of these venues can ultimately drive important social concerns into our nation's consciousness. Furthermore, by analyzing the racially charged sociopolitical thrust of Ward's play, this study pays particular attention to how *Day of Absence* inspired metatheatrical events in the form of sociopolitical protests and expressions of communal solidarity. Considering these metaperformances, my examination highlights the long-lasting cultural impact of *Day of Absence* while simultaneously considering the meaning and efficacy of the play's theatrical tactics and real-life enactments.

DAY OF ABSENCE: THE GROUND ON WHICH IT STANDS

The 1960s was an explosive era in American theatre. Lorraine Hansberry's *A Raisin in the Sun* had set the future of African American theatre alight with its historic turn on the Broadway stage in 1959, opening the doors for a deluge of black playwrights. Two of the era's most important, canon-expanding plays, LeRoi Jones's *Dutchman* and Adrienne Kennedy's *Funnyhouse of a Negro*, won Obie Awards in 1964, helping to further propel public interest in African American drama. Plays like *Dutchman* and *Funnyhouse of a Negro* pushed theatrical boundaries farther than ever before by wrestling with the era's contentious racial issues in shocking and seemingly divergent—yet surprisingly complementary—ways.[2]

It was in this fertile artistic environment that other African American artists began to garner greater attention from mainstream critics and audiences. Such was the case when Robert Hooks first produced Douglas Turner Ward's famous double bill, *Day of Absence* and *Happy Ending*, after workshopping *Day of Absence* with students from the Group Theatre Workshop. The workshop, a Harlem-based training company, was founded by Hooks in 1964 to combat the dearth of opportunities available for the development of young urban talent. Assisted by the vision and leadership of seasoned actors and directors such as Barbara Ann Teer, Ron Mack, and Hal DeWindt, the Group Theatre Workshop was described in a 1965 *New York Times* article as a "unique improvisatory acting academy for teenagers without the money for formal dramatic school and, in most cases, without a penchant for classes in the usual sense of that word."[3] Members of the group met once a week at Hooks's loft apartment, and while the majority of the young participants were black, there were also Puerto Rican, Chinese American, and white members. This diverse collection of young artists not only hailed from local New York neighborhoods, but some even made their weekly treks to Hooks's apartment from as far away as Long Island and New Jersey, where they spent three to four hours each session developing their acting craft.[4]

By the fall of 1965, the Group Theatre Workshop had been running for over a year, propelled by the passion of its leadership, eagerness of its students, and the generosity of a few financial benefactors. In its efforts to train young actors, the group also created opportunities for writers to experiment with new work. This practice not only expanded the group's developmental programming, but it ultimately earned its members unexpected attention from local theatre critics and aficionados. In fact, it was after a local critic watched the group perform an excerpt from *Happy Ending* that Robert Hooks was inspired to produce Douglas Turner Ward's work with a professional cast.[5] Taking on the daunting task of theatre producer (an uncommon role for African Americans at the time), Hooks armed himself with what he knew would be formative, cutting-edge work: a double bill featuring both *Happy Ending* and *Day of Absence*. Boasting an impressive cast, the two one-acts featured Douglas Turner Ward and Robert Hooks, in addition to a host of other legendary theatre artists: Esther Rolle, Frances Foster, Lonne Elder, Arthur French, Barbara Ann Teer, and Moses Gunn.[6]

Curiously, there has been limited discussion among scholars regarding the presentation of *Day of Absence* and *Happy Ending* as companion pieces. Although the two plays were originally presented together in a twin bill at the St. Marks Playhouse, critical treatments on Ward's national debut have often focused on *Day of Absence*, with far less attention paid to *Happy Ending*.[7] Both plays interrogate whiteness and white-black relations, thus their partnership in production is not only thematically appropriate, but it illustrates a conceptual symmetry that enriches and complicates an audience's understanding of America's racial dynamics during the 1960s. The complementary dynamic of the two plays is particularly befitting since Ward wrote

Happy Ending in a concerted effort to create a companion piece for *Day of Absence*.

> I didn't plan to write [*Happy Ending*] as a play until I realized that *Day of Absence* wasn't long enough for a night of theatre ... so I needed a companion piece to fill out the bill. I knew *Day of Absence* was so unique in so many ways that I couldn't see it being on the bill with some other play—some other writer's play. I knew it needed its own companion piece. It needed a brother-sister relationship with another play; they needed to be harmonious together. So I thought about what other idea I had that could go along with *Day of Absence*, and I immediately thought of this real-live experience that I had with my aunts.[8]

And thus *Happy Ending* was born. Although the focus of this chapter precludes an in-depth examination of *Happy Ending*, I believe it is important—dramaturgically speaking—to briefly attend to it in order to demonstrate how the twin billing of these plays highlight their interrelated messages about whiteness and racial relations.

One of the major components of institutional dramaturgy is the need to frame a production in relation to its theatrical companions (i.e., the dynamics revealed through twin bills, works in a repertory, a production season, a play series, or festival). The manner in which plays are linked may reflect practical concerns such as financial resources, but such choices also allude to an institution's "branding" through preferences of style, genre, or subject matter. The pairing of *Day of Absence* and *Happy Ending* is no exception. Both pieces address the inflated cultural capital of whiteness and, when placed in tandem, also offer exacting intracultural critiques that may not be as apparent when the pieces are received separately. While unequivocal in their interrogation of white dominance, both plays also address the survival strategies blacks have utilized in order to navigate the facade of America's constructed racial hierarchies.

While Ward's *Day of Absence* takes place in various locales throughout a small southern town, the whole of *Happy Ending* takes place in the kitchen of a humble yet nicely equipped Harlem tenement. When the play opens the audience sees two African American sisters, Ellie and Vi, who appear to be wrestling with a devastating loss. It is soon revealed that the women's employers, the Harrisons, are divorcing due to Mrs. Harrison's repeated sexual indiscretions. The women are then joined by their nephew, Junie, a young man who expresses indignation and shame in response to his aunts' presumed blind loyalty and apparent subservience to their white employers. After initially tolerating Junie's scorn and ridicule, both Ellie and Vi retort with gentle verbal vengeance: they reveal, with unabashed pride, that they are not the trustworthy domestics that they appear to be but rather are cunning entrepreneurs who have taken full advantage of the Harrisons' incompetence and gullibility. They also remind their nephew that his acceptance of their financial support and many lavish gifts (such as hand-me-downs from Mr. Harrison) makes him a beneficiary of their supposed subservience. The play ends "happily" when it is discovered that the verbal machinations of Ellie and Vi have once again managed to keep the Harrisons' marriage intact, thereby saving their jobs and their standard of living.

Ward's *Day of Absence* also dutifully addresses the fallacies of racialized hierarchies, but it underscores its story line with the visual potency of theatrical whiteface. The premise of *Day of Absence*, on the surface, is relatively simple: a small southern township awakens to discover that all their "negro" citizens are missing. Shock and confusion soon lead to anxiety and chaos as the white townspeople recognize how essential black folks are to their day-to-day lives: white women prove to be ill-equipped to take care of their children and households; the absence of sweepers and sanitation workers leads to civic disarray; respected authority figures and treasured family members—folks who had been "passing"—suddenly disappear from their homes and official posts; and the entire infrastructure of this small, unnamed "Everytown" erodes. In hopes of affecting the blacks' return, the town's mayor delivers a desperate radio broadcast—a plaintive plea that eventually leads to angry and demanding outbursts directed toward the missing population. Following the mayor's broadcast, pandemonium ensues, and the small town is overcome with violence and riots. However, the next morning the play's sole black character, Rastus, mysteriously appears, signaling the return of the blacks—but not necessarily signaling a restoration of the town's social order. The play closes with a taunting sense of open-endedness: the playwright does not offer an explanation to the white townspeople or theatre audience as to why and how the black folks vanished, where they had been, and whether or not such an enigmatic exodus could happen again.

In varying yet complementary ways, *Day of Absence* and *Happy Ending* expose the erroneous nature of racialized myths, particularly those associated with whiteness. Both plays dismantle iconic images of the servile black domestic, attack the presumed purity of white womanhood, and expose the ways in which whiteness can be a disabling rather than empowering characteristic. Furthermore, both plays suggest unsettling possibilities to white audience members. Among the most pertinent assertions are (1) that black folks are the ones that are *really* running things, and (2) that black folks have omniscient knowledge of white people and their ways. These suppositions, based on the unilateral intimacy forged by a long history of white domination and black subjugation, were potently addressed by W. E. B. DuBois in 1920 when he turned his ruminations from the souls of black folk to contemplate the "souls of white folk."

> Of them I am singularly clairvoyant. I see in and through them. I view them from unusual points of vantage. Not as a foreigner do I come, for I am native, not foreign, bone of their thought and flesh of their language. Mine is not the knowledge of the traveler or the colonial composite of dear memories, words and wonder. Nor yet is my knowledge that which servants have of masters, or mass of class, or capitalist of artisan. Rather I see these souls undressed and from the back and side. I see the working of their entrails. I know their thoughts and they know that I know. This knowledge makes them now embarrassed, now furious! They deny my right to live and be and call me misbirth! My word is to them mere bitterness and my soul, pessimism. And yet as they preach and strut and shout and threaten, crouching as they clutch at rags of facts and fancies to hide their nakedness, they go twisting, flying by my tired eyes and I see them ever stripped,—ugly, human.[9]

Seemingly activating DuBois's words through the antics of Vi, Ellie, and Rastus, Ward metaphorically strips his white characterizations of undue superiority and unearned privilege.

Through their dramatic exposés, *Happy Ending* and *Day of Absence* can be read as championing revolutionary ideologies, yet they also feature elements that complicate easy assumptions regarding black empowerment. In fact, a day before the play's New York debut, Robert Hooks commented, "I rather think that 'Happy Ending' is not going to be the image of the Negro in the theater that many of the Negro middle-class want to see, and it may also disturb some whites who'll feel impelled to run home and check their maids."[10] Perhaps Hooks recognized what later scholars would identify as Ward's wielding of a "double-edged sword": "[*Happy Ending*] is considerably more than an extended vaudeville sketch as some critics regarded it.

The whites are vicious and parasitically dependent upon the blacks for their existence. The blacks must counter parasitism with parasitism in order to survive."[11]

Affirming the intended complexity of his characters as well as the layered critique they invite, Douglas Turner Ward shared how *Happy Ending* was actually inspired by his real-life experiences.

> Junie is based on me. It's a critique about him—his revolutionary 1950s, 1960s ideals, thinking that he is so advanced—but he is not "getting it." Junie is really me taking a stab at myself. My instinct was out of my own superficial perspective. I am taking a jab at my own conceit—that my consciousness, my value system, and all of that were so superior [to those of my aunts]. I was the new Negro, the new black, the revolutionary black, and I immediately interpreted their behavior as if *they* were backwards. Yet at the same time I was ignoring the fact that I hadn't bought a suit for so long because my aunts provided me with so much. I had been broke, and hungry, and they had fed me. And therefore it was their complex survival practice that kept us alive and intact. So they weren't living of off scraps, they were far superior. . . .
>
> [Blacks of my generation] were sort of one dimensional in appointing a dichotomy between the older generation and the younger generation. And as far as I'm concerned [now], there [was] never that separation. They were never as one dimensional as we thought they were, and we were never as complex as we thought we were. Junie was my satirical critique of myself. His final coming to consciousness is him accepting the complicated truth about all of us. It is his consciousness that is raised. The aunts are not lacking consciousness; it is his superficiality that is questioned.[12]

The critical reflections on intracultural disparity in *Happy Ending* also have their counterpart in *Day of Absence*. In *Day of Absence*, however, Ward's commentary on intra-communal discord is expressed through the character that seems the most tenuous—the seemingly acquiescent character of Rastus.

In a potent act of "disidentification,"[13] the subservient Rastus refuses to answer the queries of the "white crackers" Clem and Luke. After claiming complete ignorance of all recent events, he offers them (and the audience) a hint of a smile, leaving the more perceptive Luke to question whether or not life as he knew it has really resumed. When asked about the character Rastus, Ward emphasized his dualism, underscoring the necessary intracultural critique he signifies.

> Rastus is a walking stereotype. To bring Rastus back is to bring back the epitome of the black stereotype, *but* the revolutionary aspect of it is that he comes back and, on the surface, seems like the same old Rastus, right? But in two lines, a couple of words, a posture, "Don't rightly know, Mr. Luke," and then he straightens up, he stands up straight. And he says, "... just goes to show you how time kin fly"—that one line—no bumbling, no hesitating, no stumbling over words, he stands up straight, breaking the stereotype. That sudden breaking of the stereotype is *within* the stereotype. So, if Rastus is part of that absence, then we really are doing something 100 percent unified because if Rastus went along with it, then that means *all* black people can be critical of their behavior. If [people like Rastus] are part of the plot, then the plot is complete.[14]

And so, through the characters of Junie and Rastus, Ward animates contradictions and distinctions within African America, while offering audiences the opportunity to discern between rhetoric and action.

The complexity of Junie and Rastus, however, also invites us to consider the way *Happy Ending* and *Day of Absence* both conclude with an intriguing ambivalence. Although *Day of Absence* may suggest a "happy ending" for black and/or liberal white audience members by proposing that blacks have more agency than is generally recognized, the black population's reappearance does little to dismantle the play's world of institutionalized racism. Rather than initiating a structural or ideological revolution, the blacks in *Day of Absence* ultimately reassume their roles in society—just as Ellie and Vi, out of their need for their white employers, return to their posts in the *Happy Ending*. With the black characters returning to their previous states of existence, both plays ultimately speak not only to *white dependence* on black people but to *black dependence* on whites as well. Rather than arguing for separatism or a reversal of racist hierarchies, the plays resist simplistic representations of a black-white divide and invariably argue for a new vision of black-white relations.

Regardless of the many ways in which *Day of Absence* and *Happy Ending* complement one another, most critical attention has been paid to *Day of*

Absence. This tendency may be due to the fact that the use of whiteface in *Day of Absence* offers a more visually titillating experience than the realistic *Happy Ending*; the heightened theatricality of *Day of Absence* simply makes it an easier conversation piece. While the inherent spectacle in *Day of Absence* readily attracts attention, the play's persistent appeal—evidenced by a recent swell of scholarship[15]—also pays tribute to how its form relates to its content. Ripe for further analysis and consideration, *Day of Absence* not only portrays mythic ideals surrounding whiteness, but it dismantles these perceptions through utter absurdity, offering an imaginative and still fertile ground with which to explore racial politics.

THE THEMATIC RIFFS ON WHITENESS IN WARD'S *DAY OF ABSENCE*

In a 2004 interview with the performance scholar and artist Daniel Banks, Ward spoke about the dramaturgical structure of *Day of Absence*, "It played on riffs—what the White critics didn't understand was the riffs. Duke [Ellington] could take an idea and then play all kinds of riffs around it, but still the singular through line."[16] In taking Ward's jazzlike dramaturgical approach to heart, one can see how *Day of Absence* reveals a number of familiar "riffs" on whiteness, thematic refrains that are frequently echoed in the vernacular and scholarly discourses of critical whiteness studies. Among the tropes of whiteness that *Day of Absence* animates and interrogates is, of course, the titular suggestion of whiteness in relation to absence, but it also addresses the association of whiteness with normativity, supremacy, privilege, purity, terror, and death.

Perhaps it goes without saying that the title of Ward's play, *Day of Absence*, immediately prompts its readers and audiences to contemplate the meanings of absence *and* presence. The play's plot is built around the disappearance of the town's black characters and the notion of white vacuity is ironically expressed through the *absence* of blackness. As alluded to earlier, the deprioritizing of whiteness in the play (as expressed by the white characters' lack of skills, from parenting to politicking) is dramatized when the whites are forced to act for themselves. Without black people to do life's most fundamental and ubiquitous work, the white townspeople are infantilized, thereby reversing age-old stereotypes. The play's logic discloses how the bodies and inner lives of laboring blacks, widely unnoticed and unrecognized by white people on a day-to-day basis, has led to a black "invisibility" that is only acknowledged once it has absconded. Strikingly, however, only when the *hypervisibility* of whiteness is articulated through black absence is whiteness revealed as overesteemed and ineffectual. Though physically "present," the whitefaced characters in *Day of Absence* embody yet another type of absence through their apparent futility.

In challenging assumptions of the everyday, *Day of Absence* interrogates the very premise of whiteness as being normative. The fact that Ward disrupts the extraordinariness of a southern town with a fantastical happening that is *marked* by whiteness defies the notion of whiteness as the unmarked standard. This defamiliarizing of whiteness is further propelled by the play's use of theatrical whiteface, a strategy that assures that whiteness is framed as abstract and disconcerting, thereby effecting a sense of alienation rather than assumed familiarity.[17]

Also emblematic of futile and estranged whiteness is the play's young married couple, John and Mary. As lights rise on the sleeping couple, "Loud insistent sounds of baby yells are heard,"[18] yet despite their baby's plaintive cries, both parents remain in bed until John—unable to ignore the cries any longer—awakens his wife. Both parents, it turns out, are still recovering from a "head-splittin' blow-out" the night before,[19] but even without their subsequent hangovers it becomes clear that neither parent is prepared, equipped, or truly willing to attend to their young child's needs. Instead, as the baby continues to cry, the two desperately lament the apparent absence of their domestic and nanny, Lula. Dumb struck and panicked by the scenario, the countenances of John and Mary are shaken. Referring to her baby, Mary yells for John to "SMOTHER IT!,"[20] while John responds by questioning whether the baby really is his child. Tempers escalate further between the couple when Mary's culinary skills prove to be as poor as her maternal ones. After choking on the breakfast Mary prepares, John pummels her with words.

> JOHN: When I married you, I thought I was fairly acquainted with your faults and weaknesses—I chalked 'em up to human imperfection . . . but now I know I was being extremely generous, over-optimistic and phenomenally deluded! You have no idea how useless you really are!
> MARY: Then why'd you marry me?!
> JOHN: Decoration![21]

In referencing the unearned valuation that Mary once held in John's deluded eyes, Ward addresses the unearned valuation of whiteness—a sense of worth and idealization that was based on surface assumptions rather than substance. This undeserving adulation is reinforced by the play's Club Woman, who states that the travails experienced by Mary represent the unraveling of "Southern Bellesdom." The Club Woman asserts that this undoing "might very well prophesy the collapse of our indigenous institutions.... Remember—it has always been pure, delicate, lily-white images of Dixie femininity which provided backbone, inspiration and ideology for our male warriors in their defense against the on-rushing Black horde. If our gallant men are drained of this worship and idolatry—God knows!"[22]

Not only is the absence of blacks troubling the domestic sphere, but the day-to-day business operations of the town are deeply affected by the disappearance of fundamental, and too often ignored, civic workers. Although the blacks' "invisibility" may have precluded an immediate recognition of their sudden exodus, the realization of their absence slowly dawns on the whites, as expressed by Clem: "Now, every morning mosta people walkin' 'long this street is colored. They's strolling by going to work, they's waiting for the buses, they's sweeping sidewalks, cleaning stores, starting to shine shoes and wetting mops—right?! ... Well, look around you, Luke—where is they?"[23] Admitting to how "scarifying" this realization is, Clem's discomfort is experienced by all those whose livelihoods are indebted to the constant aid and assistance afforded them by the service of black people.

Speaking of the massive impact of the blacks' disappearance, the Industrialist tells the mayor that "Seventy-five per cent of all production is paralyzed," with losses felt in business-related maintenance, manufacturing, and consumption.[24] Later in the play, the television Announcer (a "Huntley-Brinkley-Murrow-Sevareid-Cronkite-Reasoner-type" and the *only* character that the playwright suggests should be portrayed by a white actor) further reveals the oblivious perspective of the white townspeople when he likewise reports of "Factories standing idle from the loss of *non-essential workers*. Stores shuttered from the absconding of *uncrucial personnel*."[25]

As the leader of the town, the bumbling Mayor Henry Lee epitomizes this excessive yet previously underacknowledged dependence on black people. Shouting over a cluttered desk, the mayor demands the presence of a number of black workers. He calls for Mandy to straighten up his desk and for Rufus to knock dust off his shoes and then complains that he had to dress himself due to JC's absence, fix his own coffee without May Belle, drive himself to work without Bubber, and sexually accost his own wife in the absence of Sapphi[ire].[26] Suffering from a general sense of disarray without the exploitation of black labor and bodies, the panic of the mayor and his staff escalates when they realize that it is not just domestics and municipal workers who have gone missing. And with that turn, the myth of white purity is also dissected with Ward's pen.

Beyond disclosing the moral and ethical trespasses of the play's white characters, the notion of white purity is interrogated through the historical fact of racial passing. As the story line unfolds, the mayor is informed that some of the town's most notable citizens have disappeared, and thus biological purity also becomes a source of contention and concern for the townspeople. Among the missing who are revealed to be "Secret Nigras" are the vice mayor, two City Council members, the chairman of the Junior Chamber of Commerce, the City College All-Southern halfback, the chairwoman of the Daughters of the Confederate Rebellion, the local beauty queen, and "numerous other miscellaneous bodies."[27] The sheer numbers and positions of individuals who have "infiltrated" the ranks of white citizenry speak volumes with regard to deconstructing notions of what white "looks like," as well as destabilizing assumed whiteness as hierarchical status. Thus, in tandem with the ubiquitous dependence whites have on blacks, *Day of Absence* pointedly asserts, "Southern identity and culture are so thoroughly defined by blackness, it would be disastrous, apocalyptic, to separate black from white."[28]

Far from glamorizing the cultural capital of whiteness, the white characters of Ward's imagination repeatedly fail to exhibit any characteristics that may be interpreted in terms of emotional, psychological, ethical, or intellectual supremacy. The "country crackers," Clem and Luke, whose actions are described with words such as "drowsy" and "lethargically," come across as sluggish simpletons. The tempestuous John and Mary exhibit failings in their interpersonal relationships and familial life. And, like the mayor, others—whose titles, appointments, and categorized whiteness supposedly suggest a certain cunning and intellect—are among those who ultimately fail to rise to levels deemed worthy of admiration and privilege. Pushing the issue of unjustified and unjust privilege to its comic limit, Ward even features an indignant white supremacist, Mr. Council Clan, who expresses ironic outrage over the fact that the blacks were not forced out but rather appear to have left of their own volition: "Ain't supposed to do nothing 'til we tell 'em. Got to stay put until we exercise our God-given right to tell 'em when to git!"[29]

Although the presence of Mr. Council Clan in *Day of Absence* is one of Ward's many farcical strokes, the visual intimation of a red-robed Ku Klux Klan member inescapably alludes to America's history of racial violence. Thus, the trope of "whiteness as terror" is symbolized, if not actualized, through the inclusion of the Klan figure. Strikingly, however, *Day of Absence* also incorporates references to "white terror" and violence in other, less clichéd ways. In addition to conjuring acts of white terrorism, *Day of Absence* stages the terror *of* whites who fear the deprivation of black bodies to command or subjugate. The unbridled fears coalesce through the news reports of all-white mob violence and riots offstage, thereby offering Ward the opportunity to mock stereotypes regarding black aggression by suggesting a different type of source of anxiety and dread.

Marvin McAllister's reading of *Day of Absence* deftly addresses the way in which Ward exploits the fear of racialized mob violence in the 1960s. Observing the way Ward depicts the riotous outbreaks that take over the town, McAllister points out how the playwright "takes the anger, frustration, and nihilism associated with urban blackness and attaches it to southern, small-town whiteness."[30] It is this reversal of white terror that *Day of Absence* signifies on with Ward's revisioning of "white flight." Playing off the way desegregation efforts are routinely met with the significant departure of white families, "Ward stages unglued whites 'flying' toward black contact, as the rest of the nation scrambles to protect their cities, and their Negroes, from suffering the same mysterious fate."[31]

The fate whites dread in *Day of Absence* is one that annihilates their comfortable way of life. Thus, the whiteness that befalls the citizens of Ward's Everytown brings forth the suggestion of "death" in multiple ways. There is, of course, the total paralysis of civic life, which suggests the town's looming destruction and demise. The impending danger of the citizenry's crippling stasis is articulated most pointedly by the television Announcer who reports on the deaths among the town's elderly: "[D]ozens of decrepit old men and women usually tended by faithful nurses and servants are popping off like flies—abandoned by sons, daughters and grandchildren whose refusal to provide their doddering relatives with bedpans and other soothing necessities result in their hasty, nasty, mess corpus delicties."[32] And later the Announcer returns to this conjuring of whiteness as death when he offers his final description of the devastated town and its inhabitants: "The city: exhausted, benumbed.—Slowly its occupants slinked off into shadows, and by midnight, the town was occupied exclusively by zombies. The fight and life had been drained out.... As our crew packed gear and crept away silently, we treaded softly—as if we were stealing away from a mausoleum.... The Face of a Defeated City."³³

Of course, in turning to the notion of the city's defeated "face," one must address how Ward's masterful, rifflike plays on whiteness are punctuated through the play's concerted use of theatrical whiteface. The use of whiteface as a theatrical strategy was by no means a foreign concept by the time *Day of Absence* debuted.³⁴ Taking full advantage of the visual vocabulary engendered by earlier whiteface performances, Ward also created his own signal differences. According to his stage directions, he wanted all the characters in *Day of Absence* (with the exception of the Announcer and Rastus) to "whiten up."

> Play is conceived for performance by a Negro cast, a reverse minstrel show done in white-face. Logically, it might also be performed by whites—at their own risk. If any producer is faced with choosing between opposite hues, author strongly suggests: "Go 'long wit' the blacks—besides all else, they need the work more."³⁵

Despite the theatrical precedents and comic potential posited by Ward's use of whiteface, published reviews of *Day of Absence* did not always measure up to the general zeal the public had for Ward's play. Moreover, many of the more pointed criticisms were directly related to the drama's engagement with transracial performance.

Among the less than enchanted reviewers was Michael Smith of the *Village Voice*. Smith, who made it clear that the work was not to his liking, expressed surprise that his fellow audience members seemed to enjoy it so thoroughly.³⁶ *New York Times* critic Howard Taubman also expressed dissatisfaction with Ward's playwriting and the ensemble's acting: "Under Philip Meister's direction the acting is often too broad, and the actors have evidently been encouraged to use Negro diction so exaggerated that they are difficult to understand and their shafts often go astray."³⁷ Taubman did, however, close his review with some praise for Ward's work: "Nevertheless, Mr. Ward is on the right track. Laughter can be as effective as anger in telling white America what the Negro has on his mind."³⁸ Aside from recognizing the sociopolitical thrust of *Day of Absence*, the denunciations of Ward's use of satire and exaggerated effects stand in marked contrast to the observations of several other prominent reviewers.

For instance, although the *New York Herald Tribune*'s critic, Herbert Kupferberg, was not overly exuberant about the twin bill (he, like Smith, suggested that there were "in" jokes that he did not get), he did refer to Ward's speech as Mayor Henry Lee as one of "sheer satiric intensity," even naming it the "most biting, incisive moment" of the evening.[39] And then there was Tom Prideaux, the theatre editor of *Life* magazine, who expressed wholehearted enthusiasm, offering nothing but praise for Ward's double bill. Calling the productions "a gust of fresh air among racial plays," Prideaux credited Ward's comedic turns for their theatrical, as well as metatheatrical, affects.

> By caricaturing the whites, with their Southern drawls and brainless bombast, just as outrageously as Negroes are often caricatured, *Day of Absence*, I felt, nudged the audience, which was mixed Negro and white, a little closer together.[40]

Similarly, the *Baltimore Afro-American* not only referred to *Day of Absence* as a "very funny play" but also observed:

> All colored characters are made up in whiteface and their Southern white dialect leaves nothing to the imagination. Turner's radio plea to the absent colored people is, to my way of thinking, one of the classic moments of the theatre. Turner is a thespian to watch and his pithy Herculean writings are fantastic.[41]

These affirmations stand in line with the laudatory summation of yet another major review, printed in *The New Yorker*.

> While Mr. Ward uses very broad farce to spook the Southern establishment, nothing less, perhaps, would work out, since at times the Southern realities teeter on the edge of farce themselves. Mr. Ward and all his fellow-actors struck me as superb entertainers, and you'd be well advised not to miss them.[42]

In light of *Day of Absence*'s more complimentary assessments, the misreading (or mishearing) of Harold Taubman in the *New York Times* and the acknowledged cluelessness of the *Village Voice*'s Michael Smith symbolize a concern many African American artists had about the way the predominantly white media received their work. A common apprehension was whether or not—due to their own naïveté or conscious resistance—white critics, particularly those considered most influential, were culturally literate enough to objectively judge African American theatre.

Black artists were also concerned about the way white reviewers compared white and black dramatists, often positing black playwrights as inferior followers of white writers.[43] This type of bias was illustrated by Martin Gottfried of *Women's Wear Daily* when he compared *Day of Absence* to Jean Genet's *The Blacks*. With unfettered disdain, Gottfried wrote:

> The theatrical thematic affect of a Negro in whiteface is enormous and could only be conceived by a royal artist like Genet. Ward's borrowing of it was presumptuous and his application of it to a play whose attitude basically is peevish, makes it obscene. *Day of Absence* is an elaborate pout.[44]

Perhaps Gottfried's reference to *The Blacks* was due, in part, to the fact that Genet's critically acclaimed play had its own American premiere at the same location only four years earlier. The relatively recent premiere of *The Blacks* may have left *Day of Absence* particularly ripe for critical comparisons. Genet had experienced a great deal of success with his 1961 American debut of *The Blacks*, a play that also featured black actors in whiteface. *The Blacks* not only premiered at the St. Marks Playhouse, but Douglas Turner Ward acted in its highly successful off-Broadway production. Ward's intimate familiarity with Genet's work was, by his own admission, a huge influence on his own playwriting, though not in the way critics often assume.

With eager openness, Ward is quick to share how Genet's *The Blacks* induced a watershed moment by encouraging him to prioritize his own artistic aims versus acquiescing to outside pressures.

> Genet was not a direct influence in terms of trying to copy his style or in terms of whiteface or anything like that, but he influenced me in terms of my freedom of expression.... I thought that if Genet had the precision to take, for instance, a widespread stereotype of the black male and then verbally use it, openly, without any apology or reservation, that meant that I should never let anybody censure whatever I was writing, whatever point of view I was expressing.[45]

In reflecting on his decision to employ whiteface, however, Ward does concede that Bertolt Brecht was a major source of inspiration.

> When I decided to write *Day of Absence* as a play it was simultaneous with the idea of *how* to do it—the style, the form—so the whiteface was almost contemporaneous with my decision to write it as a play. So the style and form of it was already there because of the combination of Genet and Brecht. The way that Brecht looked at theatre as an important way to look at issues in the real world, Brecht's theories of alienation, and his ideas in relation to the audience—not being oversentimentalized and so forth ... so it was all that: style, form, worldview, and the embrace of a theatrical form combined with Genet's expressiveness.[46]

And, without doubt, there was yet another factor informing Ward's use of whiteface: blackface minstrelsy. Recognizing the political climate of the time, and addressing the tumultuous history of racial representations in American theatre, Ward's strategic use of whiteface was also a very conscious attempt to reinscribe the narratives of blackface minstrelsy. In the words of the playwright, "It was my revenge on them [white people] for Black-facing us."[47]

If these considerations were not impactful enough, Ward also understood how his use of whiteface in *Day of Absence* augmented a number of insightful assertions, among them the seemingly insurmountable distance yet inescapable interconnectedness between blacks and whites. It is this latter point that Brandi Wilkins Catanese addresses in her compelling discussion of Ward's play.

> [T]he use of whiteface in *Day of Absence* allows Ward to define and criticize whiteness ... [and] the crisis induced by the supposed absence of blacks—when combined with the actual presence of their performing bodies under the white greasepaint—theatrically demonstrates the impossibility of imagining or representing American whiteness outside of some relationship to blackness. ... With these [casting] instructions, Ward makes clear that the de-naturalizations of theatrical and social whiteness are essential to the play's meaning.[48]

As Catanese concisely observes, Ward's play offers a biting "meta-critique of American racial politics" by illustrating that whites are dependent on blacks within the most private and public spheres of their lives, that blacks are equal contributors to the success and structure of American society, that intimacy between racialized groups is a reality, and that racial purity is a socially constructed fallacy. By embodying whiteness via black bodies, and thus challenging the concept of "real" white bodies, Ward's play powerfully destabilizes traditional notions of whiteness while exposing the intrinsic relationship between whites and blacks—a relationship that cannot be visualized or imagined without conceptualizing the other.[49]

In choosing to frame Ward's use of whiteface as a simple visual gimmick gone awry, critics such as Gottfried failed (or chose not) to recognize the multiple ways the use of whiteface underscored the play's conceptual framework, a web of thematic threads that extend out of Ward's central aim to interrogate whiteness. The visual effect of whiteface is particularly poignant when the issue of "passing" arises in the play. The immediate visual gag, of course, is the fact that the characters in the play—characters performed by black actors—are supposedly the town's real (as opposed to passing) whites. But beyond the narrative of passing, the imagery of white concealing black is also anxiety producing; it visually signifies an uncomfortable truth for many white people: there are those who may appear white but are really black "underneath" (it may be someone they know—or, worse yet, their own unacknowledged reality).

Considering these layered articulations, it becomes clear that it is not simply the inclusion of whiteface in *Day of Absence* that supports the play's multiple disclosures, but it is also the manner in which the whiteface is styled that underscores the play's meaning. According to Ward's original design intentions, the makeup used on the actors does not fall within a spectrum of color that could be identified as a natural "fleshtone."[50] Instead, the makeup is a bright white, and, similar to the whiteface makeup described in the set directions for *Funnyhouse of a Negro*, it was designed to have a decidedly unnatural appearance.[51] Rather than simply suggesting a communal affiliation among the white characters, the whiteface in *Day of Absence* signifies a simulated whiteness that is so unreal that it highlights the illusory nature and impossible truth of pure whiteness through its very presence.

It is this same deployment of whiteness that the celebrated African American novelist Ralph Ellison suggests in *Invisible Man* (1952). While I hesitate to assert a direct or overt correlation between the imaginings of Ward and Ellison, I do believe that they were similarly inspired to demonstrate how perceptions of whiteness are dependent on perceptions of blackness—a conceptual trope that is threaded throughout the work of African

American artists. In *Invisible Man*, the mythic purity of whiteness is articulated through the novel's famous "Optic White" scene in which the novel's unnamed protagonist is schooled by Kimbro, the supervisor at the Liberty Paint Company. Kimbro boasts to Ellison's protagonist that the paint company's premier product, "Optic White," is "the purest white that can be found." In describing Optic White as a color that is "as white as George Washington's Sunday-go-to-meetin' wig and as sound as the all-mighty dollar," Ellison's fictive scene, like the whole of *Day of Absence*, not only mockingly marries notions of whiteness to American patriotism but simultaneously reveals that the myth of ultrawhiteness is ultimately dependent on the presence of blackness.[52] This phenomenon is underscored when the novel's protagonist learns that the creation of Optic White paint requires ten drops of "dead black" in each bucket, thereby revealing that Optic White is not really "pure" at all. In writing about this Optic White scene, Harryette Mullen offers an analysis that also resonates when applied to Ward's creative intentions in *Day of Absence*.

> The American myth may rely for its potency on the interdependent myths of white purity and white superiority, but the invisible ones whose cultural and genetic contributions to the formation of American identity are covered up by Liberty White, those who function as machines inside the machine, know that no pure product of America, including the linguistic, cultural, and genetic heritage of its people, has emerged without being influenced by over three hundred years of multiracial collaboration and conflict.[53]

In the case of Ellison's *Invisible Man* and Ward's *Day of Absence*, the concept of "optic whiteness"—a visually potent, unambiguous whiteness that is, nonetheless, dependent on blackness for its very expression—is enunciated in different ways but works toward the same conceptual affect. Further accentuating Ward's use of *optic whiteface* is the fact that the bright base makeup used in the original productions of *Day of Absence* was drawn *within* the outline of each actor's face as if portraying an ill-fitting mask. Fashioned in this way, the brown tones of the actors' faces, ears, neck, arms, hands, and legs were blatantly exposed—visually reminding audience members, in the words of Mullen, of the "machines inside the machine."

The conscious choice to disclose the blackness of the players beneath their makeup is highly efficacious. In clearly suggesting that the optic white-

Mayor Henry Lee. Douglas Turner Ward's *Day of Absence,* directed by Carlton Molette, Florida A&M University, 1967. (Photo courtesy of Carlton Molette.)

face is masklike, the actors intentionally reveal the mask of whiteness as both shield and fabrication while presenting black bodies as masters over whiteness in a Bahktinian reversal of power. Exposing the constructed nature of whiteness, the style of the makeup reveals the powerful relationship between form and content, reinforcing the way the design's strategy emboldens the play's thematic through-line on the constructed nature of our racialized identities.

While the base color of the whiteface makeup used in the original *Day of Absence* production was ultrawhite, the makeup design did not lack nuance or detail. The differing ages and idiosyncrasies of the characters were suggested by the application of various facial characteristics, all the while paying homage to the play's suggested color scheme. For example, since Ward had specified that "This is a red-white-and-blue play—meaning the entire production should be designed around the basic color scheme of our patriotic trinity," characters boasted blue eyebrows or exhibited wrinkles drawn in red and blue.[54] Although the whitefaced male characters in Ward's debut production all performed without hairdressing (revealing the natural texture of their dark, tightly curled hair), their female counterparts all wore wigs. This is evidenced by the character Mary, who appeared in a blond ringlet wig, and the telephone operators, who wore matching bright-red wigs, giving them a decidedly "Raggedy Ann" appearance. Continuing this emphasis on the doll-like veneer of Ward's characters, some directors choose to employ *yarn* wigs for both male and female characters, as in the case of Carlton Molette, whose productions of *Day of Absence* (at Florida A&M University in 1967 and the University of Michigan in 1976) featured this constructed aspect.[55]

Despite the variations described here, the common visual refrain among productions of Ward's play is the doll-like and clownish stylization of the whitefaced characters.[56] Ward's stage directions, exemplified by his description of the incompetent young mother, Mary, have undoubtedly inspired the frequent use of doll-like visages. Writing that Mary could well be portrayed with a "Kewpie-doll face, ruby-red lips painted to valentine-pursing, moon-shaped rouge circles implanted on each cheek," Ward's notes clearly suggest the style and manner in which he envisions his whiteface characterizations. I would argue again that the artifice inherent in such costuming reveals Ward's intention to disclose the fallacies of whiteness. Unlike the ways in which some early blackface performances attempted to construct and perpetuate racist representations of blacks *as* authentic, Ward's whiteface is a transparent performance that highlights the inauthentic nature of both blackface and whiteface.

John and Mary. Douglas Turner Ward's *Day of Absence*, directed by Carlton Molette, Florida A&M University, 1967. (Photo courtesy Carlton Molette.)

Strikingly, Ward's description of Mary also offers readers an opportunity to again reflect on *Invisible Man* by way of the novel's own "kewpie character." When describing his protagonist's sighting of the forlorn white dancer in *Invisible Man*'s Battle Royal scene, Ellison's writes:

> The hair was yellow like that of a circus kewpie doll, the face heavily powdered and rouged, as though to form an abstract mask, the eyes hollow and smeared a cool blue, the color of a baboon's butt.... I wanted at one and the same time to run from the room, to sink through the floor, or go to her and cover her from my eyes and the eyes of the others with my body; to feel the soft thighs, to caress her and destroy her, to love her and murder her, to hide from her, and yet to stroke where below the small American flag tattooed upon her belly her thighs formed a capital V.[57]

On seeing the clownish visage of the kewpie-doll-like dancer, Ellison captures his protagonist's entangled feelings of desire and disgust. By evoking the image of "the small American flag" tattooed on the dancer's belly, Ellison conceivably creates a conceptual blueprint for Ward's *Day of Absence*. Ellison's kewpie-style dancer personifies a seductive, inaccessible, and tormented nation. Similarly, the white characters in *Day of Absence* may initially strike audience members as innocuous and ineffectual, but—draped in the red, white, and blue colors of the American flag—their eventual expressions of resentment and antagonism ultimately betray the truths that lie beneath their dollish exteriors. Like Ellison's passage on the kewpie dancer, the whitefaced characters in *Day of Absence* animate America's complicated racial relations by dramatizing dueling feelings of desire and disgust, love and hate.

The deliberate uses of doll-like imagery in *Invisible Man* and *Day of Absence* are heightened, and particularly befitting, choices. In thinking of the more sinister manifestations of doll-like images, Allen S. Weis's observations regarding the haunting properties of dolls in popular culture seem particularly resonant when applied to *Day of Absence*: "The doll, simulacrum of the body, is an object of the most profound psychic projections, the ultimate floating signifier. As such, it is particularly adequate to express, and to counteract, that most empty and final of signifiers, *death*."[58] The doll-like/deathlike quality of Ward's optic whiteface is further highlighted by the Announcer's final description of the devastated inhabitants as "zombies," underscoring the trope of "whiteness as death." Perhaps these death-oriented visual and thematic ruminations contributed—consciously or unconsciously—to any unrest or displeasure experienced by those less enamored with Ward's play. The playwright himself, however, points to another reason that some critics disavowed *Day of Absence*. He asserts, quite simply, that white folks were not used to seeing their own whiteness staged and critiqued; they were not accustomed to such public censure.[59]

Of course, as evidenced by the commercial success of *Day of Absence*, a great many audience members—white and black—enthusiastically embraced Ward's optic whiteface and broad strokes. In creating "a reverse minstrel show," Ward recognized that the theatrical power of his play would double: the application of whiteness to brown bodies would obscure problematic narratives associated with both whites and blacks. While a handful of theatre reviewers staunchly resisted this dramatic exploration, history reveals that audience reaction to the now famous double bill was overwhelmingly positive. *Happy Ending* and *Day of Absence* ran for 504 performances (more than fifteen months) at the St. Marks Playhouse, and the impact went far beyond impressive ticket sales. With the notable success of their initial productions, Robert Hooks and Douglas Turner Ward were quickly transformed from relatively unknown dramatists to high-profile community activists and artists. This, in turn, would take *Day of Absence* from the stage to the small screen in an unprecedented television event: the 1967 premier episode of the PBL.

A BIG DEBUT ON THE SMALL SCREEN: THE PUBLIC BROADCAST LABORATORY

Taking advantage of the critical spotlight on *Happy Ending* and *Day of Absence*, the desire to develop black artistry became a major—and very public—goal for all those involved in the production of Ward's plays. In fact, even before the official debut of the twin bill, Robert Hooks was directing the public's attention to the needs of African American artists. In a *New York Times* feature on the Group Theatre Workshop (a preview piece that preceded the November 15 opening of the double bill), Hooks laid out the history, mission, and goals of the workshop. His vision for its future was to see the company benefit from nonprofit status and gain substantial foundation support. While the need for a stable artistic home for the workshop was publically articulated by Hooks in the article, the dialogue did not stop there.[60]

Nine months after opening his plays at the St. Marks Playhouse, Douglas Turner Ward wrote an urgent and forceful article for the *New York Times* titled "American Theater: For Whites Only?"[61] The opinion piece begins by recognizing a recent flood of accomplished Negro playwrights, citing Louis Peterson, Lorraine Hansberry, Ossie Davis, James Baldwin, and LeRoi Jones.[62] Despite the various acknowledgments and accolades black theatre artists were receiving at the time, Ward's op-ed article cautioned his readers to recognize the relative dearth of opportunities for black actors, playwrights, and directors working in the world of American theatre, a direct consequence of their racialized marginalization: "By his mere historical placement in American society, the Negro exists as a disturbing presence, an embarrassment to majority comfort, an actuality deflating pretenses, an implicit witness and cogent critic too immediate for attention."[63] Moreover, Ward's words invoked the sentiments of W. E. B. DuBois,[64] in that he, too, decisively urged for the creation of theatre by blacks, for blacks.

> [T]he screaming need is for a sufficient audience of *other Negroes*, better informed through commonly shared experience to readily understand, debate, confirm, or reject the truth or falsity of his creative explorations. Not necessarily an all-black audience to the exclusion of whites but, for the playwright, certainly his primary audience, the first persons of his address, potentially the most advanced, the most responsive or most critical. Only through their initial and continuous participation can his intent and purpose be best perceived by others.[65]

At the close of his article, Ward reinforced his assertions by rephrasing the sentiments that Hooks had expressed nine months earlier, reminding the reading audience of the fact that black artists needed professional homes if true advancements were to be made.

> If any hope, outside of chance individual fortune, exists for Negro playwrights as a group—or, for that matter, Negro actors and other theater craftsmen—the most immediate, pressing, practical, absolutely minimally essential active first step is the development of a permanent repertory company of at least off-Broadway size and dimension. Not in the future, but now.[66]

Notably, Ward's remarks not only continue along the conceptual trajectory initiated by DuBois, but they also target the same issues that the great American playwright August Wilson raised thirty years later in his famous Theatre Communications Group conference speech, "The Ground on Which I Stand."[67] As if trying to curtail the criticisms that would later be hurled at Wilson,[68] Ward wrote, "This is not a plea for either a segregated theater, or a separatist one,"[69] clarifying his broader goal of inclusivity by insisting that if whites were open to supporting black theatre, he would be equally supportive of their patronage and participation.

The vision articulated by both Hooks and Ward came to fruition when Hooks, Ward, and Gerald S. Krone (a white theatre manager and producer who had previously worked for the Group Theatre Workshop) won a $434,000 grant from the newly formed Ford Foundation. They pledged to use the grant to improve and expand on the work begun by the workshop and christened their new collective the Negro Ensemble Company (NEC).[70]

The vision of the NEC captured the attention of the Ford Foundation and also drew interest from another burgeoning, cutting-edge organization: the PBL. Like the NEC, the PBL—a programming arm of National Educational Television—was indebted to generous funding from Ford.[71] Touted as a nationwide experiment featuring noncommercial, journalistic programming, the PBL enticed its potential viewers with an intriguing marketing campaign, one that highlighted its promise to cover controversial and provocative topics. At the time, the PBL was cited as being "easily the most widely promoted and advertised venture in the annals of non-commercial TV."[72] One part of its extensive marketing campaign was an advertisement that ran in the Sunday edition of *the Washington Post*.

> PBL's goal is to demonstrate every Sunday night just how inventive, provocative and important Public Television can be. It will offer two hours (or maybe more) of incisive reporting, examinations of the arts and sciences, live drama, strong opinion and probing comment. It will venture into subjects commercial television has not touched. It will be completely free of commercial interruptions and advertiser influence.
>
> PBL will use television as it's never been used before to deepen understanding and to offer new perspectives on the issues and events of our time. It will call upon the best minds in the academic world and public life, top dramatic talent and proven broadcast journalists headed by PBL Chief Correspondent Edward P. Morgan.[73]

The remainder of the PBL's *Washington Post* ad offered an impressive teaser of no less than twenty topics, each followed by one or two sentences that suggested the approach to the subject matter. The titles of future episodes disclosed a range of material that went from the curious (such as "Trading Stamps: Trick or Treat?," "Groucho Goes to Washington," and "Are You Eating Yourself to Death?") to the controversial ("Vietnam: The House Divided," "George Wallace's America," and "Is the Roman Catholic Church in Trouble?").[74] The debut program, however, would attack a decidedly controversial subject: race. Inspired by the upcoming 1967 mayoral elections in Cleveland, Boston, and Gary, Indiana (in all three cases, racial factors exacerbated the political conflicts), the PBL fashioned an evening of programming that would highlight both real-life drama and drama on the stage, making Ward's *Day of Absence* one of its featured segments.

According to the *New York Times*, the public television stations in Boston (WGBH-TV) and Cleveland (WVIZ-TV), were among the more than one hundred that were originally prepared to air the PBL series in its entirety, but on learning that attention would be drawn to the racially charged mayoral campaigns, both stations "expressed concern" with regard to providing "fair coverage in accordance with the Federal Communications Commission's established requirement for equal time for candidates in political races."[75] To satisfy this requirement, the Boston and Cleveland stations decided to edit the program and remove any references to the mayoral campaigns, thereby avoiding accusations of biased reporting prior to the elections.[76]

While the trepidation of the Boston and Cleveland channels was related to the issue of political coverage, other stations—such as the educational station housed at the University of Georgia—refused outright to air the laboratory's debut show, with all indications suggesting that the Georgia station was particularly resistant to the presentation of *Day of Absence*. Claiming that the PBL had failed to inform station employees of its programming details in a timely manner, the manager, Dr. William H. Hale Jr., asserted that the PBL had not been given the station enough time "to arrange for a supplementary program offering a balanced perspective on the racial issue."[77] Moreover, Hale expressed concern that there was an inherent regionalism at play in the composition of PBL: since all the PBL board members hailed from the Northeast, he felt that they would be "unfamiliar with the Southern perspective" and that the programming "did not embrace the diverse viewpoints of other geographical areas."[78]

Although Hale's anxiety regarding the late notice of PBL's programming plans was clearly articulated, less clear is how his station could conceivably have presented a more "balanced" perspective in response to *Day of Absence*. How would such a dramatic or journalistic angle be actualized? Would an opposing segment demonstrate that the day-to-day presence of black people was *not* essential to civic life in America, or would an acceptable counter-presentation reveal that whites were, in fact, central to society's ubiquitous machinations? If so, how would the latter viewpoint present a newsworthy perspective? Didn't these vantage points already dominate the cultural texts of the time?

What is known is that the University of Georgia was not alone in its refusal to air the first PBL episode. In fact, all ten of Georgia's noncommercial stations, five of South Carolina's, and seven of Alabama's refused to telecast the program due to the planned subject matter. A handful of additional stations cited other reasons, such as a lack of funding or the inability to connect to the necessary relay circuits, for not airing the show.[79] In the end, 29 of 119 public stations ended up dropping the PBL broadcast from their schedule.

Strikingly, not only was the unease surrounding the presentation of Ward's *Day of Absence* expressed by independent broadcast stations, but it was also a dynamic that fostered internal strife within the power structure of the PBL. According to newspaper accounts, the head of the laboratory's editorial policy board, Edward W. Barrett (who, ironically, was on a "leave of absence" from his post as the dean at Columbia University's Graduate School of Journalism), was displeased with the decision to air *Day of Absence* from the very beginning. Barrett's objections to Ward's play were repeatedly framed as "theatrical, not political, and ... the chief complaint was the quality of the show."[80] Nevertheless, the laboratory's executive director, Av Westin, defended the decision to move forward with the airing of the play. Steering away from questions regarding the quality of the presentation, Westin focused on how *Day of Absence* served as "one form of Negro expression" that fulfilled the PBL's aim of addressing the larger issue of race relations.[81]

Recognizing that the PBL's leaders expressed a lack of confidence in the theatrical quality of *Day of Absence* raises even more questions. What, exactly, were they hoping to accomplish with the presentation of *Day of Absence* if they were not wholly convinced that this particular "form of Negro expression" would appeal to television audiences? If both Barrett and Westin had issues with the quality of the play, how were they staging—or more appropriately "setting up"—the work for its racially diverse television audience? In other words, what do these decisions reveal about the ways in which the program's institutional dramaturgy affected the reception of the play?

Before engaging in this line of questioning, however, one also must fully consider the entirety of the debut PBL program. Although *Day of Absence* was certainly a major part of this initial broadcast, the material that framed the play undoubtedly contributed to the way it was received by its various audiences. The program in its entirety featured several segments: (1) a journalistic account of the mayoral campaigns in Gary, Cleveland, and Boston; (2) a contentious and emotionally charged dialogue between white and black Chicagoans; (3) the televised performance of *Day of Absence*; and (4) the PBL's much buzzed "anticommercials"—advertising spoofs that commented critically on the claims of products such as aspirin and 100 mm cigarettes.

In reviewing the premier episode and reflecting on its contents, I believe that the material, structure, and delivery of the PBL program inevitably affected the ways in which *Day of Absence* was interpreted and received by viewing audiences. Just as the juxtaposition of *Day of Absence* and *Happy Ending* in a single viewing experience shapes the way the themes and motivations of each piece are understood, the PBL version of *Day of Absence* was placed in a context that influenced its reception. Undeniably, the PBL's televised presentation served its goals and effectively highlighted a number of tropes and messages found in Ward's play. However, as part of a wider broadcast, the conceptual complexity of *Day of Absence* was diminished by the PBL's programming agenda. Thus, the significance of the laboratory debut not only lies in its role in presenting *Day of Absence* to a national audience, but it also serves as an intriguing example of how institutional dramaturgy (i.e., the metatheatrical and experiential context of a performance) can invariably influence an audience's understanding and appreciation of a work.

THE MAYORAL CAMPAIGNS OF 1967

The PBL debut begins simply enough: an unseen narrator informs the audience that the evening's program will explore a "black-white dialogue."[82] When the PBL correspondent, Edward P. Morgan, formally appears onscreen he characterizes the current conditions of racial unrest by offering an anecdote that ends with the observation, "Americans still are not talking to each other." Citing the lack of dialogue as a "communications problem," Morgan asserts:

> Black and White Americans are shouting at each other. In the vicious babble, too few are listening. Everybody should be. The noise pierces the heart of our society with a simple issue. How can a democracy survive with a dual system of justice in which some people—white people—are more equal than others? Impatient Negro extremists have burst the boil of frustration with violence. Some frightened whites have answered with the backlash of bigotry. The theme of our black-white dialogue, or non-dialogue, is painfully relevant.[83]

Pronouncing the PBL's effort "to show the awful width of the communications gap and the urgency of bridging it," the broadcast turns its critical eye—and camera lens—on several heated 1967 mayoral elections.

The first words uttered by Tom Pettit, the PBL journalist covering the mayoral election in Gary, Indiana, further underscore the atmosphere of dissension expressed earlier by Edward P. Morgan: "Gary, Indiana, is a microcosm of America's urban problems, and this weekend it is a symbol of the country's failure to establish a dialogue between black and white." Raising provocative queries (the same sorts of questions, notably, that were uttered during Barack Obama's presidential campaign in 2008), Pettit asks, "Can a black man be elected despite his color? Should a black man be elected mayor *because* of his color? Can a white man oppose a Negro without exploiting the race issue and vice versa?"

Prompted by these questions, the aid of retrospection offers present-day audiences the opportunity to fully recognize the relative rarity of blacks gaining prominent political positions in the 1960s. While this truth would clearly resonate in its day, the troubled tone of the PBL's election coverage further primes audiences for the accentuation of this rarity as theatrically portrayed in the forthcoming presentation of Day of Absence. In Ward's play, the whitefaced mayor, Henry Lee, is a potent reminder of the lack of black civil leadership due to historic and systematic discrimination. Mayor Lee even directly addresses this history when he happily reminds the play's television Announcer of the eventual demise of Reconstruction: "Carpetbaggers even put Nigras in the Governor's mansion, state legislature, Congress and the Senate of the United States. But what happened?—Ole Dixie bounced right on back."[84] Thus, the rhetoric of the whitefaced mayor further reifies an expectation to exclude blacks from political spheres rather than entertain the potential for change.

America's history of racial inequity, initially raised by the PBL reporter's opening queries, is further addressed when Pettit delves deeper into the Gary election campaigns of Richard Gordon Hatcher and Joseph Radigan. Hatcher, an African American lawyer and president of the Gary City Council, was running against Radigan—a white furniture dealer with no previous experience in politics. Despite the vast disparity in the candidates' political activities and educational backgrounds, Pettit notes, "It is generally agreed in Gary that if Richard Hatcher were white he would be a sure winner." According to the news coverage, the racial identity of the candidates was not only a major issue *between* political parties but also an issue *within* the Democratic Party. In spite of his preparatory experience, Hatcher was denied local support by fellow Democrats. In fact, the county chairman of the Democratic Party, John J. Krupa, wryly dismissed Hatcher, asserting that the African American lawyer has "learned a trick of making [a] profession out of being a Negro like Martin Luther King, Stokely Carmichael, H. R. Brown, and people of that ilk." Furthermore, Krupa, clearly attempting to foster public anxieties, put on record that he was prepared to call out the National Guard and state police if a Hatcher loss led to riots.

With public uprisings such as the Harlem riots of 1964, the Watts riots of 1965, and the Detroit riots of July 1967 still lingering in recent memory, possible election-related riots seemed to dominate the public imagination. To underscore this point, the segment includes a scene in which Hatcher, shortly after speaking to a small, all-white audience, is asked about whether or not he is concerned about the possibility of violence erupting if he is not elected. Hatcher attempted to assuage the fears of the inquisitor—as well as the trepidation of the television audience—insisting that violence would not ensue and expressing his confidence that the American public, black and white, would behave with civility and composure, regardless of the election outcome. As noted earlier, it is the fear of violence, erroneously ascribed to black folks' supposedly riotous nature, that Ward derides in *Day of Absence*.[85] Fortifying rather than assuaging these rampant fears, the PBL reporter closes his piece with a curious transition.

> On election day, the National Guard will be on standby, federal investigators will be on duty, but the damage to the city has already been done. The truth of it is that in 1967 Richard Hatcher could not avoid the race issue any more than John F. Kennedy could have avoided the religious

issue in 1960. And the race issue both helps and hurts a Negro candidate, as Carl Stokes is finding out in Cleveland.

The PBL broadcast then shifts its focus to the Cleveland mayoral contest between a black democrat, Carl Stokes, and a white republican candidate, Seth Taft.

Giving relatively little attention to the fact that Seth Taft is the grandson of former president William Howard Taft, the PBL reporter, Greg Shuker, focuses inordinately on Cleveland's African American candidate, highlighting a number of Stokes's unscripted campaign moments. Shuker also makes the pointed assertion that Stokes's campaign is "two pronged," suggesting that the candidate's talking points are framed differently depending upon the racial makeup of his audiences. At face value, Shuker's commentary reinforces a troubled assumption: that black folks simply want Stokes elected *because* he is black and whites—unlike their black counterparts—have serious concerns about civic issues. Moreover, the inference that such a two-pronged political platform is even necessary invariably confirms the PBL's claim regarding the "awful width of the communications gap" between blacks and whites.

The PBL's final mayoral race segment, reported by Austin Hoyt, offers a notable deviation in terms of race-inflected politics. The mayoral contest in Boston is between two white Democratic candidates: Louise Day Hicks and Kevin White. Despite the fact that both mayoral candidates are white, the Boston race is highly racialized: Hicks is a staunch and highly vocal opponent of desegregation programs, while her opponent has chosen to focus on less contentious issues such as rent control. Undoubtedly, the inherent theatricality of Hicks's controversial campaign prompted the PBL cameras to focus predominately on her incendiary persona. Highlighting her well-worn campaign slogan, "You know where I stand," the Boston segment captures multiple moments that effectively represent the city's civil unrest and Hicks's uncompromising racial politics.

> The supporters of Louise Day Hicks for mayor of Boston: they're from the ethnic enclaves of a pot that never melted. They're older, less well educated, and poorer than those that vote against her. She calls them her "little people" and says she'll protect them. Protect them from the urban renewal bulldozer, the big banker, the universities taking property off

the tax roll. But what school committeewoman Hicks makes clearest to them is that she will protect their neighborhoods from the Negro by preserving neighborhood schools. That she wants to appeal a state law that says no school can be predominately Negro as more than fifty schools in Boston are. That she's dead against proposals to bus Negro children into white neighborhood schools. To her critics, she is the George Wallace of the North. To these people, who helped her to a primary victory over nine men, she is a savior from South Boston.

To further illustrate the tone of Hicks's campaign, the camera cuts to some of her devoted followers: two white women who express their confusion over Boston's current political climate. The women readily assert that prior to the migration of blacks from the South, Boston's blacks were "happy" with the city's segregation—a fictional utopia that Hicks is fervently hoping to reestablish if elected mayor. Thus, as a northerner with Confederate-style sympathies, Hicks ultimately symbolizes the real-life political embodiment of the fictional mayor in Ward's *Day of Absence*. Like Hicks, the character of Mayor Henry Lee represents white glorification of a nonexistent past of "fond memories" and "happy associations" between whites and blacks.[86] In pure politicking mode, Mayor Lee broadcasts his thinly disguised racist rhetoric to the masses, and, despite the sly packaging of his words, he—like the candidate Louise Day Hicks—makes it very clear where he "stands."

A mere two days *after* the airing of the tension-filled PBL episode, the votes in the three elections would be cast and history would be made. Despite the contention displayed in the PBL coverage, Richard Gordon Hatcher would beat the white furniture dealer, becoming the first African American mayor of Gary, Carl Stokes would beat Seth Taft and become the first African American mayor of Cleveland, and Kevin White—the first mayoral candidate in decades to receive an endorsement from the *Boston Globe*—would beat the staunch segregationist Louise Day Hicks. Although the eventual results of these mayoral races would offer television spectators hope regarding the future of race relations in America, these results were not foreseeable on November 5, 1967, the night of the PBL's initial airing. What the sensational coverage of these historic mayoral campaigns did do, however, was to directly confront a national audience with the racial anxieties that marked the social and political climate of 1967. The stories behind these campaigns, however, were only a part of several PBL segments that highlighted America's racial disparities. While the mayoral segment addressed the *political* campaigns of a few, the following segment—a black-white dialogue between Chicago citizens—addressed the *personal* campaigns of many.

CHICAGOANS SPEAK: "A BLACK-WHITE DIALOGUE"

At the start of the next segment, the voice of the unseen narrator is heard again: "The race issue. That's all you hear about these days. Tiresome sometimes, but you can't escape it. But in all the talk about race, is either side talking to the other? Where is the dialogue?" The PBL commentator then asserts the need for "confrontation," the chance to "talk, directly, to each other." With these words of explication, the program turns to a studio in Chicago in which one hundred ideologically diverse residents are gathered. According to our narrator, the audience members range from "militants and moderates, some who say now, some who say never," all of whom have gathered to engage in a highly charged—and often very personal—debate on race.

Yet before the discussion formally begins, the segment cuts to an orchestrated preface: a video and audio clip created by the self-proclaimed black nationalist and Chicago resident Russell Meek. Far from inviting, Meek begins his piece with undeniable antagonism: "You want to know what in the hell a ghetto is like? You want to know what in the hell it's like to live on that stinkin' West Side of Chicago? Well, me and my little black brother are gonna show you, Whitey. Watch this." As the segment continues, Meek prompts spectators to watch a dramatic prelude to the forum that will follow: a self-authored, voiced, and directed minidrama/documentary. And while Meek initially seems to target "Whitey" with his words, the viewing audience soon learns that he is an equal opportunity offender, not only disgusted with the ways of white folk but also expressing little tolerance for black folk that fail to share his nationalist ideology.

Meek's brief docudrama reveals that that he lives on Chicago's West Side (ostensibly "the ghetto"), loves Stokely Carmichael, believes that "nonviolence is the philosophy of the fool," and would "rather die on [his] feet than live on his knees." The piece (which, again, was under Meek's "complete control" according to the narrator) offers this entrée into Meek's personage while also providing a visual tour of his West Side neighborhood. The camera spends a great deal of time scanning the neighborhood's most disappointing aspects: garbage-filled streets, dilapidated buildings, and the hollow eyes and crouching bodies that represent victims of extreme poverty.

Nevertheless, the lens does not totally limit its gaze to expressions of defeat or despair. It also offers examples of progress and defiance. Emphasizing the latter, Meek briefly interviews a few West Side teenagers. These young men talk of being tired of the distressing circumstances that surround them, arguing—with black nationalist rhetoric—that the solution to the social ills around them can only be cured through "complete separation" of the races. Meek applauds the young men while denigrating the integrationist politics of more mainstream African American leaders.

This video piece serves as a disquieting prologue to the actual "Chicago Forum"—a carefully contained event in which white and black Chicagoans confront each other in a no-holds-barred discussion. Among the notable characters present for the conversation are the aforementioned Russell Meek; two of the teenagers featured in Meek's video; and the Reverend Henry Mitchell, a local black minister from Chicago's West Side whom Meek repeatedly attacks for his integrationist politics. Tempers fly between and within the racial groups, with some of the greatest tensions expressed between Meek and Mitchell. Mitchell, championing his spiritual doctrine, advocates "Christian love," but he lacks the verbal acuity, wit, and poeticism exhibited by Meek. Meek's dynamism is undeniable, and his verbal alacrity obliterates the reverend's sincere attempt at peaceful persuasion. In the end, the reverend appears far weaker—in presentation and power—than the unrelenting black nationalist.

Mitchell's acquiescence, relative to Meek's characterization, is a disconcerting display for those with either antiblack *or* integrationist sentiments. Meek's obliterating militancy (he skewers the likes of Martin Luther King Jr., Whitney Young, and Roy Wilkins) leaves little room for the program to display an African American "middle ground." Meek also wholeheartedly dismisses Christian tenets, arguing that Christianity is a white man's faith, a means of controlling and oppressing blacks rather than a means of hope or communal galvanization. Notably, this critique of Christianity arises later in *Day of Absence*. In Ward's play, the tellingly *un-Christian* sentiments of Reverend Reb Pious seem to support Meek's perspective. Pious contends that Christianity is the key to combatting the "deep-rooted primitivism" of blacks: "Now, at last, you can understand the difficulties of the Church in attempting to anchor God's kingdom among ungratefuls.... Despite all our aid, guidance, solace and protection, Old BeezleBub still retains tenacious grips upon the Nigras' childish loyalty—comparable to the lure of bright flames to an infant."[87] After witnessing Meek's potent presentation, as well as Mitchell's less than stellar performance, audiences may have been erroneously primed to interpret Ward's treatment of black Christianity in a negative light rather than as an invitation to recognize the nuances and complexities of Christianity in relation to black history.

Although the staging of the forum and its various characters ensured that polarities would abound, there were some genuine attempts among the attendees to make links across racial lines. For example, a white woman proudly asserts that her nineteen-year-old daughter has just married a "Negro boy" and her son married a Chinese girl; a white, male schoolteacher from Chicago's West Side affirms one of Meek's talking points by arguing that the challenges faced by poor blacks are far greater than the challenges faced by poor whites; and another white woman clumsily—yet sincerely—asks Meek, "How do you go about not alienating the white man that has been for you through violence?" Despite the woman's sincere overture, Meek—as if representing the black race—staunchly rejects any efforts toward racial coalition and admonishes the white audience member: "We don't want you to love us. . . . We don't love you."[88]

The attempt of white speakers to bridge the communication gap is theatrically challenged not only by Meek but by his teenage minions. Two of the young men who were previously filmed in Meek's documentary present fiery opinions regarding the racial climate. They firmly reject the notion that blacks have a chance to work their way up the economic ladder and blast integrationist efforts as Uncle Tomism. In fact, as if to terminate any discussion of potential racial unification, at one point the youngest boy proudly proclaims, "I am for violence."

There were, of course, points and counterpoints offered throughout the debate. One particularly intriguing counterperformance to Meek's nationalist rhetoric was the staunch declarations offered by a white woman from the East Avondale Community Council.

> I arose from this neighborhood. I lived in the slums. I'm not ashamed of it, and, you know, nobody helped me get where I'm at. I scrubbed floors. I scrubbed floors, it doesn't make any difference. The friends that I graduated with have jobs and homes just as I have now, and they were colored. And they had a chance; they sat right next to me in class. The teacher listened to them just like she listened to me. And it was that same, that same house that you showed me on that film. So, then, I am the same as these boys here. 'Cause I seen little white kids as well as little

colored kids together digging out of garbage cans, not separately.... So what about me? Am I a poor white person, God help me, give me mercy? I want white power then!

Despite what could be perceived as persuasive passion, the councilwoman's neoconservative perspective fails to resonate with Russell Meek. Rather, Meek responds by asserting that the issue of analogous white poverty and marginalization is moot: he couldn't care less about white people, and, moreover, he believes that both whites and blacks need to solve their *own* problems respectively.

In thinking of the *Day of Absence* presentation to follow, the councilwoman's denial of her privileged whiteness can easily be identified with the Social Welfare Commissioner in Ward's play. Insisting on the acknowledgment of white deprivation and victimization, the Commissioner Aide in *Day of Absence* readily transposes the problems facing blacks to whites, noting, "Disruption of our pilot projects among Nigras saddles our white community with extreme hardship."[89] Moreover, in dismissing the way institutionalized racism hinders the socioeconomic progress of the black community, the aide attributes the predicament of blacks to lack of personal agency: "We pioneered in enforcing social welfare theories which oppose coddling the fakers. We strenuously believe in helping Nigras help themselves by participating in meaningful labor. 'Relief is Out, Work is In,' is our motto."[90] Thus, both *Day of Absence* and the PBL broadcast feature white characters that espouse a "pull yourself up by your bootstraps" ideology, one that stirs sentiments on both sides of the racial divide yet offers no resolution.

Of course, resolution was never a stated goal of the PBL staff—they only articulated a desire to stage a "confrontation." Yet and still, there were moments throughout in which potential solutions were raised, if not championed. Case in point: when the forum's moderator, Dave Dugan, brings up the fact that Martin Luther King has been proposing to "tie up the cities" as a nonviolent tactic, Meek immediately discounts the efficaciousness of such strategies: "You don't tie up a city. There's no such thing as massive civil disobedience." Jumping into the conversation, a black religious leader and social worker by the name of Reverend Davis pushes the possibility further: "What if every Negro employee of the CTA [Chicago Transit Authority] picked one day in September to get sick. Wouldn't that tie up the city?" Meek bleakly responds, "No, they'd get fired; they'd get white folks in their place." In his refusal to engage in dialogue, Meek's impetuous response also fails to heed two facts: boycotts can indeed make a difference, the Montgomery bus boycott of 1955–56 being a superlative example; and white folks *are not* eager to take on the tasks normally executed by blacks. Also of interest is the fact that in dismissing the communal power of boycotts Meek foregrounds a dismissal of the very premise of *Day of Absence*, the programming segment that is soon to follow.

With much said, positions staked, and nothing resolved aside from the staging of the confrontation itself, the Chicago Forum bestowed certainty on only one issue: the seemingly irresolvable nature of the nation's racial divide. Creating the only type of resolution possible under the staged circumstances, the PBL program transitioned from Chicago back to the PBL studio, revealing a panel of three white men: two white broadcasters and an interviewee, a Harvard psychiatrist, Dr. Robert Coles.

When one of the broadcasters asks, "What do you make of all this?," Coles responds enthusiastically, noting that he is glad he "interrupted [his] Sunday to come and watch" the PBL program: "I've never seen anything quite so real and vivid and—in a sense, historical—as this film, because in this film I saw everything that is going on in America today, beautifully shown." With diplomatic urgency, Coles expresses his wish that more whites could be exposed to the material at hand: "[T]hey don't understand how Negroes feel, and I think they don't know how they feel. I think this film shows white people how they feel." He also admits his own discomfort with the televised exchanges: "I found myself getting nervous, a little apprehensive, twinging. . . . I think it gets to you." Attempting to distance himself from white liberals who fail to recognize their own conflicting sentiments regarding race, Coles continues:

> I think white intellectual liberals are often very blind to their own arrogance, which takes the form of condescension, which takes the form of a kind of naive, innocent, almost ingratiating kindness, which is infuriating to someone who's hungry, who's been rebuffed again and again. We saw the classical scene here of a woman who's offered her daughter to the Negro race. . . . [T]his lack of comprehension doesn't make her an evil person, doesn't make her a bad person, doesn't make her a stupid person; it makes her an ordinary human being who has the kinds [sic] of blindness, the kinds [sic] of self-defense, that we all have to have in order to survive some of these very rancorous, abrasive, annoying truths.

Adding that "we are going through a terribly painful, wrenching, and difficult . . . [time]," Coles offers the illustrative yet unfortunate analogy of a parent-child relationship, suggesting that whenever children (in his analogy, black people) break away from authoritative and controlling parents (white people), there will always be unavoidable difficulty and pain related to the restructuring of the relationship.

Thus, despite Coles's efforts to bring a relatively progressive perspective to his analysis, the viewer is left with yet another paternalistic overlay. His analogy suggests the inevitability of, and innate separation between, blacks and whites rather than promoting the promise of potential unification. Befittingly, it is at this point that the PBL moderator, Edward P. Morgan, reiterates the program's focus on America's communication gap in order to introduce its next segment: the controversial airing of Douglas Turner Ward's *Day of Absence*.

TELEVISING *DAY OF ABSENCE*

As the introductory credits for *Day of Absence* begin, the camera captures the play's studio set. While the set directions written for the theatre specify "No scenery is necessary—only actors shifting in and out on an almost bare stage," the PBL broadcast of *Day of Absence* not only used set pieces but also utilized monochromatic black and white flats to suggest the multiple locations featured in the play.[91] Delineating spaces such as a street corner, the mayor's office, and the interior of Mary and John's home, the PBL set's stark set pieces appear as larger-than-life cartoon sketches. Outlined and detailed in black, the one-dimensional white flats have a playful, comical appearance, clearly underscoring the fantastical—and satirical—impulse of the play. Creating a milieu of exaggeration and artifice, the various walls—glorified dividers—symbolize the social divisions explored in the play's text. Moreover, in highlighting its own constructed nature, the set underscored the various themes of "construction" throughout the play. With the artificiality of a dollhouse, the set also suggests a certain fragility—a visible vulnerability symbolic of America's own tenuous social circumstances.

The taped version of *Day of Absence* stayed fundamentally true to the original script, although the change in venue invited some obvious alterations. For example, the medium of television allowed for a studio set, the editing of transitions, the cutting of shots from scene to scene, and camera close-ups. The PBL version of Ward's play was also invariably shaped by what preceded and followed its televised presentation. To that end, just as the Chicago Forum and its "expert" respondents preceded the *Day of Absence* segment, the play's conclusion was punctuated with a brief exchange between Edward P. Morgan and the historian John Hope Franklin.

> MORGAN: Professor Franklin, not as a drama critic but as a historian, will you write us a review of *Day of Absence*?
>
> FRANKLIN: It reminds me of an article which the Reverend Dr. C. K. Marshall of Mississippi wrote in eighteen hundred and sixty-five, just a few weeks after the end of the Civil War, remarking on the prospects for the survival of the Negro in the United States and freedom. Dr. Marshall predicted that as of the first of January, nineteen hundred and twenty, the last Negro would disappear from the United States.[92]
>
> MORGAN: May I ask you if the play, *Day of Absence*, is dated or is it telling something of our time; is it contributing something to the dialogue between black and white?
>
> FRANKLIN: It's extremely difficult to have anything about the South, or indeed about the United States, that is dated so far as race relations are concerned, so far as the relations between Negroes and whites is [sic] concerned. For what is remarkable is that some of the same views which were held 150 years ago regarding Negroes and their relationships with whites are held today. I think particularly of this kind of ambivalence which is reflected in the play. That on the one hand, the Negro is somehow indispensable, he is desperately needed, but on the other hand there is the tendency to put him away and to disregard him and to fail to recognize that he is a human being and that he has certain aspirations and, indeed, certain rights. Only by, I think, understanding the message that Mr. Turner [sic] seems to be conveying—mainly of the persistence and the prevalence of these cancerous forces of American life—only by recognizing this, can one really begin to understand what is necessary in order to do anything about it. . . .
>
> MORGAN: As a Negro and as a historian and as a distinguished American, are you optimistic or pessimistic about the course of this dialogue?
>
> FRANKLIN: It depends upon the day that I get up and what I see and

feel at that particular time. May I say that I'm not terribly optimistic at the present time.

Although Franklin's sincere, if not encouraging, reflections are his own, they also work to reinforce the broadcast's thematic refrain of racial dissonance and national disunity.

As if to provide a bit of levity, Franklin's brief interview is followed by one of the PBL's acerbic pseudo commercials. However, the chief correspondent, Morgan, soon concludes the program with a sobering commentary.

> Last week a Negro GI just back from Vietnam warned we better do something about all the little Vietnams flaring through American cities. Is there a more monstrous paradox than this: while we invest our substance in blood and bullets in a war nine thousand miles away for justice and freedom, we have yet to fulfill these basic goals at home.

In conjuring the notion of "home," Morgan challenges America—as a nation—to address the "little Vietnams" that prevent national unity, while subtly encouraging *Americans*—those individuals watching the program from the comfort of their living rooms—to join the fight for social justice. With this moral charge, the debut program of the PBL comes to an imposing end.

According to newspaper reports, ninety stations aired the PBL broadcast as initially planned, although responses to the program were strikingly uneven. Jack Gould of the *New York Times* summed up critics' general ambivalence toward the airing when he glibly noted that the show "had flashes of provocative heat but far more moments of journalistic and theatrical ineptitude."[93] This is not to suggest that the PBL completely failed to instigate passionate responses from viewers. According to New York's Channel 13, between fifty and sixty complaints about the program were received, while a telephone operator estimated the number of complaint calls to have been closer to one hundred.[94]

There was also praise for the PBL. Describing *Day of Absence* as "piercing, though not always subtle," the *Washington Post* reported on the "brilliance" of the PBL's initial effort and offered special commendations for the exchange between white and black Chicagoans. Affirming the unresolved tension as a compelling and necessary construct, the reviewer wrote:

> It captured the reality of race relations without illusions; neither "good taste" nor hopes for social harmony were permitted to conceal the antipathies and frustrations, the raw, visceral reactions that can easily touch off explosions of physical violence.[95]

Another enthusiastic review came from the assistant executive director of the National Association for the Advancement of Colored People (NAACP), Dr. John Morsell, who was quoted as saying that he thought the PBL broadcast was "very interesting and much of it excellent."[96]

But the *New York Times* was a little more critical of the PBL episode.

> The segment confirmed in compelling terms the existence of strident attitudes, the ambivalence of white liberals and the generation gap among Negroes. The confrontation could have been a springboard for truly illuminating analysis: the laboratory would have been better off to recognize the sequences as a beginning for discussion and not an end.[97]

Other reviews, including those by the PBL's own leadership, were not even that generous.

Av Westin (the executive producer of the PBL, who defended the decision to air *Day of Absence*) received telegrams that praised the debut program as "some of the most exciting and frightening TV in many a year," yet Westin himself gave the initial broadcast a "C plus."[98] Westin's ambivalence was matched by the Ford Foundation's TV consultant, Fred. W. Friendly, who applauded the fact that the PBL put it on the air, but conceded that "they made a lot of mistakes. It was disappointing."[99] While the PBL's leadership did not openly share the nature of its disappointment, it is clear that opinions ranged widely.

A central and consistent issue of criticism among those who did share their thoughts circulated around the inclusion of *Day of Absence*. And while several reviewers commented on the length of the play, the harshest criticisms were in reference to Ward's use of whiteface.

> The central quarrel with Mr. Ward, unhappily, is his failure to realize that he had a brilliant idea that, on television at least was hampered by his insistence on Negro performers appearing in visually clumsy whiteface....

> By having members of the Negro ensemble theater wear whiteface, he added a completely understandable but nonetheless an extraneous critique of the minstrel show. Had he had a white cast sincerely convey the sense of alarm over the disappearance of the Negroes, he would have achieved in the close-up of television a work of much greater impact.[100]

The assertion that the play's whiteface was "extraneous" demonstrates a failure to recognize the centrality of Ward's layered commentary. Instead of addressing how the use of whiteface speaks to the symbiotic relationship between blacks and whites, the fallacy of racial purity, or the absurdity of *all* racial stereotypes, Jack Gould's critique hinged on reading whiteface as a mere inversion of blackface minstrelsy. Gould was even more biting in a follow-up article, published six days later.

> *Day of Absence* was tiresomely long and largely defeated its worthwhile theme by having member of the Negro Ensemble Theater appear in whiteface, which on the home screen shattered the credibility of a not uninteresting idea.... They wound up satirizing themselves more than the whites.[101]

Gould's disparagement is strikingly similar to Gottfried's condemnations of the stage play two years earlier: in both instances, the reviewers failed to recognize the ways whiteface reinforced Ward's manifold critiques.

This censure suggests an inability—or resistance—to confront the play's various and variable meanings. Rather than considering the truths highlighted through the use of whiteface, the spectacle of optic whiteface, as a relatively unusual theatrical strategy, became the "straw man" that white critics could belabor rather than addressing Ward's more substantial and implicative commentary. In suggesting a straw man effect, I contend that Ward's critical presentation of whiteness was too discomforting for many white reviewers; the discrediting of Ward's whiteface allowed them to uniformly dismiss the greater considerations featured in his work. Such a hasty dismissal fails to recognize that *Day of Absence*, unlike the material that accompanied it in the PBL program, is far from "black and white." As a parodic piece, *Day of Absence* carried a much different tone than the serious-minded mayoral campaign coverage or the black and white dialogue in Chicago. And, although the PBL anticommercials did inject some comedic flair into its debut episode, these short treatments were far from ambiguous in their statements: they clearly condemned the exorbitant costs of name-brand aspirin and admonished the notion that 100 mm cigarettes were any healthier than their carcinogenic forefathers. *Day of Absence* was far more sophisticated. It may have presented an unequivocal critique of white privilege and dominance, but it also used its humor to expose complacency on both sides of the racial divide. As most evident when it is paired with its original companion piece, *Happy Ending*, Ward's *Day of Absence* is not a one-sided condemnation of America's racial dynamics: a close analysis reveals a play that acknowledges the impossibility of separatism and calls for a revisioning of both inter- and intraracial relations.

While I would concede that the initial PBL broadcast was highly successful in actualizing its stated goal of creating "confrontation," I would also argue that its institutional dramaturgy failed to serve the complexity of Ward's Obie-winning play. In my estimation, the nuances and bipartisan elements within *Day of Absence* were diminished when the PBL placed the play within a performative context that constantly reiterated the notion of racialized polarities and chasms. Throughout the broadcast, the PBL transmitted a liberal political viewpoint that fervently aspired to meet the goal of racial equality, yet in its televised staging of the nation's tumultuous race relations the program ultimately expressed disillusionment about the real possibility of racial unification. Within such a context, audiences—particular white audiences—may have been primed to transpose these divisive sentiments onto Ward's play, viewing *Day of Absence* through a lens of futility instead of one of possibility.

Whether or not the PBL producers had particular dramaturgical intentions is unknown, but if they had consciously sculpted the program's framing, Douglas Turner Ward was not privy to these plans. When Ward and the NEC had agreed to perform *Day of Absence* on national television, they were not offered any programming details.

> We had no idea that *Day of Absence* was going to be part of this whole event with all these other elements as a part of it. . . . I was just interested in doing a great production of *Day of Absence*, but I didn't know how it was going to be shown. By the time they told me about the whole evening, I had no idea how it would impact *Day of Absence* . . . . I was probably a little concerned about *Day of Absence* being part of everything only because, you know, artistic work that does [have] its own solitary presentation might get swallowed up or affected by attitudes about the

rest of the stuff.... *Day of Absence* was in the last hour, and by the time it came on, some kind of way it was going to be affected; [I knew that] the content of the other stuff may impact how *Day of Absence* was perceived or seen. But that was not my initial worry because, fuck it, all I wanted to do was make sure that *Day of Absence* was done to my approval, my liking. And by the time we had finished, I was very satisfied by what we had done.[102]

Emboldened by the "freedom of expression" lessons he learned from Genet, Ward's major concern with the PBL program was to have his artistic voice heard and to that end the national debut of his play served its purpose. Through the course of one evening, *Day of Absence* was disseminated and popularized among an even wider audience, further impressing itself on the psyches of black viewers in unexpected and highly efficacious ways. While the drama surrounding its television debut may have faded from collective memory, the premise and meanings of *Day of Absence* have remained ever present in our political and artistic imaginations.

THE PERSISTENT PRESENCE OF *DAY OF ABSENCE*

Two years after *Day of Absence* aired on public television, the NEC restaged the play as part of the theatre company's 1969–70 season. The year 1969 was also the year in which the phrase "day of absence" resonated beyond the world of theatre to refer to a political strategy within the world of social justice—a transposition befittingly symbolized by the creation of Black Solidarity Day. In fact, Dr. Carlos Russell, the community activist and Brooklyn College professor who founded Black Solidarity Day, was directly inspired by the premise of *Day of Absence*.

> What happened in 1969 was that across this country there was the unbelievable and unresponded to reality in which young black men and young black women, and young white men and women were being killed.... We had to find a way to be involved without necessarily picking up a gun. We knew then that America was essentially a capitalist country. We also knew that black people were the laborers, the foundation, the column of a capitalist system that was exemplified by our enslavement. So we had to come up with a concept. How do we deal with this? How do we save

the lives of young people and at the same time, derail the oppression that was killing us and destroying the universe? Well, Douglas Turner [Ward] had written *Day of Absence*, and I said, "Wow, look at that!"... I remembered that Malcolm had preached that we were not oppressed because we were Baptists or Methodist. We were oppressed because we were black. So I came up with a notion: what if we came together around our blackness? Thus, Black Solidarity Day. What would happen if black folks stayed home one day? They didn't go to work. The buses wouldn't run. The subways wouldn't run. The banks wouldn't work. The people that lived on Long Island couldn't come to New York City; they'd have to stay home and mind their own children. So let's talk about black solidarity.... So let us bring together black folk, irrespective of their political persuasion, and let's see if we can cripple, stop this country at least for one day. And I said let's do it the day before the election."[103]

In creating Black Solidarity Day, Russell recognized that the blacks in Ward's play "absented themselves as if moved by a spiritual force," and he hoped to harness "that element of magic which has always been a tradition with our people" in order to embolden the sense of familial kinship and responsibility necessary to inspire activism and change.[104] Accordingly, Russell urged African Americans to demonstrate both their communal solidarity and their invaluable presence by taking a single day to refrain from participating in the larger society (namely, by abstaining from work or patronizing white-owned establishments).[105] With poetic purpose, Russell also asserted that this official day of absence should regularly take place on the Monday before Election Day each November, thereby highlighting the political significance and impact of African American citizenry on the nation. The mantra adopted for Black Solidarity Day reflected this strategic aim: "By your absence make your presence felt."[106]

While Black Solidarity Day has not been consistently observed, organized events such as rallies, panels, featured speakers, concerts, and artistic presentations often mark the occasion. Typically, these activities aim to celebrate community while addressing the persistent sociopolitical concerns of black people. Strikingly, Black Solidarity Day has evolved in unexpected ways, becoming an event of note at predominately white universities such as the State University of New York at New Paltz, Evergreen State College, Tufts University, Stony Brook University, Binghamton University, and Yale University.[107] Through panels, workshops, and guest speakers, these institutions of higher education use the concept of Black Solidarity Day to affirm the contributions of blacks to the American landscape but also to promote a sense interracial solidarity and community building.[108]

Certainly, the most publicized Black Solidarity Day was October 16, 1995—the day of the Million Man March/Day of Absence in Washington, DC. The event—initiated by the minister Louis Farrakhan—was designed to address the economic, social, and political concerns of African Americans by focusing on three central themes: "atonement, reconciliation, and responsibility."[109] Although Farrakhan and his organizers did not choose to hold their march on Black Solidarity Day, they did employ its mantra, "By your absence make your presence felt," as an organizing call.[110] Moreover, in the days, weeks, and months following the Million Man March, a great deal of journalistic ink was spilled referencing Ward's *Day of Absence*, including an article in the *Washington Post* in which reporter Jacqueline Trescott called Ward's play "one of modern theater's most incisive contributions to the sociology of black-white relationships." Within her article, Trescott featured commentary from several of the original cast members of *Day of Absence*, including Douglas Turner Ward, who noted, "Every time anybody comes up with a protest and asks people to stay away from work, people remember it.... So seldom does a work of art continue to have that kind of direct relationship to people's desire to attain some sort of freedom."[111]

Despite acknowledging the currency of the play's premise within sociopolitical circles, the question of whether or not the play is "dated" still frequently arises. Even during the time of the Million Man March, when the premise of *Day of Absence* seemed to resonate in both practical and metaphorical ways, the question of whether the play itself was still timely was addressed with surprising reflections from audiences and theatre makers alike. In fact, in his program article note for Baltimore's Center Stage, director Marion McClinton was refreshingly forthcoming about the contested nature of his approach and vision for the theatre's 1995 production of *Day of Absence*.

> I have been wrestling with this play since I agreed to direct *Day of Absence*. One of the most important questions that I had to ask myself was whether or not the play had become dated.... So I have gone through a lot of different concepts, because we are living in interesting, intriguing times. The millennium is less than half a decade away. The last presidential election of the 20th century is at hand. A line of distinction has been drawn in the sand, and nobody is backing down from anyone.

While McClinton eventually conceded that the play "is still very 1965," he also recognized that *Day of Absence* contains essential and lingering truths.

> Maybe the continued brilliance of Mr. Ward's play is that in a time when common ground is essential to our survival as a nation, he has provided it on the field of comedy. He has shown us ourselves and the sillinesses of our present course. He has also given us a warning, to either laugh together or lose the ability to laugh forever.[112]

As McClinton suggests, the still pressing need for our nation to unify for the sake of its survival remains a timely concern. Moreover, the divisions in need of suturing have only proliferated in the public's consciousness, going beyond black and white to include other ethnic identities, as well as concerns regarding gender, class, religion, and sexuality.

Thus, the intersectional nature of our nation's current sociopolitical complexity clearly demonstrates how these challenges—far beyond a simplistic white-black dyad—still aggravate a sense of national unity. It is for this reason that Ward himself questioned the current relevance of *Day of Absence* in Trescott's *Washington Post* article. Although he recognized the significance of the play with respect to immediate events (namely, the Million Man March), Ward questioned whether its premise would still be valid in post-civil-rights America. Expressing his doubt that a complete absence of black folks would actually cripple society, Ward asserted, "We are disposable." Moreover, he proposed that if he were to rewrite the play he would likely "take it in the opposite direction" because "They have found other people to do the (dirty) work. Now it's like we are a nuisance. They would like to see us disappear."[113]

Ward's comments referenced the fact that the manual and unskilled labor once provided by black workers was (and *is*) increasingly being provided by recent immigrants and other minorities. In recognizing this shift, he was suggesting that the answer to creating a more contemporary *Day of Absence* might be to alter the play's ending. I would suggest, however, that it is the very fact that the "disappeared" of Ward's play could now easily represent another minority group that powerfully reveals the play's persistent currency. Moreover, adjusting the casting to reflect America's new demographics could provide an even more powerful lens with which to study the pervasive and wide-reaching effects of imperialism and colonialism. Rather than disempowering Ward's initial premise and intention, such an adaptation would highlight the omnipresent consequences of white privilege and the insidious dynamics of contemporary racism. "Whiteness"—and all its myriad meanings and unearned liberties—must be interrogated and revisioned beyond the binary of black and white because it is a conceptual force that impinges on multifarious groups and communities. In fact it is this truth that inspired the 2004 *A Day without a Mexican*—a film that shares an uncanny conceptual resemblance to Ward's *Day of Absence*.

A Day without a Mexican is a satiric exploration of what transpires when the state of California is suddenly confronted with the fact that its entire Latino/Latina population has mysteriously vanished. In the film, Latinos (all of whom are erroneously referred to as Mexicans) disappear, presumably vanquished through the presence of a mysterious pink fog that rolls over the state. The absence of farmers, nannies, cooks, domestic workers, day workers, criminals, and even illegal border crossers puts the state in a frenzy, dismantling the order of things and exposing the dependencies and shortcomings of those who are left to muddle through their day-to-day lives without the aid of essential workers. Like *Day of Absence*, the vanished eventually return—with no apparent knowledge of how they disappeared or where they had gone. The impact of their absence, however, affects their families, friends, and communities in significant and highly personal ways, leading to an unexpected cinematic rumination on the power of identity politics and cultural associations. In the end, *Day without a Mexican* offers an antiessentialist commentary: communal affiliation cannot be appointed by archaic notions such as biology or blood quantum, but rather such socially constructed categories are contingent on an individual's personal identification with a particular culture.

When *A Day without a Mexican* was released in 2004, there were occasional public comparisons made between the film and Ward's play despite the fact that the makers of *A Day without a Mexican* claimed that they had no previous knowledge of *Day of Absence*.[114] Yet and still, the obvious commonalities between the works speak profoundly to their persistent and relevant messages, a fact expressed by the film's leading actress and cowriter, Yareli Arizmendi.

> You know what was fantastic, is when we came out with a short, everybody kept referring us to *Day of Absence*. And we had never really heard of it. It just goes to confirm that—the reason the idea was so powerful for the film, is because it's very basic. We've all felt that, either as a cultural group, or as child, or as an adolescent, I mean—it's basically like do

you see me, do you appreciate me, do you value me? And what if I wasn't here, then you'd be crying. But it comes from a real desire to be appreciated, to be told that, you know, it does make a difference that you're on this earth.[115]

Just as *Day of Absence* and *A Day without a Mexican* were conceived from similar sentiments, the film—like the play—inspired real-life responses in the form of "A Day without a Mexican" protests. While "A Day without a Mexican" boycotts have not received as much national exposure as Black Solidarity Days, they have made significant impressions in particular regions. Among the most notable protests were the Arizona business boycotts in May 2010 in response to debates on the state's immigration laws. These particular protests paid full tribute to *A Day without a Mexican* by taking place on May 14 and 15—the same days on which the Latinos vanished in the film. Thus, just as the economic boycotts of African American organizations and communities have continuously referenced Ward's *Day of Absence*, Latino organizations and protesters are now relying on the public's knowledge of *A Day without a Mexican* to help galvanize community activism.

And yet the parallels between Douglas Turner Ward's *Day of Absence* and Sergio Arau's *A Day without a Mexican* do not end there. It is intriguing to consider the way in which Arau and cowriter Arizmendi echo one of the central thematic elements found in Ward's play: the call for people of color to engage in self-empowering introspection. Through its obvious interrogation of whiteness, *Day of Absence* encourages its black viewers to reflect on the cultural habits that facilitate the traditional structure of our racial hierarchies. Using its theatricality to the fullest extent, *Day of Absence* calls on black people to do more than simply recognize their own value; it calls on them to take action by coming together and demanding their due worth. Like Ward's play, *A Day without a Mexican* initially relishes humorous displays of white incompetence, but the story line eventually shifts to focus on the potential effects of cultural pride, solidarity, and self-empowerment. Thus, both of these artistic works take a similar conceptual journey, one that begins with intercultural concerns and closes with a call for intracultural activism. In so doing, both work to revision racial relations within the context of their own times, revealing how much has changed—and stayed the same—since 1965.

CHAPTER TWO

Staging Hegemonic Whiteness
The Bluest Eye and the Performative Paradoxes of (In)visibility

Chapter 1's focus on Douglas Turner Ward's canonical play *Day of Absence* offered readers the opportunity to consider critiques of whiteness through a stage play and its eventual adoption into a televised format. Although the same players were involved in both productions of *Day of Absence*, shifts in relation to context and institutional dramaturgy ultimately informed the way Ward's play was framed and received within these different venues. This chapter also explores the affect and potential of theatrical adaptations that critique whiteness through an analysis of Lydia Diamond's stage version of Toni Morrison's *The Bluest Eye*.

Further inspired by the absence-presence dyad discussed in chapter 1, my analysis of *The Bluest Eye* reveals a number of ways in which Diamond's version of Morrison's novel animates contesting perceptions of white (in)visibility while also considering how the process of adaptation from literature to embodied performance necessarily demands dramaturgical negotiations of omission and addition. Moreover, the process of adaptation highlighted in this chapter addresses the work of two different genres (literature and performance), as well as the artistic sensibilities of two different authors.

While much will be said about Lydia Diamond's translation of *The Bluest Eye* into an embodied performance, one must readily acknowledge that Morrison's novel already stands as an intriguing example of performative writing; it is, unquestionably, a literary work ripe for theatrical adaptation. From Morrison's pointed use of typographical design to the sight-related metaphors she filters throughout the novel, *The Bluest Eye* is infused with tropes of spectatorship—of seeing and not being seen. The varying styles of these textual references coalesce to disclose the devastating consequences of privileging perceptions of whiteness, demonstrating how racist belief systems are powerfully transmitted through ocularcentric mediations.

Acknowledging the way Toni Morrison's novel constructs—and is constructed by—a number of interrelated themes, this chapter focuses on the novel's tropes of absence, presence, and visibility/invisibility as witnessed through the stage adaptation's carefully selected text and dramaturgical strategies. The stage play, as a piece built around the envisioned audience/spectator, *embodies* Morrison's thematic treatments of absence and presence by actualizing the invisibility and *hyper*visibility of whiteness. Accordingly, Diamond's adaptation of Morrison's novel becomes a performative expression that produces the very thing it describes.[1] By dramatizing selected narratives from Morrison's novel, the play compels spectators to consider the theoretical concepts of white visibility and invisibility while simultaneously offering them the opportunity to experience this paradoxical construction of whiteness for themselves. And while this chapter reveals how the (in)visibility of whiteness—a major trope in critical whiteness studies—is a dominant and structuring theme in the stage play, it also entertains other familiar themes within the discourse of whiteness, among them whiteness as beauty, privilege, normative, and terror inducing.

Like other performance texts addressed in *Coloring Whiteness*, Morrison's story was published long before critical whiteness studies was created as a formal field of theoretical inquiry and exploration, yet it is rich with concepts that are routinely addressed in the scholarship of race studies. The play, set in Lorraine, Ohio, in 1941, chronicles the tragic tale of a young black girl, Pecola Breedlove. Pecola's tumultuous life is shaped by interdependent oppressions (racism, sexism, and abject poverty) which, exacerbated by a dysfunctional family unit, contribute to her compromised self-image and eventual psychotic break.

The details of Pecola's story unfold through contrapuntal narratives throughout the course of the play, a style of storytelling in which various characters create the semblance of a singular tale. The play's primary narrators, however, are the MacTeer sisters (Claudia and Frieda)—the school-age peers of Pecola. Within mere minutes of the play's opening, Claudia and Frieda disclose a primary and abhorrent fact to the viewing audience: Pecola was impregnated by her father. With that stark truth voiced to the audience, Frieda continues, "There is really nothing more to say—except why," at which point Claudia asserts, "But since the why is difficult to handle, one must take refuge in how."[2]

The aforementioned phrasing of *the why* versus *the how* in *The Bluest Eye* has been frequently addressed by critics in their discussion of Morrison's original text, and, like the novel, the stage adaptation takes its audience through various scenes and scenarios that attempt to present "the how." "The why," as suggested by both texts, is impossible to articulate in logical terms. Victims and victimizers (they are often one and the same) in *The Bluest Eye* act and react according to that which is *illogical*—that is, the inequities and biases that arise from racism, classism, and sexism. By depicting *the how*, however, both the play and novel reveal the tragic circumstances that Pecola endures.

Unlike the deep, selfless, and unquestionably "tough" love the MacTeer girls receive from their parents, Pecola's parents are bedraggled vessels of self-contempt and confusion. Her mother, Pauline Breedlove, escapes from the disappointments of her life by seeking refuge in the white family for which she works, all but abandoning her own children. Her father, Cholly Breedlove, is a man whose parentless upbringing and perpetual subjugation has emotionally and psychologically castrated him to the point that he consistently tries to assert a false sense of virility through violence. In the case of both Pauline and Cholly, expressions and practices of white superiority and systematic racism have so deeply affected their psyches that they accept these biases as truths and, in turn, impart their own sense of self-hatred to their daughter—a self-hatred that is consistently reinforced by the mediated images and experiences of racial prejudice that Pecola faces every day.

Throughout the play, "the how" of Pecola's ideological inheritance is revealed through a number of pivotal scenes—moments that are contingent on the conceptual and theatrical twin binaries of visibility-invisibility and absence-presence. Before detailing the ways in which notions of invisibility and visibility are activated in *The Bluest Eye*, however, I find it useful to establish how the trope of white (in)visibility is often addressed within critical discourse. In his foundational text, *White*, Richard Dyer succinctly attends to the dueling and contradictory characteristics of so-called whiteness.

> White identity is founded on compelling paradoxes: a vividly corporeal cosmology that most values transcendence of the body; a notion of being at once a sort of race and the human race, an individual and a universal

subject; a commitment to heterosexuality that, for whiteness to be affirmed, entails men fighting against sexual desires and women having none; a stress on the display of spirit while maintaining a position of invisibility; in short, a need always to be everything and nothing, literally overwhelmingly present and yet apparently absent, both alive and dead.... Thus it is that the paradoxes and instabilities of whiteness also constitute its flexibility and productivity, in short, its representational power.[3]

Throughout *White*, Dyer delves into the ways notions of whiteness evolve from privileging "the spirit" over corporeal realities of the body. Related to this is the observation that qualities of whiteness are often posed by what whiteness *is not*, thereby relegating whiteness to a kind of absent, spectral presence. To a great extent, these aforementioned paradoxes can all be placed under the explicatory rubric of whiteness's (in)visibility.

Certainly, the *invisibility* of whiteness has been heralded as both fact and falsehood.[4] While innumerable scholars have duly interrogated and defied the idea of whiteness as invisible or absent, the trope continues to persist—if only to challenge its veracity. The argument of invisibility is contingent on the well-acknowledged fact that whiteness is set as the paradigmatic standard (a concept I elaborate on in chapter 5 through my study of presumed aural whiteness), a standardization that grants whiteness an obscuring ubiquity—an inevitable power. In the words of Richard Dyer, "Whites must be seen to be white, yet whiteness as race resides in invisible properties and whiteness as power is maintained by being unseen. To be seen as white is to have one's corporeality registered, yet true whiteness resides in the noncorporeal."[5] As this chapter reveals, it is the omniscient and noncorporeal notion of whiteness that is dramatized in *The Bluest Eye* stage play. Although there are several white characters in Diamond's adaptation, the play never calls for their embodied presence—at least not through the use of live, *human* bodies.

What the play also discloses, however, is that as useful as the trope of white invisibility has been in articulating practices of normalizing whiteness, it has also been directly challenged by other, equally compelling revelations regarding the *hyper*visibility of whiteness. This contrasting understanding of whiteness is taken up by *The Bluest Eye* with due diligence. Both the novel and the play reveal the ways in which ubiquitous representations of white people (as portrayed in print culture, Hollywood cinema, and even the toy industry) underscore the hypervisibility of whiteness in contrast to the subjugated status and diminished mediated representations of black people. Moreover, this sense of hypervisibility becomes particularly potent when the presence of whiteness is transformed from markedly conspicuous to absolutely terrorizing.[6] To this end, *The Bluest Eye* animates the way the psychological trauma resulting from a terrorizing act of white-on-black violence festers rather than subsides, only to mutate and resurface as a devastating act of black-on-black violence.

As a play, the form of *The Bluest Eye* works in tandem with the story's content to reveal the power of symbolic spectacle. Just as Morrison organizes the movement of her novel by noting the changes of the seasons, Diamond employs this organizational strategy within her adaptation. The play's chronological movement from autumn to winter, spring, and summer is clearly noted by the costumes of the MacTeer girls. Claudia and Frieda wear brown dresses in autumn, blue dresses in winter, white and pastel-accented dresses in spring, and green dresses in summer. Juxtaposed against the MacTeer dresses, however, is the tainted white dress that the most victimized character, Pecola, wears throughout the length of the play.

As written in Diamond's stage directions, audience members are first offered the opportunity to recognize whiteness—or, rather, the lack of whiteness—in what is described as Pecola's "dingy loose fitting white dress."[7] Despite the suggested matching bow, Diamond's description is crafted so that audiences recognize that the dress is distressed. It is not only dirty but ill-fitting; it was not made for her brown body to wear. Thus, Pecola's dress reflects her social position in layered ways: she, like her dress, is viewed as impure (due to both the markers of her race and the sexual abuse she will later endure); and, like her ill-fitting dress, her physical characteristics do not conform to society's expectations of physical beauty. Moreover, the condition of Pecola's dress presents the audience with the opportunity to question the (lack of) resources available to her, in material terms as well as in relation to her lack of physical and/or emotional care. Pecola's appearance immediately signifies a sense of deprivation, the depth of which becomes all the more startling when she turns to reveal her profile and the audience is suddenly and dramatically confronted with a visible sign of this young girl's pregnancy.

Readily utilizing physical bodies and design elements to suggest symbolic meaning in *The Bluest Eye*, the play also purposefully exploits the *absence* of these same types of visible elements to comment on racialized *invisibility*.

This strategic oscillation dramatizes paradoxical notions of absence/presence and visibility/invisibility in relation to racial construction. Highlighting several key moments from the novel, the stage version of *The Bluest Eye* embodies these contesting tensions and contradictions, thereby revealing the forces and ideologies that shape the life of Pecola and the play's other central characters.

Among these pivotal passages is a scene in which the audience witnesses Pecola's heartfelt pleas to God, a moment that explicitly conjures the theme of (in)visibility. Displeased with her embodied blackness and the disparagement she experiences because of it, Pecola prays for the disintegration of her corporeal form: "Please, God. Make me disappear. Please, please, please, please, God. . . . Please, God. Make me invisible. . . . Please, please, please, please, please."[8] Pecola then addresses the audience, giving further credence to her desire *not* to be seen.

> If I squeeze my eyes shut, real tight, little parts of my body go away. I have to do it real slow like, then in a rush. First, off my fingers go, one by one, then my arms disappear, all the way to my elbows. My feet now. Yes that's right good. My legs go all at once. Above my thighs is the hardest part. I have to be real still and pull and pull and pull . . . [and] when my stomach goes away the chest and neck follow 'long pretty easy. The face is hard too. Almost done, almost. But my eyes is always left.[9]

Pecola's fantasy is a confounding one. At once, she yearns to disappear, to rid herself of the body that designates her as other in order to experience the privileges relegated to what is deemed normative, yet she also knows that such fantastical yearnings are impossible. Even within the confines of her imagination, the seductive dream of not being seen cannot be completed because her "eyes is always left." Pecola's eyes, representing the instruments with which she envisions the world and her role in it, will not let her escape herself, therefore intimating that beauty is not only in the eyes of the beholder but also in those of the beheld. Consequently, Pecola—as unworldly as she may be—clearly recognizes that the way she *sees* must be fundamentally altered. Lacking the sophistication to unpack the machinations of hegemonic dogma, she articulates this latent understanding in a different way, concluding that the solution can be found in a physical, rather than ideological, transformation.

> It don't matter how hard I try, my eyes is always left. And I try. Every night I pray for God to deliver me blue eyes. I have prayed now going on a year, but I have hope still. I figure God is very busy, and I am very small. To have something wonderful as that happen would have to take a long, long time. Blue eyes like Shirley Temple, or Mary Jane, on the Mary Jane candies. Or Jane in the primer at school.[10]

With Pecola's wishful naïveté comes the false belief that if she were gifted with blue eyes she would not only see herself differently but her physical transformation would also affect the ability of others to fully appreciate her presence: people would finally "really look at" her, and—perhaps most significantly—no one would ever be prone to "do bad things in front of those pretty eyes."[11]

Moving drastically from wishes for invisibility to the fantasy of being hypervisible and thus *"really seen,"* Pecola's contradictory thoughts reveal her tumultuous emotional state, as well as the paradoxes associated with whiteness. For her, being black is to be framed in a specific and disparaging way. She seems convinced that the way to resolve her experience of abjection will be found through the comfort of being unmarked—being "invisible" in terms of not being categorized as a racial or ethnic other. However, she also recognizes that whiteness, ubiquitously highlighted as worthy of notice and attention, inscribes one as a "politically visible subject."[12]

This latter understanding of whiteness becomes apparent when Claudia, in the role of narrator, recounts Pecola's experience with the white store owner, Mr. Yacobowski. Observing that Mr. Yacobowski "looks but doesn't really see Pecola," Claudia notes how Pecola's blackness—in the eyes of Yacobowski—becomes a present absence. Claudia goes on to describe the abstracted nature of Yacobowski's vacant stare.

> It's a total absence of human recognition, a glazed separateness right behind his eyes. Pecola has seen interest, disgust, even anger in grown male eyes. But this vacuum has an edge. An edge of distaste that lurks in the eyes of all white people. The distaste for her blackness, because what else could it be, is right there, in his bottom eyelid.[13]

As described, Yacobowski doesn't *see* Pecola as a human subject; he fails to recognize her as worthy of his respectful attention. Yacobowksi utters no sound as he engages in an exchange at the counter, choosing not to acknowledge Pecola's polite address beyond the perfunctory act of accepting her money. Moreover, the described scene between Yacobowski and Pecola is heightened by its pure performativity: we never see Yacobowski in this narrated scenario—he is a spectral presence, given life through words alone.

Strategically vacillating between what is and what is not seen, Diamond's adaptation animates Sandra L. Richards's compelling ruminations on "the absent potential."[14] Observing that "the unwritten, or an absence from the script, is a potential presence implicit in performance," Richards asserts that "one must write the absent potential into criticism; that is, in addition to analysis of the written text, one must offer informed accounts of the latent intertexts likely to be produced in performance, increasing and complicating meaning."[15] Her critical reflections work in two complementary ways when applied to the staged production of *The Bluest Eye*. In heeding the recognition of the absent potential, she reminds us to consider how the meanings of embodied performances are not solely bound within, and created through, the limited perimeters of the written text. Second, Richards reminds us of how material absences (the lack of an embodied presence or the absence of props and stage signs) also offer meanings in relation to the literary content and sociopolitical context of staged plays. In relation to *The Bluest Eye*, the former is exemplified by the complete absence of a visible white presence (i.e., the absence of white actors or images of white people) within the play.

Although Yacobowski is never embodied, his presence and the ramifications of the scene powerfully invoke the interdependent dimensions that have historically contributed to black female subjugation in American society: exploitation of black female bodies for capital gain, the refusal to grant black women power and status within social and political discourse, and the negative imagery surrounding black women and their embodiment.[16] While Yacobowksi readily takes advantage of Pecola's presence inasmuch as it serves his own fiscal interests, he fails to recognize the value of black girlhood/womanhood of its own accord—a limiting perspective that is wholly determined by the subjugated individual's racialized position.

Of course, a centralizing current throughout *The Bluest Eye* is the way in which perceived beauty and perceived ugliness are relegated according to racialized categories. Pecola's wish to be invisible and, likewise, her inability to be recognized under Mr. Yacobowksi's gaze underscores how the blackness of Pecola and her parents has cast them as "ugly" according to the mediated scripts of popular culture. However, as Morrison qua Diamond pointedly asserts, the members of the Breedlove family are not *truly* ugly.

Rather, they have come to believe in their ugliness; they are convinced of its facticity purely through their own "conviction."

> CLAUDIA. The Breedlove's ugliness was a unique kind of ugliness.
> FRIEDA. No one could have convinced them that they were not relentlessly and aggressively ugly.
> CLAUDIA. Except for Cholly,
> FRIEDA. Whose ugliness had more to do with his behavior . . .
> CLAUDIA. Mrs. Breedlove and Pecola wore their ugliness, put it on, so to speak, although it did not belong to them.
> FRIEDA. You looked at them and wondered why they were so ugly; you looked closely and could not find the source.
> CLAUDIA. Then you realized it came from conviction. Their conviction. It was as though some mysterious all-knowing master had given each one a cloak of ugliness to wear, and they had each accepted it without question. The master had said, "You are ugly people." It was a truth supported by every billboard, every movie, every glance.
> BREEDLOVES. "Yes,"
> CLAUDIA. They had said.
> BREEDLOVES. "You are right."
> FRIEDA. And they took the ugliness in their hands, threw it as a mantle over them, (BREEDLOVES *put on sweaters/jackets, blankets*) and went about the world with it.[17]

In the preceding exchange, Claudia and Frieda assert that the Breedloves—victims of an Althusserian construct of consent[18]—accept their socially assigned ugliness "without question" or resistance. Their indoctrination into this belief system conjures the sentiments famously described by Frantz Fanon in *Black Skin, White Masks*, thereby animating the self-alienating process of interpellation for black citizens within an ideological system that privileges whiteness and denigrates blackness. Speaking from the vantage point of the disenfranchised other, Fanon writes:

> My body was given back to me sprawled out, distorted, recolored, clad in mourning in that white winter day. The Negro is an animal, the Negro is bad, the Negro is mean, the Negro is ugly. . . . I become aware of my uniform. I had not seen it. It is indeed ugly. I stop there, for who can tell me what beauty is?[19]

Just as the MacTeer sisters refer to socially presumed ugliness as literal garments, the words of Fanon also underscore the way in which the truths of beauty are hidden under the cover and weight of hegemonic opinion. Yet and still, in both instances there is also the insistence that if one accepts these cloaking mechanisms, they create their own willful blindness to alternative truths. As described by Louis Althusser, the Breedloves exemplify those that meet the hail willfully (an imagined encounter that is animated by the verbal response of the Breedloves), thereby highlighting how they have subjectified themselves.

Moreover, while discussion regarding the Breedloves' supposed ugliness offers us the opportunity to address the insidious nature of consent, it also suggests how the Breedloves assume the nature of a performative identity. Similar to Judith Butler's assertion that gender performance (and the reception of gendered identities) is the result of "constituting acts,"[20] the ugliness of the Breedloves is also the result of constituting acts—the consequence of *becoming* what one is *deemed*. Acquiescing to racist ideology, the Breedloves adopt the behaviors that support rather than challenge the status quo. In so doing, the behaviors expressed by the Breedloves not only "constitute" their ugliness, but they also contribute to furthering qualitative judgments associated with racial difference.

The aforementioned scene is born from the pages of Morrison's novel, but it should be noted that Diamond's dramatic adaptation presents theatre producers with a unique challenge and opportunity to further explore perceptions surrounding physical beauty. In *The Bluest Eye* novel, Morrison offers the following details regarding the Breedloves' appearance.

> The eyes, the small eyes set closely together under narrow foreheads. The low, irregular hairlines, which seemed even more irregular in contrast to the straight, heavy eyebrows which nearly met. Keen but crooked noses, with insolent nostrils. They had high cheekbones, and their ears turned forward. Shapely lips which called attention not to themselves but to the rest of the face. You looked at them and wondered why they were so ugly.[21]

Describing their noses as "keen," Morrison asks us to envision noses that are relatively aquiline—an observance that is later underscored in the novel when Pecola reflects on how her own nose "was not big and flat like some of those who were thought so cute."[22] While the narrowness of the Breedloves' nasal bridges may align their features with a more Eurocentric idea of beauty, Morrison gives us the "but": their noses are "crooked" and feature "insolent" nostrils, suggesting a flare that is more readily associated with typical negroid features. The perception of the Breedloves' physical irregularities are further substantiated with ears that "turned forward," and although Morrison grants them "shapely lips," this attractive characteristic proves to be more problematic than appealing in that they "call attention" to the peculiarities of the "rest of the face."

With the description of particular idiosyncrasies, the ugliness of the Breedloves is neither confirmed nor denied. Diamond, writing for the theatre (and thus, quite aware of the improbability of securing actors that naturally match character descriptions) is far less pointed in her descriptions, yet she does emphasize the need for gradations in skin tone. In describing Pecola, Diamond writes, "It is imperative that she have very dark brown skin," following with a note that both Mrs. Breedlove and Cholly should also be "dark brown."[23] Notably, in contrast to Morrison, Diamond offers no remarks that could be perceived as suggesting a qualitative judgment in relation to the Breedloves' features. She does, however, specify that Maureen Peal should be "Light skinned" *and* "very pretty"—thereby making it clear that one does *not* necessarily mandate the other.[24] Echoing Morrison's conscientiousness, Diamond recognizes the complexities of intraracial color consciousness. With that simple "and," she reveals how public perceptions of one's physical features can either be conflated with—or distinguished from—one's skin color among "color-struck" folks. That is to say, the intracultural politics of color consciousness often engage in ever-shifting, perpetually unstable, and highly subjective judgments that not only take into account skin color (light to dark) but also consider details such as hair texture (straight to kinky) and facial features (keen to broad). Any precarious combination of these discriminating factors works to create a sliding scale of physical attractiveness in accordance with Eurocentric ideals.

Both Diamond's specificity regarding Maureen and lack thereof regarding the Breedloves offer theatre makers an expansive opportunity when it comes to casting. In taking up Diamond's descriptions, theatre makers may—consciously or unconsciously—further perpetuate societal conflations that equate darkness with ugliness (and, conversely, beauty with lightness) or they can purposely work toward dismantling such racialized assumptions and expectations. I would be remiss not to note, however, how often the issue of casting skin color gradations in the American theatre becomes a source of frustration for African American dramatists and performers. While some casting agents may not (or choose not to) recognize skin color difference in an effort to champion an antiracist, "color blind" world vision, such a tendency may result in a polar effect, one in which the failure to recognize difference is suggested as a homogenizing "they all look alike to me" attitude.[25]

In practical terms, when casting decisions regarding the Breedloves are made, theatre makers must ask themselves how the casting of these characters can create or destabilize depictions of beauty and ugliness as they have been historically represented. How may casting choices perpetuate (mis) perceptions of what "white" versus "black" features *look like* pertaining to, as well as beyond, the epidermal surface—and how do casting agents prioritize the absence or presence of particular features? Certainly, aesthetic judgments are always subjective, but one cannot disregard the blatant or subtextual messages that a production may be transmitting regarding an actor's visage. Does an actor possess highly unusual, exaggerated, or (in the words of Morrison) "irregular" facial features and, if so, according to what standard or model? Are the actors cast as the Breedloves particularly attractive, thereby powerfully animating the way their actions—versus their outer countenances—are the true source of their perceived ugliness? Moreover, how different *should* the skin color gradations between the characters be? While the playwright notes that the members of the Breedlove family should have noticeably dark skin, how distinctive should their brown skin appear in relation to that of the MacTeer girls? If a casting agent chooses to assign actors who share the same hue, will it work against the play's intentions or will the audience be better equipped to understand that the source of the Breedloves' self-disdain is a matter of conviction?

While such questions may seem cursory, they are not. Rather, they speak to the very tangible opportunity theatre has to embody and make visceral the inter- and intraracial politics that still persist beyond the stage. Such a prospect was not lost on Lydia Diamond.

> I think the politics of race, over time, becomes an even more slippery thing to talk about, like, as we think we're becoming more liberal, and as we are actually really becoming slightly more sophisticated around issues of diversity, we're also not always equipped with the tools to do the social dissection of the subtleties of race. And so it is harder, I think, for this generation of students to have a conversation about skin color, and how

those images play out, having not had those conversations previously, so that when they come to you they're often having that for the first time.²⁶

In producing Diamond's adaptation of *The Bluest Eye*, not only are theatre makers presented with the opportunity to dramatize the everyday ways in which racial imaginings shape our aesthetics (and aesthetics shape our racial imaginings), but we are also presented with the opportunity to answer or confound Fanon's heart-wrenching query, "for who can tell me what beauty is?"

Such an opportunity is a rich one, especially considering the ubiquitous ways in which white beauty and privilege have been championed through varying modes of both consent and coercion. In the case of Morrison's novel, one of the most profound and oft-analyzed exhibits of acculturated racism is symbolized by the allusions to the Dick and Jane primers created by William Elson and William Gray. While the Dick and Jane readers were eventually updated to reflect a more racially and culturally diverse America, the original primers of the 1930s (up through 1965) feature decidedly white characters and model nuclear families (a working dad, stay-at-home mom, two kids, and a faithful pet), thereby failing to duly represent those who live outside these supposed descriptors of all-white suburbia. Debra Werrlein writes, "In fact, beyond the occasional appearance of a 'savage' Indian, they never feature nonwhite Americans. The Dick and Jane books in particular exist almost entirely outside of history—as if no thing and no time exists beyond the suburban present. They therefore treat American childhood as an abstraction that excludes all but white middle-class children."²⁷

As Werrlein and others attest, the popularity of the Dick and Jane books did far more than simply teach children the fundamentals of reading—they also taught children fundamental lessons about America's racial hierarchies. The Dick and Jane primers not only "primed" black subjects to understand their place, or lack thereof, in American society, but their lily-white, elitist representations—void of any semblance of diversity, hardship, or struggle—also championed a picture of familial and civic life that was so fantastic that it was not even an attainable reality for the white middle-class children it supposedly represented.²⁸ The racist and classist allusions that are implicit throughout the early primers serve as powerful conceptual touchstones for Morrison's novel, reminding readers of the pervasive and devious ways in which prejudice, bias, and self-contempt are taught and disseminated among the most youthful of masses.

Highlighting the role of discursive spheres in cultivating social perceptions, Morrison opens her novel by interrogating the cultural sway of the Dick and Jane readers, as well as the power of the written word. Morrison duplicates, and then progressively disturbs, familiar passages from the readers in order to reveal the fact that the representations within the books are, in truth, skewed. She does this by incorporating the art of typography to translate this sense of imbalance, manipulating three versions of a single passage from a Dick and Jane reader. The first passage is printed as a full paragraph, void of the original primer's signature illustrations. The passage that follows is comprised of the same words and language, yet it is distinctively marked by the compression of the words in each sentence and the absence of appropriate punctuation. The third paragraph violates the legibility of the passage altogether, revealing a complete blurring of words and a total absence of spacing and punctuation.

Taking her performative cue from Morrison, Diamond uses the play's spoken language and embodied characterizations to create the same effect and meaning as Morrison's written word. In the play, Pecola begins reading the first line from a Dick and Jane reader: "Here is the house. It is green and white. It has a red door it is very pretty."[29] Pecola's lone figure is then joined by her parents, Mrs. Breedlove and Cholly, who begin a simultaneous recitation. They, in turn, are joined by additional characters—Frieda and Claudia, Maureen, Mamma, and Soaphead Church—who, one by one, create an extended Dick and Jane narration comprised of the original book's perfunctory, elementary sentences. Increasingly the choral delivery becomes *"frenetic, no longer in unison,"* ending with Pecola having the last words and seizing the moment with the disturbing image of her pregnant silhouette: "(*PECOLA turns, we see in profile that she is pregnant, she closes the primer. Lights and sound out*)."[30]

While Diamond's adaptation only utilizes a few of the sentences featured in Morrison's prologue, she uses the audible cacophony to replicate the sensation that Morrison's performative text induces in its reader. Diamond's frenetic chants suggest the personal and interpersonal discord that will be revealed as the play unfolds, especially in relation to the "perfect" images conjured by signifyin(g) on the early Dick and Jane readers. Although the nature of the aural recitation in this scene is notable, it is also important to recognize how these spoken cues are emboldened by the physical presence of the primer.

Pecola's large, red primer is a constant visual and thematic refrain throughout the dramatic work—a poignant prop in numerous scenes. Although red in color, it is the proverbial "black book"—a sacred tome that symbolizes the desired yet unattainable. In fact it is during some of the most painful times that Pecola resorts to the idyllic and wholly inaccessible representations of domestic and national bliss found in the Dick and Jane primers. A dramatic articulation of Pecola's reality in contrast to the idyllic world of Dick and Jane occurs in the midst of a violent bout between Pecola's parents. Pecola reads from the primer during this altercation, her innocent visage and voice piercing the poisoned atmosphere to create a clear polarity. As the *"highly choreographed slow-motion fight"* between Cholly and Mrs. Breedlove ensues, Pecola attempts to escape this violent dance through the contrived simplicity and sanctity of the pictorial display she holds in her hands.[31]

Just as the Dick and Jane reader symbolizes a mode of fantastic escape for young Pecola, the glamour of Hollywood pictures serves as both a means of escape and a source of torment for Pecola's mother, Mrs. Breedlove. When Mrs. Breedlove initially married Cholly and moved away from Kentucky and the life she had known, she found "comfort and company in the cinema."[32] With obsessive adoration, she became a follower of starlets such as Jean Harlow, even trying to mimic Harlow's countenance and hairstyle. Enamored by the glorious lifestyles she witnessed on the screen, Mrs. Breedlove became convinced that she would find happiness by emulating the images she saw in the motion pictures: "I started to spend all my housekeeping money on clothes and some nice things for the house to be more like them happy white people in the pictures."[33] What Mrs. Breedlove soon recognizes, however, is that she will never be empowered to *be* "like them happy white people." The impossibility of achieving the sense of freedom, luxury, and privilege enacted on the screen is due to the universal inaccessibility of such staged representations, an imagined existence that is compounded by the limits of race and class.

The full disclosure of these limits becomes clear to Mrs. Breedlove when she loses her front tooth: "There I was, five months pregnant, trying to look like Jean Harlow, and my front tooth's gone. Didn't care no more after that. I settled down to being ugly, and goin' to them pictures just made me more ugly."[34] Encapsulated within the visual image of losing a (white) tooth, both Mrs. Breedlove and the reader/viewer are confronted with the myriad meanings cast by such a concrete, material absence. Not only does the loss of Mrs. Breedlove's tooth further compromise her ability to represent idealized notions of white, feminine beauty, but its loss also directly indicates her outsider status by underscoring her compromised economic situation. As a victim of abject poverty, Mrs. Breedlove's lost tooth becomes more than a marker of her neglect and exclusion; it also signifies the material consequences of inadequate health care and citizen status. Thus, the *absence* of a tooth—part of one's skeletal/structural foundation—speaks to the structural absence of black bodies within the play's social and civic landscape. Moreover, for Mrs. Breedlove this visible incarnation of absence and lack is not simply the constant reminder of what she does not *have*, but it is also a constant reminder of who she *cannot be*.

The recognition of Mrs. Breedlove's personal voids, from the empty space left by her missing tooth to her inability to be perceived as a "viable, political subject," further underscores how her embodied blackness represents a status of lack. In the world of the play, black bodies inordinately find themselves as consumers rather than producers, as the affected rather than the effective.[35] This is a debilitating dynamic that was of particular interest to Diamond.

> I think a huge portion of racism in general has been a very successful PR [public relations] campaign that the Western Caucasian has worked over the whole world, really—and certainly the way these images have imposed themselves on the reality of these poor black people, it's profound. And I'm fascinated—not consciously so in writing the adaptation of *The Bluest Eye*—but in general in my work, and even more recently, I'm really, really fascinated with our definitions of beauty, and the way the ideas of media and celebrity play out.... I think it's very present in the world of the piece, in the world of the novel.[36]

Accordingly, it is the truth of America's "PR campaign" that is literally reflected on Mrs. Breedlove's visage when the play's stage directions note that a "*movie-screen effect plays across MRS. BREEDLOVE'S face.*"[37] This pointed stage direction animates how the "absent presence" of whiteness impresses itself on black bodies, visually articulating how Mrs. Breedlove's consuming adulation of Hollywood images is described in the novel.

> She was never able, after her education in the movies, to look at a face and not assign it some category in the scale of absolute beauty, and the scale was one *she absorbed in full from the silver screen*.... It was really a

simple pleasure, but she learned all there was to love and all there was to hate.[38]

Thus, as compelling as it may seem for a director or designer to incorporate *real* film images within this scene, it seems dramaturgically critical to resist such an urge. As Diamond has penned it, this moment underscores the paradoxical nature of whiteness by demonstrating the cunning ways white preference and privilege have been historically mediated and perpetuated. The audience watches Mrs. Breedlove literally *absorbing* the images of whiteness that are projected on her face—images that are "invisible" (we are not made privy to what she sees) yet profoundly consequential to how she understands and reads herself.

While Mrs. Breedlove's relationship with Hollywood imagery calls attention to how ideas of beauty are pronounced and reiterated through the media, *The Bluest Eye* also reveals the way in which young people are equally—if not more—vulnerable to images of celebrity. With a "like mother, like daughter" parallel exploration, *The Bluest Eye* traces Pecola's fascination with Shirley Temple, a fanatic attraction that is counterbalanced by Claudia's insistent animosity toward the famous child star. While Pecola celebrates the partnered dancing between Bill "Bojangles" Robinson and Shirley Temple (as featured in the films *The Little Colonel* [1935], *The Littlest Rebel* [1935], *Rebecca of Sunnybrook Farm* [1938], and *Just Around the Corner* [1938]), the romanticized union between Temple and Bojangles triggers Claudia's deep-seated animosity.

> Mr. Jangles wasn't supposed to be dancing with that white girl. He was *my* friend, *my* uncle, *my* daddy. He should have been soft-shoeing it and chuckling with me. At least with someone who looked like me.[39]

Claudia's resentment stems from an awareness of how whiteness, epitomized by the young Shirley Temple, is celebrated throughout the popular narratives of the cinema *and* society. Moreover, in the frame of the Temple films themselves, there is no space or representation for someone who "looked like" Claudia, nor is there space created for *any* analogous images in which young black women can see themselves.

Even as the play reveals the prevalence and idealization of white bodies in popular American culture (as indicated through allusions to the Dick and Jane readers or the films of Jean Harlow and Shirley Temple), Diamond does not suggest that these images should be featured in the theatrical design of the play. The decided absence of white actors and iconic representations of white bodies speak profoundly to their pervasiveness: the mere naming of white celebrities conjures collective memories and/or communal understanding. Moreover, the choice not to materialize the media-related images of Dick and Jane, Jean Harlow, and Shirley Temple aid in *The Bluest Eye*'s work toward interrogating and destabilizing the perpetuation of racist facilitations. The antihegemonic efforts of *The Bluest Eye* are underscored by Diamond's refusal to further affirm or propagate these mediated images by restaging them for an audience's consumption.

When it comes to addressing ideological consumption via acts of consumerism, *The Bluest Eye* also makes use of a highly symbolic yet "generic" product: the "annual blond, blue-eyed Christmas doll" Claudia receives from her well-intentioned parents.[40] Claudia becomes overwhelmed with the problematic proposition such a doll presents. She recognizes that society's scripts offer her limited ways to interact with her doll: "What was I supposed to do with it? Feed it? Rock it? Bathe it? Be its mother?"[41] In fact, in Morrison's novel, Claudia's thoughts forthrightly express a general distaste for the very idea of *performing* motherhood: "I had no interest in babies or the concept of motherhood. I was interested only in humans my own age and size, and could not generate any enthusiasm at the prospect of being a mother. Motherhood was old age, and other remote possibilities."[42]

Although this general disparagement of motherhood is not directly expressed in the play, the audience is fully empowered to consider this sentiment—as well as Claudia's resistance to "other remote possibilities." As scripted—and given the visual display of the young girls handling the Christmas doll in question—Claudia's internal monologue suggests that the social roles she is expected to fulfill leave her few pleasurable options. She recognizes that any "true-to-life" reenactments would cast her in the subservient (and ultimately undesirable) role of being a nursemaid or mammy, for according to America's racial designations, the doll's whiteness precludes Claudia from being able to fully imagine herself in the role of its mother. Unwilling to cast herself in the position of a domestic or caretaker—even in the realm of the imaginary—Claudia wholeheartedly rejects the doll and expresses her discontent with the injustice it represents. Ripping it apart, piece by piece, she vents her rage: "I wanted to commit a systematic dismembering of real little white girls to understand what magic it was that they weaved on others. What made people look at them and say 'Awwww,' but not see me at all? Why was I invisible next to little white girls in pleated skirts and white knee-highs?"[43] With deliberate destruction, Claudia disarticulates the doll's inanimate form, seeking to unravel an even greater enigma by deconstructing the ideological mechanics of white preference and prejudice.

Despite Claudia's agitation, both Frieda and Pecola remain forever enamored by white dolls and anything else that bears a Shirley Temple–like mystique. However, the most committed fan is Pecola, whose fascination with portrayals of white femininity is expressed not only through her love of white dolls and Shirley Temple but also through her naive idealization of the fictitious Mary Jane candy girl. Just as Pecola consumes inordinate amounts of milk so she can drink it from Frieda's Shirley Temple cup, she relishes the purchase and consumption of Mary Jane candies, eating them as if the ritualistic process of ingesting the sugary treats could somehow impart to her the magical qualities of the fictional figure.

> Before I eat my Mary Janes, I look at each one. Each pretty little girl. Each girl's name is Mary Jane and she has blonde curls and big blue eyes. And she looks at me with those pretty eyes and she is my friend.... I eat the candy, and it is almost like I am Mary Jane.[44]

Powerfully conjuring bell hooks's phrase "eating the other," Pecola's devouring of Mary Jane candies is a curious expression of both desire and resistance.[45] On the surface, the ingestion of the peanut-flavored chews pays tribute to Pecola's phantasmic friend, an enticing symbol of all that Pecola deems to be sweet and good. She takes these candies and the images they conjure—the intangible body and spirit of Mary Jane—into her mouth with the relish and dedication of a Communion rite. Divine as this gastronomic experience may be for Pecola, it also bears the marks of aggression and conflict. After all, she is *chewing* Mary Jane, masticating until the evidence of "each pretty little girl" is ground to oblivion and swallowed. This imagery brings to mind the words of cultural studies and foodways theorist, Kyla Tompkins.

> That violence is deployed through biting or eating returns us forcefully to the role of the mouth in fixing and unfixing racial embodiment. The desire to bite both materializes and minimizes bodily violence; it inflicts pain, but it appears to do so only at the precise and relatively small point where human mouth meets human flesh; it is not shooting, cutting, or whipping. And yet biting is primarily a violence of childhood: it enacts

the desire to destroy the other by consuming her, by obliterating the signs of her existence, or, at the very least, by reducing her physical presence in the world one mouthful at a time.[46]

Framed accordingly, Pecola's eating of the Mary Jane candies is an expression of desire and resistance, love and hate. Thus, the metaphor of "consumption" becomes activated in many, layered ways: Pecola becomes the ultimate consumer, taking in a smorgasbord of troublesome ideologies—an unbridled binge that can only result in agitation and pain.

Striking, too, is the nature of Pecola's blind endearment toward both Shirley Temple and Mary Jane, for she projects a characteristic of white girlhood (blue eyes) onto these images even though they are not actually present. In other words, despite the fact that Pecola insists that all her favorite heroines have blue eyes ("Blue eyes like Shirley Temple, or Mary Jane, on the Mary Jane candies. Or Jane in the primer at school"),[47] neither Shirley Temple nor the Mary Jane caricature actually possesses blue eyes (Temple's eyes are green, and the hair and eyes of the cartoon-sketch character, Mary Jane, are so dark they appear to be black).[48] Regardless of these factual discrepancies, Pecola's unwavering insistence on imaginings of whiteness creates a false memory and reshapes truths to abide by a cultural trope within and beyond her own recollections. This repeated refrain not only assigns blue eyes to specific, citational images of white celebrity but simultaneously—and erroneously—conflates blue eyes with whiteness.[49]

Although they are woven throughout the text, the tensions and sentiments that revolve around Pecola's vision of idealized white girlhood culminate within the play when Frieda, Claudia, and Pecola encounter Mrs. Breedlove's young (and, in the play, nameless) white charge. Diamond's stage directions effectively describe the novel's little Fisher girl just as Morrison penned her: "*The little GIRL wears [a] pink sundress and pink fluffy bunny bedroom slippers.*" However, the playwright also offers—through the character of Claudia—an impression of the young white girl that is not found in Morrison's novel: "If her hair wasn't long and straight and blonde and her eyes blue instead of green, I might have mistaken her for Shirley Temple."[50]

Once again, the iconic figure of Shirley Temple is shorthand for unearned white privilege and mediated perceptions of whiteness, a whiteness that is brimming with youth and femininity, and fueled by consumer culture. The particularities of Shirley Temple—as both a real person and the representative of Hollywood fantasy—are as irrelevant in the social fabric of the play as they were to the media machines in real life. What is essential (and essentialized) in the eyes of Pecola is the way in which Temple symbolizes an indisputable mythic whiteness. The mention of Temple's manufactured image alludes to the ideal model of American youth culture: its promise, purity, and innocence. This is made particularly clear by the stage play's acknowledgment of the obvious *difference* between the described visage of the young white girl and the famed child actress she supposedly resembles. While Mrs. Breedlove's charge may be blonde, she does not have Temple's signature ringlet curls; moreover, we are told her eyes *are* actually blue (while, again, Temple's eyes were green). One can presume that Diamond's pointed allusion to Shirley Temple not only is included as a dramaturgical strategy (it creates a through-line by reinforcing the play's earlier reference to the iconic actress), but it also echoes Pecola's similar conflations of semiotic whiteness. Claudia's reference to Shirley Temple is not prompted by any true resemblance; rather it suggests that any exemplar of youthful, white femininity adequately satisfies the requirements needed to gain Temple's status: she's white, therefore she's right.

Diamond further interrogates the construction of whiteness by indicating that the white girl in the play should not be portrayed by a live actor, but rather the character should be represented *"by a white, life-sized doll, manipulated by the actress who plays MAUREEN PEAL, wearing an identical outfit."*[51] This dramaturgical strategy not only harks back to Ward's use of doll-like imagery in *Day of Absence*, but it alludes to a number of instances in African American performance in which whiteness has been theatricalized on the stage using dollish images.[52] In representing the white girl in this manner, the doll—in tandem with the matching outfit worn by the actor—moves beyond the parameters of what is traditionally referenced as "whiteface" to exhibit a nontraditional form of whiteface, a *nonconforming whiteface* in the guise of a puppetlike, full-body mask. Accordingly, although Claudia recognizes that she cannot "commit a systematic dismembering" of real little white girls in the same way she dismembers her Christmas doll,[53] this representation of the little Fisher girl does offer a way to imagine the possibility of black authority over whiteness. While the reliance on a black body to affect the doll's movement dramatizes the fact that white people have profited from the labor of black bodies, this fully embodied, nonconforming whiteface also intimates that black people are often the unacknowledged and unrewarded "puppet masters" of white civic life—a suggestion that is also addressed in Douglas Turner Ward's *Day of Absence*.

The act of manipulating the doll figure in *The Bluest Eye* play not only interrogates representations of whiteness, but it serves as a symbolic surrogate for the few expressions of black-over-white empowerment found within Morrison's original story. Among these moments in the novel is a scene in which Morrison sheds light on Pauline Breedlove by offering an intricate explanation as to why she finds such pleasure and pride in being a caretaker in the Fisher household. While Pauline's domestic work allows her to witness a world of wealth and privilege, her position of servitude also demands that she conduct business on behalf of the family—a role that gives her a relished sense of authority.

> The creditors and service people who humiliated her when she went to them on her own behalf respected her, were even intimated by her, when she spoke for the Fishers. She refused beef lightly dark or with edges not properly trimmed. The slightly reeking fish that she accepted for her own family she would all but throw in the fish man's face if he sent it to the Fisher house. Power, praise, and luxury were hers in this household.[54]

In Morrison's novel, Pauline shields herself from the day-to-day indignities of racism behind the whiteness of her employers. Diamond retains and animates this dynamic through the shielding of a black body behind a white doll—an artful allusion that ties the work of the novel to the play through her use of nonconforming whiteface.

Also significant is that the black actor's handling of the white doll offers the visual representation of black bodies as *coconspirators* in the creation of mythic whiteness—a possibility that is epitomized by the way Pauline Breedlove prioritizes whiteness over blackness (a process of reproduction that is materialized through her daughter Pecola). Embodying this phenomenon, the actor that plays Maureen Peal is the one that actually holds the white doll—a scenario that also prompts audience members to consider Maureen as both a victim *and* a perpetrator of failed mimicry and intraracial prejudice. In the particular world of *The Bluest Eye*, Maureen Peal—Pecola's fair-skinned and well-to-do classmate—is both privileged and penalized by her socioeconomic status and light skin color. She receives undue attention from her peers and teachers and is, in turn, handicapped by her unearned privilege, unable to make substantive connections within her community. Without the emotional and psychological satisfaction of healthy relationships, Maureen, like the doll, is a pretty package void of true substance.

Pauline Breedlove and the Fisher girl. Toni Morrison's *The Bluest Eye*, adapted by Lydia R. Diamond, directed by Walter Dallas, University of Maryland, College Park, 2010. (Photo courtesy of Walter Dallas.)

Yet, as was made clear by the celebrated director Walter Dallas, the use of the doll image in the staged enactment of *The Bluest Eye* also speaks directly to the young Fisher girl's own victimization. Essentially a pawn of the power structure, she—willing or not—is indoctrinated into a belief system that insists on qualitative judgments about race *and* gender. It is this sense of paradox and duality that Dallas attempted to underscore when he made the pointed decision to use a ventriloquist doll in his 2010 production of *The Bluest Eye* at the University of Maryland.

I always envisioned the little white girl as a very real person who, however, was also a super entitled mouthpiece, the voice of a misguided, hateful, fearful community that first infected, and then spoke through her. [She is] an innocent defiled by a society fearful of its own guilty shadow. She, therefore, saw herself and was seen, even by the audience, and especially by those who wanted the freedom her white skin assured, as a cutie-pie, Shirley Temple doll of a thing. She, too, was victim, reduced and trapped into a ventriloquist doll, doing no more or less than had been taught and expected.[55]

Dallas's sensitivity to, and awareness of, the intersecting forms of oppression that violate both black *and* white lives stands perfectly in line with Morrison's own authorial intentions and affects. In one of the novel's first scenes, Morrison introduces us to the MacTeer sisters' "next-door friend," Rosemary Villanucci. Depicted throughout Morrison's novel as more "foe" than a "friend," Rosemary is also presented as a figure that epitomizes intersecting oppressions. While she is white and relishes in the benefits of unearned privilege, she is still limited by her socioeconomic status, gender, and youth. After noting how Rosemary taunts both Claudia and Frieda with the bread she is consuming, Claudia gives voice to these confounding complexities.

We stare at her, wanting her bread, but more than that wanting to poke the arrogance out of her eyes and smash the pride of ownership that curls her chewing mouth. When she comes out of the car we will beat her up, make red marks on her white skin, and she will cry and ask us do we want her to pull her pants down. We will say no. We don't know what we should feel or do if she does, but whenever she asks us, we know she is offering us something precious and that our own pride must be asserted by refusing to accept.[56]

Notably, Morrison offers these ruminations early in her novel. In so doing, she prepares her readers to enter the world of *The Bluest Eye* with an understanding of the nuanced set of relations and circumstances that shape all of its characters—both black and white. With Rosemary Villanucci, Morrison suggests both the privilege a young woman finds in her whiteness and the vulnerability that comes with her age and gender. Clearly a victim of sexual exploitation and abuse, Rosemary functions with an awareness, if not an understanding, of her own subjugation, and she is conditioned to be all too ready to continue her victimization. In offering to expose herself to the

MacTeer girls, Rosemary acquiesces to her circumstances and positions herself to further perpetuate such behaviors. This seemingly nominal scene in Morrison's text reveals the cyclic nature of abusive forces and foreshadows the revelations of the similar cyclical dynamics to come.

Despite all indications that Rosemary's life is far from idyllic, the "arrogance" and "pride of ownership" that plays across her lips still suggest the illogical tenets of white supremacy. The interrogation of this logic is pointedly underscored through the *alternative* stage directions Diamond offers in relation to the white doll scene previously discussed. While Diamond initially proposes that the Fisher girl may be represented by an actor's puppeteering, she follows that by also suggesting that the girl could be represented through the use of a stationary doll and a voice-over.[57] In this potential version of nonconforming whiteface, the complete absence of a *live* body further emphasizes the doll's inanimate nature—and the little white girl's lack of agency. Staged this way, the scene answers the frustration Claudia voices earlier in the play when she disdainfully reflects on receiving her Christmas doll: "What made people look at them and say 'Awwww,' but not see me at all? Why was I invisible next to little white girls in pleated skirts and white knee-highs?"[58] Although the answer to this painful query is never directly articulated in the novel, Diamond uses the play's framing of spectatorship to visibly enunciate a response: there is nothing inherently special about little white girls other than the social capital of their whiteness. Accordingly, the doll's countenance underscores the absurdity of the pedestal on which Mrs. Breedlove has placed her white charge. Moreover, the voice-over reveals the same set of contradictory impressions yielded by the characters of the queen and duchess in Adrienne Kennedy's *Funnyhouse of a Negro*: while relaying the impression of an omnipresent and all-powerful force, the girl is essentially powerless aside from the sense of sovereignty others choose to give her.

Representing a lack of real power, the absent presence of the inanimate doll reinforces the play's portrayal of hegemonic whiteness as simultaneously intangible and impactful. Continuously building on this refrain, Diamond employs other sight-related strategies to portray two of the play's most disturbing scenes, both of which revolve around carefully crafted depictions of sexual violence. The first of these scenes is a flashback in which the gentle, sensual explorations of a young Cholly and his childhood friend, Darlene, morph into an ugly act of denigration and defeat. The scene begins with tenderness: within a field of muscatine grapes, Cholly and Darlene come together "as natural and sweet as the night had become."[59] However, the moment is lost when a group of white men force Cholly to "simulate what had before been beautiful and was now something ugly and confusing."[60]

Once again Diamond's stage directions create a dueling sense of white invisibility and power. Noting that Cholly and Darlene *"react to the men who we do not see,"*[61] Diamond suggests the presence of whiteness through visual and audible cues. "Splashes of white light" and a few "muffled and stylized" voices from offstage are the only indicators of the white men's incorporeal presence.[62] Though absent from the staged scene, the power and dominance of these white men are uncontestable, leaving an irreversible impression on their victims. The shame and horror associated with Cholly's feigned act of penetration are dramatized as a dual rape: he is forced into performing a sexual act just as Darlene is forced to receive him. This abominable event fleeces Cholly of his sense of masculine virility and strength, psychologically and emotionally castrating him. Impotent to fight against the deadly threat imposed by the pack of white men, the innocence of both Darlene and Cholly is stolen in mere minutes. The play does not disclose how this event shapes the life of Darlene (nor does the novel), but audience members are asked to understand that this episode emasculates Cholly while simultaneously skewing his moral compass. The fact that the white perpetrators are never seen by Cholly, Darlene, or the audience contributes to the way the play repeatedly animates notions of (in)visibility. This difficult scene also sets the stage for another disturbing episode: the rape of Pecola at the hands of her father.

Narrated by Soaphead Church and Claudia, the incestuous rape scene begins when Cholly, in a drunken stupor and suffering from a "confused mixture of his memories,"[63] is unable to distinguish between feelings of discomfort, pleasure, revulsion, guilt, pity, love, impotence, and power. Crippled by his compromised judgment and damaged psyche, Cholly rapes his daughter. The playwright is very specific in her vision of this daunting scene, purposefully noting in the stage directions that Cholly and Pecola are *"never touching or moving."*[64] In fact Diamond's "Playwright's Note" at the top of the published script explains in detail the importance of *not seeing* the rape in explicit terms.

> I worked hard in this adaptation to approach the story as a tale of the damaging trickle-down effect of a rather crippling societal racism, not merely as the story of a dysfunctional family and community. I feel strongly that this most serves the intention of the book and also serves

the dramatic intention of the play. *To this end, I think it is very important that the piece be spared graphic, realistic representations of sexual violence.* ... As soon as we are made to watch a heinous act of incest on stage, we are forced to assimilate that act first and foremost. We lose sight of its place in the story and ultimately end up diminishing the tragic effect of the act itself as well as obscuring Pecola's story.[65]

Although some productions of *The Bluest Eye* have chosen to illustrate the rape scene more realistically, most have honored Diamond's artistic vision.[66] For example, in describing the Cholly-Pecola rape scene in Steppenwolf's debut production, Harvey Young and Jocelyn Prince note that the characters' choreography was in a "stylized, nearly expressionistic manner."[67] Writing of Cholly's "exaggerated slow motion," Young and Prince describe how the characters "began to circle one another ... like a stalker or a predator" before standing still through the most incriminating parts of the narration.[68] The authors rightly conclude that Diamond's insistence on the characters never touching may have been shaped by the fact that a more realistic representation of the rape scene could "render it unsuitable" for the school-age audiences for which the piece was originally intended.[69]

While the need to address concerns about the debut production undoubtedly informed Diamond's dramaturgical choices, the decision to avoid any explicit representation of the rape also honors Toni Morrison's original intentions and helps to further underscore the play's theatrical treatment of (in)visibility. As specified, the play brings purposeful attention to what we literally do and don't see, and the meanings therein. On the surface, we are asked to recognize that a horrendous act of black-on-black violence transpires; however, the playwright does not want us to simply fixate on the grotesque images that erupt from this conclusion. Rather than focusing on the visualization of this abhorrent act, Diamond wants us to *see* that invisible forces drive Cholly's actions. That is, Diamond's stage directions highlight the unseen and underrecognized ideological perversity that has driven Cholly to this level of abasement and self-loathing. Prompting her audience to recognize the psychological subjugation and violence experienced by Cholly and those like him (the underprivileged victims of societal racism), Diamond's insistence on *not* seeing the actors touch necessarily shifts the emphasis—but not the horror—of the scene from a specific heinous act to the publically sanctioned, ubiquitous acts of societal and institutionalized racism at the root of Cholly's derangement.

THE INFLECTIONS OF MEMORY: ABSENCE, PRESENCE, AND THE NEGOTIATIONS OF ADAPTATION

Despite the inherent theatricality of *The Bluest Eye*, it was not until 2005 (thirty-five years after the original publication of Morrison's novel), that *The Bluest Eye* was transformed into a stage play. The Diamond adaptation was commissioned by Chicago's Steppenwolf Theatre Company for two of its special programs: the Steppenwolf for Young Adults (SYA) program and New Plays Initiative (NPI).[70] The merging of these programming initiatives was done with two finite goals in mind: (1) to develop work that would attract a younger and more demographically diverse audience to Steppenwolf's stages and (2) to create a piece that would be suitable for Black History Month.[71] However, the tremendous critical and commercial success of *The Bluest Eye*'s debut production, along with Toni Morrison's blessings, opened the possibilities for the stage adaptation of Morrison's novel to become a main stage event for theater groups across the country.[72]

The success of the stage play is indebted to the greatness of the original novel, as well as to Lydia Diamond's skill as a dramatist. Just as Morrison's novel engages with words and the *performance* of words on the page, Diamond's aural and visual adaptation translates the original narrative into a breathing, multi-sensory montage. As I have demonstrated throughout this chapter, Diamond's theatrical rendition of *The Bluest Eye* offers a unique opportunity to explore how the absence, as well as the presence, of visual cues can powerfully stage white privilege as both an ideological construct and a visceral, materialized fact.

For Diamond, the impetus to adapt *The Bluest Eye* into a play was propelled by her desire to interrogate the persistent absence of positive African American imagery within American popular culture.

> *The Bluest Eye* is the story of a young African American girl and her family who are affected in every direction by the dominant American culture that says to them, "You're not beautiful; you're not relevant; you're invisible; you don't even count."
>
> That is what is painful in the novel—the way in which our country has dealt with race, the way in which the power structure has hurt us, and the way in which it has made us hurt ourselves. Often enough we Afri-

can Americans don't get the opportunity to say "This is the source of my dysfunction, and it's not all my fault."

> To be shown that when you are young is painful, horrible. On the other hand, it is very affirming to have all these things made *very clear and relevant*; things that I knew were sick and wrong, things that touched me in *these intangible ways, all made clear* just by having the lives of people like me represented in literature.[73]

Diamond's reflections champion the way in which access to and distribution of Morrison's story can provide an affirming experience for the people to whom (and for whom) *The Bluest Eye* speaks. Her comments not only reveal how racialized identities are highlighted or diminished in popular culture, but they also help us understand that her decision to adapt *The Bluest Eye* was driven by a need to make the contentious history surrounding African American representation "very clear and relevant." Just as Morrison's novel records the intangible yet ever affective forces that inform both black and white lives, the stage adaptation of *The Bluest Eye* offers us yet another opportunity to document and destabilize oppressive belief systems. Giving Morrison's novel a new kind of visibility through embodied expression, Diamond's takes the intangible forces of which Morrison speaks and gives them form in an unparalleled and decidedly accessible way.

When considering the issue of form, I would be remiss if I did not take a moment to fully address how the stage play's form (a memory play) and formation (an adaptation) also speak to ideas of absence and presence. Modeled after the novel, the stage play is narrated by several characters, all of which offer retroactive reflections to weave together the *how* of Pecola's story. Thus, the memories that make up the play are selected and selective on two levels: in terms of what the characters choose to share with the audience and in terms of what the adaptor chose to retain from the original piece of literature. As such, the impressions, anecdotes, and recollections portrayed in *The Bluest Eye* are evidence of both subjective and collective processes of erasure and emphasis.

In terms of the way the content of the play and novel utilize memory, one must consider how the play's narrators are empowered to recall events and emotions they did not actually witness or experience for themselves. In wrestling with the *how* instead of the *why*, the narrators (Claudia, Frieda, and Soaphead Church) guide the audience through a number of formative events in the lives of Cholly, Darlene, Mrs. Breedlove, and Pecola. As visible specters and commentators throughout these various enactments, the staged presence of the narrators and their stories provide visual evidence of others' subjective experiences. In this way, *The Bluest Eye* stage adaptation captures the structure of the novel, a collection of contrapuntal narratives, thereby serving as an illustrative example of memory in action. Acknowledging the various ways the absence and presence of collective memories shape the play's form and content, it is also fitting to consider how directorial choices can further highlight the play's thematic through-lines. This consideration invites me to reflect on Walter Dallas's repeated stagings of *The Bluest Eye* (four separate productions, all of which used a strikingly sparse set) and how these signature productions served the play's tropes and strategic enactments of absence/presence and invisibility/visibility.[74]

Supported by the fact that Diamond's stage directions specify moments in which people or actions should not be seen, each of Dallas's productions (for the Plowshares Theatre in Detroit; Lorraine Hansberry Theatre in San Francisco; Freedom Theatre in Philadelphia; and, most recently, University of Maryland, College Park) pushed this concept even further by utilizing very little in terms of sets and props. In part Dallas concedes that his preference for such sparse staging was born of his own artistic training and experience.

> I have always believed that all I needed to create theatre are an actor or two, an audience, visibility, and a good story. It's all I had as a poor kid in Atlanta when two coke bottles were my cast; I was writer, producer, director, choreographer, dramaturg, voice overs, and Master of Ceremony. All I had was that story, an invented relationship, and the desire to seduce my audience into believing; or to suspend their disbelief. Chicken or egg. By telling the story of *The Bluest Eye* with no set, the audience—and actors—could really focus on what is really most important: the story about these adroitly drawn characters, their amazingly intense relationships, people to people, people to community, community to society, society to this fertile time in American history.[75]

Although Dallas's *ability* to effectively stage *The Bluest Eye* with relatively few stage properties may have been informed by his experience and formal training, his *choice* to do so also speaks to the play's emphasis on (in)visibility. Appropriately, Dallas capitalized on the absence of *things* and focused on the players' bodies to create dramatic, emotionally charged tableaus onstage. As

Stage tableau. Toni Morrison's *The Bluest Eye*, adapted by Lydia R. Diamond, directed by Walter Dallas, University of Maryland, College Park, 2010. (Photo by Stan Barouh.)

an audience member, these silhouettes immediately brought to my mind the silhouette work of the African American artist Kara Walker. Walker, known for her own racially charged motifs, dramatizes some of our nation's most disturbing stereotypes by crafting black cutouts against white backgrounds. In Dallas's production of *The Bluest Eye*, the Breedloves were cast against the airy blue of an unadorned stage. As witnessed in the accompanying image, the Breedloves' bodies are affected by unseen forces, and the sudden lack of corporeal detail (the lighting makes it impossible to see the particulars or contours of individual faces) suggests that their forms become "stand-ins" for all those who are similarly victimized—or victimizing. Moreover, as Dallas's own musings assert, the lack of detail and minutia allows the play's scenes to flow seamlessly into one another with an almost stream-of-conscious fluidity. In lieu of material distractions, the pictures painted before the audience are sutured together to visually punctuate the primacy of the characters and the potent meanings of the play's carefully selected enactments.

Of course, the very nature of a novel to stage adaptation demands that the adapting artists and potential audience members be prepared to create and witness a piece that is notably different from the original work. For

Diamond, part of the process of adapting *The Bluest Eye* was accepting that difficult cuts and omissions had to be made.

> I'm always aware of the missing voices in the play. . . . I hate that Junior can't be in the play; he's important, but there was no way to develop him as thoroughly as he would need to be, and not just be another boy doing something bad to Pecola. Similarly, the prostitutes—I missed them a lot, but again, there was no way in a ninety-minute play to develop them, and not have them just be the prostitutes. They couldn't have a place onstage if I couldn't serve them by fully rounding out their character arches—and there just wasn't time.[76]

As Diamond laments, some of the play's omissions are significant, yet such deletions were also necessary to create a tight and cohesive theatrical piece. Sammy (Pecola's brother), the "whores" (including Maginot Line), Mr. Henry (the MacTeers' boarder), Junior (one of Pecola's most notable antagonizers), Rosemary Villanucci (the next-door neighbor), and Samson Fuller (Cholly's father) are among the notable characters that are absent in Diamond's stage adaptation. The fact of these absences, in tandem with the spirit of Diamond's own reflections, attests to the difficulties faced by adaptors. These challenges are taken up by the theatre artist/practitioner Jocelyn Prince and theatre and performance scholar Harvey Young in their article "The Politics of Lydia Diamond's Adaptation of Toni Morrison's *The Bluest Eye*."

In discussing the artistic politics surrounding the adaptation process for the play's Steppenwolf commission, Prince and Young assert how the adaptation of novels into stage plays can be an arduous process, one that presupposes a number of aesthetic and political quandaries. Wrestling with the inherent challenges in adapting *The Bluest Eye*, they pose—and answer—important artistic queries.

> How do you create a theatrical event—even as a faithful adaption—from a mostly descriptive text? If theatre is driven by dialogue and physical action, then how do you wrestle with the challenges posed by continuous first-person narration? The answer, for Diamond, was to maintain Morrison's tone of address and import it onto the stage. Her characters also speak in first-person, direct address. This choice preserves Morrison's *absented presence* as the authorial guide, who takes the reader and,

now, theatergoer through the play. . . . In addition, the descriptive narrative structure likely made the play easier to adapt and, indeed, stage. Entire characters and subplots can be omitted, years can pass, and new locations can be introduced, thanks to the re-orienting function of first-person direct address.[77]

While key characters may have been sacrificed for the benefit of the playscript, Diamond's adaptation preserves the author's voice and assures that the central themes and conflicts within the world of the novel ultimately find their expression in the stage play. Morrison's own absent presence is maintained throughout the course of the play's unfolding, yet Diamond still manages to seize a number of opportunities to omit, as well as insert, notable elements in her theatrical adaptation.

In terms of textual additions, it is important to note that there are innumerable moments in which Diamond rephrases language from the novel or necessarily gives voice to the psychic utterings of Morrison's characters. Consciously and conscientiously shaping elements from the book to best fit the context and demands of live performance, Diamond succinctly synthesizes and translates the novel's sentiments and metaphors into a carefully crafted (and often original) array of exchanges and monologues. Among Diamond's notable additions is a scene that has no counterpart in Morrison's novel: a monologue by Pecola in which she addresses poisoning the dog at the behest of Soaphead Church. In their analysis of the adaptation process, Prince and Young give due attention to this added scene, detailing the multiple dramaturgical goals it serves: (1) the monologue allows the theatre audience to witness Pecola's subjectivity; (2) it highlights the symbolic parallels between Pecola and the condemned canine; and (3) it functions as an explicatory bridge for the following scene, in which Pecola—recognizing her role in the dog's demise—finally succumbs to the comfort found in her psychotic break.[78]

While all these dramaturgical strategies serve the form and function of the play, it is the way in which the monologue underscores the parallels between Pecola and the abject animal that I find most resonant. Both Morrison's novel and Diamond's play reveal the contempt that Soaphead Church feels toward his landlady's dog and, thereby, impart to their audiences an understanding of the dog's outsider status—an experience of repudiation that is likewise endured by the dog's human counterpart, Pecola. A relatively brief yet incredibly effective interlude, Pecola's monologue describes the dog's death and her accidental role in it. As such it mirrors and serves as a powerful proxy to a number of analogous metaphors found in Morrison's novel, all of which speak to white hegemony in parallel and complementary ways.

Some of these metaphoric moments are found in both the novel and the play, among them Pecola's ruminations on dandelions, the wildflowers she initially sees as beautiful. In the play, Pecola's musings occur during her walk to Mr. Yacobowski's vegetable stand: "I wonder why pretty yellow dandelions is called weeds. I like them. They strong and grow fast and don't hurt no one."[79] Yet two short scenes later—soon after she endures Mr. Yacobowski's cold, vacant stare—Pecola succumbs to the belief system of others and determines that dandelions are, indeed, undesirable: "Come to think of it, maybe they are weeds. Yes, they are ugly. Ugly weeds. Nobody would think a weed is pretty. You would have to be stupid to think a weed is pretty. (*She stomps on the dandelion, crushing it into the ground*)."[80] The stage play also dramatizes another floral analogy that originates in the novel; the story of the marigolds.

When the audience first meets Claudia, she tells us that marigolds did not bloom in the fall of 1941. In the play's final moments, however, Claudia reflects more profoundly on the absence of marigolds that year, assessing that the fault was not found in the way *she* planted the seeds but rather in the earth itself.

> I even think now that the land of the entire country was hostile to marigolds that year. This soil is bad for certain kinds of flowers. Certain seeds it will not nurture we acquiesce and say the victim had no right to live. We are wrong, of course, but it doesn't matter. It's too late.[81]

Similar to Pecola's submission to the popular thought that dandelions should be abhorred rather than appreciated, Claudia's reflections on the absence of marigolds allude to the widespread effects of systematic racism. As Morrison intimates, our nation's racist doctrines (the "soil") stifle the blossoming of minoritized bodies and minds; these unyielding perceptions can prevent the truth of black value and beauty to come to light. While both flower analogies, and the prose used to express them, are found within the novel and the playscript, the novel has several other like-minded riffs that are absent from the stage adaptation. Among these are Morrison's prose regarding the Breedloves' sofa and her description of Pauline Breedlove's rotting tooth.

Relaying yet another "how" from Cholly's life story, Morrison takes a moment to describe how he was forced to pay for a damaged sofa, thereby revealing the ubiquitous and emasculating inequities faced by black men in America. Explaining the Breedloves' lack of pride in the ownership of the damaged goods, Morrison writes:

> And the joylessness stank, pervading everything.... Like a sore tooth that is not content to throb in isolation, but must diffuse its own pain to other parts of the body—making breathing difficult, vision limited, nerves unsettled, so a hated piece of furniture produces a fretful malaise that asserts itself throughout the house and limits the delight of things not related to it.[82]

As described, the family's despair moves beyond its disregard for a single item of furniture. The couch becomes a symbol of the family's victimization and, most pointedly, Cholly's sociopolitical impotence. The unrest and disparagement Cholly feels not only spreads throughout the house, infecting all its inhabitants, but it alludes to the contagion of negative thought, revealing how bias can take hold and permeate throughout an entire community.

Likewise, Morrison's description of Pauline Breedlove's sore tooth serves a similar end. While Diamond's adaptation addresses Pauline's lamentations over the loss of her tooth, Morrison's novel also reflects upon the *process* of that loss by associating the metaphor of decay to the dynamics of racial prejudice.

> And then she lost her front tooth. But there must have been a speck, a brown speck easily mistaken for food but which did not leave, which sat on the enamel for months, and grew, until it cut into the surface and then to the brown putty underneath, finally eating away to the root, but avoiding the nerves, so its presence was not noticeable or uncomfortable. Then the weakened roots, having grown accustomed to the poison, responded one day to severe pressure, and the tooth fell free, leaving a ragged stump behind. But even before the little brown speck, there must have been the conditions, the setting that would allow it to exist in the first place.[83]

With a clearly rooted analogy (pun intended), Morrison once again asserts the power of hegemonic thought when she claims that "there must have been the conditions" that would allow the festering and proliferation of something so insignificant to cause such irreparable damage.

These stories of the marigolds, dandelions, couch, and tooth become material signifiers of the conceptual contagions that infect the Breedloves and permeate our nation's psyche. With dramaturgical considerations of space, time, and cohesion, however, Diamond was confronted with the practical need to truncate or totally excise these expressions while still maintaining the novel's definitive critique of white hegemony. Although those who have yet to read Morrison's novel may be none the wiser concerning any discernible adjustments, audience members who are familiar with the original work may readily recognize the discrepancies between the two artistic productions. Subsequently, the play has the potential to activate yet another experience of remembrance: in the wake of their spectatorship, informed audience members of *The Bluest Eye* are given the chance to revisit—and perhaps revise—their earlier impressions due to the story's adapted form.

There is also a richness to be gained by having the ability to examine and contrast original source material with an adapted work. As I have suggested elsewhere, the process of adaptation creates textual palimpsests that offer us the opportunity to "read between the lines" and analyze artistic works through, as well as beyond, their intertextual relationships.[84] This grants us the chance to analyze how our dramatic texts and canons develop, and, more significantly, it empowers readers to critically evaluate how the choices made during the adaptation process reflect our social, political, artistic, and commercial influences, past *and* present.

And, finally, the practice of adaptation encourages us to ask a fundamental dramaturgical question with regard to our past and present: "Why *this* play, now?" In posing this question to *The Bluest Eye*, we acknowledge that Morrison wrote her novel in 1970, over thirty years before Diamond's 2005 stage adaptation. The critical responses and emotional resonance of the adaptation disclose part of the answer to the aforementioned query: not only is the work artistically rich, but the issues presented in *The Bluest Eye* still persist, despite the phenomenal progress that has been made in terms of both our social and our racial politics. Nevertheless, we are not always eager to recognize and acknowledge the existence of these persistent, and embarrassingly backward, ideological constructs. Enamored of our celebrated advancements, we are often too willing to ignore the damaging perceptions that continue to affect how audience members envision themselves and others. Thus, the staged presentation of *The Bluest Eye* offers an opportunity to stimulate the consciousness of audience members who—like Pecola—are too easily seduced by a dangerous, peace-granting fiction.

For *The Bluest Eye* protagonist, Pecola, this denial is far from innocuous: it catapults her into a realm of madness. As revealed in both the novel and the play, the many psychological and emotional pressures endured by Pecola eventually take their toll. Wounded by her twisted truths and finding salvation in fantasy, Pecola chooses to deviate from facticity and embrace the notion that she has, indeed, been given the blue eyes for which she has long yearned. This delusion proves the definitive tone of Morrison's assertion: "[S]he would never know her beauty. She would see only what there was to see: the eyes of other people."[85] Thus, not unlike the heroine of Adrienne Kennedy's *Funnyhouse of a Negro*, Pecola becomes yet another tragic model of "racial madness"; her relinquished sanity represents the *maddening* consequences of racial bias and prejudice on the human psyche.[86] This closing evidence of Pecola's madness also exemplifies the performative paradoxes of visibility and invisibility that are presented throughout *The Bluest Eye*: the tragedy of Pecola, and of her world, is the tragedy of those who see a presence where there is an absence and perceive an absence where there is a presence.

Thus, true to Morrison's novel, Diamond's adaptation of *The Bluest Eye* critiques the skewed perspectives of racism and the unstable, contradictory constructions of whiteness. This critique permeates both the play and novel, but the genre of the stage play, buoyed by Diamond's nuanced and insightful treatment of the given material, offers the opportunity to fully embody and enact the paradoxes of (in)visibility that are so essential to Morrison's story. By dramatizing fragmented memories and activating visual cues that denote both absence and presence, Diamond's dramatic adaptation of *The Bluest Eye* takes full advantage of the opportunity to present both experiential and theoretical understandings of whiteness and hegemonic ideology. In so doing, it not only enacts its own performative utterance, but—true to its paradoxical nature—it reveals what still remains to be seen *and* unseen.

CHAPTER THREE

Whiteness as "Becoming"
The Corporeal Crossovers of Daniel Tisdale and Michael Jackson

The previous two chapters of *Coloring Whiteness* wrestled with tropes of whiteness as they journeyed through the process of artistic adaptation. Chapter 1's examination of *Day of Absence* chronicled the transformation of a live stage play into a televised performance, and chapter 2's study of *The Bluest Eye* considered the transition of a literary novel to its staged interpretation. In both instances, the transitions discussed—whether in relation to the narratives' changing genres or the temporal shifts marked by these various productions—reveal progress as well as problematic truths. One of the most discomforting and persistent truths addressed in the preceding chapters is that the undue prioritizing and privileging of whiteness continues in the here and now.

What is particularly remarkable about "the here and now," however, is that advances in technology, medical science, and the beauty industry *can* make a brown-eyed black girl's dreams of having blue eyes come true (or at least *appear* to come true). Through the use of tinted contacts, hair dyes, bleaching creams, or even cosmetic surgery, racialized features *can be* manipulated and manufactured with relative ease. In this day and age, the potential to experience a phenotypical transformation is more than just fantasy bound by a book, play, or film. What was once the material of creative fiction is now a very real possibility, and innumerable people—artists, cultural activists, entrepreneurs, and everyday folk—are now actively exploiting, critiquing, and experiencing these real-life, embodied "adaptations." Such is the case of Tracey E. Goodman.

Armed with his company's motto, "We turn minorities into majorities," Tracey E. Goodman, entrepreneur extraordinaire and president of Transitions, Inc., took a grassroots approach to marketing by advertising his company's services on several New York City street corners. Claiming that Transitions, Inc. had the wherewithal to change the phenotypical appearance of its customers—and thereby ensure them financial and personal success—Goodman peddled his wares to pedestrian passersby on Wall Street, in Times Square, at Astor Place, and on 125th Street and Lenox Avenue. With visual aids such as before and after portraits, brochures, posters, charts, flyers, and sample products, Goodman (a light-skinned, green-eyed, auburn-haired, and sharp-featured African American male) passed out promotional material and described the variety of services offered by his company. After hearing of the techniques employed by Transitions, Inc. (services ranging from skin bleaching and cosmetic surgery to linguistic and behavioral training), bystanders responded in widely disparate ways. Some passersby exploded with indignation while other observers attentively listened and gathered the written materials in hopes of becoming future clients. Unbeknownst to either group, however, Tracey E. Goodman was *not* the president of Transitions, Inc. In fact, he did not exist at all: not only was he a fictional character, but Transitions, Inc. was a fictional company. Thus, rather than responding to an enterprising entrepreneur at work, both groups of unsuspecting pedestrians had inadvertently become invaluable participants in a performance piece, *Transitions, Inc.*, enacted by the Harlem-based artist Daniel Tisdale.

Using the artwork of Tisdale, as well as the corporeal and performance texts of the famous pop star Michael Jackson, this chapter explores the impulses and anxieties engendered by the idea of black bodies transitioning into "whiter" ones. In revealing how these metamorphoses and alterations—both fictional and factional—are associated with social and fiscal value, this chapter examines how whiteness and the notion of "becoming white" are ostensibly conflated with the American Dream. Through a detailed analysis of selected visual texts, I use the transformative performances of both Tisdale and Jackson to highlight—and question—the packaging, marketing, and consumption of whiteness in America, illustrating the ways in which the phenotypical markers of whiteness are associated with access, entitlement, and transcendence. I argue that these artists offer audiences the opportunity to interrogate how the mediated images of black bodies have been historically perceived, both *inter-* and *intraracially*, by activating perceptions of whitening in their work. Through their appropriation of visual cues that are habitually conflated with whiteness, both Tisdale and Jackson challenge unilateral readings of authentic blackness, invariably complicating easy assumptions regarding contemporary expressions of African American identity.

THE PERFORMATIVE PALIMPSESTS OF DANIEL TISDALE

Originally born and raised in the Los Angeles area, Harlem-based Daniel Bretton Tisdale is an artist, educator, and fervent political activist. A masters graduate of the Otis/Parsons School of Design, Tisdale is the founder and acting president of the National Visual Artists Guild, a union designed to secure the rights and benefits of visual artists. While deeply entrenched in his creative work, Tisdale's activism extends beyond the art world. In 2003 he created *Harlem World* magazine, an online journal dedicated to Harlem news and insights, and in 2013 he was selected by the NAACP to receive the Game Change Award. Tisdale served as a New York State committee member in the Seventieth Assembly District in the mid-1990s, and he has participated as an active board member and associate of innumerable organizations, including the Los Angeles Poverty Department (LAPD), the National College Art Association (CAA), the New York Foundation for the Arts (NYFA), and the Independent Publishers Association (IPA).[1] For Tisdale, however, the roles of artist, activist, and politician are one and the same, as is evident from even a cursory review of his work.

While Tisdale engages in many different artistic genres (photography, installations, drawings, and performance art), his projects are always inspired by a particular social or political theme. From his Warholesque photo montages of a 1930s lynching to repeated frames of the Rodney King beating and his critically acclaimed installation *The Black Museum* (in which products signifying "blackness"—such as hot combs and dashikis—are displayed), Tisdale's work often prompts his audience to reflect on America's racial dynamics. The provocative nature of his art has resulted in its display in over one hundred galleries and museums worldwide, among them the Smithsonian Institution, the Whitney Museum of American Art, the New Museum of Contemporary Art, the Studio Museum in Harlem, the Institute of Contemporary Art in Boston, and the National Civil Rights Museum in Memphis, as well as venues in Canada, Egypt, Europe, Israel, Russia, and South Africa.[2] Nevertheless, Tisdale's work is still relatively underrecognized beyond New York art circles and has been the subject of just a handful of major reviews (one of the most prominent being the descriptive account penned by Kobena Mercer in *ArtForum* in 1992).³ Those who have had the chance to experience Tisdale's work, however, are offered a memorable opportunity to contemplate how perceptions of race affect our social networks.

One of the most interesting examples of Tisdale's artistic queries is his street performance *Transitions, Inc.*, in which he takes on the outrageous personae of Tracey E. Goodman. Particularly intriguing is *Transitions's* "layered" form: the performance incorporates pieces from Tisdale's earlier artwork as essential props. Created and presented as part of Creative Time's 1992 City Wide Project Series, the conceptual seeds for *Transitions, Inc.* were actually planted by Tisdale's visual art series *Post Plantation Pop* (1988) and *Sign of the Times* (1989). Both series consist of portraits that have been altered in order to comment on societal assumptions regarding race and gender. Considering our postmodern moment, Tisdale's use of portraiture to define and redefine notions of identity proves to be especially resonant.

Commenting on postmodernism portraiture, art historian Shearer West writes that it is a medium that increasingly wrestles "with social masks and the ways individual identity can be submerged or obliterated by surface or stereotype."⁴ Just as West describes how other artists have used portraiture to challenge "the inescapability of social stereotypes," Tisdale's work animates "the notion that even the identity of a single individual can be multifaceted and subject to fluctuating interpretations."⁵ As both products and producers of contemporary pop culture sensibilities, artists such as Tisdale have

> found portraiture an appropriate medium to convey the sense that, in the late twentieth century, no individual has a single, definable identity.... Because of these philosophical and social paradigm shifts, the experimentations with identity and role-playing within portraits have become a fundamental part of late twentieth- and early twenty-first-century portraiture.⁶

Certainly, Tisdale's portrait artwork grants him an ideal opportunity to engage in "experimentations with identity and role-playing."

For example, in *Post Plantation Pop* and *Sign of the Times* Tisdale manipulates the facial features of a number of individuals, juxtaposing "before and after" pictures to suggest the metamorphoses of racial identities. In *Post*

Whiteness as "Becoming"

Robeson, by Daniel Tisdale, from the *Post Plantation Pop* series, 1988. (Courtesy of Daniel Tisdale.)

Plantation Pop, he does this by modifying the photographs of sacred African American icons. In *Sign of the Times*, however, he alters the pictures of both known and lesser-known figures of varying racial identities.[7] While the whole of these art series feature a number of different metamorphoses, for the purpose of this chapter's focus, I would like to turn my attention to two pieces from Tisdale's *Post Plantation Pop* series, both of which suggest racial "whitenings": *Robeson* and *Malcolm X*.[8]

In Tisdale's *Robeson*, the title figure is cast against a kente-cloth-like backdrop. The "before" photographic image of Paul Robeson features the legendary artist/political activist in a stoic pose. The "after" picture beside it, however, reveals numerous changes. By altering the original photograph, Tisdale makes Robeson's skin appear lighter and smoother. His hair, formerly a bit uneven, is aligned, and the contour of his hairline is transformed into a sharp widow's peak—an angularity that is further accentuated by shaped eyebrows and a thinned nasal bridge. The lips of the after Robeson are also thinned, and, by accentuating his cheekbones, his lips now appear to disclose the hint of a mischievous smirk. His eyes, formerly dark brown, are translucent and suggest—even though the picture itself is black and white—that his irises are now blue. The final Tisdalian touch is that Robeson's unadulterated chin now features a deeply cut cleft. Without question, the after picture of Robeson effectively creates a feeling of dissonance and disjuncture between the images, distancing viewers from the more familiar visual and textual narratives associated with the civil rights activist.

The son of a runaway slave, Paul Robeson (1898–1976) was not only a political figure but also a celebrated athlete, scholar, singer, and actor. However, nothing has concretized our perception of Robeson's strength and virility more than his legacy of social activism. In the late 1930s, he began an ardent campaign for international civil rights, speaking out against racism in America and for the rights of working people and organized labor unions across the world. As a supporter of the Communist Party, Robeson's remonstrations—and the controversy surrounding them—adversely affected his career. Not only was he blacklisted from performing in American venues, but in 1950 his passport was revoked, thereby preventing him from making a living elsewhere. When his passport was reinstated eight years later, time had taken its toll: no longer a favored player in the public imagination, Robeson's career was essentially over.

Even during the strongest period of his career (1924–45), Robeson's image as a performing artist was a contested one, particularly in terms of what his presence meant and symbolized in relation to blackness. As Richard Dyer articulates in *Heavenly Bodies: Film Stars and Society*, Robeson's successful career as a "crossover" star "insisted on his blackness"—that is, it demanded that he expressed a racial essence that was invariably marked and transmitted by the music he sang and characters he played.[9] As Dyer notes, those who lauded Robeson framed his crossover status as a symbol of racial progress and possibility, while others saw the famous performer as a "sellout" whose portrayals reinforced perceptions of black atavism, primitivism, and intellectual inferiority.[10] Despite the contradictory views of Robeson at the height of his commercial success, a commonly shared belief is that he endured a "tragic fall" in the eyes of the public by his career's end. As observed by his biographer, Martin Duberman:

> Robeson had been viewed for a number of decades as the symbolic, "good Negro," as proof that the system worked, as proof that there was no significant prejudice in this country. But Paul Robeson not only stepped over the line of being the good representative Negro, but he strode across the line. He insisted on being openly political and insisted on remaining true to his principles, even after the world shifted and changed around him.[11]

Echoing Duberman, Rob Nagel writes that Robeson was "widely vilified and censored for his frankness and unyielding views on issues to which public opinion ran contrary."[12] Despite the personal consequences, Robeson was uncompromising in his critique of the US government, staunchly advocating social and political change. It is this rigid, unrelenting fortitude that has secured perceptions of his defiant masculinity within more complimentary reflections on his life. It is also this conformance that is countered by Tisdale's transformed *Robeson*.

Similarly, Tisdale's *Malcolm X* drastically revises the way we envision yet another African American leader. Born Malcolm Little in 1925, Malcolm X, like Paul Robeson, has come to symbolize the strength and fortitude of black manhood. When he was named minister and national spokesman for the Nation of Islam (NOI), he used his position and increasing notoriety to speak forthrightly about conditions in a racially divided America. Despite the contentious and controversial nature of his earlier, separatist rhetoric, Malcolm was steadfast in expressing his views—that is, until Elijah Muhammad silenced him. In light of disturbing revelations about Muhammed, Malcolm resigned from the NOI in 1964 and established his own religious organization. When he undertook a pilgrimage to Mecca later that year, it was an experience that not only changed his perceptions of white people but gave him an entirely new perspective on the future of America's race relations. Like Robeson, Malcolm began expanding his vision of civil rights on a global scale. However, his murder in 1965—at the hands of three NOI members—ended his revolutionary call for national and international unity.

Outspoken, unflinching, and courageous, Malcolm X has symbolized the dogged strength and resilience of black masculinity. In his oft-quoted eulogy for Malcolm, actor/activist Ossie Davis offered these words.

> It is not in the memory of man that his beleaguered, unfortunate, but nonetheless proud community has found a braver, more gallant young champion that this Afro-American who lies before us—unconquered still. I say the word again, as he would want me to: Afro-American— Afro-American Malcolm. . . . Malcolm had stopped being a "Negro" years ago. It had become too small, too puny, too weak a word for him. Malcolm was bigger than that. Malcolm had become an Afro-American and he wanted—so desperately—that we, that all his people would become Afro-Americans too. . . . Malcolm was our manhood, or living, black manhood! This was his meaning to his people.[13]

As evidenced by Davis's reverential remarks, the image of Malcolm X, a heroic symbol of black manhood, has become synonymous with racial pride and cultural integrity. This imagining of Malcolm, however, is not evidenced in Tisdale's alterations—a transformation that is strikingly similar to the metamorphosis witnessed in *Robeson*. At the hands of Tisdale, Malcolm—whose naturally light skin and auburn hair earned him the nickname "Detroit Red" during his wild and reckless youth—undergoes an intentional whitening. Ridding Malcolm of his signature horn-rimmed glasses, Tisdale drastically tempers his skin color, divests him of his goatee and mustache, and thins his broad features, most noticeably his nose. Suggesting, as in the case of Robeson's transformation, a small widow's peak, Tisdale also heightens Malcolm's new look by emphasizing a cleft chin and intimating that his eyes are now a clear blue. In both instances, the "after" pictures of Robeson and Malcolm X not only undermine perceptions of their corporeal blackness, but their seeming feminization also challenges general assumptions regarding African American masculinity.

Tisdale's before and after portraits of Malcolm X and Paul Robeson may obfuscate the original images, yet their distortions also help reveal how masculinities are read outside of the context of a white, male body. In describing the sundry typologies to which black men have been relegated, David Marriott asks, "What does it mean to be seen, or be seen to be, a 'type'? Can the idea of type be used to question the process of being typecast, stereotyped?"[14] Bringing Marriott's queries to life, Tisdale's visual play with images of renowned black men troubles the convenient categories often used to classify what they look like—and therefore what they *are* like. By reinscribing the familiar likenesses of Malcolm X and Paul Robeson with lighter skin and thinner features, Tisdale not only alters the appearance of these particular icons, but he also challenges images related to the physicality (and nature) of all black men. Moreover, by "cutting away" his models' features to diminish the perception of their masculinity, Tisdale portrays a racial transformation and simultaneous castration, thereby disclosing the peculiar ways in which our variable understandings of masculine virility are informed by notions of racial embodiment.

Acknowledging the public's emotional investment in the legacies of both Malcolm X and Paul Robeson, Tisdale's "after" portraits also draw attention to the way in which notions of racial purity impact assumptions regarding cultural and sociopolitical allegiances. On one hand, the altered images of Robeson and Malcolm suggest a level of cultural assimilation that actually

Malcolm X, by Daniel Tisdale, from the *Post Plantation Pop* series, 1988. (Courtesy of Daniel Tisdale.)

affirms the aesthetic standards and ideologies of an oppressive and racist society. In so doing, they enact an artistic rendering of what I refer to as *naturalized whiteface* (cosmetic alterations presented on the "everyday" stage). Through the use of elaborate makeup, plastic surgery, or even medical technology, naturalized whiteface suggests an intentional effort to adopt phenotypical markers typically associated with whiteness. This is not to say that the whitening of these visages is in any way "natural looking." Rather, these machinations are initiated and stylized to suggest a desire to conform to the aesthetic strictures that prioritize whiteness, thereby resulting in features that are deemed white—or at least "whiter."

Seen this way, the assumption of whitened features could be read as the imagined acquiescence of Robeson and Malcolm to societal expectations and preferences, thereby alluding to a reverence for whiteness and, subsequently, a denouncement of blackness. Beyond a mere transition, the machinations portrayed in Tisdale's portraits not only suggest an intentional *becoming*, but the very conceit of their before and after framing implies that the subsequent images should be perceived as marked improvements. Accordingly, the resulting image is posed as preferential, thereby perpetuating and substantiating the premise that whiteness represents beauty and the aesthetic ideal.

In the case of Robeson, such framing readily speaks to the criticism that he compromised himself—and presentations black manhood—for the sake of professional gain. As succinctly described by Dyer, denigrators of Robeson (Harold Cruse being among the most pointed) argued that he was "too integrationist, too concerned with adapting himself to white cultural norms, too far removed from the real cultural concerns of black people, and too little aware that cultural development is not a thing of the spirit alone but is rooted in material conditions, the necessities of funding and support usually absent in black communities."[15] This interpretation complements Tisdale's rendering of Robeson, but then again the politically ostracized Robeson of the late 1940s and 1950s was far from an "assimilationist," and it is that potent, and more recent, memory that frequently circulates in the public imagination.

Likewise, Tisdale's before and after depictions of Malcolm X echo what social psychologist Alex Gillespie refers to as the "conversion narrative" or "metamorphosis narrative" that serves as the template for Malcolm's autobiography.[16] Paramount to the public's understanding of Malcolm, as Gillespie elucidates, is that notions of change and transformation propel his story. Not only did he experience a number of ideological conversions that affected his lived and performed realities (he was born Malcolm Little, became Detroit Red, converted to Minister Malcolm X, then transformed himself again to become El-Hajj Malik El-Shabazz), but the latter incarnations also represent an emblematic struggle to effect social and political change.[17] Despite the compelling metaphors and allusions, what we think we know of Malcolm X (and El-Hajj Malik El-Shabazz) stands in contradiction to Tisdale's "after" picture of the slain leader.[18] Thus, in the case of both renderings by Tisdale (*Robeson* and *Malcolm X*), spectators are urged to recognize that they, as audience members—and not just the men in question—are implicated as participants in the conceptual economy created by America's sociopolitical circumstances and the perpetuation of white, hegemonic thought.

Also of note is that the method Tisdale used to create *Robeson* and *Malcolm X* can also be framed as actually activating familiar tropes of whiteness, namely, tropes of absence and presence. Starting with a picture of his chosen subject, Tisdale fashioned his images through repeated erasures and alterations in order to create the final product. Done by hand, this painstaking and time-consuming process was one that Tisdale learned while working as an advertising production director in the 1980s for *Interview* magazine. While under the tutelage of Andy Warhol, he recognized how Warhol's own interest and emphasis on portraiture was particularly influential.

> Warhol would take photos and make portraits. He would clean it up—remove moles, remove lines. He had a reputation that you would always look better than you did in real life. It was unique to the culture of *Interview* magazine at the time. Warhol was "into" beauty—he was giving the first makeovers. If you scrounge up the photographs in those periods, you'd see. They didn't have Photoshop in those days. It was handwork: rub at the photos with instruments like tweezers or you would scratch at the photograph. Or, if there was a white face, you could paint over it or scratch out a line to expose the white of the paper underneath. Painting, scratching, or airbrush—the technology didn't come until the early '90s. Of course, that is the long tradition of portraiture of famous people—it never looked like the actual person; it was always more beautiful.[19]

Employing the techniques he learned while working at *Interview*, Tisdale applied the now antiquated methods of rubbing and scratching to his portraits. Through deletions and addendums, Tisdale cultivates his models' appearance, and, just as Warhol's famous portraits "never looked like the actual person," the work invariably relishes the awareness of difference.

Among art reviewers, however, this perception of difference often resulted in descriptions of Tisdale's work as creating "deracialized" images. Unsurprisingly, such nomenclature fails to recognize whiteness or cues of whiteness as raced, further disclosing how whiteness is routinely associated with normality or standardization. Contrary to these suppositions, it is important to recognize that Tisdale's artistic machinations do not highlight "deracialization" but rather ascribe a process of "reracialization." In Tisdale's hands, the after images do not reflect an absence of racial markers but rather the reinscription of racialized features, namely, a conversion that suggests the whitening of what are deemed to be more "negroid" characteristics.

Of course, the methods used to make Tisdale's images are unknown to most viewers, and thus, as pictorial palimpsests, these final images veil the history of their creation. In doing so, however, they also ultimately perform the line of inquiry that shapes Tisdale's own artistic explorations.

What does it mean to be African American, Native American, etc.? It's an authenticity issue. My work definitely asks: is there a before to the before? Where do we say the original starts? There is a continuum, an evolutionary process. Before she was a European woman, her family came from Greece. Then there's another layer before that. So I'm just asking those questions. What's interesting is the journey of the answers because there's never one answer that sums it all up—there are so many other layers.[20]

Rather than making immediate, sweeping changes to a singular image, Tisdale's portrait-making process engages in the same notion of "layering" that inspires his artistic queries. Moreover, in working with the images of celebrated individuals, he purposefully emboldens audiences with a sense of recognition, which helps shape the unspoken question, "Is there a before to the before?"

The notion of authenticity is made immediate and visceral through these artistic turns. Tisdale's work demands that spectators recognize the fabricated quality of the "after" images while also offering them an opportunity to reconsider the original quality of the "before" images. By engaging in the uncanny, that is, by making the familiar unfamiliar, distant and strange, Tisdale creates a conceptual dissonance that allows his audience to simultaneously acknowledge and critique the all too familiar citations that engender and affirm our concepts of racial identity. In *Robeson* and *Malcolm X*, for example, audience members are encouraged to ask themselves, "How *real* are the before images?" While the after images are clearly counterfeit, does the juxtaposition of the before and after images and their obvious incongruity inevitably disclose more about the chosen figures—and the audience's cultural investment in these individuals—than the before pictures alone?

These queries demand that we question the ways in which physical markers are used to authenticate or renounce cultural membership. They also draw attention to the marketing, packaging, and consumption of phenotypical appearance. Tisdale's use of icons from African American history ensures that we—his audience—recognize our participation in their commodification. The very fact that the before images are so familiar to us speaks to their value within the economy of popular culture. The images of legendary leaders and activists carry with them their own particular histories, and their insistent reproduction informs the public as to how their lives and legacies "should be" presented and received.[21] If, as Marianna Jenkins insists, the primary purpose of portraiture "is not the portrayal of an individual as such, but the evocation through his image of those abstract principles for which he stands,"[22] what does Tisdale's creative license disclose about how the public identifies—and identifies with—these figures? How do changes in surface appearance symbolize or signify cultural integrity, allegiance, or betrayal? In what ways do all of us, as individuals, make ubiquitous "transitions"—whether they are visible or behavioral—to successfully navigate through our own social networks? Tisdale's work, self-consciously irreverent, challenges the conceit of cultural decorum by playing with and against sacred images from the annals of African American history. In doing so, he prompts a multilayered line of inquiry that spares neither blacks nor whites from introspection.

Recognizing the public's investment in the images of Paul Robeson and Malcolm X, the juxtaposition of Tisdale's before and after pictures also effectively animates the laws of representation and excess as addressed by the performance scholar Peggy Phelan.

> Representation follows two laws: it always conveys more than it intends; and it is never totalizing. The "excess" meaning conveyed by representation creates a supplement that makes multiple and resistant readings possible. Despite this excess, representation produces ruptures and gaps; it fails to reproduce the real exactly.[23]

Cued by Phelan's conjectures, Tisdale's portraiture reveals the problematic status of representation. Conveying far more than just the physical likeness of Robeson and Malcolm X, the familiarity of the "before" images gives credence to our public narratives about their private lives. However, these pictures are not totalizing—they fail to fully encompass the characters of these men and the contours of their existence. Thus, while we are quick to recognize that the after pictures of Robeson and Malcolm clearly revel in excess, we must also recognize that the before pictures are equally unsuccessful in capturing a concise reading of these legendary figures. By presenting obvious addendums and erasures in his after portraits, Tisdale's work reminds us of the inherent inefficacy of *any* visual representation to secure a complete and unbiased understanding of a subject—regardless of how much it supposedly resembles the original model.

Encapsulating the notion of corporeal transitions and metamorphoses, Tisdale's portraits also reflect shifts in contemporary science and medicine.

Although George Schuyler famously parodied the idea that scientific procedures could foster race changes in *Black No More* (1931), the fact is that Tisdale's fictional work riffs on present-day, real-life referents and alludes to the medical and scientific realities of our current cultural moment. We are living in a time when visual markers of race, age, and gender *can* be altered and reinscribed. Tisdale exploits the very real malleability of physical racial signatures, simultaneously commenting on the economic machinations behind the industries that make these types of transitions possible. In other words, Tisdale's before and after work illustrates how the meanings and values placed on visible signs of racial membership produce and disperse cultural *and* economic capital. In an attempt to interrogate this dynamic even further, Tisdale pushed his inanimate artwork into decidedly animated territory by transforming *himself* into the character of Tracey E. Goodman for the street performance *Transitions, Inc.*

TRANSITIONING INC.: ANIMATING THE INANIMATE ART OF DANIEL TISDALE

Appearing as the character Tracey E. Goodman in *Transitions, Inc.*, Tisdale not only uses his before and after art portraiture as evidence of his fictitious characters' company, but he also uses his own body to reveal the persuasive power of visible racial signatures. Born with hazel eyes and light-brown skin, Tisdale conceded that ubiquitious responses to his own more Eurocentric features actually contributed to the inception of *Transitions*.

> At first the idea was that I'd rather talk about myself when talking about the issue of race. Because when I start with myself, no one can really argue with that. People would comment on my eyes, comment on my skin. For me they are not an issue. To me, I looked at them as deformities. To me it's not really about how I, in theory, would originally look. It's an abnormality if you think about what has come together to make us who we are today. We are a mixture of everybody. I don't look at that as a negative. So the performance came from that, from creating a dialogue.[24]

Oscillating back and forth between qualitative statements (from "not an issue" to "an abnormality," then back to "I don't look at that as a negative"), Tisdale's own spontaneous response reveals the complex and sensitive issue

Daniel Tisdale as Tracey E. Goodman in *Transitions, Inc.*, New York City, 1992. (Courtesy of Daniel Tisdale.)

of color consciousness. Despite the fact that he says "We are a mixture of everybody," he cites his own fine features and light skin color as "deformities," suggesting that he, too, is affected by the common belief that essentialized racial configurations are "normal" while variations are "abnormal." Ironically, Tisdale's own contradictory thoughts disclose the angst and apprehension that underscore his artistic objectives.

In order to fully activate the goals envisioned by his performance, Tisdale created the pretense and character of Tracey E. Goodman. Embodying the character of Goodman (and thereby parodying what a "good man" should look like), he accentuated his own physical traits by lightening his hair and applying makeup in such a way as to thin his nose and create the illusion of even sharper, more aquiline features. In doing so, he hoped passersby would immediately recognize that Tracey E. Goodman—borrowing from the popular Hair Club for Men motto—was not only the president of *Transitions, Inc.* but also a client.

Despite the grandiose claims espoused by Tisdale's alter ego, the staging of his performance was a relatively humble endeavor. A small public address system, a cassette player playing Frank Sinatra's "New York, New York" and

Prince's "You Got the Look," and a simple folding table adorned with sample products, brochures, and business cards completed the *Transitions* set. With microphone in hand, Tisdale (as Goodman) threw out catchphrases ("To be a success is to make the 'transition' from one culture to another!") and bombarded passersby with flyers that detailed his pseudo company's procedures, products, and philosophy. According to the official yet revealingly simple company flyer, Transitions, Inc.'s New Contours Sculpting System is "used for refining the nose, lips, eyes and buttocks (reduction) with laser surgery." The Skin "Appeal" Peel, Whitener, and Bleach by Dr. Palmer is used to "peel, lighten and bleach away all unwanted major or minor dark areas," and the "Happy, Not Nappy" 100% Human Hair Extensions and Bone Strait Hair Relaxer allowed customers to "say goodbye to 'bad' and 'kinky' hair and say hello to exciting *new* 'good hair.'" Attending to the more ephemeral aspects of racial transitioning, Goodman also offered the New Philosophy and Name Specialization component for "individual or group mental flossing," a process that promised to be "the icing on the 'crossover' cake" by ensuring "a total mind and body makeover."[25]

While Tisdale's performance addressed racial anxieties by asserting that white features are aesthetically superior (a conceit that is inherent in the suggestion of "good" and "bad" hair, for example), Tisdale's improvised script focused less on idealized beauty and more on the economic benefits of corporeal race changing. As Tracey E. Goodman, Tisdale's animated display supported the claim that whiteness is associated with greater prosperity, access, and privilege through an assortment of promotional materials, including charts, statistics, and testimonials. Fervently addressing the crowd regarding the value of whiteness, Goodman's rhetoric reinforces K. Sue Jewell's contention that "the determination of positioning on the social hierarchy of discrimination is based on how closely individuals approximate the race and gender of the privileged class."[26] Likewise echoing the assertions of Kobena Mercer, *Transitions, Inc.* capitalized on the belief that "Opportunities for social mobility... involve the negotiation not only of socio-economic factors such as wealth, income, education and marriage, but also of less easily changeable elements of status symbolization such as the shape of one's nose or the shade of one's blackness."[27] Primed by such observations, Tisdale's character exploited these social expectations and anxieties, hoping to convince his audience that those "less easily changeable elements" could, in fact, be changed with ease.

Espousing phrases such as "I want to give the average person the opportunity to succeed, with cultures that are affordable," Tisdale/Goodman referenced the issue of "affordability" not only as it related to the expense of the procedures, but also as it related to cultural commerce by insinuating that passersby of color could not "afford" to let such an opportunity pass. Taking advantage of existing anxieties, *Transitions* readily utilized stereotypes regarding race, class, and culture by actively equating a whiter appearance with responsible citizenship—or, at the very least, the public perception of responsible citizenship. Such was the pretense staged by Tisdale's conjured testimonials of "Will Carpenter" and "Lee Roy Jonson."

According to Goodman's brochures, the presumably black Will Carpenter enthusiastically quipped, "I've noticed less and less door lockings as I cross the street," and the illusory Lee Roy Jonson echoed this sentiment when he was quoted as saying, "[W]omen have stopped clutching their purses as I walk by." In addition, several other fictional clients praised Goodman for granting them the opportunity for career and life changes. These testimonials were supported by elaborate graphs that supposedly detailed the claimants' demographics and measured their subsequent success, all of which was contrasted with the statistics of individuals and ethnic groups that did not use the products and services offered by Transitions, Inc. The accompanying paperwork (i.e., Tisdale's interactive props) made Goodman's point clear: social status and material wealth can only be gained by people of color if they undergo a visible process of cultural and racial assimilation.

Dependent on a history of visual and textual citations, Tisdale's performance was an explicitly staged commercial that, on the surface, "sold" whiteness just as it aimed to expose the ubiquitous, capitalist nature of consumer culture—a culture greatly informed by belief systems that create insatiability and desire.

> And what you see—not just with black people, but everyone—is an issue of advertising. In advertising you deal with photos, the resulting image was never the original image. Never what was originally there. In the end, it's all "beautiful people." It's all about a commercial—the body contour, the "body beautiful"—that's what plastic surgery serves. And commercials are all about choices. They're about making you look good, to spin it around, to look one way.... The whole idea about advertising is to make you want what you don't have, to be unsatisfied with yourself. Your hair is too long, your hair is too short, you're too big, too small, you're too black, you're too blonde. I turn that into a performance.[28]

Incorporating both the images and the products of contemporary pop culture into his performances, Tisdale seduces his audience into experiencing the way perceptions regarding racial and sexual identity are made, unmade, and valued through embodied visual signatures. As noted by Lynell George of the *Los Angeles Times Magazine*, the discomfort that arises from Tisdale's art "forces participants to confront, on the spot, the scope and texture of that uncomfortable quandary: What should one give up to achieve success in contemporary American society? The varied responses of those critiquing from the sidelines mirror the real-life incertitude of people enmeshed in this cultural gamble."[29]

In some cases, what follows is the actual creation of potential clients—that is, some audience members actually buy the *Transitions* sales pitch.[30] Absorbing the performance and its rhetoric, these audience members not only become active participants in *Transitions*' conceptual negotiation, but the promises of transformation also ignite the imaginations of those yearning to participate in the "American Dream."

> There was this Hispanic brotha with his family, and this was at the Astro place stop. He was with his wife, two kids. He was right in front. He wanted blonde hair and wanted to get rid of his accent. He didn't want it to be permanent. He just wanted it to be temporary so he could get a job. It was funny when he first started talking about it because I thought he was joking, but then it was sad because you realized that what he was focused on was that he wanted a job. He had bills to pay, mouths to feed.[31]

By expressing his interest in *Transitions*' services, the audience member substantiated the line of inquiry presented by Tisdale's performance. Fair-minded reflection on Tisdale's anecdote obliterates assertions that one's racial pride or cultural allegiance is inherently affirmed or compromised by the way one amends or accentuates one's corporeal self. Fully recognizing the reality of economic forces—that within our capitalistic society people's livelihoods are affected by perceptions of belonging and not belonging—complicates easy assumptions regarding the way we actively choose or do not choose to have our racial and/or cultural identities perceived.

Accentuating the economics of opportunity (and the politics therein), Tisdale claims that his primary aim is to prompt a flurry of different responses—from personal introspection to antagonistic outbursts and hopeful inquiries—in order for all of us to learn from one another and create greater tolerance for differences.

> I try not to judge, that's why I say about my work, "I try to ask questions." I'm not trying to grab anybody by the shoulders and say "You know, you need to not do this." Who am I to criticize? Who am I to say anything if they feel more comfortable, if they feel better. If they feel that it empowers them in some way, who am I to criticize? But I do try and critique that in an open forum. If I had their same history, I might do the same thing and I would want somebody to give me the opportunity to search for a way to answer some of the same questions I have. There is, however, a price that you pay for all that. There are always prices to pay for searches of inquiry.[32]

Insisting that his work does not necessarily critique the desire for racial transitioning but rather "critiques the critique," Tisdale maintains that he is interested in interrogating the judgments passed on those that desire to transition rather than critiquing the desire to transition itself.

The open-ended, provocative way in which Tisdale presents his work has, unsurprisingly, caused passersby to express outrage over what they deem to be a legitimate business presentation. In fact, during the time he was presenting *Transitions*, Tisdale had strategically placed copies of *Malcolm X* around New York City (in subway corridors, on poles, and on the sides of brick buildings). The posters were uniformly torn down within a twenty-four-hour period—acts of resistance that he interpreted as the greatest of compliments. As an actor in a partially scripted and mutable dialogue, Tisdale relies on a spectrum of possible responses from his audiences—all of which are spontaneous and uncensored—in order to actualize his performance. His spectators are the unsuspecting yet essential ensemble members that ultimately provide the opinions that Tisdale resists offering. Disparate and ultimately inconclusive, his ever-shifting performances reflect, but do not necessarily deflect, the tumultuous nature of American's ongoing racial dialogues.

And that, in part, marks "the price to pay" for Tisdale. The artist's determined ambivalence and the content, structure, and staging of his performances run the risk of reinforcing and perpetuating the very concerns they attempt to address. Although some audience members recognize *Transitions* as a performance or, at the very least, become aware of the true nature of the display when they witness Tisdale's postshow discussion (a conclusion that is only awarded to those who catch the end of the hour-long presentation), other passersby observe segments of *Transitions* without ever detecting or discovering its artifice. What, then, do those unsuspecting audience members take with them as they continue down the street, turn the corner, or go down into the subway? Without the appropriate frame of reference, *Transitions* is primed to reinforce, rather than interrogate, long-held stereotypes and racial assumptions. Regardless of intentions, the commercial throughline in the work can easily sell the notion that more Eurocentric features are, indeed, ideal. This premise is reinforced by the fact that all Tisdale's visual texts champion the need to change "blackened" bodies rather than rehabilitating "whitened" minds.

Haunted by its uncertain impact, what is unequivocal about Tisdale's artistic machinations is that they contribute to the discourse of identity politics by asserting the malleability of identity. Ideal texts with which to examine the thematic evolution of contemporary African American performance, Tisdale's work encapsulates the conceptual premise and promise of our present "transitional" moment while addressing the fact that the parameters of identity—and identification—have always been inexact and unfixed. Moreover, as an African American artist highlighting the ubiquitous reality of naturalized whiteface (for such expressions are, indeed, found in everyday life among everyday people), Tisdale complicates easy assumptions about how whiteface expressions are used in contemporary life and art. Invoking notions of postmodernism and popular culture, his art is, literally, a "sign of the times," reflecting an era in which the complexity of African American identities is symbolized through a confluence of fluid and ever-proliferating signatures—by nature as well as by design.

CORPOREAL CROSSOVERS BY THE CROSSOVER KING: THE ITERATIONS OF MICHAEL JACKSON

While Tisdale's guerrilla performances were reinforced through various real-life props such as over-the-counter skin whiteners, relaxer kits, and hair extensions, the visual/performance artist also used the very real before and after portraits of the world famous pop artist Michael Jackson to stake his claims. Boasting that "THE JACKSON FAMILY remain Transitions,

Inc.'s NO.#1 clients since 1986," Tisdale's character, Tracey E. Goodman, promoted the association between his fictitious company and Jackson's commercial success. Strategically placing a picture of a young Jackson (ca. 1969) next to an image of Jackson thirty years later, Tisdale used Jackson's well-documented physical transformations to offer striking and compelling proof of the fictitious Tracey E. Goodman's claims. While more sophisticated spectators immediately recognized *Transitions* as a performance, for others the inclusion of Jackson in Goodman's presentation suspended, rather than engendered, disbelief.

Considering both the nature of Tisdale's work and the time in which he was presenting *Transitions*, it is particularly fitting that Jackson's visage was integrated into Tisdale's street performance. On viewing the before and after portraiture that Tisdale created *prior to* the creation of *Transitions* (pieces that were then integrated into the latter performance), one can readily recognize that Jackson's ever-changing features influenced the style and fashioning of Tisdale's art—cookie-cutter transformations that echo one another and speak to the assembly-line aesthetics of contemporary pop culture. Although Tisdale initially insisted that his "after" portraits were not intentionally designed to resemble one another,[33] upon further inquiry and introspection he credits the mirroring of these images to the use of a singular, albeit subconscious, template. Through his hours of careful layering, erasing, and drawing, Tisdale concedes that he inevitably replicates "a certain kind of chin, a certain kind of nose, light eyes, light skin, a certain kind of lips"—all of which subsequently suggest Jackson's exaggerated facade.[34]

From his young adulthood onward, changes to Jackson's physical appearance were obvious and widely noted. The nature and number of Jackson's cosmetic surgeries resulted in aberrant facial features—exaggerated contours and sharp angles that denoted a contrived ambiguity in terms of both race and gender—and his broad nose was repeatedly altered to such a degree that stories often circulated that it was at risk of collapse. His skin, far from a natural complexion, appeared blanched and traumatized. Although there has never been a consensus or definitive answer as to what motivated Jackson's attraction to plastic surgery, Elizabeth Haiken expressed the common public opinion, "[I]f he is not trying to look white, he is at least trying to look less black,"[35] thereby fulfilling one of the characteristics of naturalized whiteface.

Tisdale's use of Jackson to signify the success gleaned from a corporeal crossover was, of course, poetic on many levels. After all, the man hailed as the "King of Pop" could also be championed as the "Crossover King." A crossover, in the field of musical production, generally describes a solo artist or group that has "crossed" perceived racial or cultural boundaries by appealing to the popular-music-loving masses and, in so doing, has achieved a significant degree of commercial success. Furthermore, as David Brackett suggests, "Some see the idea of crossover as utopian, a metaphor for integration, upward mobility, and ever-greater acceptance of marginalized groups by a larger society."[36] For many, Jackson is the paragon of crossover success.

As a product of the strategic grooming of Berry Gordy's Motown machine, Jackson and his brothers were fashioned to appeal to a mass audience, a mission supported by their projection on the small screen in the form of talk show appearances, as well as their own animated cartoon series.[37] However, while Jackson experienced success as a member of the Jackson Five, his accomplishments as a solo artist are unparalleled. Prior to his death (which prompted a dramatic spike in the sales of his music), he had sold in excess of 750 million records worldwide, earned 8 platinum or multiplatinum albums, had 13 number-one singles and 47 songs on the *Billboard* Hot 100, won 13 Grammys, received the American Music Awards' Artist of the Century Award, was inducted into the Rock and Roll Hall of Fame (twice—once as a Jackson Five member), and was cited by *The Guinness Book of World Records* as the Most Successful Entertainer of All Time.[38] Although one could trace Jackson's meteoric rise to solo superstardom to his 1979 album *Off the Wall*, by most accounts it was Jackson's explosive 1983 appearance on the television network MTV that secured his crossover status and helped to propel his legendary career.[39] Unapologetically homogeneous at the time, MTV was primarily focused on propagating rock (read "white") music. However, evidence of Jackson's commercial viability challenged MTV's original mission and inspired significant changes in its programming. And the rest, as they say, is *HIStory*.

Thus, from the vantage point of the music industry, Jackson epitomized the very meaning of *crossover*. He was a global phenomenon, and his worldwide achievements obliterated any notion that his music was racially or geographically bound. Yet, after acknowledging the enormity of his career, we can also readily reflect on the other ways in which crossing over was an identity theme that dominated both the life and the artistic expressions of Michael Jackson.[40] Jackson's crossing theme was persistently expressed through his own physical machinations, as well as through visual cues and expressions that supported his music. Throughout these endeavors and efforts—evidenced through his body and in his music videos—he continuously presented visual refrains that returned to themes of morphing and metamorphosis.

BODILY TRANSITIONS: TRANSGRESSING THE BORDERS OF RACE AND GENDER

When one reflects on Judith Butler's assertion that performativity is not a single act but "repeatable operations," Michael Jackson proves that these operations are literal as well as figurative. Although he admitted in his 1987 autobiography, *Moonwalk*, that he had undergone two rhinoplasties (nose surgeries) and had an artificial cleft put in his chin, he repeatedly denied additional surgeries—an admonishment that was clearly refuted by his physical appearance.[41] Even a novice gaze could detect the various surgeries Jackson had undergone, among them several nasal surgeries, eye surgery, and what appeared to be cheek and chin implants.[42] Just as Tisdale's renderings are created gradually, through a process of layers and addendums, Jackson's face—a human canvas—had undergone transformations through a graduated process of surgical edits and revisions, thereby emboldening the concept of naturalized whiteface.

Eventually appearing almost as if a caricature of himself—or, in the words of Susan Willis, "as a simulacrum of himself whose moment of appearance signals the immediate denial of the previous Michael Jackson,"[43] the entertainer's countenance seemed marked by exaggeration. Aiding in this aforementioned assessment was the dramatic lightening of his skin.

When public scrutiny first began to address the change in Jackson's skin color, his manager—and Jackson himself—explained the phenomenon as being a result of a rare skin disorder, vitiligo. Vitiligo, a disease of the immune system, attacks the cells that produce melanin, causing white or pink blotches to appear on the skin, and, in extreme cases, most of the sufferer's natural pigment is removed. Despite Jackson's insistence that he suffered from vitiligo, the public was often resistant to accepting this rationale as a worthy explanation for his lightened visage, particularly since the other changes in Jackson's facial features appeared to be so intentional.[44] Moreover, many critiqued Jackson's apparent choice to undergo depigmentation treatment over the application of dark makeup, arguing that it proved he preferred "looking white" to "looking black." Regardless of how one situates the change in his skin color, Jackson's conjuring of vitiligo raises the very real possibility of a "natural" crossover in an individual's racialized appearance. Thus, whether intentional or not, Jackson's vitiligo narrative aggravates unstable yet still-held perceptions regarding the validity of visual racial signatures. Cast in the role of a racial iconoclast, Jackson's corporeal likeness overthrows traditional and institutionalized beliefs regarding the ways one can—or cannot—undergo a racechange.[45]

Some of our most accomplished cultural thinkers have addressed, with serious engagement, the social concerns and consequences raised by Jackson's amorphous, ever-changing features. When Marjorie Garber, for example, took note of Jackson's multiple cosmetic surgeries and accompanying accoutrements ("his glittery clothes, his long lustrous hair, and the fact that his singing and speaking voices have become higher rather than lower over the years") she was one of the first scholars to consider how the entertainer "has literally remade himself as a figure for transvestism."[46] Jackson's gender bending persona never ceased to draw attention, prompting scholars to wrestle with his seemingly paradoxical performance. His "simultaneous ultrasexuality and asexuality . . . mark simultaneously his art and his awkwardness."[47] Writing along this same conceptual trajectory, Cynthia J. Fuchs applied Homi K. Bhabha's concept of *"productive* ambivalence" to Jackson, effectively surmising how he embodied the crossing of both racial and gendered signals.

> Bhabha writes that the "colonial subject" is produced in discourse, articulated through "forms of difference—racial and sexual." . . . That is, the "forms of difference" he articulates are multiple and interdependent: continuums of race, class, sexuality, gender, and age inform the ambivalent representation known as "Michael Jackson."[48]

Confirming this observation through his analysis of Jackson's video *Thriller*, Kobena Mercer begins his study with the following acknowledgment: "Neither child nor adult, not clearly either black or white, and with an androgynous image that is neither masculine nor feminine, Jackson's star image is a 'social hieroglyph,' as Marx said of the commodity form, which demands, yet defies decoding."[49]

Echoing the various versions of this prominent refrain, Michael Awkward recognized Jackson's "surgical and cosmetic assaults on American constructions of race and gender,"[50] yet he also astutely asserted that Jackson's visage concurrently resists *and* confirms these constructions. In so doing, Awkward suggests that we consider how Jackson's intentional modification of visual racial signifiers (hair, skin, features) may actually represent a "transformative intervention" that doesn't *diminish* the representation of blackness, but rather *expands* our understanding and imagining of blackness.[51] With rhetorical savvy, Awkward offers the following query regarding Jackson.

> "[D]oes his stance serve as a critique of other's [sic] critiques of his putatively deracializing transformations by suggesting, in his manipulation of the viewer's access to his visage, that the human body has come to represent an extremely malleable surface and that others' efforts to read his altered state as a manifestation of an absence of racial pride are themselves operating in terms of limited notions of blackness?"[52]

Awkward's question succinctly echoes the position that Daniel Tisdale holds with regard to his *Transitions* performance. Instead of assuming that a passerby who exhibits an interest in Transitions, Inc. is unquestionably enamored with whiteness (and, therefore, is disparaging blackness), Tisdale encourages his audiences to complicate their own interpretations of naturalized whiteface and, ideally, critique their own critiques. As expressed by Awkward, one way to approach naturalized whiteface is to understand how altered and/or alternative expressions of embodied blackness may actually champion, rather than deny, the proliferation and expansion of black identity. Seen in this way, any attempt to police the boundaries of blackness is not symbolic of racial pride, but rather it can be viewed as a subjugating and oppressive act in that it insists that one's blackness must be confined and constrained by essentialist parameters.

Following a similar line of thought, Eric Lott reveals how one can interpret Jackson's *Black or White* video as an attempt to illustrate the pervasiveness and prevalence of the African diaspora in America by reminding audiences of African American contributions to music history (and, thereby, verifying Jackson's own reclamation and appreciation of his African ancestry).[53] The nuanced positions of Awkward and Lott speak directly to my reading of Jackson's crossover status, asking us to resist interpreting Jackson's modes of crossing as an attempt to wholly reject his blackness. After all, as noted by both Willis and Awkward, such an aspiration would be nearly impossible: the public will always know that Jackson was once a brown-skinned boy from Gary, Indiana. Likewise, a *true* crossover can never engage in passing. As we know from cultural studies and the social sciences, passing (in any form) fails as a strategy for integration and acceptance since it is "thoroughly invested in the logic of the system it attempts to subvert."[54] Instead, by challenging public perceptions about the myriad possibilities of black artistic expression *and* embodiment, Jackson fostered an awareness of the ubiquitous, intrinsic, and often "invisible" African presence in America. His performances not only expanded the reception and possibility of experiencing blackness in America, but they represented global dispersions that also bore the promise of reimagining ideas of blackness across nations.

VIRTUAL TRANSITIONS: MEDIATED RUMINATIONS ON AN IDENTITY THEME

Many of the aforementioned considerations of Jackson's corporeal performativity (on- and offstage, as an extravagant artist, as well as a human canvas) were crafted in the early 1990s, yet despite the passage of time and circumstance, Jackson's physical appearance still invites interest and reflection. The endurance of our fascination is, in great part, due to the fact that the dramatizations of Jackson's manifold crossings persist throughout his work, as evidenced in a number of his short films, beginning most notably with the video *Thriller* (1983). As previously noted, the success of the album *Thriller* was a major videographic and pop cultural event. The video of the same name is also significant in that it is the first of Jackson's short films to explicitly animate the concept of "crossing over"—a major identity theme in Jackson's oeuvre—via physical metamorphosis.

In his analysis of the metamorphosis scenes in *Thriller*, Mercer specifically addresses how the transformations of the *character* "Michael" (first into a werewolf and later into a zombie) can "be seen as *a metaphor for the aesthetic reconstruction of Michael Jackson's face.*"[55] He writes

> The metamorphosis could thus be seen as an accelerated allegory of the morphological transformation of Jackson's facial features: from child to adult, from boyfriend to monster, from star to megastar—the sense of wonder generated by the video's special effects forms an allegory for the fascination with which the world beholds his reconstructed star image.[56]

Asserting that *Thriller* can be read as a metaphor for Jackson's multiple experiences of transformation, Mercer also suggests that we consider how the video—particularly the awe and wonder inspired by its cutting-edge technology—serves as a fitting instrument with which to arouse and signify our fascination with Jackson's celebrity. Moreover, Mercer offers an insightful exploration of the video's "intertextual dialogues between film, dance and music," illustrating how the short film "draws us, the spectators, into the *play* of signs and meanings at work in the 'constructedness' of the star's image" while also demonstrating how it "'visualizes' the music."[57]

Thriller was the first of Jackson's celebrated videos to disclose the artist's fascination with metamorphoses, but it certainly was not the last. Among the videos that explicitly conjure the identity theme of crossing over via physical transformations are *Smooth Criminal* (1988), in which Jackson (with the help of a "lucky star") is transformed into a sports car, a giant robot, and then a spaceship while fighting an evil drug lord; *Speed Demon* (1989), in which Claymation is used to portray Jackson turning into a trickster rabbit figure, followed by physical transformations into well-known celebrities such as Sylvester Stallone, Tina Turner, and Pee-Wee Herman; *Remember the Time* (1992), in which Jackson is transformed from a robed peasant to a pile of golden sand and then to a mesmerizing performer; and, of course, the video *Black or White* (1991), which famously utilized cutting-edge digital morphing technology.[58]

For the sake of this chapter, Jackson's music video for *Black or White* is particularly fruitful to analyze. Not only do the lyrics of *Black or White* express Jackson's desire to eradicate racial distinctions, but even more strikingly, its use of morphing technology creates the illusion of figures "transitioning" from black to white and male to female. In doing so, Jackson's video echoes the inanimate work of Daniel Tisdale in that both artists manipulate visual texts to animate the contentious concept of fluid racial identities.

The opening scene of Jackson's *Black or White* video offers its audience a "bird's-eye view" of a neatly designed neighborhood in white suburbia.[59] When the camera enables us to see inside one of these homes, we find a father, played by George Wendt (also known as "Norm" from *Cheers*, the highly popular television series of the early 1980s and 1990s), sitting on a cushy chair in front of a TV. Meanwhile, the 1980s child star of *Home Alone* fame, Macaulay Culkin, portrays a rambunctious kid who is blasting loud rock music while dancing on his bed. Immediately the stage is set for audiences to note the constructed contrasts presented in the video. Culkin is a decidedly white child (racial ambiguity is never a question with him) listening to hard rock (read "white" music), yet he is also a celebrant of Michael Jackson as evidenced by the poster that hangs on his wall. The hard rock refrain that opens this scene soon becomes the core of the song *Black or White*, thereby immediately staging the notion of hybridity through the presentation of differencing genres and cultural representations.

Overflowing with images of "white Americana" (the artifice of the neighborhood is clearly a manufactured model, thus, literally, signifying a "model neighborhood"; the father is watching a baseball game; and the living room is filled with suburban kitsch), the disruption of this ideal family occurs when Culkin's character rebels against his father's demand that he turn off his music. Instead, Culkin's character amps up the speakers to such a degree that his father's chair is ignited and rocketed into space. Wendt's character—still sitting in his armchair—lands in Africa among spear-carrying natives. It is at this point that the musical portion of the *Black or White* video truly begins, launched by the introduction of Michael Jackson, who suddenly appears and begins dancing among the African hunters.

Clad in black paints and a white top, Jackson dances between the dark-skinned warriors, serving as a bodily bridge between the African men and the white body of Wendt. Jackson appears as a living suture that has the power to bridge and meld disparate cultures. Indebted to the magic of film editing, Jackson's body travels through several global locales, serving as the embodiment of a personified hyphen. The video enables Jackson to bridge scenes and link cultures by dancing from one sutured space to the next. Traveling between a group of Thai women, pow-wowing Native Americans, South Asian dancers, and leg-kicking Russians, Jackson remains the central figure of interest, acting as a binding force at the site of each transition. As spectators we never lose sight of him, and we are absorbed by the (in)ability to detect fully the exact moment and points of metamorphosis—a visual experience that introduces the conceit that there are no rigid racial boundaries.

This collection of morphing scenes is followed by the image of two babies—one a brown-skinned black baby and one a blonde white baby—sitting on top of the world and seemingly conjuring the song's refrain: "If you want to be my baby, it don't matter if you're Black or White." As euphemistic as the lyrics may be, what is particularly interesting is that even though the preceding scenes seem to obliterate binary constructions of race and culture, the *unsung* representatives (those who are not neatly categorized as "black" or "white") are ultimately positioned *between* the African warriors and the high-kicking Russians. They are made peripheral due to their staged liminality, and therefore they invariably substantiate the presentation of habitual binaries.

Jackson's direct interrogation of race and racial identity is also presented when the singer is flanked by Culkin and several other children of various racial backgrounds while sitting on the steps of a New York–style brownstone. Adorned in hip-hop attire and striking various hip-hop poses, Culkin's character begins lip-synching the voice of a presumably African American, adult rapper.

> It's a turf war on a global scale
> I'd rather hear both sides of the tale
> See it's not about races, just places,
> Faces, where your blood comes from
> Is where your space is, I've seen the bite get duller
> I'm not gonna spend my life bein' a color.

Within this short riff, Jackson encapsulated his well-advertised ideology: he would rather "hear both sides of the tale," deconstructing the perception of spatial (and aural) boundaries in order to eradicate notions of racial difference.[60] Due to his privileged economic position, Jackson occupied a space in which he could purchase the transition of his own racial signatures; the stain of his previous physical markers remained but became considerably "duller" in his attempt to escape being understood as "a color."

Following Jackson's short and personalized exegesis on race, the most technologically celebrated portion of the video occurs: the morphing sequence. It is at this point that Jackson's *Black or White* exemplifies the postmodern pop culture sensibility found in the work of Daniel Tisdale. While Tisdale's work was directly influenced by Jackson's physical alterations, Jackson's video—created several years after Tisdale's *Post Plantation Pop* series—became another popular citation that reiterates and confirms Tisdale's highly charged notion of racial "transitioning."

What makes *Black or White* especially compelling in relation to Tisdale's portraiture is that its morphing technology brings the actual *process* of these physical transformations to life. The technique, as explained by Ron Alcalay, was initially expensive to execute but relatively simple to achieve: "[T]he programmers place grids over two dissimilar objects, connect the intersections of the grids, and stretch or compress the sections, in order to create a continuum of intermediary forms and colors."[61] While the viewing audience is witness to the morphing, the transformations occur so quickly that it is impossible for the naked eye to identify the seams, breaks, and points of modification. Tisdale's artwork differs in this regard because the stark contrast between "before" and "after" is strikingly apparent and the after images omit the process of their creation. Nevertheless, the premise and process of Tisdale's transformations are the same in that they are both created through graduated (if not gradual) change.

Tellingly, however, the modifications in both Tisdale's art portraiture and Jackson's video focus on the face.

> The face, as unique, physical, malleable and public, is the prime symbol of the self. It is unique, for no two faces are identical, and it is in the face that we recognize each other, and identify ourselves. The face is physical, and therefore personal, yet it is also "made up," "put on" and subject to fashion.[62]

The face—a malleable symbol—is fetishized, standing in for the body and its markers of racial, sexual, or national identity. By using morphing technology to vividly show the similarities among different racial categories, *Black or White* also challenges the visual cues that indicate femininity and masculinity. From a large East Asian male to a black woman, a red-haired white woman, a dread-locked black man, an South Asian woman, and then back to a black woman, the morphing continues, covering a wide spectrum of perceived markers. Moreover, in limiting the audience's gaze to the face, the bodies of the morphing figures—and, thus, further evidence of their biological sex—is excised from the spectators' view. Sex and gender are visually cut out of the equation, and "e-raced" by Jackson's discourse of physiological racial distinctions.

At the conclusion of this notable morphing sequence, the *Black or White* video takes a metatheatrical turn. Viewers observe what seems to be the conclusion of the film: as the camera continues to roll, we see the cast and crew of *Black or White* clearing out the studio, but then a black panther strolls, undetected, through the scene and into the darkness of night. Within this extension of the video, two things are underscored. First, the *constructedness* of Jackson's utopic vision—its imaginary, "model" status—is once again revealed to the viewer. Second, the morphing technology is used yet again as the image of the panther morphs into the form of Jackson himself. This is an ironic morphing in that it highlights Jackson's own duplicity, contrasting the loaded political and social associations conjured by a black panther (alluding to the ardent black nationalism often attributed to the Black Panther organization of the 1960s) with a shot of an alley cat—the nonthreatening, effeminate, and "lost" image commonly attributed to Jackson.

In portraying these transformations of race and gender (and even species—the latter being a conceptual thread to which I will soon return), Jackson's visual evocations seem to suggest the instability of such distinctions by emphasizing the similarities, rather than the differences, among us. Writes Lott, "The sequence imagines race mutable, the burden of this construction lifted; boundaries between self and other are permeable even as the particularity of faces and races is stunningly present."[63] In so doing, both Jackson and Tisdale (their actual bodies as well as Jackson's video and Tisdale's art portraiture), reflect our fascination with—and fear of—the impending collapse of society's organizational categories.

This fear of collapse can be understood as an expression of "binary terror." In her article "Binary Terror and Feminist Performance: Reading Both Ways," Vivian Patraka, in dialogue with Jill Dolan, coined the term "*binary terror*," defining it as "the terror released at the prospect of undoing the binaries by those who have the most to gain from their undoing."[64] A further elucidation of this sociopsychological assault is articulated by Rebecca Schneider, who wrote:

> The terror that accompanies the dissolution of a binary habit of sense-making and self-fashioning is directly proportionate to the social safety insured in the maintenance of such apparatus of self. The rigidity of our social binaries—male/female, white/black, civilized/primitive, art/porn—are sacred to our Western cultural ways of knowing, and theorists have ... pointed to the necessity of interrogating such foundational distinctions to discover precisely how they bolster the social network as a whole, precisely what they uphold and what they exclude.[65]

I contend that it is this terror, this anxiety, that is produced and perpetuated by the works of both Daniel Tisdale and Michael Jackson. Both artists effectively represent how the body can be manipulated in order to reinscribe and/or deconstruct our dichotomous readings of race and gender. In addition, these performative texts may seem to symbolize how individuals are also psychologically terrorized. Terrorized by an acculturated sense of inadequacy, they hope to redirect—through signatures of whiteness—how their "blackness" is valued and/or interpreted by others.

That being said, it is equally important to recognize that the fascination with becoming, as illustrated by Tisdale and Jackson, undoubtedly signifies that our understanding of whiteness, like our understanding of blackness, is experiencing its own transition. With America's increasing multiplicity, long-standing fears about the impending end of whiteness have reawakened and proliferated with a vengeance. In the last decade this palpable fear has been fanned by concerns regarding immigration, census statistics, and America's precarious economy. Thus, the naturalized whiteface in the works of Tisdale and Jackson not only suggest potential reinscriptions of African American identity, but they also capture the transitioning experience—the "crossings"—currently at play with white identities. In other words, the works of Tisdale and Jackson not only suggest a whitening of blackness but also a blackening of whiteness. White, they seem to assert, may very well become "the new black."

REITERATIONS OF THE MAKEOVER: JACKSON'S SYNESTHETIC *SCREAM*

Justifiably, Jackson's *Black or White* video is often conjured when issues regarding his ever-present exploration of metamorphosis are raised. On the other side of the spectrum, the video *Scream* (1995) is a sorely underexplored text, yet it also wrestles with the notion of fluid identities. Moreover, *Scream* has the unique distinction of speaking to Jackson's own real-life need need for a PR "makeover." Admittedly, neither the song's lyrics nor the narrative of the *Scream* video directly address constructions of blackness or whiteness. However, what interests me about this less examined Jackson video in relation to the idea of "whiteness as becoming" is that it retains and expounds on an endeavor to transform one's "public face." Moreover, the conduit for this exegesis on transformation is filmed, literally, *in* black and white, thereby offering a stylistic medium that ultimately highlights both racial and gendered cues in implicit and explicit ways.

With regard to the latter, one of the most obvious—and seemingly determined—ways in which *Scream* plays with gender is in its very presentation of the Jackson siblings. The song is, after all, a duet with Michael and his younger sister, Janet Jackson. As Michael Jackson was well aware, comic fodder often revolved around the speculation that he and Janet were actually one and the same person. In fact Michael addressed this ridiculous rumor when he received the Grammy Legend Award in 1993 from Janet. With a cunning smile, Jackson was mere seconds into his formal acceptance speech when he offered this witty pronouncement: "I hope this finally puts to rest another rumor that has been in the press for too many years.... Me and Janet really are two different people."[66] Cognizant of this rumor, yet consciously playing *with* it instead of against it, the *Scream* video features the siblings costumed in strikingly similar ways. At one point, they even wear matching shiny black pants, black kneepads, and "spiked" black sweaters. Twinlike in appearance, the two Jacksons underscore this intentionally inscribed resemblance with a synchronized dance sequence. In fact one could read the quick camera cuts between Michael and Janet as a way in which the video's cinematography goads viewers into playing a hurried game of "who's who" each time the images shift, purposefully suggesting a potential "morphing" of the two entertainers. Correspondingly, the costuming and choreography serve to feminize Michael and, at the same time, defeminize Janet, thereby providing further evidence of the ability to aggravate gender boundaries. Also of note is the way the monochromatic film, aided by makeup, seems to obscure the skin color gradations between Michael and Janet. Most notable, however, is the way the black and white video augments the startling whiteness of Michael's own visage.

As for the way *Scream* addresses Michael's desire and need for a PR makeover, the video can easily be read as a response to some of Jackson's most difficult times. Produced on the heels of the child molestation allegations he faced in the early 1990s, the lyrics of the song seem to resist and refute the accusations of pedophilia while also condemning the propagation of media-propelled rumors and assertions.

> [Michael]
> Tired of injustice
> Tired of the schemes
> The lies are disgusting
> So what does it mean ...
>
> With such confusions don't it make you wanna scream
> Your bash abusin' victimize within the scheme
> [Janet]
> You try to cope with every lie they scrutinize
> [Both]
> Somebody please have mercy

'Cause I just can't take it
Stop pressurin' me
Stop pressurin' me
Make me wanna scream

As a song that argues Jackson's innocence, unjust persecution, and tortured existence, it is fitting that the video suggests a need for escape—or self-exile—from various social scripts.

Imaginatively set within the interiors of a sleek spacecraft (which appears to glide above *two* Earth-like planets), the video also nods to the popular perception of Jackson as "otherworldly." Exacerbated by his naturalized whiteface, popular media often conjured the satirical suggestion that he was, indeed, an extraterrestrial. From quips that described his "pale, made-up face," or noted that he "barely seems of this world,"[67] to conspiracy-theory blogs declaring him an extraterrestrial émigré and his hilarious cameo as the wannabe agent in *Men in Black II*, narratives related to Jackson's literal "alienness" persisted for more than two decades. Just as he used humor to dispel rumors at the 1993 Grammy Awards, Jackson's 2002 appearance in *Men in Black II* was clearly executed to poke fun at the spectacular, and sometimes disparaging, allusions that questioned his humanity.[68]

All this speaks, however, to the way in which Michael's personae and otherworldly whiteness so disturbed notions of a stable identity that his very *personhood* was publicly interrogated. Tellingly, it is the question of Michael's own humanity *and* the humanity of others that is spotlighted through the *Scream* video, a performance that depicts the siblings' efforts to transcend the entrapments of Earth, as well as the trials and tribulations associated with human existence.[69]

After establishing the Jacksons' intergalactic milieu, *Scream* follows the schema of many familiar space travel narratives by depicting Michael and Janet as if they are just rising from an induced sleep. This awakening, however, is a stress-filled event: while various lights flash and strange technotones are released, it becomes clear that both Jacksons are experiencing a sudden rush of pain and discomfort, ostensibly from the sounds coming from their earphones.[70]

But what *is* the nature of this sound? At this point in the video, we may rightly assume that Michael and Janet are hearing a sound that is so intense, and the decibel level so high, that it causes them excruciating discomfort—a high-pitched scream, perhaps? The video's visual narrative even supports this assumption: Michael himself lets out a granular scream just as the glass that had encased him shatters (or is it *his* scream that shatters the glass?). It is only later, through the lyrics accompanying Janet's spoken solo, that we are offered another way to interpret what the siblings are hearing.

> [*Janet, with earphones on*]
> Oh my God, can't believe what I saw
> As I turned on the TV this evening
> I was disgusted by all the injustice
> All the injustice
> [*Michael*]
> All the injustice

During Janet's utterance, we hear a murmur coming from the televised image of a white news anchor. While the newsman's words are hardly discernible, the written lyrics attributed to him are far more pointed and deliberate.

> A man has been brutally beaten to death by
> Police after being wrongly identified as a
> Robbery suspect. The man was
> An eighteen-year-old black male ...

In presenting a cautionary tale about presumed guilt, the anchorman's words reveal the power of propaganda. The curious fact that this exhortation is barely detectable—in the guise of a whisper rather than a forceful, audible assault—attempts to convey the particularly perilous effect of surreptitious rumor. Furthermore, the racial specificity of the victim of misidentification ("An eighteen-year-old black male") critiques racialized assumptions—a different, yet parallel, predicament experienced by Jackson since his behavioral codes and corporeal signatures were often deemed a failed representation of a "real" black man.

And so, while the lyrics of "Scream" may align with talking points from Jackson's personal narrative, the *Scream* video also reiterates his familiar tropes of crossing over and metamorphosis by drawing attention to the construction of cultural imagery and the (de)construction of iconic status. The scene in which these thematic crosscurrents merge is in the video's art gallery sequence. While this visual vignette received relatively little attention from critics,[71] I would argue that it clearly signifies on the morphing instances found in previous Jackson videos while also reveling in his established interest in the cross-pollination of various artistic mediums. Moreover, *Scream*'s art gallery sequence is distinctive in that it stages Jackson's desire to merge artistic disciplines by incorporating familiar representations of *visual art*. As such, the video fully animates Phillip Brian Harper's theory of the "synesthetic strategy in Afro-American culture"—that is, it utilizes "one mode of sensory perception in a context normally reserved for another," thereby speaking further to Jackson's crossover potential and appeal.[72]

The synesthetic scene in question opens by revealing a virtual viewing space within one of the spaceship's narrow passageways. The austere, sterile appearance of the spaceship's interior supports the suggestion that this virtual gallery is a site of objectification versus utilization. Soon Michael and Janet take on the role of "gallery curators" by taking hold of the remote control that regulates a revolving exhibit of (what appear to be) iconic masterpieces. Accordingly, when the gallery doors initially open Michael is casually straddling an overstuffed white chair as if staged on a pedestal. Moving from his posed position to the position of highly engaged spectator, Michael "clicks" the remote to make a self-portrait of Andy Warhol suddenly materialize. Another click and the Warhol transforms into a Jackson Pollock painting. The scene cuts to capture the image of the white chair/pedestal spinning, but on mobilizing again we see that Janet now occupies the seat of governance. Her presence prompts the camera's eye to now reveal the likes of an Easter Island Maori head, which then morphs into a Buddha sculpture, followed by a sculpture of a Gothic era figure. Michael reassumes control of the remote, choosing again to view the Pollock painting, which then appears to morph into René Magritte's *The Son of Man* (1964). The video frame cuts to Janet, then back to Michael: sans any other recognizable masterpieces, *they alone* become the last visible relics of the gallery's ever-changing exhibit. This close to the scene prompts the video's audience to later ponder whether or not the Jackson siblings are curators and/or consumers of the art that is displayed or if they are part of the collection—characters objectified by the greater society.

While the morphing sequence in *Black or White* can be seen to serve a utopic vision of "We are not so different," the morphing sequence in *Scream* offers additional commentary. *Scream* seems to suggest that artwork—or perhaps any image—can be easily manipulated, transformed, substituted, relegated, or demoted by a simple change in whimsy—thereby reminding us of the highly constructed nature of social signs and status. We are given a brief moment to consider the *idea of art* and the cultural capital placed on things and representations rather than the art itself. This is particularly resonant if we acknowledge that audience members may not actually recognize the art pieces featured in the gallery. The Warhol, Pollock, Maori, and Magritte *may seem* familiar to us as specific pieces (but are they "real" or just copies of the real?), and the Buddha and Gothic sculptures are not as easily labeled or categorized, falling instead into the *ideas* of East and West; symbols of cultural capital and the various hierarchical categories that follow. Used as visual representations, these pieces are ultimately indefinite articles portraying definitive artifacts; we assume their iconic status, yet they may be misleading—if not purely empty—signifiers.

While the art and artists featured in the *Scream* gallery scene are conspicuously displayed, there is yet another iconic masterpiece whose existence is alluded to through the title and imagery of the video: Edvard Munch's painting *The Scream* (1893).[73] One of Munch's most famous paintings, *The Scream* is often posited as a paradigmatic example of expressionist art and the movement's thematic interest in isolation and internal anguish.[74] In fact, if one accepts the conjecture that Munch's work often explored the "conflict between man and urban life" and the theme of "sexual conflict" (two major themes of nineteenth-century symbolic art),[75] the conceptual citation offers an interesting riff with which to consider Jackson's own artistry and inspirations. Even at face value, knowledge of the image resonates within the video, presenting yet another way in which Jackson inscribed meaning through the use of visual art and iconic imagery.[76]

In considering the many ways in which Jackson utilized art and iconography to validate and/or interrogate the significance of visual citations, we find ourselves returning to the presentation of his own embodiment. Case in point: the opening video short for Jackson's *HIStory II* DVD (1997). The *HIStory II* teaser is an intriguing visual prologue considering the constructed nature of Jackson's iconic status. Similar to the overture in Jackson's *HIStory* DVD (vol. 1), the second collection begins by focusing on the fervor and magnitude of his fandom. The introductory bit consistently oscillates between shots of Jackson's fans shouting and weeping and the detailed staging of a military-style procession led by the acclaimed pop star. The pageantry (replete with a countless uniformed "soldiers" who execute choreographed footwork and engage in artillery acrobatics with martial precision) leads to the ultimate spectacle: a ceremonious unveiling of a gigantic sculpture of Jackson himself. With phallic presence, the enormous sculpture looms over the masses. This transparent, propagandistic gesture establishes Jackson not only as a cultural icon but also as a figure of cultural iconography. Yet, through this unveiling, Jackson actually emphasizes the artifice that is his own self-fashioning: he presents himself as both an artistic subject and a sculpted object *of* art—a knowledge that was never lost on the public, but perhaps one that became more pronounced once he was lost to us.

A PERSONAL POSTSCRIPT (OR, MICHAEL JACKSON'S ULTIMATE MAKEOVER)

I first began to think about Michael Jackson and his multifarious makeovers long before I conceived writing *Coloring Whiteness*. At the time of his death in 2009, I had already scribed most of the thoughts in this chapter, but Jackson's passing—and the media response to his death—prompted me to think of his various transitions in different ways. My thoughts were propelled further by seeing him anew through the eyes of my son and daughter (then six and two years old, respectively), both of whom had little exposure to Jackson prior to the news of his death. I simply had not talked about him, nor—I admit—played his music. However, with the onslaught of media attention in news stories, marathon videos, and televised specials, my children started paying attention and asking questions. When my son, Trey, finally asked, "Who is Michael Jackson?" (because, as evidenced by the blitzing media, Jackson seemed like someone he ought to know), my husband answered the question by playing the *Smooth Criminal* video on YouTube. In less than the 4:45 minutes it took for that video to play, my children became some of Jackson's youngest fans.

Following this divulgence, my husband and I began to play Jackson's music for our children, but we said very little about him. They knew nothing of the child abuse allegations surrounding him, Bubbles the chimp, the oxygen chamber, or any other news befitting of tabloids or legal attention. However, it wasn't until I overheard a conversation between Trey and his best friend, Malcolm, that I fully realized that Jackson was experiencing a renaissance in the public eye—a rebirth aided by tragic circumstances. Intrigued with how young people seemed to read (or *not* read) what I deemed to be Jackson's obvious eccentricities, I decided to conduct an informal interview, starting with "Who is Michael Jackson?"

TREY: He's the best singer—
FCC: He's the best singer? [*to Malcolm*] Who do you think he is?
MALCOLM: Uh, a performer.
FCC: A performer. Interesting. What's the difference between a performer and a singer?
MALCOLM: He sings *and* dances to the music.
FCC: So, what would you tell someone who doesn't know anything about Michael Jackson?
TREY: He's the best in the world!
FCC: The best in the world?
MALCOLM: The best *performer* in the world.
FCC: Now, how do you know that—did someone tell you that?
TREY & MALCOLM: [*in unison*] No, no.
FCC: Then how do you know that?
TREY: We're smart. We got brains. You think we don't have brains? [*points to his head, giggling*].
FCC: But there are other singers and dancers—what makes Michael Jackson the best in the world?
MALCOLM: Because he practiced and practiced—
TREY: —and practiced and practiced until he died.
FCC: And do other people like Michael Jackson?
TREY: Yes! He's the best!
FCC: Well, how do you know people like Michael Jackson?
MALCOLM: I saw a statue of Michael Jackson! It was on the iPod Touch.
FCC: Okay. Who built that statue?
TREY: Michael Jackson.
FCC: So let me ask you another question. What do you think about how Michael Jackson looks?
TREY: Brown and then white.
FCC: He's brown and then white?
MALCOLM: He turned different colors.
TREY: He turned his nose and face and stuff.
FCC: How do you know that?
TREY: Because we can see his face and his nose is acting funny. His nose is like this [*pinches his nose*].
FCC: And is that okay?
MALCOLM: Yea, we still like him.

TREY: He's the best singer!—
MALCOLM:—because it doesn't matter what you look like.
TREY: Yea, [*starts singing*] it doesn't matter if you're black or white ... [*giggles*].[77]

This exchange fascinates me (personal interests aside) for a number of reasons. It strikes me that these two six-year-olds had readily accepted the popular postmortem narrative that Jackson was "the best performer in the world." Both had undoubtedly heard this attribute through various media outlets and, from what they had witnessed, it appeared to be uncontested truth (especially for those who were "smart" and "had brains"). Yet even without the benefit of critical distance or the wisdom of more advanced age, there is still an implicit recognition that Jackson was also a mediated self-construction. Malcolm recognized that the statue of Jackson wasn't real, but rather an image on an iPod, and Trey surprisingly asserted that the effigy was created by Jackson himself, thereby prompting us to reflect again on Jackson's own hand in sculpting—literally and figuratively—his iconic persona.

And finally, when asked about Jackson's physical machinations, both boys insisted that even though Jackson had "turned different colors" and "turned his nose and face and stuff" he should still be regarded in artistic terms (because, in the utopic words of Jackson himself, "it doesn't matter if you're black or white"). This latter sentiment, the idea that Jackson should—first and foremost—be remembered in terms of his artistry, informed the various memorials, remembrances, tributes, and events that occurred soon after his death. While this may seem to be an all too typical response to the passing of a celebrity, I would argue that it is also evidence of our ongoing fascination and *active participation* in the seemingly ubiquitous remakings of Michael Jackson.

While the deluge of Michael Jackson coverage will undoubtedly continue to proliferate in years to come, a selected examination of just a few memorial tributes reveals his public refashioning. One of these was an NBC/MSNBC star-filled special that aired on July 6, 2009. This live event featured celebrities such as Brooke Shields, Usher, Stevie Wonder, and Mariah Carey; however, there were two additional appearances that received a considerable amount of media coverage following the gala: the practiced oration of Reverend Al Sharpton Jr. and the unscripted, but particularly sensational, words of Michael Jackson's then eleven-year-old daughter, Paris.

Al Sharpton Jr., known for his verbal alacrity, offered the media a potent sound bite that was repeatedly aired. Directing his words to Jackson's children, he said, "There wasn't nothing strange about your daddy. It was strange what your daddy had to deal with, but he dealt with it."[78] Greeted with a round of applause, Sharpton's words pointed a finger at the American public for Jackson's tumultuous life, presumably incriminating us for being cogs in a media machine that simultaneously exalted and destroyed the late singer. Even more spectacularized than Sharpton's remarks, however, was the viral repetition of Paris Jackson's tearful tribute to her father. Yet, before touching on Paris's emotional pronouncement, I must pause to consider how she, along with her older brother Prince and her younger brother Blanket, invariably contribute to Jackson's persistent performance of naturalized whiteface by also serving as accouterments in real-life acts of nonconforming whiteface.

By most accounts, Paris and her brothers do not possess what is typically identified as "Afrocentric features." In fact, without evidence to the contrary, an uninformed passerby would probably assume that the older two siblings are white—or at least not black. When Michael Jackson was alive, he insisted that he was the biological father of all three children (the first two, Prince and Paris, were birthed by Jackson's former nurse and ex-wife, Debbie Rowe, and the third child, Blanket, is said to have been birthed by a surrogate). What is far more intriguing to me than the facts of the children's parentage is how their more Eurocentric features inform readings of Jackson's own corporeal mask. Like the performative palimpsests of Daniel Tisdale, Jackson's children and perceptions of their whiter/whitened bodies are now conceptually inscribed on one's reading and interpretation of Jackson's own performative body. Despite our knowledge that Jackson was once a brown-skinned boy from Gary, Indiana, his memory and legacy—embodied by Prince, Paris, and Blanket—are framed in a decidedly different way. As real-life adornments and dressings, Jackson's children can be seen as *living* dolls conceptually akin to the life-sized doll used in Lydia Diamond's adaptation of *The Bluest Eye*. This conjecture does not diminish the love Michael had for his children, but rather it acknowledges that, despite intentions or genuine affection, the bodies of Prince, Paris, and Blanket serve as obscuring, masking agents for their father. As props in a performance of everyday life, Jackson's children inevitably emboldened his naturalized whiteface through their fully animate and involuntary acts of nonconforming whiteface.

The visual pronouncement of Jackson's three children may have conjured moments of speculation for audience members during the live NBC/MS-NBC tribute, but it was what Paris *said* that really struck a chord with viewers: "Ever since I was born, Daddy has been the best father you could ever imagine. And I just want to say I love him so much."[79] Of all the tribute's presentations, Paris's spontaneous and heartfelt declaration was among the most riveting in that it was so unexpected, yet it fulfilled the modi operandi of familiar Jackson narratives by painting another "new face" on the superstar. While it was common knowledge that Jackson bore the title of father, the American public had yet to fully embrace the idea that he was an *appropriately* loving, involved, and participatory (read: healthy) paternal figure. Paris's personal tribute to her father was, for many viewers, a revelatory moment in that it offered an alternative way of reading Jackson, inevitably serving as a formative event in his most current metamorphosis.

Another manifestation of Jackson's latest transformation was birthed and dispersed by his tribute at MTV's 2009 Video Music Awards (VMA). Madonna, one of the music industry's most celebrated stars (and a notable self-fashioner in her own right), opened the evening's events by offering a deliberate and personal accounting of Jackson and his legacy.

> Michael Jackson was born in August, 1958. So was I. Michael Jackson grew up in the suburbs of the Midwest. So did I. Michael Jackson had eight brothers and sisters. So do I. When Michael Jackson was 6 he became a superstar and was perhaps the world's most beloved child. When I was 6 my mother died. I think he got the shorter end of the stick.
>
> I never had a mother, but he never had a childhood.... [H]ow do you recreate your childhood when you are under the magnifying glass of the world for your entire life? There is no question that Michael Jackson was one of the greatest talents the world has ever known.... That when he sang a song at the ripe old age of 8, he could make you feel like an experienced adult was squeezing your heart with his words. That the way he moved had the elegance of Fred Astaire and packed the punch of Muhammad Ali. That his music had an extra layer of inexplicable magic that didn't just make you want to dance but actually made you believe that you could fly, dare to dream, be anything that you wanted to be. Because that is what heroes do. And Michael Jackson was a hero.[80]

In relating what she shared with Jackson, Madonna rhetorically crafts a conceptual merging of the two celebrities that not only suggests their common ground but also attempts to recuperate the more wayward impressions of Jackson.[81] Unequivocally exalting Jackson as "one of the greatest talents the world has ever known," Madonna compares him to the well-respected figures of Fred Astaire and Muhammad Ali (the latter, it should be noted, also went through several transformations in terms of public reception before becoming, as he is now, one of the most revered athletes of all time). Jackson is, Madonna declares, "a hero"—and this declaration was met with the thunderous applause of the VMA attendees.

While Madonna's speech firmly frames Jackson as an exemplar, she positions him in the role of victim with equal fervor. She reminds the audience that Jackson, like Pinocchio (a fairy tale figure who also embodies the motif of transformation), never had a chance to be a real boy. Furthermore, she declares that he was "plagued with insecurities," that she witnessed both his "vulnerability and his charm," and, above all, that despite his superstar status he was "a human being." And then, like Sharpton, Madonna's tribute becomes a pointed critique of the world audience.

> Then, the witch hunt began and it seemed like one negative story after the other was coming out about Michael. . . . I know what it's like to feel helpless and unable to defend yourself because the roar of the lynch mob is so loud that you are convinced your voice can never be heard. . . .
>
> When I first heard that Michael had died. . . . [a]ll I could think about in that moment was that I had abandoned him. That *we* had abandoned him. That we had allowed this magnificent creature that once set the world on fire to somehow slip through the cracks. While he was trying to build a family and rebuild his career, we were all busy passing judgment. Most of us had turned our backs on him.[82]

Thus, in the wake of Jackson's death, the presentation of him as a victim—of public obsession and rejection, as well as drug-dealing physicians and unscrupulous associates—is morphing his mediated memory away from the "Jacko Wacko" images that dominated the press in the last decades of his life. This latest evolution is a sanitizing transmutation that allows us to once again fully embrace Jackson and his artistry. It is on this note that Madonna ends her tribute, noting that her children, ages four and nine, had also become obsessed with Jackson: "There's a whole lot of crotch grabbing and moonwalking going on in my house. And, it seems like a whole new generation of kids has discovered his genius and are bringing him to life again."[83]

Aptly phrased, Madonna's suggestion that young Jackson fans are "bringing him to life again" recalls the icon's penchant for re-creation and renewal. And, without question, these expressions of reimagining Jackson were further propelled by the release of the Spike Lee–directed Sony picture *This Is It*. Named after the fifty sold-out concerts Jackson was scheduled to perform in London prior to this death, the musical film features edited material from eighty hours of rehearsal footage that was taped from April to June 2009. With the tag line, "Discover the man you never knew," early advertisements for the film boasted that it would give audiences a "privileged and private look at Jackson as he has never been seen before"[84]—ostensibly promising yet another opportunity for us to reenvision him. And in this way, *This Is It* did not disappoint.

Amid peeks into the spectacle that never had a chance to fully actualize itself before a live audience, *This Is It* portrayed a side of Michael Jackson that many people—fans and foes alike—had never imagined. His presentation in *This Is It* is remarkable in that it discloses a strong-minded, authoritative (dare I say "masculine"?) side of Jackson that had rarely been propagated as part of his stage persona. Presenting him as polite yet forceful and unwavering, *This Is It* frames Jackson as a singular visionary who earned and demanded respect. The narrative that he was ever plagued with insecurities or uncertainties seems at direct odds with the personality that lights up the screen in the concert documentary. Of course, while *This Is It* is one of the more recent chapters in Jackson's drama to be marketed, packaged, and sold, it will certainly not be the end of his story. If we have learned nothing else in Jacksonian discourse, we have learned that it is inherently metamorphic, and, as such, the title of this 2009 documentary would have had less commercial appeal—but been far more accurate—if it had been called *This Is It, for Now*.

CHAPTER FOUR

"*Mixing It Up*"
Enacting Whiteness in the Comedic World of Dave Chappelle

The artistic machinations of Daniel Tisdale and Michael Jackson chronicled in chapter 3 revel in the notion of race changing by suggesting the possibility of transitioning from one racial category to another. Through fictional and factual presentations of naturalized whiteness, both Tisdale and Jackson prompt us to imagine the potential migration between corporeal classifications of race. These visual manifestations, however, are never complete. They imply the *possibility* of perceived transformation, but the traces of their performed transfigurations are always present in their artistic palimpsests; their processes and processions ultimately hint at a sense of liminality and "in betweenness." Of course, in betweenness is part and parcel of human evolution and experience. To that end, one of the greatest and enduring fictions of race changing is the implication that there is a sense of biological purity that can be compromised or altered in the first place. Addressing this fallacy, this chapter acknowledges the always-already nature of human in betweenness through the comedic critiques of stand-up comedian and actor Dave Chappelle. Examining the ways in which Chappelle's comedy engages with whiteness in order to address "mixedness," this chapter reminds us that mixed-race identities are not only constituents within African American communities, but they shape and form American culture.

In its critical turn to interracial identity through the lens of comedy, this chapter also offers a complementary contrast to the preceding chapters by examining work with a decidedly different tone. Chapters 2 and 3 offered particularly sobering material, especially in terms of the tragic dramas associated with Pecola in *The Bluest Eye*, the would-be clients of *Transitions, Inc.*, and the tumultuous life and death of Michael Jackson. Similar to chapter 1's discussion of *Day of Absence*, however, this chapter bears witness to the fact that artistic critique need not be melancholy in order to be powerfully relayed. Rather, satire and comedy are equally effective (and sometimes even more so) in the task of documenting, as well penetrating and transforming, our psyches. Attesting to this, American studies scholar Lawrence E. Mintz wrote on the merits of stand-up comedy, "[H]umor is a vitally important social and cultural phenomenon . . . [and] the student of a culture and society cannot find a more revealing index to its values, attitudes, dispositions, and concerns."[1] Certainly there are countless comedians whose work serves as an effective barometer of the sociopolitical milieu of their given eras. In the early twenty-first century, Dave Chappelle stands as one of those significant figures, not only for his major accomplishments as a stand-up comedian and actor, but most notably for his role as the creative force behind the hit television series that carried his name: *Chappelle's Show*.

Chappelle's Show received both critical and popular praise for its unabashed take on traditionally taboo subjects. Although it addressed a range of potentially contentious issues (from venereal disease to "pimp fashion"), the trope of race dominated the series, providing material for complex, race-centric discussions in a relatively innocuous, accessible way. For Chappelle's imagined community audience, the outrageous scenarios and purposeful use of racial signifiers interrogate society's rigid and prejudicial understandings of identity. However, Chappelle's comedy is also ripe for damaging misinterpretation, for if its nuances are lost on an ill-informed public, his work can be used to reinforce, rather than subvert, biased ideologies.

What makes Chappelle's comedy particularly apropos within the context of this book is that his interrogations of race are often accomplished through his use of theatrical whiteface and familiar tropes of whiteness. While no racial or cultural designation is "safe" from Chappelle's acerbic comedy, his semiotic and thematic plays on whiteness are especially effective in their efforts to disrupt the status quo of our racial imaginings. Moreover, his humorous exegeses on whiteness (as witnessed in sketches such as "Clayton Bigsby" and "The Racial Draft") offer striking contributions to the complex discourse around mixed-race politics and identities. "Clayton Bigsby," for example, features the ideological and entrepreneurial antics of a black white supremacist—a skit that grants viewers the opportunity to consider nonconforming whiteface enactments while also considering the cloaking possibilities that arise from racially mixed identities. In "The Racial Draft," Chappelle stages a draft system—akin to the process used in professional sports—in which civic players are denied the power to claim identities for themselves, but rather are assigned to teams according to objective designations of membership and belonging. Throughout the skit, "The Racial Draft" uses exaggerated portrayals of race (including tinted whiteface) to dramatize and question the dominance of, and dedication to, monoracial narratives despite our increasingly subjective multiracial realities.

Through a critical analysis of these sketches alongside well-known and lesser-known historical and popular narratives, this chapter illustrates how Chappelle's irreverent comedy challenges rigid and antiquated notions of biologically based racial absolutes. In doing so, these sketches invariably advocate a more nuanced recognition of identity, one that destabilizes our reliance on biological links or phenotypes in order to consider more expressive modes of membership and belonging. As comedic vignettes emboldened with serious-minded strategies, the sketches in *Chappelle's Show* are not easily categorized. Accordingly, their design also reveals the "mixed nature" of Chappelle's dramaturgy—a humor marked by syncretic paradoxes and absurd incongruities. But again, while Chappelle's comedy is clearly designed to critique racial essentialisms, one could—if they so chose—interpret or utilize it in a contrary manner, thereby illustrating a *regressive* versus progressive position on race and racial difference. This is the slippery slope on which *Chappelle's Show* slides, one that became so precarious that Chappelle voluntarily stepped down from the peak he had climbed, descending from television's greatest heights at the zenith of his career. By briefly considering how the termination of *Chappelle's Show* induced the very anxiety-raising issues this program originally aspired to tackle, I close this chapter by highlighting how Chappelle's comedy illustrates the ways in which performances—onscreen and in everyday life—simultaneously represent and engender dialogues about racial transgressions and/or the requirements of racial membership.

COMIC GROUNDS: READING RACE, CULTURE, AND THE US CENSUS IN THE WORLD OF DAVE CHAPPELLE

To understand Chappelle's comedy as intended, we need to revisit the way phenotypical traits (such as skin color, facial features, and hair texture) have traditionally guided our perceptions of race. These perceptions, often erroneously understood in terms of "biology," have, in turn, fostered assumptions regarding the physical, intellectual, and/or moral differences between groups of people. While it is often used as a way to explicate or understand human variability, this notion of *race as biological* is highly problematic. Though frequently used as a convenient descriptive tool, the conceptual shorthand of assigning racial categories according to an individual's corporeal characteristics is by no means definitive or precise. Demonstrating the faulty logic of biological race, the biological anthropologist Alan H. Goodman presents a number of reasons why racial categories are ultimately an ineffective way to catalog human variation.

1. Race is not an evolutionary concept (it doesn't account for evolutionary change).
2. "Cutoff" points for racial traits are arbitrary, and there is overlap between designated groups.
3. Traits within racial groups (e.g., skin color) vary.
4. Statistically speaking, within-group variation is even greater than "between-group" variation.
5. Classifications themselves are influenced by space and time (e.g., the way the terms *black* versus *colored* are used in America and Africa).
6. In using "race," social definitions and lived experiences are fused with biological concepts, and therefore issues of culture inevitably shape ideas of race.[2]

Like Goodman, many critical race theorists (David Theo Goldberg, Howard Winant, and Michael Omi among them) recognize that the concept of race has changed—and continues to change—over time. Understandings of race have been temporal and dynamic, formed through and by various processes and strategies. While Omi and Winant have given us a concise and common working definition of *race* ("race is a concept which signifies and symbolizes social conflicts and interests by referring to different types of human bodies"),[3] they are among those who acknowledge how the concept of race has been used to articulate and explain human difference in a number of ways. Used in these contrasting ways, the *idea* of race has had a major impact on social organization and identificatory practices. To this end, Omi and Winant have articulated how "racial projects" function to manufacture and promote ideologies that link social structures and cultural representations: "A racial project is simultaneously an interpretation, representation, or explanation of racial dynamics, and an effort to recognize and redistribute resources along particular racial lines."[4]

Laying racial projects bare, the sketches in *Chappelle's Show* consistently demonstrate why *race* is such a slippery and capacious term, one that is dependent on specific contexts and agendas in order for its application to have translatable meaning, however temporal and contingent. *Chappelle's Show*, through its seemingly nonacademic, vernacular form, effectively animates the theories of innumerable scholars by illustrating why the idea and perception of biological race is troubled. Equally efficacious, however, is the way Chappelle's humor reminds us of the seriousness with which scripts regarding perceived racial differences are taken. Long-held assumptions about racial difference still manifest themselves through our material, if not biological, realities. Despite the common recognition that racial categories are not fixed and absolute, we have yet to abandon our allegiance to them. The increased recognition among scientists, cultural critics, and laypersons that race *is*, indeed, a social construct has not prevented us from "checking the boxes." Rather, as clearly illustrated by the changes made to the US Census in 2000, it has simply created *more* racial boxes to check rather than diminishing our fascination with racial distinctions.

The adjustments made to the 2000 census reveal how social perceptions regarding racial categories are shifting yet still contingent on the idea that discrete categories can exist and then combine to create something new. With the refashioning of the census report in 2000, respondents had the opportunity—for the first time—to claim more than one race or, if preferred, check the box labeled "Some other race." In total, the US Census Bureau offered six fixed racial categories for respondents to claim: (1) White *alone*, (2) Black or African American *alone*, (3) American Indian and Alaska native *alone*, (4) Asian *alone*, (5) Native Hawaiian and Other Pacific Islander *alone*, and (6) Some other race *alone*.[5] Respondents that checked more than one of these boxes, however, were then identified as members of a seventh group, referred to as the "Two or more races" population, thus resulting in a total of seven racial classifications.

What is most relevant about the 2000 census in relation to this chapter, however, is the fact that the selection of these categories was based on *self-identification*: the answers of the census respondents reflected what they "consider themselves to be."[6] As recorded by the US Census Bureau, "changing lifestyles and emerging sensitivities among the people of the United States necessitate modifications to the questions that are asked. One of the most important changes for Census 2000 was the revision of the question on race and Hispanic origin to better reflect the country's growing diversity."[7] However, despite the acknowledgment of multiraciality in the census, 97.6 percent of respondents indicated that they belonged to "one race." A decade later, when the 2010 US Census results were divulged, the majority of Americans (97.1 percent) still described themselves as belonging to one race.[8] The slight drop in "one race" constituents from 2000 to 2010 may be considered, in part, with the increase in those who reported themselves as belonging to "Two or more races." Between 2000 and 2010, those claiming to be bi- or multi-racial rose from 2.4 percent to 2.9 percent among the total respondents. In more accessible terms, this translates into a marked change: from 6.8 million people to 9 million people self-identifying as "mixed" within a decade—an indisputably significant increase.[9]

What is particularly resonant, moving the detailed statistics aside, is that we are left with quantitative evidence that discloses how Americans remain deeply invested in dichotomous identifications such as white/black and, correspondingly, male/female, straight/queer. Despite the opportunities to embrace the facts of our multiplicity, our census reports continue to reveal our awareness of, yet resistance to, racial ambiguity. I would also argue, however, that Americans' long-standing discomfort with the notion of mixedness is also paired with our persistent fascination with the notion of racial amalgamation. It is this simultaneous discomfort and fascination that, I believe, is underscored and animated by a number of comedic sketches in *Chappelle's Show*. While humorously substantiating the *insubstantiality* of biological race, *Chappelle's Show* wittily dramatizes how antiquated notions of racial difference—and their subsequent material impact—play out in the economic, political, and social structures of American society.

Chappelle's sketches not only target ideas of race through references to lineage and blood quantum, but they also call attention to the more ethereal aspects of racial discourse, namely, the *performance* of racial identity and the politics of cultural identification. Accordingly, they utilize and expand on critical race and gender theories, demonstrating how the conduct and belief systems associated with racial identities are learned and reiterated through ritualized behaviors and constituting acts.[10] Chappelle's sketches exploit this knowledge, prompting us to recognize that cultural enactments and expressions are socially constructed rather than essential or biologically inherited characteristics. This is one of the central ideas traced through Chappelle's "Clayton Bigsby" and "The Racial Draft." With a simultaneous consideration of lineage and ideology, these sketches attack corporeal notions of race with comic ferocity. However, while they both use spectacles of whiteness and tropes of mixedness to propel their performative exegeses, they do so in strikingly divergent ways.

SKETCHING "CLAYTON BIGSBY"

> I still haven't been canceled yet ... but I'm working on it. And I think this next piece might be the one to do it. This is probably the wildest thing I've ever done in my career. And I showed it to a black friend of mine; he looked at me like I had set black people back with a comedy sketch. Sorry.[11]

With that tongue-in-cheek pseudo apology, Dave Chappelle readied viewers for the unforgettable character of Clayton Bigsby. Spoofing the reputable PBS news program *Frontline*,[12] the sketch features a blind white supremacist who has become one of the most prominent leaders of the White Power Movement. The audience soon learns, however, that Bigsby is not a *Frontline* feature story simply because of his esteemed position among his extreme followers, but rather his rocket rise to fame (or infamy) is particularly fascinating because he is, in fact, African American.

While the weight of Chappelle's "Clayton Bigsby" sketch relies heavily on the fact that both Clayton Bigsby and his devotees are originally ignorant of Bigsby's corporeal blackness (he is blind, and his admiring public only sees him when he is donning a Ku Klux Klan [KKK] robe), the sketch's obvious deconstruction of race and racialized perceptions is enhanced by its ploys with language. Chappelle reinforces the visual gags within the "Clayton Bigsby" sketch with a purposeful exploitation of language, a strategy that is evidenced by the fact that the sketch actually opens with a joke based on the presence of *words* rather than the visible presence of raced bodies. As the sketch begins, the serious and deliberate voice of a fictitious *Frontline* journalist, Kent Walker, can be heard, bringing to life the cautionary words that become visible within the borders of the television screen.

Warning

For viewers sensitive to issues of
Race, be advised that the following
Piece contains gratuitous use of

the "N" word.
[*pause, quick blackout, with the words again becoming visible and voiced*]

And by the "N" word, I mean
Nigger.
[*soon followed by*]

There, I said it.

There is a slight taunting, challenging cadence to the speaker's assertion, "There, I said it." Although the verbal addendum immediately invokes laughter, the narrator's unprovoked retort carries with it a sense of disregard toward any possible resistance or offense. This suggestion of indifference is particularly loaded if it is aligned with the audience's likely presumption that the speaker is—as he soon proves to be—white. Moreover, there is an unstated assumption that the voice, belonging to the *Frontline* reporter, is necessarily unbiased and therefore has permission to use a word like *nigger* without fear of repercussions because journalistic exactitude allows such contextually specific phrasing.

Nevertheless, the speaker's pronouncement of *nigger* invites a number of questions regarding what is appropriate and justified—and in what context. Thus, while the perverse conflation of Clayton Bigsby's "black body" and "white mind" is at the heart of this particular skit, the manner in which the sketch opens with the use of *nigger* immediately alludes to its thematic refrain by drawing attention to the idea of "mixed messages." Using *nigger* as a touchstone, Chappelle (like innumerable comedians, past and present) successfully animates the inter- and intracultural debates regarding what Randall Kennedy has referred to as "the strange career of a troublesome word."[13] It is widely understood that *nigger* is a disparaging term, but—as evidenced throughout popular culture—it has also been championed by some as a term of affection, community, and defiance. In rallying *for* its use among black Americans, it has been heralded as a mode of sociopolitical subversion, a term that actively subverts and signifies on racist meanings to create its own signal difference. With this coded understanding, the context of *who* is using it, *how* it is used, and even how it is *pronounced* (nigger or nigra versus nigga) imbues it with varied meanings. As a rhetorical strategy, *nigger* offers the listening public a way to define boundaries and interpret notions of exclusion and inclusion beyond visual clues of imagined membership. Thus, in the "Clayton Bigsby" sketch, Chappelle uses language—as epitomized through the word *nigger*—as the initial way to disrupt our understanding of race and racial categories. It is, after all, through language that our racial categories are expressed, translated, formed, and perpetuated; it is language that reveals ideological positions, just as effectively as it obscures and cloaks them. Language informs our ideas of race just as profoundly—and ineffectively—as does our reliance on visual clues.

Because of *nigger*'s particular social history, its manifold significations resonate in distinct ways throughout Chappelle's "Clayton Bigsby" skit. *Nigger* not only suggests disparate ideologies, but its contested meanings parallel the contradictions that Chappelle's title character, Bigsby, *embodies*. The sketch artfully conjures the contention of the word *nigger*, evoking and building on the term's vernacular elasticity and paradoxical elements by connecting *its* dueling meanings to the dualities that Bigsby, the black white supremacist, personifies.

As a conceptual seed, the contentious nature of *nigger* is subsequently dramatized throughout the sketch, beginning with a scene that directly follows the introduction. When *Frontline*'s reporter, Kent Walker, finally appears on the screen, his words further accentuate the audience's sensitivity to *nigger* as he formally introduces the program's feature story.

> For the last fifteen years, a man named Clayton Bigsby has been the leading voice of the white supremacist movement in America. Though not sold in any major bookstores, his books *Dumptruck, Nigger Stained, I Smell Nigger,* and *Nigger Book* have sold over six hundred thousand copies combined. Despite his popularity, very few have ever seen him due to his reclusiveness. But in an effort to bring his message to a wider audience, he agreed to give his first public interview ever to *Frontline*.

Excessive in its use, and buoyed by the actor's deadpan delivery, the monotonous announcement of the various "nigger" titles becomes a joke in itself, suggesting the hateful origins of *nigger* while simultaneously making the term comically ineffectual through its vacuous repetition. The concurrent viciousness and impotence of *nigger* is then exploited yet again when Chappelle's character Clayton Bigsby finds himself outside a gas station surrounded by a small group of white men. Unaware that the racist epithets and threats that he hears from the white men are actually being directed toward *his* black body, Bigsby joins the men in their barrage of insults, mistakenly thinking that he is accosting a black passerby when, in actuality, he is ostensibly harassing himself.[14]

As readily noted by *Frontline*'s Walker, "the confusion did not end there," and the mockumentary shifts to an exchange between Clayton and three white teenagers when the youths' car stops at a traffic light next to Bigsby's truck. Hearing the hip-hop bass kicking from the teenagers' vehicle, Bigsby begins yelling at the youths, referring to them as "jungle bunnies" and "nigras." Seemingly awestruck by the sight of this older black man hurling racial epithets at them, the young men initially appear to be speechless, but then we discover that their apparent incredulity is actually shocked delight: "Did he just call us niggers? Awesome!" Elated with their honorary nigganess, the young men celebrate with high fives and handgrips. These playful turns on *nigger* throughout the "Clayton Bigsby" sketch exploit both the power and the incapacity of racially charged language in our contemporary moment. Taking advantage of the opportunity to revel in the various mixed messages that are received and intended with the term *nigger,* Chappelle does what he does best: he simultaneously critiques and celebrates the absurd ideas—and words—that continue to promote and shape our racial beliefs.

Although the question of language fittingly sets the stage for Chappelle's "Clayton Bigsby" sketch, the success of the piece is unequivocally built on a dependence on visual cues, especially in terms of how race is worn on the body. To be certain, body-oriented humor dominates the breadth of Chappelle's comedy in explicit ways. In the "Clayton Bigsby" sketch, a great deal of humor is derived from the confusion Bigsby engenders as he navigates the world as an antiblack African American man unaware of the reality of his own blackness. Until Bigsby unceremoniously reveals his black body (a revelation that proves as shocking to him as it is to his followers), his performance of whiteness proves, retrospectively, to be a fantastic paragon of passing. Bigsby not only passed as white among throngs of white racists, but by living ignorant of his corporeal blackness he managed to pass as white *to himself.*

What make Bigsby's layered and lifelong acts of passing possible are the manipulative powers, persuasions, and paucity of two senses: hearing *and* sight. The most obvious and impactful of these senses, of course, is Bigsby's blindness—his inability to see. However, while his blindness prevents him from seeing the truth of his own corporeal form, it is both the *presence and absence* of language that further shapes how he sees the world. Having been raised among whites who harbored racist sensibilities (we learn that he was raised in an all-white orphanage), Bigsby absorbed the rhetoric of his immediate surroundings. The assumption of his community's racist beliefs shaped the way he interpreted his own identity, as well as how he categorized others. As a white supremacist, language and rhetoric continued to be a factor in Bigsby's acts of passing. While his followers may have been ignorant of his racial appearance, it was his command of language, exemplified by his oratorical presentations and incendiary publications, that helped to obscure how others perceived him.

While Bigsby is highly successful as an orator and mouthpiece for racist discourse, his success as a leader in the White Supremacist Movement is also dependent on the cloaking and concealment of his black body. It is only with the full-body masking of his KKK uniform that Bigsby manages to successfully navigate and pass through public forums in which the difference between being identified as white or black could be the difference between life and death. Thus, in utilizing racist rhetoric, as well as the symbols of traditional Klan garb, Chappelle's "Clayton Bigsby" offers us yet another opportunity to frame and consider whiteface performance. Enacting forms of nonconforming whiteface, it encourages us to consider the multiple ways white identity is displayed for primed audiences.

RACIST RHETORIC AND TERRORIZING COSTUMES: KKK THEATRICS AS WHITEFACE PERFORMANCE

The KKK, a white supremacist organization founded in Tennessee in the mid-1860s, has always expressed its tenets and mission through performative means. Common to most of its activities—whether created for the purposes of entertainment, terror, or a combination of both—is its highly theatrical rituals and expressions. After all, both real-life and fictional stagings of Klan activities employ a foundational element found in theatrical contexts: dramatic conflict. This may be due to the fact that the KKK—as a symbolic entity as well as a vehicle for cultural ideologies—owes its earliest manifestations to a familiarity with performance culture and stagecraft. As historian Elaine Frantz Parsons reveals, the consciously theatrical tendencies of the KKK can be traced to its founders, several of whom played musical instruments and participated in communal, performance-related activities.[15] Furthermore, presentational aspects of the Klan, from its dizzying array of costumes and signature accessories to its legendary acts of intimidation and violence, offer further evidence of theatre's influence on its members. As Parsons concisely notes, "It is an understatement to say that the Klan used performative elements in its attacks; performative elements largely produced the movement."[16]

Understanding the inherent theatricality found within the Klan's tactics, many scholars have explored correlations between blackface minstrelsy and the KKK's public performances. Reconstruction era members unabashedly borrowed the tenor, tone, and tricks of blackface minstrelsy to simultaneously titillate and terrorize the American public.[17] Among their favorite appropriations, however, was the act of "blacking up"—a seemingly mirthful practice that enabled white Klansmen, like the white stage performers that inspired them, to simultaneously discredit and control supposed black bodies under the gaze of the public eye. This mode of blackface costuming was also politically strategic: it aimed to obscure the identity of white Klansmen and serve their claims that it was renegade blacks, not white radicals, who tormented communities with their violence.

Illustrative of these methodic efforts are the testimonies of many witnesses, some of which are included in the *Report of the Joint Select Committee to Inquire into the Condition of Affairs in the Late Insurrectionary States* (1872). Throughout this collection are found eyewitness accounts attesting to the Klan's practice of "blacking up." One such witness was forty-one-year-old Joe Brown. Born into slavery in Virginia and living in White County, Georgia, at the time of his courtroom testimony in October 1871, Brown traveled to Atlanta to provide an account of the Klan's attacks on his family. At one point in the testimony, Brown refers to an episode in which his wife saw two Klansmen whose identities were clear despite their use of blackface.

> ANSWER. My wife saw two men disguised as they came across below our house and up by the house. They made out they were black men, and spoke to my wife to see if she knew them. . . .
> QUESTION. You say this man Bailey Smith was supposed to have shot Mr. Cason?
> ANSWER. On the same day he was disguised Mr. Cason was killed.
> QUESTION. And they thought your wife would testify against him?
> ANSWER. Yes, sir. He came up to fool her and pass himself off as a black man, and she said, "Bailey Smith, I know you." That is the way he knew my wife knew him, and he told his Klan to come back on us and run me and her out of there.[18]

Brown's testimony illustrates how the practice of blacking up did not necessarily prevent Klansmen from being recognized, although such efforts did foster opportunities to distract attention from whites and unduly cast suspicion on blacks.[19]

The historically grounded associations between the performance of racial mimicry (specifically, blacking up) and KKK activities are ingeniously exploited and reversed through Dave Chappelle's nonconforming whiteface act. By "whiting up" Clayton Bigsby in KKK garb, Chappelle enacts his own mirthful yet politically strategic performance. His presentation, under the gaze of a public eye, controls a potent symbol of white supremacy while mockingly discrediting its principles, thereby making the ignorance and logic of such hate groups appear as absurd as the scenario itself.

This observation foregrounds the fact that while Klansmen openly denigrated blackness, the thrust of their unruly behavior was aimed at performing and championing whiteness—a performance that was most immediately displayed through Klan attire. Although many of these early displays were inspired by the imagery of "haints," ghosts, or devilish, unnameable creatures, these costumes (particularly the iconic white gowns) "indicated inner whiteness—a whiteness for which white skin was a necessary but not sufficient prerequisite."[20] It is this indication of the wearer's "inner whiteness" that Chappelle dramatically parodies in his sketch. Bigsby's whiteness is assumed due to his racist rhetoric and white KKK garb, thereby dramatizing a white racial designation that is totally independent of phenotypical whiteness.

As Chappelle's "Clayton Bigsby" sketch discloses, early KKK members performed whiteness through their intimidating antics and costuming; however, they also staged the significance and perception of whiteness by repeatedly flaunting their immunity to social and legal repercussions. Despite some resistance, the explicit absence of civic and penal consequences was palpable evidence of the authority and privilege whites held. Klansmen rarely faced punishment for their actions, and it is this glaring inequity—and the message it sent to both blacks and whites—that was perhaps the Klan's most commanding performance of power. The absence of consequences illustrates white privilege and reinforces the paradox of white (in)visibility. While the marked and often ostentatious costumes of its members may have obscured their identities (therefore animating their attempts to be both visible and invisible), Klan propaganda emphasized that its "empire" should be "invisible." Early KKK organizers insisted on a level of discretion that even forbade printing the organization's name for fear that this would result in unwanted validation or exposure.[21] Valuing the image of their organization as an ethereal, intangible, omnipotent force, early Klansmen exploited this impression of omnipotent authority to destabilize the potential for resistance and/or anti-Klan allegiance across racial lines. Fearful of black empowerment, racial solidarity, and miscegenation, the Klan geared its discriminatory practices toward the subjugation of blacks and the reinforcement of white power.

The Klan's disdain for black-white relations makes its performance of whiteness particularly intriguing because, in many respects, these enactments relied on carnivalesque constructs that actually animated, rather than discouraged, notions of miscegenation. After all, in *Rabelais and His World*, Mikhail Bakhtin famously declared that carnival is "the sum total of all diverse festivities, rituals and forms of a carnival type" and a "syncretic pageantry of a ritualistic sort."[22] Reveling in the disintegration of binaries, carnival is marked by the fact that

> [a]ll things that were once self-enclosed, disunified, distanced from one another by a noncarnivalistic hierarchical worldview are drawn into carnivalistic contacts and combinations. Carnival brings together, unifies, weds, and combines the sacred with the profane, the lofty and the low, the great with the insignificant, the wise with the stupid.[23]

Through inversions, integrations, reversals, and substitutions, the carnivalesque embodies the conflation of polarities to create unsettling, yet celebrated, amalgamations.[24] Although this disintegration of absolutes can be easily be traced through various types of Klan activity, it is striking to also note that the roots of carnivalesque traditions within the United States— those carried on by Klan members—speak directly to the conceit of cultural mixture and amalgamation.

While the history and rituals of early Klan performances necessitate an acknowledgment of the carnivalesque, Chappelle's sketch also calls on the carnivalesque in its reversals and fusions. I am particularly struck by how Bakhtin's theory applies to Chappelle's comedic refrains on "mixedness"—a trope that is uniquely amplified through the personification of Clayton Bigsby. In the character of Bigsby, however, it is not the concept of *biological* mixedness that is dramatized (an exploration that *is* addressed in "The Racial Draft"); rather, Bigsby's symbolic mixedness represents the incongruity of a *black body* conjoined with a racist, *antiblack mind*. The inconceivability of this mixture, along with Bigsby's complete violation of the status quo, is so overwhelming and impossible to fathom for Bigsby's crowd of white supremacists that the revelation of his blackness results in absolute chaos.

This fateful moment arrives when Bigsby's devotees demand to see their leader's face. Bigsby, swept up in the euphoria of the crowd's enthusiasm, readily responds and pulls off his hood—an act of disclosure that is met with screams of astonishment and horror. So shocked and disgusted is the crowd that some members cover their eyes and vomit. One man's incredulity is so great that his head explodes, causing blood to spray around the room. And then there is stunned silence—a silence full of both disbelief and terror.

As a *black* Klansman, Bigsby horrifies his white audience members with his *actualization* of all that they fear: he successfully infiltrated the extreme fringes of white society, he assumed (and was granted) a position of leadership and authority over white subordinates, and he engaged—with his white wife of nineteen years—in interracial sexual congress. These facts are so terrorizing to the gathered white supremacists that Bigsby's exposure brings forth a scene befitting a B-horror film. With spectacles of vomit and blood, Chappelle's "Clayton Bigsby" extends its engagement with Bakhtinian theory. Theatricalizing the notion of "the grotesque body," this over-the-top scene "displays not only the outward but also the inner features of the body: blood, bowels, heart and other organs."[25] The sheer crudeness of this bit reverses the intimations of black fright and terror that are traditionally associated with early Klan activities. Twisting the circumstances to create a parodic episode of *white* fright and terror, the "Clayton Bigsby" sketch uses outrageous comedy to signify on both the physical and psychological coercion and violence Klan victims experienced.[26]

At the close of the Bigsby sketch, Kent Walker offers a concluding (but hardly surprising) assessment, starkly stating that "irreparable damage has been done to [Bigsby's] reputation and in many ways, the White Power movement." The *Frontline* journalist also notes that Bigsby's personal life suffered from the revelation of his blackness, noting that he filed to divorce his wife on the indefensible grounds that she was "a nigger lover." And so, when the fictional Bigsby account comes to its official end, the viewing audience is once again privy to a carnivalesque deconstruction. Like the mock crowning and subsequent decrowning of Bakhtin's carnival king, the revelations of Bigsby's blackness—the birthing of his black body amid the expelling of blood and bodily fluids—symbolize a concurrent death and renewal.[27]

While Bigsby's perceived whiteness and authoritative position in the movement suffer from a certain and sudden demise, the awakening of his consciousness simultaneously represents a beginning as he is forcefully birthed into his blackness *and* the experience of abjection that often comes with it.

By engaging in the discourse of mixedness, Chappelle's "Clayton Bigsby" ultimately underscores the contemporaneous belief that racial identity is performative rather than essential. This central mode of thought is found in many of Chappelle's comedic presentations (including, as I shall discuss, "The Racial Draft"). Throughout his vignettes, the comedian and his supporting actors present skits that ultimately challenge the belief that one's "whiteness" or "blackness"—as evidenced by physical appearance and/or behavior—is an intrinsic, categorical reality. In demonstrating how the biological notion of race is often erroneously conflated with the idea of cultural socialization, Chappelle's comedy exploits a common fallacy while also targeting anxieties regarding membership and authenticity.

A BLACK WHITE SUPREMACIST: "HOW COULD THIS HAPPEN?"

Prompting its viewing audience to discern between perceptions of race and culture, Chappelle's "Clayton Bigsby" voices *and* poses a significant rhetorical query: "How could this happen, a black white supremacist?" At first consideration, a black KKK member undoubtedly strikes many audience members as ludicrous—the comedic invention of Chappelle's outrageous humor. Such an assumption, in turn, gives credence to the claim that Americans find Chappelle so funny because his comedy "represents alternative worlds and scenarios that are simply too far-fetched to possibly be true."[28] Despite the rightful core of such an assertion, I would argue that one of the principal elements of Chappelle's comedy is that it often reminds us that reality can, indeed, be just as strange—if not stranger—than fiction. In fact, some of Chappelle's most ridiculous dramatizations are rooted in the very things people *really do* think, say, or do (just not in "mixed" company). Proof of this is the seemingly far-fetched scenario of a black white supremacist. After the initial laughter it induces, Chappelle's "Clayton Bigsby" skit invites audience members to acknowledge the painfully real expressions of self-hatred that actually exist within some minoritized communities, thereby contributing further to our understanding of how whiteness has been performed and imagined. This brings us to the fascinating case of Leo V. Felton.

Leo V. Felton, a neonazi skinhead, made viral news in April 2001 after being arrested for using counterfeit money. The counterfeiting story itself was not particularly titillating, but Felton's criminal activities became more sensational when the police learned that the counterfeiting scam was part of a grandiose scheme to finance the destruction (via bombings) of targets affiliated with both Jewish and African American communities, all in hopes of igniting a "racial war." As if that wasn't sensational enough, the *real* page-turning aspect of the tale was that the police discovered that Felton—"a member of a self-described Aryan Order known as the White Order of Thule"[29]—was of African descent, far surpassing the supposed requirements of America's one-drop rule.[30] The relatively fair-skinned Felton was not just "a little bit" black—he was biracial, born of a black father and white mother.

Felton's father, a black architect, and his mother, a former nun of Jewish ancestry, were briefly married but then divorced when Felton was two years old. Following the divorce, Felton's mother embraced a lesbian identity, and she and Felton moved in with her female lover and her lover's two white children. According to reports, the complex negotiation of social identities and familial configurations was difficult for the young Felton to manage, especially considering the predominately white, heteronormative, middle-class neighborhood in which he was being raised. While negotiating difference is something with which most people must wrestle, it was especially difficult for Felton in that he also exhibited, from an early age, a number of behavioral deficiencies.

When Felton was just ten years old, he attacked a black boy with a knife after being called a "half breed." This incident led his mother to commit Felton to the Psychiatric Institute of Washington. Following his stay, his mother continued to insist that Felton had a number of emotional and psychological anomalies, and—despite the objections of individual therapists and Felton's father—she repeatedly sent her son to psychiatric facilities throughout his teen years. Both Felton and his father claim that he didn't have any psychological issues *before* these various institutional stints, but by the time he was fourteen, the periods spent in these institutions—and *away* from his family—had left him feeling irreparably "angry, confused and antisocial."[31] Felton's compromised temperament, along with the disastrous influence of equally troubled friends, drug abuse, and criminal activities, led to a moral disintegration that eventually gave birth to his pure, unadulterated racial hatred.

But this brief biography still brings us back to the question: "How could this happen, a black white supremacist?" How does someone of African ancestry come to hate his blackness so profoundly? How does he become a leading member of the White Order of Thule, an Aryan organization devoted to "violent action as a way of advancing a white power agenda to *rid the United States of a multi-racial society* and its perceived Jewish influence"?[32] As it turns out, Felton believed it was his own troubled experience of mixedness that spawned his white supremacist beliefs. In a letter to the *Boston Herald*, he wrote: "I am what I am.... Contaminated, falsely condemned, and alienated from my comrades. But a lover of Nature nonetheless, and a lover of the West, and ever an unrepentant enemy of the multicultural myth."[33] According to ethnographer and cultural essayist John L. Jackson Jr., Felton's tortuous story and feelings of self-contempt can be read as a "retooled version of Hollywood's classically tragic mulatto."

> In a postmodern "Imitation of Life," Felton's mixed-race ancestry made it so hard for him to fit in with other black children that he chose, instead, to pass for white.... The doubled counterfeiting (passing off fake money while passing off a faked whiteness) was lost on no one. How could Felton know his interracial family history and its implications for his own social identity, especially in the context of America's one-drop rule of hypodescent, and still choose to pass as a skinhead, still identify with white supremacy so unabashedly and violently?[34]

Leaning on the explanations offered by Felton himself, we come to understand that he clearly made a distinction between his material, corporeal self and his African American heritage, and what he deemed to be of greater significance and import: his spiritual and ideological self. In a letter to *New York Times Magazine* reporter Paul Tough, Felton credited the philosophies of Francis Parker Yockey as traced in the work *Imperium* (published in 1948 under the pen name Ulik Varange). In *Imperium* Yockey asserts, "Race is, in the first instance, what a man feels"—it is about spirit rather than biology.[35] The fact that Felton *chose*, then, to blame his blackness for his woes ultimately speaks to flawed logic. While Felton understood that racial and cultural affinities go beyond "blood and biology," his own discriminatory logic disrupts this central premise with a vetting process that relies on physical and biological signatures to determine racial essence and human value.[36]

We may never understand, exactly, why Felton *felt* he was white rather than black, but we do know that his prison stints, and the highly segregated prison population, led him to feel that he needed to make a choice and that whiteness felt—to use a popular idiom—"more like right." The immediate assumption by most inmates that Felton was white certainly helped facilitate that choice, and as someone who always struggled to belong, Felton believed that claiming whiteness—and, specifically, joining the white supremacist community—would grant him the feeling of inclusion for which he had long yearned. Thus, as the journalist Paul Tough asserts, Felton earnestly thought that "[b]y defending white culture, he would literally become white—as pure as anyone else who shared the same beliefs."[37]

Taking up the gauntlet to defend whiteness, Felton preached his supremacist beliefs to fellow prisoners, and—like the fictional Clayton Bigsby—dispersed his ideologies through the power of pen and paper. He not only charged his followers to read volumes on volumes of theoretical, philosophical, and Aryan-friendly texts as a means of further indoctrination, but he also created a propagandistic comic book about renegade, racist revolutionaries. Reminiscent of Clayton Bigsby, Felton's volatile performance underscores the way the accoutrements of literary and audible rhetoric can perform whiteness. In addition, Felton adopted strategies associated with nonconforming whiteface by acquiring visible accessories associated with white supremacist ideologies. Similar to the way Chappelle's Clayton Bigsby embodied whiteness through the use of KKK garb, the olive-skinned Felton (who prior to his public outing credited his "ethnic look" to being one-quarter English and three-quarters Italian) relied on his body tattoos to articulate both sentiments and his desired racial status.[38] By inscribing signs of whiteness *on his skin*, the real-life Leo V. Felton adorned his body with a permanent uniform of whiteness, thereby exceeding the temporal efforts of the fictional Clayton Bigsby. With this epidermal costuming, along with his authored treatise, Felton successfully portrayed the corporeal identity of his choosing, presenting himself as a *white* white supremacist leader among his followers.

Of course, like Clayton Bigsby's unveiling, Felton's ride on the white supremacy train came to a screeching halt. In Chappelle's sketch, the journalist Kent Walker asks Clayton's assistant, Jasper, about revealing the truth to Clayton, and Jasper replies, "Listen man, he's too important to the movement. If I tell him he's black probably kill himself just to be one less nigra around. His commitment is that deep." Although such a retort is a source of laughter in "Clayton Bigsby," the public exposure of the real black white supremacist, Felton, did result in his attempted suicide. After failing to cut his jugular vein with a prison-issue razor, Felton spoke of his devastation and desperation: "You have to understand, my level of investment in the cause—it was existential for me. My existence was bound to this idea. It was what I understood to be the purpose in my life. The fact of my fractured lineage was something that I thought was a burden I could bear within myself. As long as it was something I kept to myself, it wasn't a problem."[39]

Felton's assertion that the truth of his black heritage "wasn't a problem" as long as he kept it to himself is, well, evidence of *many* problems—not the least of which is his self-loathing and dogged commitment to racist ideologies. What Felton's temporal performance of oppressive whiteness also reveals, however, is the ease with which whiteness can be performed and received if the right script is enacted before a yearning, ripe audience. Our borders of belief are incredibly permeable and dependent on what we *choose* to recognize. Felton chose to recognize his whiteness, not his blackness, just as those around him chose to read the various signs that supported his white identity versus his potential "otherness."

The troubled biography of Leo V. Felton also suggests that, in part at least, time away from parental consideration and individual attention may have exacerbated his psychopathic leanings. Chappelle may very well have been inspired by the details of Felton's story, thereby informing the depiction of Clayton Bigsby as an orphaned child raised in the Wexler Home for the Blind for the first nineteen years of his life.[40] It is Bigsby's complete lack of familial intimacy and self-knowledge that makes his metaphoric blindness possible, a fact underscored by Bridget Wexler, the orphanage's headmistress, when Kent Walker interviews her.

> WEXLER: He was the only nigra we'd ever had around here, so we figured we'd just make it easier on Clayton by just telling him—and all the other blind kids—that he was white.
> JOURNALIST: And he never questioned it?
> WEXLER: Why would he?

While the audience may briefly reflect on the rhetorical question "Why would he?," a query that raises proliferating queries (e.g., did he ever notice the texture of his hair—and would he even necessarily understand how that might indicate racial otherness?), we are also struck by the simplicity of this retort. Why *would* someone who cannot distinguish between the visual signatures of race assume that he or she was a member of a racial minority? Or, in the case of Felton, if given the choice *not* to claim what he deemed to be inferior, why would he? Thus, the black bodies of both the real-life Felton and Clayton Bigsby not only reveal how whiteness is performed but also dramatize the manufactured and ephemeral nature of white power. Accordingly, these real-life and real-life-inspired stories remind us of the words of Michele Elam (a critical race theorist and literature scholar whose insightful reading of Chappelle's "The Racial Draft" complements my forthcoming analysis): determinations of race are "not of visibility but of vision."[41] Subsequently, it is not simply what one *can* or *cannot* see, but rather *how one chooses to see* (or chooses *not* to see) that really matters.

SKETCHING "THE RACIAL DRAFT"

Among the many Chappelle skits that target the issue of how we choose to see race (or, alternately, how others choose to see it for us) is "The Racial Draft" (2004). Based on the premise that different racial groups should be able to negotiate their memberships through a draft process similar to that of the National Football League (NFL), "The Racial Draft" reveals the strategic maneuverings of Asians, Latinos, blacks, Jews, and whites as they attempt to bolster their strength and competitive edge. In his stand-up-style opening for this popular sketch, Chappelle offers the following premise.

> You know what's cool about being an American? We all mixed up. I'm talking about genetically. We all got a little something in us, right? And then some people it's more than others and then that's when we get to arguing. For instance: my wife is Asian. I'm black. And we argue about which half of Tiger Woods is hitting the ball so good. Derek Jeter is another guy like that. Halle Berry is somebody else. We have got to stop arguing about who is what! We need to just settle this once and for all. We need to have a draft! That's right, I said it.[42]

Although delivered with decidedly humorous intentions, Chappelle's comic proposal powerfully reveals the "values, attitudes, dispositions, and concerns" of our current cultural moment.[43]

The format of Chappelle's "The Racial Draft"—which includes three male commentators (two of whom are white, the third being Chappelle)—pays homage to the NFL draft in form and concept: the order of the Racial Draft, like that of the NFL, is in *reverse*, thereby reflecting the comparative success of each team.⁴⁴ In other words, the most unsuccessful team in the league (and therefore the most "handicapped" in terms of ability and reputation) has the first draft pick while the most successful team of the previous year has the final pick. Not surprisingly, in the controversial and self-reflexive world of Dave Chappelle, blacks have the distinguished honor of picking first.

The spokesperson for the blacks is a Jerry-curled, red-suit-wearing, sunglasses-clad man (performed by the hip-hop artist and actor Mos Def), who saunters up to the podium ready to reveal the first pick of the draft. Adorned with physical accoutrements that suggest not only his cultural but also his socioeconomic position (his incredibly flashy attire suggests urban "pimp fashion" rather than conjuring images of middle-class black America), Mos Def's character names Tiger Woods as the blacks' chosen one. The irony of this pick is likely not lost on Chappelle's audience: early in Woods's career the golf phenom emphasized his own sense of mixedness by forthrightly claiming a "Cablinasian" (Caucasian, black, and Asian) identity, thereby making it known that he wasn't interested in being drafted into any single racial category. However, the Tiger Woods of Chappelle's imagination rejoices at the prospect of acquiring "official, 100 percent blackness" and on delivering a heartfelt acceptance speech, closes his remarks with an urban-influenced "fushizzle."⁴⁵

Woods's eager acceptance of his designated blackness plays on the public's imagination at the time of the skit's creation (2004). Adorned in his trademark golf attire, Woods is not only a self-proclaimed symbol of perceived biological mixedness, but he represents a type of cultural mixedness as well. As the world's most celebrated golfer, he also stands as a symbolic embodiment of an elite, "country club" sport that had historically excluded African American athletes.⁴⁶ While institutionalized racism may no longer prevent blacks and other minorities from teeing off at the golf course, other limitations in terms of access and cost still prevent minoritized groups from having a significant presence in the golf world, especially in comparison to their involvement in football and basketball. Unlike basketball (which requires of its players relatively little equipment—a ball, a milk carton, and some sort of pole can suffice), golf is not easy to learn, nor is it accessible; moreover, the cost of golf equipment, course entry, and lessons is exorbitant. Golf is, in no uncertain terms, a sport that is financially prohibitive for many people, regardless of color, and considering the socioeconomic realities of most black people in America, it should not be surprising that it is considered a "whiter" sport than some others.⁴⁷ Thus, the characterization of Tiger Woods offers Chappelle's audience the opportunity to consider not only how racial performance is perceived in terms of phenotype but also how it is enacted through access, affluence, and behavioral codes (including dress and language).

Throughout "The Racial Draft," Chappelle uses the sketch's comedic format to simultaneously address and trouble biological and cultural inscriptions related to racial difference and mixedness. To that end, the question of blood quantum or racial percentage is originally raised when Woods is drafted and then continuously revisited throughout the sketch, as exemplified by the moment in which the Jews draft the "half-black, half-Jewish" musician Lenny Kravitz. Since traditional Jewish law demands that Jewish identity is claimed through the matrilineal line (or formal rabbinical conversion), the Jewishness of Kravitz is in question since his black mother is not Jewish. With his drafting, however, Kravitz—sans conversion—is catapulted into the category of "100 percent" Jewish.

The ability to draft racially mixed celebrities into realms of supposed purity continues when it is the white delegation's turn to choose its draft picks. The two white commentators begin to speculate over whether they should draft Halle Berry or Mariah Carey (both of whom are the products of white-black interracial unions). Rising to speak for the white delegation is Dave Chappelle—in tinted whiteface. The only performer cast outside his "real" race, Chappelle's signature whiteface character is crafted as an obvious exaggeration of racial difference.⁴⁸ Wearing a sculpted gray synthetic wig, Chappelle's naturally brown skin, eyebrows, and mustache are floured down to a dusty, pale hue. Completing this physical transformation is the comedian's preppy outfit: a buttoned-up, checked jacket; a beige tie; gray slacks; and cream shoes.

While Chappelle's portrayal of the white delegate in "The Racial Draft" has a few specific nuances (e.g., his attire), it exhibits a characteristic common among Chappelle's other whiteface characters: they are always poorly inscribed—and purposefully so. Chappelle's use of theatrical whiteface never attempts to create a convincing, passable white visage, but rather the tinted whiteface—like the tinted whiteface in *Funnyhouse of a Negro*—is intentionally crafted to comment on the artificial, constructed nature of racial designations. In tandem with his tinted whiteface, Chappelle accents his simulated signatures of whiteness by shifting his vocal cadence and carrying his body in a stifled and awkward manner. Moving "with tightness, with self-control, self-consciousness," Chappelle's bodily expressions enliven Richard Dyer's assertion that white people are trained to carry themselves "upright" and with an "unrelaxed posture, [with] tight rather than loose movement."[49]

In "The Racial Draft," these multiple racial indicators are made immediately apparent when the white delegation leader approaches the podium. Instantaneously, Chappelle's character is unceremoniously greeted with a murmur of "boos" from the crowd—an antagonistic response that initially seems rooted in nothing other than the delegate's white presence. However, the white representative soon earns his unwelcoming reception when he offers his own impertinent response: "Will you cut the malarkey, I'm talking. There's a white man talking up here! Silencio! Ungawa!" The silencing of the crowd after the Spanish "Silencio!" and pseudo-African exclamation "Ungawa!" speaks less to the delegate's rhetorical effectiveness (a quick camera scan of the audience reveals expressions of confusion and annoyance) than it discloses his own naïveté and ignorance. Ordering the audience to cut the malarkey (meaning "foolish talk"), he then employs his own nonsensical language with the championing of "ungawa." The fact is that *ungawa*—presumed to be a word of African origin and therefore a command that should be understood by the African American audience members—was born out of racialized imaginings. A term created in, and popularized by, 1950s Tarzan films, the white representative's use of *ungawa* not only suggests that he assumes a Tarzanian status that is superior to the clamoring hordes on the floor (after all, there is "a *white* man talking") but underscores the theme of racial construction implicit within "The Racial Draft."[50] The delegate's insulting stance culminates when he brazenly asserts, "I'm the biggest hustler," thereby intimating that his white body symbolizes white people's history of colonial and imperialistic domination in the game of life. However, these telling words can also be interpreted to mean that *whiteness* and the notion of its inherent power and superiority are actually the world's biggest hoax—that whiteness itself *is* "the biggest hustle."

Returning to this chapter's exploration of mixedness, it is also useful to note that Chappelle's tinted whiteface—framed and performed at this specific cultural moment—is clearly neither "white" nor "black." Visually conjuring the very premise of neither/nor, the use of tinted whiteface in this particular skit resounds with irony. It also helps us recognize that transracial performance has long prompted readings of mixedness for its audiences. For example, in his notable study on blackface, W. T. Lhamon Jr. posits that blackface minstrelsy "developed distinct responses to 'amalgamation'—not by attaching but by enacting miscegenation. . . . Blackface minstrelsy was a much more complex attempt to understand racial mixing and accommodate audiences to it than either abolitionist propaganda or the counter-riots of the artisanry."[51] While blackface minstrelsy may have been a way of *imagining* the proliferation of miscegenation when interracial unions were not socially acceptable, Chappelle's whiteface, with its intentional grayness, can be seen as highlighting *the fact* of interracial liaisons in the twenty-first century.

Far from portraying a flesh-colored visage, Chappelle's tinted whiteface also bears witness to the impossibility of white purity, making plain the notion that whiteness itself is an ethereal idea, not only incapable of being garnered by those of color but also leading us to ask whether *anyone*—including self-identified white folks—are, indeed, *truly* white. In this way, Chappelle's whiteface echoes the effect of whiteface in Kennedy's *Funnyhouse of a Negro* and Ward's *Day of Absence*. Like the tinted whiteface in *Funnyhouse* or the incomplete optic whiteface in *Day of Absence*, Chappelle's made-up skin comes across as compromised and "impure." It alludes to the fact that those among us who may *represent* whiteness are, indeed, not really white at all but rather are—consciously or unconsciously—passing as such. Such a sly suggestion pays homage to Eddie Murphy's sketch "White Like Me," in which he warns the (white) viewing audience that the "really super groovy white guy" or the "really great super keen white chick" might very well "be black."[52] It also reminds us of the various ways "The Racial Draft" interrogates the philosophy of America's "one-drop" rule.

DRAFTING WHITENESS

Like Chappelle's "Clayton Bigsby" skit, the relative malleability of whiteness in "The Racial Draft" reminds us of America's "one-drop rule" by simultaneously confirming and countering its logic and legacy. In terms of legislation, the rule asserted that if someone's ancestry ranged from an one-eighth to one-thirty-second black (depending on the state), he or she was to be categorized as black. Socially and culturally, the one-drop rule quickly came to mean that any discernible or known trace of African ancestry—regardless of how minimal—made one unilaterally subject to being classified as black.

> When there is black/white mixing involved, the dominant classificatory arguments posit that interracial subjects are essentially black; essentially

mixed; essentially code-switchers, chameleons, who are able to crisscross extant color lines at whim; and a fairly rare position that considers mixed-race subjects essentially white, whether literally or figuratively.[53]

Nevertheless, in the world of Dave Chappelle, the act of crossing over the color line to inhabit and claim whiteness *is* a possibility, not only among those who are of mixed ancestry but also among those who are deemed to be "cultural mulattoes."

One of the most pointed explorations of the cultural mulatto was penned by Trey Ellis in his 1989 *Callaloo* article "The New Black Aesthetic." Within this oft-referenced article, Ellis addresses the shift in African American identity politics, art, and culture following the Black Arts Movement (BAM). Referring to this era as one that champions a *new* black aesthetic (thereby riffing on Addison Gayle's *The New Black Aesthetic*), Ellis claims that the post-BAM generation is fueled by "a mongrel mix of classes and types" whom he refers to as "cultural mulattoes."[54] While I would argue that *all* African Americans are cultural mulattoes in that we have all been "educated by a multi-racial mix of cultures,"[55] Ellis's characterization seems particularly effective in describing blacks that seem to "navigate easily in the white world,"[56] a maneuver that is *not* equally effortless for all black Americans, despite similarities in terms of socioeconomic status and educational opportunities. Also of significance is that cultural mulattoes can still be considered "wholly black" if they choose to categorize themselves as such.[57] According to Ellis, cultural mulattoes can lay full claim to their Afrocentricity because their blackness can be understood as a personal experience of being and is not contingent on an unyielding set of behavioral codes or phenotypical markers. When it comes to their sense of *African American* identity, cultural mulattoes can claim or disclaim this inherently complex and always-already mixed heritage at will and, simultaneously, exercise some measure of social fluency within a so-called white world. However, the dynamics of choice are decidedly different when it comes to the racially or culturally mixed subject's ability to actually *claim* whiteness. As "The Racial Draft" makes clear, the mixed subject has diminished agency and can only be *drafted* by the white delegation to claim a white identity, thereby disclosing how access to white membership is still contingent on whether or not whites *choose* to accept "honorary whites" into the fold.

The hegemonic authority of whiteness and its arbitrating power are upheld through the contradictory drafting dynamics of Chappelle's skit. While the strategic malleability of whiteness directly challenges our historical understanding of the white race's supposed racial purity, the overriding power of white judgment and the ability of white folks to redefine the boundaries of whiteness ultimately exhibit unparalleled power capable of trumping the very rules of its own devising. This agency is fully actualized when the white delegation finally makes its first draft pick. Despite the commentators' speculation over whether the delegates will draft Halle Berry or Mariah Carey, "The Racial Draft"'s revisionary—even revolutionary—understanding of whiteness becomes evident when the whitefaced Chappelle casts his party's vote: "We, the white delegation, are very proud to announce our pick this year: Colin Powell!" Foregoing any prioritization of blood quantum, the whites' pick comes as a surprise even to the white commentators: "What, Colin Powell is not white, he's not even an eighth white, he's 100 percent black!"

Interestingly, despite the assertion that General Powell is "100 percent black," the popular press has made occasional references to Powell's mixed ancestry. As the son of Jamaican immigrants, Powell can trace his genealogy to Scotland, Ireland, and Jamaica and thus, like many black Americans, can lay claim to a verifiable European lineage.[58] For "The Racial Draft," however, the issue at hand is not really Powell's supposed bloodline, but rather the sketch alludes to the way in which Powell's political affiliation has distanced him from the masses of black Americans, the majority of whom tended—at the time "The Racial Draft" initially aired—to vote along the lines of the Democratic Party. A moderate Republican, Powell was appointed by a Republican president, George W. Bush, to the position of US secretary of state (2001–5). Thus, he became the first person of known African descent to hold the title of secretary of state and, likewise, the first black to be appointed to the Joint Chiefs of Staff. Recognizing that America's political parties are highly racialized, Powell's *Republicanness* invariably symbolized a "whiteness" that was regarded with suspicion by many black Americans at the time.[59]

Highlighting the way racial inscriptions are shaped by our belief systems, "The Racial Draft" identifies the role of organized politics *within* identity politics. This is made explicitly clear when the black delegation accepts the whites' draft pick of Colin Powell with a single caveat: the whites must also claim Condoleezza Rice. Although Rice became the US secretary of state following Powell (therefore becoming the second black American and second woman to hold that position), at the time of "The Racial Draft" she was the national security adviser during President Bush's first term in office and, like Powell, the subject of cultural critique among those who felt that she did not represent the interests of black people. These sentiments were addressed repeatedly in the popular press, as evidenced by a 2005 *Washington Post* op-ed piece by columnist Eugene Robinson.

> Like a lot of African Americans, I've long wondered what the deal was with Condoleezza Rice and the issue of race. How does she work so loyally for George W. Bush, whose approval rating among blacks was measured in a recent poll at a negligible 2 percent? How did she come to a worldview so radically different from that of most black Americans? Is she blind, is she in denial, is she confused—or what?[60]

An even more scathing assessment of Rice's perceived "whiteness" was expressed the previous year in the weekly Internet magazine *Black Commentator*.

> Rice made it easy for the super-privileged to love themselves. Unlike coy Colin Powell, Rice did not bargain or seek her own space, but settled into the very fabric of Bushness. In so doing, however, Rice lost all power of personal agency. Having surrendered everything to the Bushes, her Blackness gradually lost its value as a cloak for her patrons' racism. . . . Rice's rich white admirers hugged and squeezed her too tightly—until there was nothing left but *them* all over her. It is common in African American circles to speak of "lost" Black souls, but in Rice's case it is almost literally true that she doesn't know where she stands and to whom she is speaking.[61]

Giving credence to these types of political commentaries, the drafting of both Rice and Powell comically reveals a black delegation that rids itself of members they deem lacking in black consciousness and culture.[62] By dramatizing the bilateral permeability of racial designations in "The Racial Draft"—a system that forgoes strict allegiance to phenotypical understandings of whiteness—Chappelle further dislodges our presumptions regarding the sanctity of whiteness, and in doing so once again reminds us of the fictions of biological race.

Thus, without ever uttering the well-worn phrase of racial authenticity, *Chappelle's Show* fully engages in its contemporaneous discourse. As noted by the historian and cultural critic William Jelani Cobb, "Those eight minutes of comedy did more to explain the state of American culture than the last dozen academic conferences on 'hybridity' and 'cultural miscegenation.'"[63] In a brilliantly blatant manner, Chappelle's ticklish tirade also illustrated E. Patrick Johnson's assertion that the rhetoric of racial authenticity—whether it is formed as a judgment passed on a person (Does he or she "look" or "act" black?) or raised in the context of theatre (What makes a "black" play?)—is guided by standards of exclusion. Blackness, notes Johnson, cannot be contained or possessed by any particular person or group, but rather "individuals or groups *appropriate* this complex and nuanced racial signifier in order to circumscribe its boundaries or to exclude other individuals or groups. When blackness is appropriated to the exclusion of others, identity becomes political."[64] In the case of Chappelle's draft, however, the politicizing—and policing—of racial identity, black or white, is based on the strategic deployment of inclusive as well as exclusionary practices. As such, Chappelle's comic vignette animates Naomi Pabst's observations regarding the contestations associated with black-white interraciality and transculturalism: "However aggressively people are appointed to this or that category of belonging, or not belonging as it often turns out, people are often just as aggressively rejected from that same category."[65] The practice of racial team building in America, we are told, is equally informed by the drafting and trading of its players—an exercise that often substantiates rather than curtails notions of hierarchy and prioritization within and between racial groups.

What "The Racial Draft" also ultimately suggests is that you can't play on two teams—a choice must be made. But this rigid drafting process, with all its conceptual inconsistencies, dismantles any guise of consistent racial categorization and demonstrates the futile absurdity of refuting our ubiquitous realities. Insisting that Tiger Woods could, or even should, become "black alone" echoes the language of the US Census by harboring designations that still adhere to strict racial lines. This takes to task our lingering allegiance to the one-drop rule or similar philosophies regarding "blood quantum": although the boxes still exist, the truth of the matter is that many of us are living outside the box. Chappelle's comedy—epitomized by both "The Racial Draft" and the "Clayton Bigsby" sketch—targets the persistent permeability of racial lines even within the most stringent of scenarios. In so doing, both sketches reveal and revel in the indisputable reality of racial transgressions and, subsequently, the ultimate impossibility of policing racial bodies.

POLICING RACE, POLICING CHAPPELLE: NO CONSENSUS AMID THE UNCENSORED

While Chappelle's comedy wrestles with some sobering and complex ideas regarding America's identificatory practices, it also employs strategic stereotypes, thereby prompting us to consider whether (paying homage to Audre Lorde) the master's tools *can* dismantle the master's house.[66] It is this issue that Harriet Margolis addresses when she explores the use of "self-directed stereotypes" and how these racialized caricatures are often employed with the very intent of "exposing their ridiculous underpinnings."[67] Taking this into account, we can see that Chappelle utilizes overenunciated images (the traditional garb and hairstyle of the Hasidic Jew or the pasty visage of Chappelle's generic white man), to purposefully overstate difference in an act of visual *disidentification*. Working "on and against dominant ideology" in order to "transform a cultural logic from within," *Chappelle's Show* consistently exaggerates the appearance of different racial and ethnic groups, purportedly animating persistent stereotypes in order to discredit them.[68] The question remains, however, whether or not Chappelle's intention is inevitably troubled by the fact that he cannot determine the way in which a reader or spectator will choose to interpret the material at hand.

As often explicated by reader response and audience reception theorists, the meanings of a text are not solely constructed by its author. A reader/viewer also imbues a text with meaning, thus—despite authorial intentions—a particular interpretation cannot be guaranteed. This is not to say that readers and audience members are wholly subjective in their responses. On the contrary, audience interpretations are greatly informed by social and cultural training, which, in turn, shapes the *interpretive communities* to which they belong.[69] While this understanding of audience reception is clearly related to notions of ideology, there is also a psychological dimension to it. Norman N. Holland, for example, argues that our interpretations can be read as a type of "coping mechanism" that not only reveals our desires and fears but also helps us to actualize or conquer them.[70] In other words, for audience members with racist leanings, the stereotypes flaunted in *Chappelle's Show* may serve to substantiate their biases. However, those who take offense with the way their racial identities are performed in *Chappelle's Show* can actively choose to seek counternarratives in the performance, including the sketches' disidentificatory practices.

The potential for varying and complex responses to *Chappelle's Show* prompts further questions regarding our current rules of engagement. Chappelle's scripted and nonscripted acts urge us to consider the role of the performer as well as the demographics of the audience. For, as Cobb succinctly notes, "The problem [with *Chappelle's Show*] was not so much the work as it was who was viewing it."[71] Cobb draws our attention to the mediated nature of *Chappelle's Show*, forcing us to consider issues of access, as well as the way the show's form impacted its public reception.

When writing about comedy, Lawrence E. Mintz emphasizes the significant relationship between form and content, noting that "the contexts and processes of joke telling are at least as important as the texts of the jokes themselves to any understanding of the meaning of humor."[72] Leaning on the issue of context (and thus returning to the issue of institutional dramaturgy addressed in chapter 1), we can recognize that the nature of *Chappelle's Show*'s televised format makes his work particularly vulnerable to misinterpretation. Chappelle comes from a stand-up comedy background in which the audience, like that of any live performance, is relatively stationary and engaged. Contemporary television viewing, on the other hand, offers audience members the opportunity to tune in and tune out on a moment's notice. Despite the fact that *Chappelle's Show* was consciously structured to incorporate moments of reflection and commentary from Chappelle, there was no way to ensure that audience members—with their remotes in hand—would linger long enough to allow their readings of the skits to be properly contextualized.

Beyond thinking of the different ways audience members interpreted Chappelle's comedy, the sketches in *Chappelle's Show* ultimately beg the question: Who has the position or authority to represent or police racial categories? Who has the power or authority to police membership—to deem who and what is authentic, fit, and worthy? Enriching this line of inquiry is the fact that *Chappelle's Show* not only featured skits that entertained ideas of social acceptance and rejection, but the phenomenon of the show itself offered another "real-life" narrative with which to interrogate the notion of representational authority. Case in point: the unceremonious cancellation of *Chappelle's Show*—and all the "buzz" surrounding it—was a highly performative act that dramatized the issues of representational authority that Chappelle's skits often addressed. By all accounts, *Chappelle's Show*, in the spirit of the performative, enacts its own utterance[73] by enlivening the very dynamic it fervently attempted to interrogate: the policing of racial identity.

While Chappelle's comedic sketches often explored issues of identity, the most powerful expression of his own identity theme (i.e., his contentious exploration of race and culture) was his highly publicized disappearing act. After being awarded a fifty-million-dollar deal by the Comedy Central network, Chappelle walked away from *Chappelle's Show*. With poetic allusions, he decided to travel to Africa to find the peace of mind that could only come from relative anonymity. Ironically, it was this sudden exodus that prompted some of the most thought-provoking Chappelle-inspired ruminations on racial performance. One of the most unusual responses to the controversy was the creation of the website www.chappelletheory.com.

The publicized "theory" claimed to explain Chappelle's unexpected departure from *Chappelle's Show*. As detailed by the website (which professes to reveal the "appalling truth"), Chappelle had succumbed to criticism, intimidation tactics, and death threats when he terminated his relationship with Comedy Central. The perpetrators of these offenses were the self-proclaimed "Dark Crusaders"—a collection of powerful African Americans in entertainment, business, and politics. Naming Oprah Winfrey, Whoopi Goldberg, Jesse Jackson, Louis Farrakhan, Bill Cosby, Robert L. Johnson, and Al Sharpton as unexpected allies, the website offers its readers a play-by-play account of the Dark Crusaders and their calculated and aggressive scheme to terminate *Chappelle's Show* based on their belief that it "reinforced negative stereotypes about African Americans, and that its content was, in the words of group leader Bill Cosby 'setting race relations back 50 years.'"[74] Among one of the more explosive details offered at chappelletheory.com is the report of a "voodoo-style" doll having been delivered to Chappelle's home in April 2003. The doll, dressed as Chappelle's blind Klansmen, Clayton Bigsby, was "riddled with safety pins, and had a noose tied sharply around his neck. Accompanying the doll was a message in a childlike scrawl that read, 'what you're doing is hurting the African American community—it needs to stop.'"[75]

The Chappelle theory was eventually revealed as a hoax, but not before it had extensively circulated among Internet users and pop culture enthusiasts. Although one can simply dismiss the website as a by-product of America's insatiable appetite for gossip (combined with our ability to spread such gossip on a mass scale), it is also generative in that the premise of the Chappelle theory echoes the very notions that *Chappelle's Show* attempted to problematize most significantly: the arbitration of cultural or racial allegiances. The strikingly disparate collection of personalities (from Whoopi

Goldberg to Louis Farrakhan) unified under the team emblem of the Dark Crusaders represented a highly suspect expression of "unity"—all they seem to have in common is their celebrity and a sense of group-sanctioned blackness. Noting that "at one time or another, each member of this loosely knit, informal group had played a key role in Chappelle's rise to stardom,"[76] the website suggests that there is, in actuality, a "racial draft" that had previously granted Chappelle membership in an elite group of black luminaries. Just as Chappelle had once been a member in good standing, he, too, could find himself drafted *out* at the whim or design of those who decide he is no longer worthy of racial membership.

As posed by the author(s) of the Chappelle theory, the threatening antics of the Dark Crusaders demonstrate the coercive and/or authoritative positions that are often inherent in the team-building practices of community formation. The very premise of the Chappelle theory hoax speaks to Chappelle's comic artistry in unexpected ways. Like "Clayton Bigsby" and "The Racial Draft," the Chappelle theory prompts the public audience to seriously consider the absurdity, subjectivity, and even danger associated with the policing of our racial and cultural identities.

CHAPTER FIVE

"*Sounding Off on Sounding White*"
Aural Whiteness, Linguistic Whiteface, and the Economics of Opportunity

When it comes to policing racial identities in America, an undue dependence on convenient, surface assumptions immediately becomes apparent. Despite our relative sophistication, most of us routinely rest on superficial markers, drawing problematic conclusions based on physical appearance (in the form of racial signatures and costuming) as well as behavioral codes. As surveyed in chapter 4, these were the troubled targets that the comedian and actor Dave Chappelle adroitly exploits and explodes (figuratively and literally) in comedic sketches like "The Racial Draft" and "Clayton Bigsby." By animating mixed-race discourse, Chappelle's creative forays deliberately "color whiteness," thereby critiquing our imaginings of both white and black identities. However, Chappelle's comedic vignettes—like the other performance texts studied in this book—rely on an audience's tendency to read performances through visual means in order to destabilize the perception of racial constructs. This chapter, however, attempts to disrupt our propensity to code and deconstruct racial identities through visible cues by focusing, instead, on how we use *audible* gestures to ascertain difference and sameness.

My long-standing interest in the "racing" of aural qualities crystalized when I was working as a freelance dramaturg for a black female playwrights group. Due to scheduling conflicts, the first script meeting with one of my assigned playwrights happened over the phone. This initial conversation started off well. I asked the playwright a number of open questions to get a greater sense of her intent, vision, and methodology, and I also shared with her what I deemed to be the many strengths of her work. She, in turn, offered me her insights and seemed appreciative of both the affirmations and the informational queries. Although this initial exchange proved illuminating in many ways, there was still one important clarifying question that needed to be answered: despite all that had been said, I wasn't quite sure *where* the play was taking place. The set directions clearly stated that it was set in a "Federal Government" office, yet there were multiple cues (a character in a doctor's coat, a skeleton, an X-ray machine) that also suggested a doctor's office. Was it one or the other? Both? As soon as my line of questioning revealed that I wasn't quite sure about the location, the conversation turned. And it turned hard.

"You know, I've shared this script with several people already. It was read aloud to the group. No one has ever asked me about the setting before."

"Yes, well, I just want to make sure that I understand what you are envisioning. Are we to understand that it's a doctor's office that happens to be *within* a federal government building?"

"No. It is *not* a doctor's office. It's a federal government office."

[brief pause]

"Okay, okay. Well, I'm wondering if . . ."

"You know, perhaps the problem is cultural. Everyone else who has read or heard my play has been, well . . . African American."

Suffice it to say, I was stung by the playwright's words. Admittedly, my first reaction was a very visceral and personal one: who was she to offer her definitive disavowal of *my* blackness? And then there was the more measured (and less emotive) reflection: what did I say that made her presume that I *wasn't* African American? Of course, I quickly recognized that it wasn't really the nature or content of my question that guided her assumption, but rather it had *something* to do with my voice.

Inspired by personal experiences like this (as well as the innumerable incidents that friends, family, and colleagues have shared with me), I have always been interested in what we hear—or what we *think* we hear. I am struck by the fact that despite the widely accepted recognition that race is a social construct, Americans still talk about what *sounds black* or *sounds white* in simplified racial terms.[1] And while these descriptives can certainly be challenged or renounced through linguistic and vocal analyses, as well as compelling anecdotal evidence, qualitative studies and experiential testimony are also routinely employed to convince us of the validity of such notions. In other words, when it comes to the idea that sound is raced, there is "something to it." But what is it, exactly, that keeps us personally invested in the idea of raced voices?

In considering the sound of race through the lens of performance, this chapter explores how racialized personae are received and perpetuated by listening audiences. Accordingly, it addresses how audiences interpret and/or determine vocal qualities as racial in both staged enactments and the performances of everyday life. While scholarly reflection on racial ventriloquism has primarily focused on the use of audible signatures to purposefully enact stereotypical representations of marginalized people, the ways audiences presume and interpret "whiteness" in the aural presentations of African American artists has not been widely studied. Framing these auditory prescriptions as "presumed aural whiteness" and "linguistic whiteface," this chapter investigates these underexplored perceptions while using the notion of capital (cultural, social, and economic) to think about personal and professional losses and gains at play when it comes to African American artists who are deemed to either "sound white" or *not* "sound black."

In pursuing this conceptual trajectory, this study asks how our awareness and reception of audible nuances might offer ways to enrich our formal performances. Such attentiveness can help us consider how "nonconforming casting" can move beyond visual representations to include diverse, unexpected, and nonstereotypical audible presentations.[2] While my exploration applies to vocal performance broadly conceived, I pay special attention to the field of advertising. Not only do commercials offer unique material with which to consider vocal performances without the visual cues of racialized bodies, but television advertisements are particularly conducive to analyzing the portrayal and consumption of racial identities. While I hope this examination prompts both performance scholars and practitioners to reconsider and redirect the various ways racialized identities are constituted in contemporary radio, television, theatre, and film, I also hope it will encourage those outside these fields to rethink our traditional (and often subconscious) constructions of race and culture.

THE CULTURAL CAPITAL OF PRESUMED AURAL WHITENESS

> I remember there were kids around my [Chicago] neighborhood who would say, "Ooh, you talk funny. You talk like a white girl." I heard that growing up my whole life. I was like, "I don't even know what that means but I am still getting my A."[3]

This anecdote, shared by First Lady Michelle Obama during a March 2009 visit to a Washington, DC, high school, was featured in a *Good Morning America* report that explored the first family's use of language. With a byline that read "Sounding Off on 'Sounding White,'" the brief segment discussed the way people attribute racial identification through speech. To "talk like a white person" (or, conversely, to "talk like a black person") is commonly understood to be a determination of whether or not one uses Standard American English (SAE) or African American Vernacular English (AAVE) and, moreover, the level of fluency with which either dialect is spoken.[4] Despite its continuing evolution, SAE (the dialect taught in schools, found in most textbooks, and used in most mainstream media and television outlets) is traditionally associated with "talking white," while variations of AAVE (the lexical choices, grammatical structures, intonations, and ever-changing vernacular popularized within African American communities) is associated with "talking black."[5]

As one might assume, scholarly explorations of talking white and talking black have most often occurred within the field of linguistics. Within that realm, a number of studies have documented the ability of listeners to name the racial self-identification of speakers. The sociolinguist Peter Trudgill recounts one study in which individuals were asked to listen to tape recordings of two sets of speakers and then racially identify each group.

> Many of the judges decided that speakers in the first set were African Americans, and speakers in the second set white. They were completely wrong. It was the first set which consisted of white people, and the second of Blacks.... The speakers they had been asked to listen to were exceptional people: the white speakers were people who had lived all their lives amongst African Americans, or had been raised in areas where black cultural values were dominant; the black speakers were people who had been brought up with little contact with other Blacks, in predominately white areas. The fact was that the white speakers *sounded* like Blacks, and the black speakers *sounded* like Whites—and the judges listening to the tape-recordings reacted accordingly.[6]

Although the experiment powerfully demonstrated that there are technical elements in speech that may indicate racial associations, it also revealed that these differences are based on learned behavior. Factors such as word choice and dialect are often the cues that guide a listener to draw conclusions about the speaker's race, but rather than being racially determined, these choices and patterns are evidence of one's acculturation, experience, and environment. They are not a result of physiological characteristics or biological racial categories. As Trudgill succinctly summarizes, "People do not speak as they do *because* they are white or black."[7] Yet and still, the fact that all language styles are learned or acquired does little to assuage the sting when one who self-identifies as black is accused of talking white.[8]

Suffice it to say, talking white has a long, convoluted, and complex idiomatic history. Referencing the work of Leon F. Litwack, Stuart Buck alerts us to the premise that the taunt of "acting white" (which has implications *beyond* speech and vocality, but is often used interchangeably with "talking white"), arose among white people who "equated black success with 'uppityness,' 'impudence,' 'getting out of place' and pretensions toward racial equality. 'He think he white' was the expression whites sometimes used to convey that suspicion, or 'He is too smart,' 'He wants to be white and act like white people,' and 'He think he somebody.'"[9] Addressing the adoption of the phrase "acting white" within African American communities, Buck traces it to an injurious consequence of desegregation: the creation of integrated school systems that failed to incorporate the talents and gifts of black teachers and administrators. The discounting of African American educators during the era of segregation not only "destroyed black schools" and "reduced the number of black principals and teachers who could serve as role models," but it also "brought many black schoolchildren into daily contact with whites who made school a strange and uncomfortable environment that was viewed as quintessentially 'white.'"[10]

This contentious legacy within the American education system has contributed to the premise that speaking in a clear, articulate, and well-educated manner is talking white. Thus, if a black person is described as talking white, even by the most well-meaning and admiring observer, the underlying assertion is that being well educated and/or articulate is fundamentally contrary to blackness or black identity. However, as Nancy Giles (the accomplished African American actor, comedian, and voice-over artist) makes abundantly clear, this problematic assumption is often perpetuated by blacks themselves.

> [O]ne of the things about it that really tickled me over the years is where you might think, on the outside looking in, that it's kind of dictated by white people deciding what's black and what's not, you know, that it's a white person's racism or preconceived notions of bigotry toward black

people. It's not just that; black people, of course, can be just as stupid and bigoted and discriminatory and misguided as white people.[11]

As Giles affirms, the accusatory element of talking white is based on a debilitating fallacy: the notion that one's cultural allegiance is suspect if one chooses to speak SAE rather than in a style or manner more closely associated with AAVE. In this instance, the practice of using SAE may strike some as evidence of a speaker's cultural betrayal—proof of the (black) speaker's deference for the "white thing" and/or of participation in a subjugation of black cultural styles.[12]

Timothy Douglas (the celebrated African American director, actor, and vocal pedagogue) similarly observes that there is a tenuously thin line on which blacks are often expected walk.

> I grew up in a lower-middle-class black family and community. My father consistently and absolutely encouraged me to get my education. What that translated into, however, was "Get good grades, stay out of trouble (out of jail), and attempt to be a good student." In comparison with my immediate family and others around me who were not interested in being diligent about their education, I sounded "different"—which was associated with sounding and trying to be "white." That resulted in my constantly being an object of ridicule. My daily survival lay in my success in the navigating of that double-edged sword of "Educate yourself—but don't be influenced by that education."[13]

The perpetuation of such a belief system confronts some African Americans with a troubling paradox: they have the desire and ability to succeed in all aspects of American life, yet they may be stymied by the false conclusion that expressing whiteness is one of the instruments they must use to be successful. It is this conflation of SAE with whiteness that Nancy Giles finds so troublesome and erroneous: "You know, it's so weird that somewhere it's decided that [white people] are the ones that own aspiration and excellence, and that for us to want to do that means that we're trying to act like [whites,] which, in the black community, is a put-down."[14]

What these responses reveal are the contested values associated with these two modes of dialect. One's potential to earn, acquire, and propagate fiscal security often correlates with the ability to speak SAE. For many Americans, SAE (compared to AAVE) represents a greater investment in the dominant markers of the middle class, and its practitioners are assumed to hold higher positions in terms of education and employment. Thus, the value of SAE is imbued with a self-propagating notion of economic and cultural capital. On the other hand, AAVE is seen as a repudiation of middle-class values and ideologies. It can be viewed as an antihegemonic expression, a deviation from what is considered the standard for corporate, academic, and "cultivated" America. Recognizing that SAE is the model against which other American dialects are measured, we are reminded of Peggy Phelan's assertion that the normative is marked with value. While Phelan considers this in relation to a gender binary, her assertions are equally illuminating when thinking about the presumed racial assignments in which SAE signifies aural whiteness and AAVE signifies aural blackness: "One term of the binary is marked with value, the other is unmarked. The [white] is marked with value; the [black] is unmarked, lacking measured value and meaning."[15]

Likewise, Pierre Bourdieu's exploration of capital—in all its layered forms[16]—also helps to illuminate the inculcated value of *presumed aural whiteness*. Bourdieu writes of the "domestic transmission" of cultural capital; that the opportunity to gain cultural capital is passed on or inherited through intimate relationships. He also recognizes that communal relationships can and do foster their own sense of social significance. There are values associated with (not) being a recognized member of a particular group and, moreover, these social networks are produced and reproduced through various ways—including language.[17] That being said, while AAVE may be considered of little value to members of a white, middle-class, mainstream public, it is not without value; it can, in fact, secure and yield what Bourdieu refers to as *social* capital within an African American community.

The complexity evidenced in the presentation and interpretation of both SAE and AAVE is exemplified by one of the world's most famous living figures: President Barack Obama. Even a brief study of President Obama offers model material for considering how cultural and social capital affects our aural performances, auditory senses, and social reception. As my earlier reference to Michelle Obama suggests, a lot of attention has been paid to the first family's speaking style, as made apparent when it was reported that the Obamas are "very adept at using language to send a quiet message."[18] While I would concur that the Obamas are skilled speakers, I resist the suggestion that their fluid use of language is an exceptional or covert strategy. Rather than being unique, the Obamas' "style shifting" is one of the most common and ubiquitous linguistic practices exercised in various ways by virtually all speakers.

Style shifting is defined as a speaker's ability and/or tendency to shift between different styles of speech within a single language, thereby distinguishing it from *code switching,* which may allude to shifts in style but also refer to the practice of switching between two distinct languages. Uniformly executed across racial and cultural lines, style shifting demonstrates an acute awareness of a speaker's audience, as well as the nature of the performative event. For example, when we talk to our friends our word choices, intonations, or expressions are likely different than those used when we speak with our parents our children, our employees, our boss, or our banker (and the list goes on). We all adjust the way we speak according to who we are speaking to and the nature of our relationship; *we all* style shift. In fact, the inability to do so could certainly be considered a social handicap.

Nevertheless, while the practice of style shifting is well understood in fields such as sociolinguistics, sociology, and performance studies, transparent evidence of its practice in the public sphere is often greeted with overwhelming suspicion—particularly when it is exercised in racialized contexts. This is evidenced in the ways in which Barack Obama's oratorical and casual speech has been interpreted, offering multiple examples of the American public's underacknowledged commitment to, yet apparent discomfort with, perceptions of transracial speech.

One of the earliest news stories about Barack Obama's speech hit the national spotlight in June 2008 when the independent presidential candidate Ralph Nader made the highly problematic assertion that Obama was trying to "talk white" as part of his strategy to win the White House. In an interview with the *Rocky Mountain News,* Nader offered the following opinion about Obama.

> I haven't heard him have a strong crackdown on economic exploitation in the ghettos. Payday loans, predatory lending, asbestos, lead. What's keeping him from doing that? Is it because he wants to talk white? He doesn't want to appear like Jesse Jackson? We'll see all that play out in the next few months and if he gets elected afterwards.[19]

On the most transparent level, Nader uses the phrase "talk white" to express his belief that Obama talks *to* white audiences (versus black audiences) by *not* addressing the concerns that disproportionately affect African Americans.[20] Yet Nader also suggests that talking white is an explicit act of silence and/or renunciation on Obama's part. In phrasing his critique this way, Nader does a disservice to whites by assuming that they would not be concerned or affected by the issues he mentions; he reinforces and perpetuates an accusatory subtext by suggesting that Obama's speaking style signifies a form of communal betrayal; and he even inadvertently conjures common tropes of whiteness by associating Obama's "talking white" with a type of absence. As politically motivated statements, the crafting of Nader's words not only attempt to link the ideology of the Green Party with the interests of minorities, but they also insinuate that Obama's political platform—his social and political values—can be gleaned from the "color" rather than the content of his speech. Framed in this way, Nader echoes the distinctions that are routinely made: talking white is bound to economic interests, while talking black is bound to social interests.

In presenting his problematic assumptions and troubled correlations, Nader also conjectures that Obama "doesn't want to *appear* like Jesse Jackson [emphasis mine]." Nader contrasts Obama against the likes of Jackson, an African American whose Carolina roots, Southern Baptist cadence, and civil rights activism popularly identify him as one who talks black. In doing so, he equates how one talks with how one appears, conspicuously conflating the perception of audible racial cues with the perception of visual racial cues. According to Nader's reading, Obama shapes his speech so as to *appear* whiter than Jesse Jackson. Nader confirmed this in other pointed ways: he previously referred to the future president as "half African-American" and characterized Obama's speaking style as less threatening than those of other black leaders.

> He wants to show that he is not . . . another politically threatening African-American politician. . . . He wants to appeal to white guilt. You appeal to white guilt not by coming on as black is beautiful, black is powerful. Basically he's coming on as someone who is not going to threaten the white power structure, whether it's corporate or whether it's simply oligarchic. And they love it. Whites just eat it up.[21]

While Nader attempted to posit Obama as a mimic man who is "not quite/not white,"[22] others have focused on an entirely different reading of Obama's speaking style by emphasizing the president's bidialecticism.

A flurry of media attention was attached to a seemingly inconsequential incident when the president tossed the casual reply, "Nah, we straight" to the folks behind the counter at DC's landmark fast-food restaurant Ben's Chili Bowl. Politico.com writer Nia-Malika Henderson considered this casual reply an example of the president's "dog-whistle politics," observing that Obama's "language, mannerisms and symbols resonate deeply with his black supporters, even as the references largely sail over the heads of white audiences."[23] Contextualizing the historic impetus for African American style shifting, the cultural critic Mark Anthony Neal notes that

> President Obama is not unique; he is representative of at least three generations of Black Americans who have mastered the practice of switching codes—folk who move fluidly and fluently through multiple linguistic communities, with the understanding that so-called mainstream American vernacular (talking white) was critical for putting Whites—at ill-ease because of their presence in the workplace or other places of business—at ease. Indeed, because we rarely see the "private" Michelle Obama we have little knowledge of how adept her own control of BVE [Black Vernacular English] is, but her husband clearly has more pressure to navigate the tensions between making a nation of folk comfortable and being read as "authentic."[24]

In contrast to Nader's use of the phrase, Neal's reference to "talking white" is presented as a synonym for speaking in SAE, a practice he traces to strategies of survival rather than mere politics. He reminds us that for blacks there was a historical deference for code switching, one that was not simply perpetuated by adherence to the laws of social capital but one that also recognized that the practice could, literally, be a matter of life or death.

This historical legacy has created a peculiar inheritance for many African Americans: an understanding of the need to negotiate the racially designated spheres in which we work and live. As Timothy Douglas suggests, it is this cultural inheritance that can influence African American consciousness, prompting us to reflect on the way our public performances are interpreted as "authentic" within and beyond our communities.

> There's a discomfort with the feeling that somehow we're betraying our authentic selves, particularly when speaking our words within the legacy of dominant culture.... But really, as black people—and by extension, most people of color in this country—we are compelled to fully absorb dominant culture—not only absorb it, but also feed it back in such a way that is deemed authentic, and we must accomplish this merely to survive—not even excel, but simply to survive![25]

Echoing Henderson's reference to authenticity, Douglas's observations point to a more contemporaneous concern with style shifting, one that is raised on both sides of the racial divide: if a speaker shifts between conversational codes, does one of these public performances represent the speaker's "real" persona? Is either mode deemed more culturally authentic?

In wrestling with this query, it must be noted that *cultural authenticity* is an oxymoron. Cultural practices are not discrete or absolute; they are ever changing and always transforming, consistently affected by the passage of time, as well as inevitable interactions and outside influences. Likewise, racialized associations are temporal, contingent on changing historical circumstances and cultural practices. Therefore, no person or practice can legitimately be designated as culturally authentic, original, or pure in form. What *cultural authenticity* can refer to, however, is how a set of performance strategies—particular to a specific time, place, and socialized group—are used as markers of both inclusion and exclusion.

Accordingly, if we bear in mind the oft-cited work of sociologist Erving Goffman, we can consider how the complex notion of authenticity is really about perceptions of power and authority: "Sometimes when we ask whether a fostered impression is true or false we really mean to ask whether or not the performer is authorized to give the performance in question, and are not primarily concerned with the actual performance itself."[26] Regardless of whether these performances are found in the world of entertainment or in presentations of everyday life, Goffman recognizes that *sincerity* is required for the successful delivery of a performance: "If a performance is to come off, the witnesses by and large must be able to believe that the performers are sincere. This is the structural place of sincerity in the drama of events. Performers may be sincere—or be insincere but sincerely convinced of their own sincerity."[27]

In further clarifying the distinction between authenticity and sincerity, cultural anthropologist John L. Jackson Jr. notes how the terms, though related, are often unduly conflated. Inspired by the writings of Lionel Trilling, Jackson writes that authenticity "conjures up images of people, as animate subjects, verifying inanimate objects. Authenticity presupposes this kind of relationship between an independent, thinking subject and a dependent, unthinking thing."[28] As such, Jackson explains how one may judge an *object* to be (in)authentic but one can never pass judgment on whether or not an object is sincere. Rather, he elaborates, "Questions of sincerity imply social interlocutors who presume one another's humanity, interiority, and subjectivity. It is a subject-subject interaction, not the subject-object model that authenticity presumes—and to which critiques of authenticity implicitly reduce every racial exchange."[29] Whereas authenticity addresses the qualitative status of *something*, sincerity privileges the perceived intent of *someone*. An affirmative judgment of sincerity is about perceiving a connection—about forging a sense of rapport, despite the differences that may exist between subjects.

Taken in this light we can see how the notion of sincerity, rather than authenticity, is particularly effective in addressing vocal performance. I would argue that the style shifting of African American subjects, like Barack Obama, models a practice of sincerity. By remaining cognizant of the registers in which one speaks, and adjusting appropriately, a style shifter attempts to forge a connection by speaking a common language, thereby emphasizing the subject-subject interaction Jackson details. As Goffman suggests, the motives behind such an act of sincerity may differ greatly, but this does not erode the fact that sincerity—and a sincere attempt to connect—is at play.

Moreover, I would argue that the practice of style shifting within today's social parameters epitomizes, rather than challenges, the notion of a performer's "real," holistic self. The judicious blending and/or shifting between SAE and AAVE is a unique identificatory marker, not only intimating that a speaker has benefited from the educational opportunities generally associated with middle or upper classes, but also revealing a personal ideology in that it testifies to the way an individual chooses to embrace nuances of African American cultural expression. When middle- and upper-class speakers utilize elements of AAVE in addition to (or intermingled with) SAE, it "indicates their social class or educational background without obscuring ethnic identity in their speech."[30] This bidialecticism is a profound representation of the historical and social realities of African Americans, one shaped by a common desire to gain both cultural and social capital within the community at large, as well as a desire to possess and maintain social capital within black communities.

The ability to shift between AAVE and SAE exhibits a sense of freedom that is awarded through a combination of communal exposure, social privilege, and scholarly training. The decision to oscillate between talking white and talking black in the public sphere, with relatively little concern as to how such linguistic choices will impact one's public reception or livelihood, speaks to the tremendous advances in post-civil-rights America, most notably our changing valuations of racialized identities. Obama's public exercise of bidialecticism reveals a greater, yet not uncontested, freedom from historic forms of racialized subjugation and prejudice because this freedom is still contingent on a speaker's *ability* to communicate using the rules and expectations of SAE. Beyond grammatical modes or lexical choices, however, there is yet another element in this mix: judgments as to whether or not someone talks white (or talks black) are also made in relation to *sound*.

TALKING TIMBRE: THE PHENOMENON OF RACIAL SYNESTHESIA

In referencing how someone *talks*, the onus is generally on the speaker, alluding to the way one employs a given language to convey one's thoughts and intentions. On the other hand, to note how someone *sounds* not only alludes to the style in which the language is transmitted but also how the texture of a speaker's sonic emissions are received and interpreted by a listening audience.

In returning to this chapter's central line of inquiry regarding the presumed value—and discernible characteristics—of aural whiteness, it is useful to reinforce the fact that this is not a biological or physiological query but rather a phenomenological one. I am attempting to explore the sensational: how we *perceive* differences between human subjects in an effort to understand the world around us. This exercise in cataloging people is an enduring human tradition; however, in terms of how we use our senses to assign racial designations, the sense of *sight* has garnered most of our scholarly attention. A notable exception is Mark M. Smith's *How Race Is Made: Slavery, Segregation, and the Senses* (2006).

Chronicling how white southerners used the "common knowledge" of their senses (not only their visual sense, but also their senses of smell, touch, taste, and sound) to construct and proliferate the belief in racial difference, Smith's work demonstrates how "non-visual senses often indexed viscera and emotion more than thought and reason."[31] Most of us can rely on personal, experiential evidence to support this assertion; we know how a flood of memories can overwhelm us with the taste of a favorite food, how the scent of a familiar cologne can coax a smile (or a frown) to our lips, or how the sound of an old-school jam can bring forth an inner exuberance that had previously lain dormant. These examples help demonstrate how our senses—in their capacity to trigger and capitalize on our emotions rather than stimulate our logic—can be used as persuasive factors when paired with ideological constructs.

Recognizing the need to come "to terms with the historical construction of race in all its forms and in all its senses," Smith's study attempts to decenter Americans' "ocularcentrism"—that is, our insistence that visuality is a superior sense to those of sound, taste, and smell.[32] Highlighting the way theorists and historians generally address the concept of race (even in terms of its disavowal) as a *visual* phenomenon, Smith argues that "the preference for 'seeing' race is as much a social construction" as the very idea of race itself, explicating how race has been constructed as something that can be smelled, tasted, and heard, *as well as* seen.[33] According to Smith, it was the threat and fact of racial passing that forcefully prompted whites to create additional ways to assign blackness when the visual evidence proved insufficient. With this development, popular knowledge held that "becoming visually whiter did not necessarily entail a dilution of the other sensory characteristics" and that blackness "was always vulnerable to sensory detection."[34]

The rules of this multisensory racial detection in the nineteenth and twentieth centuries were not always consistent (in fact, Smith offers many contradictory accounts of so-called evidence), but some of the more frequently cited assertions were that the scent of blackness was generously odorous, the feel of black skin was tough to the touch (making black people especially suitable for arduous labor), and blackness was also identifiable in subtleties of speech. As for the latter, those of African ancestry who were most successful at passing for white were those who (1) were able to keep quiet or (2) had the ability to speak with a "quick smoothness" or "sartorial elegance" uncommon to their life's station; in other words, they could "talk white."[35] In support of racist logic, little consideration was given to the fact that opportunity, in the form of education and class, informs and influences the ways in which speech is presented and interpreted. Rather than fully recognizing how vocal performance reflects the markers of access and social status, it was far more convenient (and, perhaps, more comforting) for southern whites to adhere to the belief that the sound of blackness was determined by inherent, biological differences.

Smith's focus on the senses—in tandem with the countless, ubiquitous assumptions applied to black speakers, past and present—prompts considerations beyond the issue of "talking white" to also draw attention to the sensation associated with "sounding white." But this necessitates a shared understanding of vocal qualities that cannot be adequately described in terms of grammar, articulation, or lexical itemization. How can one define or explain, for example, what the African American linguist John McWhorter refers to as the cadence of the "black-ccent . . . the subtle vocal quality that makes most black Americans identifiable as black over the phone,"[36] which in McWhorter's view, "conveys warmth, authenticity and a touch of seductive danger"?[37]

Acknowledging that the identifiable elements of the black-ccent are a "hazy concept in people's minds," McWhorter seems to be referring to what many scholars call "timbre." Although timbre is widely acknowledged as a significant vocal quality, the ethnomusicologist Cornelia Fales echoes McWhorter when she readily concedes that timbre is a "slippery concept and a slippery percept, perceptually malleable and difficult to define in precisely arranged units."[38] Elaborating on this lack of specificity, Fales writes:

> We have a peculiar amnesia in regard to timbre, but we're not deaf to timbre: we hear it, we use it—no one has much trouble telling instruments apart—but we have no language to describe it. With no domain-specific adjectives, timbre must be described in metaphor or by analogy to other senses, and this is true in many, many languages of the world.[39]

Timbre may be difficult to name and define, yet Fales provides a very useful and concise way of understanding it: "[T]imbre is a condition; pitch and loudness are things a sound *does*, timbre is what a sound *is*."[40] Similarly, John Putenbaugh writes, "*Timbre* refers to the perceptual quality of sounds," explaining that it is "*not* an inherent component of a sound, but rather, as an overall quality it is an attribute of *sensation*."[41]

After referring to both Fales and Putenbaugh, musicologist Nina Sun Eidsheim expands on the aforementioned definitions in her own work on "racialized timbre." Eidsheim acknowledges that there are corporeal differences that impact timbral quality, but, she explains, these variations are *not* racially distinctive. There are no morphological differences that indicate one's so-called racial identity.[42] Furthermore, as routinely asserted by *contemporary* vocal specialists, the differences we hear between individual vocal performances are real but not physiologically based.[43]

Among the factors that *do* affect vocal characteristics are elements that have nothing to do with the material nature of our bodily selves. Drawing on his training as a Linklater coach and vocal pedagogue, Timothy Douglas affirms this understanding when addressing the ways we apply our vocal instruments.

> If there's ever a time where one is not speaking with and through their natural voice—at its basic level it's because of habitual physical tension.

> The body has the capacity to hold onto an enormous amount of physical tension. Physical tension is nothing more than lost thought. What I mean by that is if an impulse to communicate and to share myself unleashes within me, and for whatever reason a thought comes in that says, "Don't say that" or "don't respond THAT way," the energy of the original impulse—precisely because I don't express it—doesn't go away. It remains a very real, live, living, "breathing" thing. The energy of that thought impulse literally lodges in the musculature of my body, which enfolds it and holds onto it. That's physical tension. That's basically and primarily what physical tension is—trapped or "lost" thought. There is, of course, more physiological detail that goes along with this thesis.... I just gave you a three-hour lecture in four sentences![44]

Coming from the related, yet distinct, worlds of theatre and music, the reflections of Douglas, Miller, and Eidsheim reinforce the same conclusion: on the most fundamental level, perceived vocal differences reflect how one uses one's instrument. While everyone is capable of expressing a range of sounds, individuals typically limit their own vocal performances by not exercising the full potential of their range. As Eidsheim succinctly summarizes, "The timbral differences we perceive are differences in style rather than in corporeally determined timbral destiny."[45]

Eidsheim's work on racialized timbre and vocal performance informs and echoes my own investigation into our auditory assumptions regarding the sound of speech in relation to racial identity.[46] Grounding her research in musical technology, as well as the operatic and contemporary musical performances of African American artists, Eidsheim attempts to decipher and derail our habitual tendency to name vocal performances in racialized terms.[47] She does this in two distinct but interrelated ways. She illustrates how the timbral expressions of black vocalists are often "choreographed" to satisfy the expectations of both music pedagogues and a consuming public, and she argues that the images of black operatic singers are further marketed to perpetuate the notion of an inherently "black" sound. By defining and distinguishing between the "timbre sonic" (the *sound of singing*) and the "timbre corporeal" (*the physical act* of forming the timbre sonic), Eidsheim creates concepts that can also be applied to the realm of speech. Suggesting that singers choreograph their vocal timbre (or have it choreographed for them through their training process), she directly addresses the intentionality and performative nature of vocal expressions and the subsequent issues of audience expectation and reception. Yet, notably, Eidsheim also proposes that the voice has a reciprocal effect on our readings of corporeal identities. Asserting that "vocal timbre is the sound of a habitual performance that has shaped the physical body," she proposes that vocal timbre influences how one, consciously and unconsciously, carries one's body and/or performs one's social self.[48]

All this further demonstrates that racialized voices are recognized, in part, by means of their affective nature—that is, by their seemingly visceral ability to produce an emotional, versus logical, response among listeners. Parsing the nature of these vocal sounds reminds us that once we move beyond objective linguistic markers (denoted by factors such vocabulary, syntax, or dialect) we begin to wander into a phenomenological terrain that provokes sensations and feelings rather than prescriptive evaluations. Such recognition reinforces the highly performative nature of these subjective associations and suggests the cultural investment contemporary American audiences still have in racializing vocal performance. While we might not be overtly conscious of these determinations when we hear them, we need to understand how we have been conditioned to hear sonic difference as indicative of racial difference among people—the latter having an unquestionable impact on both human relations and artistic products.

Given the historical and social factors that contribute to our imaginings of racial difference and our habitual conflation of sight and sound, I'm drawn to the neurological phenomenon of "synesthesia." In its clinical sense, *synesthesia* (from *syn*, meaning "together," and *esthesia*, meaning "perceiving") is understood as "the elicitation of perceptual experiences in the absence of the normal sensory stimulation."[49] The scientific researcher and art scholar, Cretien van Campen, notes that the legendary Greek philosopher Aristotle (384 BCE–322 CE) was among the first thinkers to recognize that, while human sensory perception must be understood in discrete ways, our senses of taste, touch, sound, smell, and sight can work together to create a unified sensory experience. According to van Campen:

> [Aristotle] assumed the existence of what came to be called a *sensis communis*, which perceives the common qualities (or qualia) in the different exterior senses. . . . For instance, we perceive brightness, rhythm, and intensity in images, sounds, smells, odors, and tactile sensations. (By the way, our notion of *common sense*, though the modern definition is slightly different, nonetheless is derived from this concept.)[50]

What is particularly notable about van Campen's research in relation to this study is his assertion that synesthetic sensibilities are not just "hardwired" in synesthetes, but they also develop through social and/or cultural factors.[51] Such a paradigmatic shift offers us the ability to borrow the neuroscientific term *synesthesia* and apply its basic premise to what I am referring to as *racial synesthesia*.[52] In so doing, I am furthering the application of synesthesia as suggested in Alice Maurice's study of the synchronization of race and sound in early cinema.[53]

In her study of African American representation in early talkies, Maurice demonstrates how the pairing of black bodies and "black voices" was received as a particularly effective example of the new sound technology. She notes that this visual-audio pairing invariably highlighted "a kind of synesthesia already at work in the representation and perception of race." Conjuring the *Oxford English Dictionary*'s definition of *color-sound synesthesia* ("When the hearing of an external sound carries with it, by some arbitrary association of ideas, the seeing of some form or color"), Maurice asserts that the "presumed perceptual link between color and sound" in the early talkies "offers the exemplary instance of synesthesia—a sensory wire-crossing helped along by imagination and the 'arbitrary association of ideas.'"[54]

While racial synesthesia is a product of our race-conscious culture, it appears that the sense of sound is particularly vulnerable to synesthetic conflation, a fact exhibited by the very way sound is "colored" in and through language. Vocal descriptions are repeatedly offered in terms that suggest a visual presentation, a fact that Eidsheim underscores when she observes how African American voices in classical music are frequently described as having a "full, heavy, broad and dark sound" while, conversely, the soubrette soprano is described as having a "light, lyrical, and slender voice type."[55] In such instances, words such as "broad" and "dark" versus "light" and "slender" suggest color as well size and shape—all of which can relate back to racialized imagery. Acknowledging the way we are seemingly bound by our habitual use of this language, Eidsheim affirms how "listening is formed through such descriptive terms. As a result of the use of language constituted by descriptive terms that lump together racialized bodies and vocal timbral qualities, categories are engendered, cultivated, and reified."[56]

Perpetuated and reinforced through the discourse of sound and the development of sound technology, the phenomenon of racial synesthesia is a potent example of society's ocularcentrism, demonstrating how what we *see* affects how we *hear*. According to Fales, this is to be expected in that there are various external factors that shape our auditory perception, visual stimuli being one of the most influential. In the process of hearing, and learning to hear, our brain classifies sounds and their apparent sources, creating an archive of audible cues that are categorized, in great part, according to timbre. We use these cues to recognize and understand our environment, but these classifications are only the brain's "best guess"—they do not accurately map the nature of sounds or the origins of their source.[57] From this we can see how racial synesthesia works similarly to Fales's broader notion of perceptualization, which she defines as "the process by which necessary interpretive elements are identified, created, and combine with acoustic properties of the environment to create auditory percepts."[58] Furthering her explication of perceptualization, Fales writes:

> [The] auditory system does indeed identify sources, but it identifies a version of the sources that may not always coincide with the version existing in the physical world. Instead, it perceives sources according to its own expectations, sources that are consistent with similar sources identified in the past, or that have characteristics typical to an environment. . . . The paradox exists because however different the perceived version of a source might be to the physical signal it represents, it is a version that works in our world, it is a version that is consistent with versions of other listeners, it is "real" enough that it allows us to deal with the physical environment.[59]

Racial synesthesia fulfills the tenets of perceptualization: we create and maintain the racial character assignments that supposedly correlate with audible scripts because as long as they remain unchallenged they "work"; they are sanctioned, via repeatable, performative acts, as "'real' enough" to give us a (false) sense of order in our world.

Although we may recognize how the phenomenon of racial synesthesia comes to be, we are still left to consider how the audible aspects of these social scripts are transcribed and translated. While it is common practice to describe the visual signatures of whiteness, what descriptors adequately name the qualifications for *sounding* (versus simply talking) white? If timbre describes a sound's effect or sensation rather than its essence, what are some of the characteristics employed to perform or presume aural whiteness?

PERFORMING LINGUISTIC WHITEFACE VERSUS PRESUMED AURAL WHITENESS

To understand the hazy characteristics of presumed aural whiteness, it is important to recognize that linguistic whiteface and the presumption of aural whiteness are not one and the same. The term *linguistic whiteface*, as I am conceiving it here, is meant to address the various elements (word choice, grammar and syntax, timbre, phonetics, etc.) that actors and comedians manipulate in order to consciously *perform* whiteness. In discussing *presumed aural whiteness*, I am emphasizing the presumption of its association with whiteness; I am commenting on its perceived qualities and insubstantiality. Thus, I am distinguishing between the ways performers consciously manipulate their voices to signify whiteness and the way one speaks in everyday life. In doing so, I am disrupting the facile connection between presumed aural whiteness and the problematic assertions of talking white or acting white. In the latter case, there is the conceptual undercurrent that the manner and mode of speech are proprietary objects of white bodies, borrowed and/or usurped by nonwhite bodies (a similar suggestion is made in relation to *whiteface minstrelsy*, as mentioned in the introduction to this volume). Both linguistic whiteface and the acknowledgment of presumed aural whiteness exploit and disempower this belief system, albeit in very different ways.

Presumed aural whiteness, represented as the standard style of speech and proliferated through all forms of media, is habitually framed as recognizable, accessible, and relatable. The constant transmission of presumed aural whiteness positions it as the inner voice of the public en masse—an acoustic proxy for our collective consciousness. As such, it is routinely employed to impress on its listeners an aura of inclusiveness in that it bears no distinguishing marks. On the contrary, however, *presumed aural blackness* is experienced as more distinct and particularized in that it fosters imaginings of both race and class; it is heard as more rigid and fixed, bound by the perceptions that harness it.

Linguistic whiteface, on the other hand, actually brings hypervisibility (or hyper*audibility*) to aural whiteness by accentuating false precepts regarding racial difference. A successful portrayal of linguistic whiteface requires the audience to be aware that it is, typically, a non-white body that is audibly performing so-called whiteness. In doing so, linguistic whiteface engages as a form of disidentification, aurally articulating the popularized view that whites and blacks necessarily speak differently. Yet the presentation of linguistic whiteface simultaneously reveals the black body's inherent ability to create "white sounds," therefore further demonstrating that any white-bodied proprietary claim on aural whiteness is a faulty one.

When linguistic whiteface is enacted in formal performance, it is frequently presented in comedic genres in which actors and comedians (exemplified by the likes of Richard Pryor, Eddie Murphy, or Dave Chappelle) take on a white persona that is distinguished by nasal-based, high-pitched, and/or overly enunciated speech. As one may expect, when these stylings are portrayed by men they often play off common stereotypes related to black masculinity in order to posit their equally exaggerated impressions of white masculinity. The nasal-based tone suggests a tense, physical awkwardness; the high pitch hints at relative femininity; while the overenunciation alludes to hyperintellectualism. Thus, if one were to assume that the reverse traits represent black masculinity, we are left with familiar and equally daunting stereotypes, which, in the simplest terms, designate black men as highly developed corporeal creatures whose strengths reside in their brawn rather than their brains.

Of course, the sounds of whiteness are not limited to these characteristics. For example, the supposed whiteness of a character may also be marked by an exaggerated southern accent in order to suggest the presence or inheritance of a Confederate ideology or, in the case of female characterizations, to intimate the presence of a hapless southern belle (both accents purposefully signifyin(g) on the history of the American South and its troubled race relations). Linguistic whiteface may also be expressed in other gendered ways. The comic portrayals of white women by black comedians may also take on a Valley Girl quality (as famously performed by Whoopi Goldberg) or the vocal portrayal of a young white woman may aim to suggest an equally vacuous—yet highly privileged—socialite (as enacted by the Wayans brothers in the Paris and Nicky Hilton–inspired film *White Chicks*).

While these vocal stylings are among the most current and readily identifiable ways in which black performers enact linguistic whiteface, there are innumerable ways in which whiteness may be aurally cued by the speech patterns of black performers. However, unlike linguistic whiteface—an act that is contingent on it being portrayed by bodies that carry the visual signatures of blackness—presumed aural whiteness is not dependent on *visible* bodies at all. That being said, it is precisely when speakers of presumed aural whiteness are identified as black that aural whiteness is exposed for what it is: a perception based on our habitual racial synesthesia. However, this type of exposure does not frequently occur, and there are mediated performances that seemingly depend on the unquestioned acceptance of disembodied, presumed aural whiteness; among them is the field of advertising.

As a genre, advertising serves as a unique barometer of our values and ideologies, for commercials are unabashedly and unapologetically race conscious by design. The promotional propaganda we receive is not always fact based, yet it is always created to appeal to our emotions and senses. Commercials strategically employ racial and cultural signatures to appeal to specific demographics; however, their frequent use of *dis*embodied voices also creates unparalleled opportunities for those involved in the field to make innovative choices in terms of vocal casting. Inspired by the possibilities that may arise through these abbreviated performances on the small screen, this chapter now turns to a crucial query: how can the purposeful casting of disembodied voices create, perpetuate, or *disrupt* racial synesthesia?

DISENTANGLING RACIAL SYNESTHESIA: CASTING NEW VOICES, HEARING NEW IDENTITIES

It is common practice for commercials to use the voices of actors *not* featured in the camera's visual frame. Identifying the sounds that are heard but not seen as *acousmatic*, the cinema scholar Michel Chion asserts, "When the acousmatic presence is a voice, and especially when this voice has not yet been visualized—that is, when we cannot yet connect it to a face—we get a special being, a kind of talking and acting shadow to which we attach the name *acousmetre*."[60] One notable *acousmetre* is the actress, comedian, and *CBS News Sunday Morning* contributor Nancy Giles. Giles is one of the few African American performers to consistently crossover in national commercial spots, thereby offering a number of well-recognized examples of *acousmetre* work within advertising. Her voice has been used for companies and products such as such as the *New York Times*, Folgers Coffee, Office Depot, Yoplait, True Value, Philip Morris USA, Motorola, Neighborhood Health Plan, Boniva, and GlaxoSmithKline, among many others. Yet, despite the great success Giles has experienced as a voice-over artist, she can also attest to how the tendency toward racial synesthesia presents unique challenges for black artists.

When Giles got her first "big break" as Private Frankie Bunsen on the Vietnam War–centered television show *China Beach* (1988–91), she had every right to believe that her newfound exposure would help catapult her growing voice-over career.

> [I had] started hearing that more celebrities, more people that were on TV, were beginning to get lucrative offers, and I thought—wow, I'm on this show, and if I put my picture on my demo tape, when that gets to an ad agency, they'd go—"Oh, it's the girl from *China Beach*," and maybe I'll generate more work. Well, what happened was, once I put my picture on my demo tape, all of a sudden, the wide variety of auditions that I was going on sort of stopped. And when I was in L.A., I was getting sent out basically for *Colt 45* and hair relaxers.[61]

Nevertheless, Giles's voice-over agency, (CESD), persisted in sending her on a wide range of auditions. With emphatic appreciation, the actress and comedian stresses how important this was to her career: "I love them so deeply and am so indebted to them for somehow having the idea that I could do a lot of things; they didn't ghettoize me, even when it could be easy to do that." Rather, CESD kept the possibilities for Giles open, sending her on casting calls for both black and white actors.

This is not to say that Giles's crossover ambitions were met without any resistance. In fact, some of the resistance she felt emanated from her fellow actors. Ever the comic, Giles manages to reflect on these experiences with an abundance of levity, exposing both the frustration and the humor in delimiting perceptions of blackness.

> It was interesting back in the late '80s, because I was one of the few black voice-over people or black actors that would sometimes go for these "general market" voice-over spots, which, back then, meant white, or what people would recognize as a white voice. But CESD would send me on those things. What I loved sometimes was going into the waiting room and seeing the white voice-over girls kind of look at me and look at each other, and then attempt to be helpful by saying to me, "Are you sitting in the right place, because I think these are the auditions for *Camay*. I think *Ultra Sheen* is actually down the hall." And I'd say, "No, you know, actually I'm here for Camay." And I would think (*playful laughter*), "And I'm going to get it too, bitch."[62]

Perhaps what makes Giles's anecdotes even more comical is the fact that her career is quite extraordinary, built from commercials for Crisco Oil (which centered on the topic of fried chicken), to the "general market" gigs that the *Camay* girls thought were destined for their voices alone. What is particularly intriguing to me is how Giles's voice is received in the "general market" commercials, especially those which use Giles's voice *layered over* images of white actors.

Initially airing on May 29, 2007, The GlaxoSmithKline commercial "Consequences" epitomizes this type of layering. It begins by offering an extreme close-up of a middle-aged white man's blue-gray eyes, then quickly changes to reveal the man's full face. The man begins speaking with a regionally demarcated northeastern accent: "My doctor said my type 2 diabetes was out of control (*the camera reveals the man's hands—he's wearing a wedding ring*), that high blood sugar increased my risk of serious complications. He said I better diet, exercise, take my medicine. (*Thoughtful chuckle.*) Yeah, yeah, I heard it all before. Well, (*big sigh*) maybe I should have listened." (*The man stands up and prepares his walking cane. It is clear that he has lost his sight as he begins to walk away.*) It is at this point that Nancy Giles's voice-over begins: "Every year up to twenty-four thousand people lose their eyesight to diabetes. Even more are at risk for stroke, heart attack, and limb loss. If you have high blood sugar, get help. Call or visit diabetes.com." (*The camera lingers on the empty, bodiless chair.*) Fittingly, the "Consequences" commercial ends with a haunting and suggestive absence, visually echoing the absence of Giles's own bodily presence.

Around the same time that the "Consequences" commercial began airing, Giles was also heard in a series of commercials, starring Sally Field, for the osteoporosis medication Boniva. While Field's celebrity and personal battle against osteoporosis makes her a fitting spokesperson for Boniva, she is also a perfect representative of the manufacturer's targeted demographic: a postmenopausal white woman.[63] The latter fact is clearly noted during the commercial, which begins with Field sitting on a bed: "I feel great, really great, even with osteoporosis. And you know what, deciding on a treatment with my doctor was almost easier than deciding what to wear tonight." At this point, a line of small print displayed on the screen notes that being "Caucasian or Asian" is among the high-risk factors for osteoporosis.

When Giles launches into her voice-over, she recites a rider that abounds with legalese: "Unlike weekly treatments like Fosamax, you only need Boniva once a month. . . . You should not take Boniva if you have low blood calcium, severe kidney disease, or cannot sit or stand for at least sixty minutes. Follow dosing instructions carefully. Stop taking Boniva and tell your doctor if you experience difficult or painful swallowing, chest pain, or severe or continuing heartburn as these may be signs of serious upper digestive problems." Following the necessary disclaimer, Field's monologue continues: "Look, having strong, healthy bones is *so* important. I've got this one body and this one life, so I'm going to do my best to get it right." With a visual text that reaffirms Field's assertion (the words "one body" appear and then fade to reveal "one life"), the Boniva commercial wittily reiterates the product's trademark phrase: "There's only one." While there may be only one Boniva, there is more than one body contributing to the collage of sounds and images that work together to create the product's televised advertisement.

Another compelling example of this "interracial layering" of voices and bodies can be found in the work of the African American actress and voice-over artist Rayme Cornell. As a professional actor, Cornell's voice work has been heard in commercials for nationally recognized products such as L'Oréal, Ford, Dunkin' Donuts, Cingular, Lifetime, WE, Oxygen Network, USA Network, MTV, VH1, BET, ESPN, the History Channel, and the Discovery Channel. Although Cornell considers the fact that her (white) adoptive parents may have influenced her racially indeterminate sound, she primarily attributes her ability to secure a wide range of voice-over work to her rigorous master of fine arts acting training. And, like Nancy Giles, Cornell credits her forward-thinking agents as the major reason why she frequently crosses the racial divide established in voice-over commercials. During our interview, she was emphatic about this last point.

> It's true ... if you can sound black *and* white you can book more across the border ... [but] agents send you out according to the call. They need to change their minds in terms of representation. I was very lucky to be mentored well. Ninety percent of the stuff I get, on the national network, isn't race specific, but advertising *is* so racially and target specific.[64]

Cornell confirmed this further by sharing a personal anecdote. For six years she served as a voice for the Republican Party. "For some reason," she said, "my voice appealed to the Christian coalition Republican sentiment." Cornell's representation of the Republican Party started with one commercial, and it went over so well that she continued to voice ads for more and more

Republican campaigns, for senators, mayors, and even presidential candidates. After six years of being "the voice" of major campaigns, she was finally asked (over the telephone) to audition for an on-camera public service announcement, at which point she asked the agency's casting director, "You've never seen a picture of me, have you?" While the two were still on the phone, Rayme faxed her headshot to the agent and soon heard hysterical laughter from the other end. Needless to say, she didn't get the audition for the public service spot.[65]

Cornell provides a fruitful example through which to consider the economics of opportunity. It is generally understood that if a casting call does not specify a racial identity (and the majority of calls do not) then the casting director is seeking a white actor—and few agents will "think outside the box" and send an actor of color. Moreover, her experience vividly demonstrates the frailty of our assumptions regarding vocal qualities and physical embodiment. While both Cornell and Giles have secured a number of major, mainstream commercial accounts, they have done so because of the atypical openness and proactivity of their agents. And since the vocal performances of Giles and Cornell are accompanied by images of white bodies and are not noticeably marked with qualities readily associated with African American expression, can we conclude that these artistic opportunities disrupt our racial synesthesia and—dare I ask—represent a "postracial" ideology?

Certainly, there has been a notable increase in transracial vocal work, one that mirrors the increasing representation of minoritized figures in stage, film, and cinema. Yet one also suspects that there is a significant amount of transracial voice work that speaks more profoundly to the goals of standardization rather than attempting to promote the perception of intercultural fusion or challenge ideas of racial distinctions. Even if a listener detects the differences between the vocal qualities of the voice-over actress and the actors on the screen, the fact remains that the voice-overs of Giles and Cornell are inextricably linked, visually, to the commercials' white actors. According to Chion, such a circumstance prompts a subliminal merging of sight and sound. He asserts that spectators automatically associate the aural qualities they hear with the images they see on the screen, and that, in so doing, the sounds—including voices—"can be immediately 'swallowed up' in the image's false depth, or relegated to the periphery of the visual field."[66] In other words, the audible elements are ultimately conflated (or, rather, usurped) by their accompanying visual images.

Conversely, it is intriguing to think of how a notably marked-as-black voice would be read and interpreted in contrast to the more ambiguous vocal performances of Giles and Cornell. How would audiences interpret an *acousmetre* who, through the use of AAVE or timbral textures, fulfills our expectations of a "black sound?" How would we receive this script of authority and knowledge against the commercials' visual representations of white embodiment? Could an obvious difference between the two types of representation—the visual and the aural—suggest that we, as black and white Americans, share more than we differ? Would the frequent use of such a visual-aural collage help to deconstruct racial synesthesia? Or would it simply create an unsettling and unexpected dissonance, one that highlights the actual artifice (and thus the biased economic interests) of the commercial and its engineers?

It is the imagining of new possibilities that law professor and cultural theorist Patricia J. Williams undertook in 1999 when she famously wrote on the topic of "racial ventriloquism." Joining the bevy of critics and viewers who scrutinized the 1999 film *Star Wars Episode 1: The Phantom Menace*, Williams rightly critiqued the vocal theatrics of a number of characters, most notably that of Jar Jar Binks. Jar Jar Binks, voiced by the African American actor and musician, Ahmed Best, was described by *The Wall Street Journal*'s Joe Morgenstern as a "Rastafarian Stepin Fetchit on platform hoofs, crossed annoyingly with Butterfly McQueen."[67] Brent Staples of the *New York Times* also wrote of the film's problematic characterizations.

> The main trouble centers on Jar Jar Binks, a digitalized alien who speaks in an exaggerated West Indian patois and lopes along in a combination shuffle and pimp walk. Binks is by far the stupidest person in the film. His simple-minded devotion to his (white) Jedi masters has reminded people of Hollywood's most offensive racial stereotypes."[68]

A deluge of similar critiques followed the debut of *The Phantom Menace*; however, it was Patricia J. Williams's article in the *Nation* that was the first to frame the film's vocal performances in terms of racial ventriloquism.[69] Although Williams's primary target is Jar Jar Binks, her artful analysis deconstructs a wide array of the stereotypical physical, racial, and ethnic vocal cues embedded throughout *The Phantom Menace*. With unrelenting insight, she lays bare the disparaging allusions made to blacks, Asians, Jews, and Arabs, as well as the sense of nobility and civility the film awards to both Jedi knights and enslaved whites.

The use of racial ventriloquism in *The Phantom Menace* epitomizes how distasteful this performative practice *can* be, yet racial/ethnic ventriloquism—though riddled with potential land mines—is not inherently problematic if executed with awareness, sensitivity, and skill. Nevertheless, the practice of racial ventriloquism often escapes critique, resistance, or attention—regardless of the quality or intentions of the performance. While protests against the *visible* blacking, browning, or yellowing of actors to portray a "racial other" quickly become viral in our contemporary times, the practice of racial or ethnic ventriloquism often goes unaddressed, thereby revealing western society's emphasis on the visual over the audible.[70] In addressing the dearth of resistance to "authentic dubbing" practices in the media, Angela Pao observes that the dubbing of ethnic voices, regardless of how exaggerated, receives relatively little attention from advocacy groups and other concerned parties because "the general public almost never knows when cross-cultural vocal impersonations are taking place." Moreover, Pao notes that in general such dubbing is utilized to convey the notion of ethnic versus racial difference, the former inducing far less controversy than the ever-explosive and polarizing issue of racial representation.[71]

After explicating the problematic ways in which *The Phantom Menace* engages in racial ventriloquism, Williams closes her observations by offering some compelling artistic queries. She wonders about the worldwide marketing of the film and whether or not the accents of the characters (and their racialized meanings) will be "translated" into other tongues. She also offers an intriguing conjecture: "[W]hat would it have taken to have used computer-generated voices, let's say—to create comic effects or menace or innocence by a mixture of accents and tones and inflections and images that were not at the expense of historically demonized groups?"[72] In raising such questions, Williams proposes a rethinking of nonconforming and cross-cultural casting in relation to vocal performance.

When the issue of nonconforming casting gained critical momentum in the mid-1980s, it was referenced as "nontraditional casting" and it championed the casting "of ethnic and female performers in roles where race, ethnicity, or gender are not germane to the character's or play's development."[73] As implied by this statement, the discourse surrounding nonconforming casting has primarily addressed the notion that the visual aspect of actors should not be a limiting factor in casting decisions. As we continue to explore the possibilities made available by casting choices, it might serve us well to consider the possibilities of nonconforming casting in terms of vocal spectrums, in addition to concerns of embodied representation. This means interrogating and challenging audiences' phenomenological responses to varying vocal qualities by going against the expectations prescribed by our habit of racial synesthesia. In doing so, performances may benefit from unexpected aural textures, offering us ways to reenvision others and ourselves by opening the ways in which we *hear* dramatic characters. The possibility of casting new voices and hearing new characters begins, first and foremost, in training—the vocal training of professional actors, as well as the way casting agents are trained to hear and find meaning in vocal presentations. As Rayme Cornell insists, "Until you change the mind-set of the agent or person representing you, things won't change."[74]

Similarly, we need to consider the ways in which actors' formal training affects the cycle of expectations in professional spheres. Reflecting on his training at the Yale Drama School, Timothy Douglas cited the dueling pressures that actors of color—and their more progressive teachers—felt when it came to creating a balance between cultural sensitivity and the traditions of their acting program.

> I do remember it was a source of tension in the formal training by the time I got to Yale Drama School. While we did not believe there was an overt intention of suppression from our all-white faculty, we did sometimes feel that we were being made to "sound white"—or to "get rid of our blackness." This was not discussed up front, but when we stopped to think about it, it's what we were left to determine for ourselves. Our instructors at Yale were very empathetic when those issues were brought up and were willing to have, and encouraging of, the conversation, but they were at a loss as how to move beyond the established system, because they had to get us accomplished at "Standard American (stage) Speech" by the time I got out of there. We were there for classical training, after all—a classical European aesthetic in origin, which held little regard of being inclusive of where we came from.[75]

And while such a reflection may strike some as being representative of a problem of representation, Douglas is quick to point out that such a dilemma also gave birth to professional opportunities that may have proved far richer than those presented to students whose speech was already associated with presumed aural whiteness.

> Now fast-forward to almost thirty years later and what I've come to appreciate about my training. I used to look at my time and training as being filled with the gaining of all kinds of Eurocentric creative capabilities that would go wasted on a black American man. However, I've come to realize that by being "forced" to work consistently outside of my cultural comfort zone, I actually received a far more comprehensive and diverse education than my white counterparts—who were rarely, if ever, asked to engage in the exploration in such an expansive way.[76]

Douglas's pointed words again conjure the value of bidialecticism, not only as a value of social or cultural capital but also as a factor in economic opportunities—one that inevitably ensures *professional* survival.

As a professional artist, the ways in which Douglas shapes his voice have been paramount in the opportunities he has accessed. Similarly, the ability to style shift, through the way one *talks* as well as the way one *sounds*, has also been instrumental to actors such as Rayme Cornell and Nancy Giles. And strikingly, while this fluency has created opportunities for them, it has also made them privy to the fact that agents and directors still insist on categorizing their talents along racial lines. In fact Giles recounts how some of her most egregiously offensive experiences transpired when she was working with black-owned agencies.

> It's a funny thing with them because over the years I have tried to push the envelope and put more of me *as me* in the spots, and tried—without saying anything—to broaden what I feel like could be their idea of how a black person sounds. I'll tell you what: they always rein me right back into, you know, "Give it more of that mmph, mmph," "More urban," "More street," "Can you give me some mm-mm-mm?" One person did this wild snapping: "I need some *snap, snap, snap, snap*—you know, give it more snazz, give it more flava!" Or sometimes: "You know what we want, you know, we want the–*girlfriend!*" I'll do it, but in a way it always makes my heart sink a little bit because I think, "You know, everybody doesn't sound that way you guys, and we could really be expanding things; we can help change perceptions if you start doing things a little differently." But then what'll happen is—this is how deeply rooted the stereotypes go—if you try something that's a little different, people say, "Why do they have white people on the black radio station? I don't want a white person doing these ads." It's like, oh my gosh![77]

And so, as with everything, nothing is simply black or white. What the experiences of everyday people, as well as the experiences of professional artists such as Timothy Douglas, Rayme Cornell, and Nancy Giles, accentuate is the persistence of blacks and whites alike to perpetuate expectations of difference in any manner of seen and *unseen* ways.

One speculates, then, about the artistic possibilities that might arise if such expectations are routinely challenged. How can the formal vocal training that actors receive interrogate rather than recapitulate static notions of what sounds should be coming from which bodies? And how might that enrich the training of all involved? Moreover, how can we take up Giles's charge and start doing things "a little differently" by having the artistic (and fiscal) bravery to persist through the inevitable, but certainly temporal, repudiations of such change?

The performance scholar and cultural theorist Peggy Phelan conjectured, "Taking the visual world in is a process of loss: learning to see is training careful blindness."[78] In recognizing the potential power of other sensory perceptions, I suggest that we also consider how these thoughtful ruminations can be activated in aural terms, for learning to *hear* is training careful *deafness*. Buoyed by assumptions and presumptions, we often unconsciously turn a deaf ear to the nuances of individuals in order to better facilitate a more familiar sense of the world. Committing to a phenomenological awareness of vocal performance frees us from the conventions and expectations that obscure real-life realities and, moreover, opens us to experience and *experiment with* new artistic possibilities.

Coda

Whiteface to Postrace?
The Artful Interrogations of Jefferson Pinder

I would like to close *Coloring Whiteness* by returning to the photograph with which this book's ruminations began. Taken during the Selma march in 1965, this photograph captures a specific moment in history, serving as a poignant reminder and symbol of the civil rights struggle in America—all powerfully translated through the marcher's strategic use of whiteface.

Now flash forward more than forty years to consider another striking image, one that similarly uses a facial canvas to evoke considerations relative to the cultural moment of its creation. Turning the pages of time and history, I would like to reflect on the convention-defying use of whiteface in the work of the visual and performance artist Jefferson Pinder.

JEFFERSON PINDER'S *AFRO-COSMONAUT/ ALIEN (WHITE NOISE)*

A multidimensional and interdisciplinary artist, Jefferson Pinder began his creative journey as an undergraduate theatre major, expanding his enthusiasm for embodied performance into the realm of studio art. After receiving his master of fine arts in painting and mixed media at the University of Maryland in 2003, he studied at the Asolo Theatre Conservatory in Florida, where he continued to cultivate his interest in merging a variety of art forms. Pinder describes himself in ways that reflect the eclectic nature of his work: he is a "folk video artist," a "performance artist," and a "visual artist," and his creations have been devised to greet audiences on walls, screens, and/or improvised stages. Over the past decade, spectators have experienced Pinder's work at an array of solo shows and group exhibits, including those held at the Studio Museum in Harlem in New York, the Smithsonian's National Portrait Gallery, the G-Fine Art Gallery in Washington, DC, the Milwaukee Inova Contemporary Art Center, the Flint Institute of Art, the High Museum of Art in Atlanta, the Bronx Museum, the Wadsworth Athenaeum Museum in Connecticut, the Showroom Mama Gallery in the Netherlands, and the Zacheta National Gallery in Warsaw. These opportunities have led to an abundance of critical attention, reviews, and analysis in prominent publications such as the *Washington Post, Atlanta-Constitution Journal, New York Times, Art in America*, and *Black Camera: An International Film Journal*.

While his work is vast and varied in style and content, there are a few identifiable threads to which Pinder seems to gravitate and revisit. Among the artist's recurring refrains is a fascination with physicality and exertion, as well as themes of escape and transcendence. These are, in fact, among the motifs that are dynamically addressed in Pinder's short film *Afro-Cosmonaut/Alien (White Noise)*. Notably, *White Noise* was created in 2008 for the High Museum of Art's exhibit *After 1968: Contemporary Artists and the Civil Rights Legacy*. Designed as a companion piece to the Atlanta museum's photographic exhibit *Road to Freedom: Photographs of the Civil Rights Movement, 1956–68, After 1968* challenged its artists (all of whom were born, fittingly, *after* 1968), to use their work to explore how the Civil Rights Movement had impacted the creative expressions of African Americans. In a written statement that accompanies *White Noise*, Pinder expounds on his inspirations, as well as his process.

> *Afro-Cosmonaut/Alien (White Noise)* is an escapist video narrative that ends in destruction when the protagonist plummets back to earth after a mystical space journey. Like Icharrus, the epic fall comes after reaching a brilliant zenith that is both mesmerizing and lethal. This white-face Butoh inspired performance is a crude metaphor of the civil rights legacy. Taking cues from experimental films, I plant myself within my work and ask my viewers to watch the images of propulsion and power. Utilizing time-lapse animation, *White Noise* consists of over 2,000 photographs. Each frame of the piece is an individual pose. All together they form a

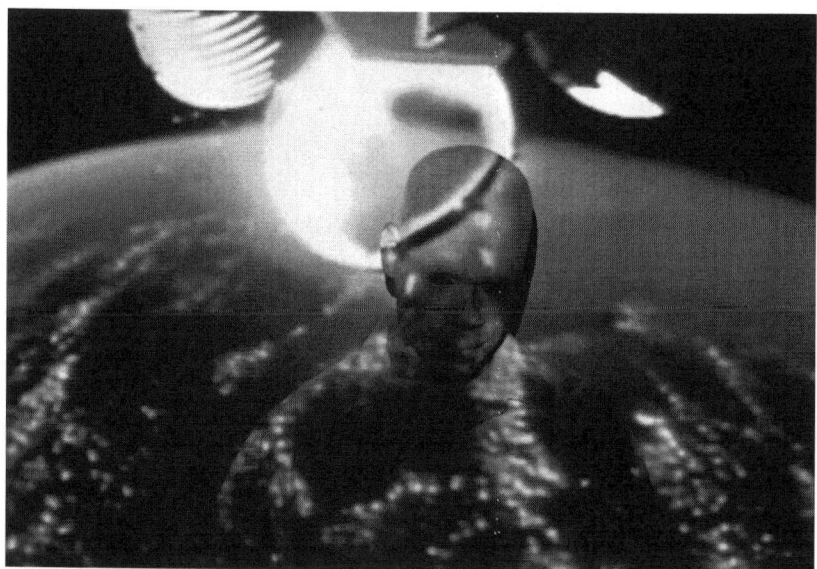

Jefferson Pinder, *Afro-Cosmonaut/Alien (White Noise)*, 2008. (Courtesy of Jefferson Pinder.)

continuous flow of activity. The sequence, which happens in exaggerated time, draws attention to the physicality of the performance and the identity of the figure represented.[1]

What is particularly striking about *Afro-Cosmonaut/Alien (White Noise)* in the context of this book, however, is the "white-face" Pinder references. In fact, *White Noise* not only utilizes a stunning, unconventional whiteface performance, but it actually features an act of "whiting up."

As *White Noise* begins, we hear the distinctive strumming of a stringed instrument, followed by a visual and audible "countdown" of numbers flipping across the screen. With the music still playing, we soon see Pinder's face against a white backdrop. Void of any revealing expression, Pinder proceeds to take a paintbrush and coat his brown skin with a thick, opaque white liquid. Frame by frame, he paints his face and neck and, aided by the stark white shirt he is wearing, he obscures the specifics of his body until he animates the notion of "white invisibility." The white coating on Pinder's face looks so impenetrable and the stark surroundings appear so all encompassing that it prompts this viewer to query: is he actually encased, that is,

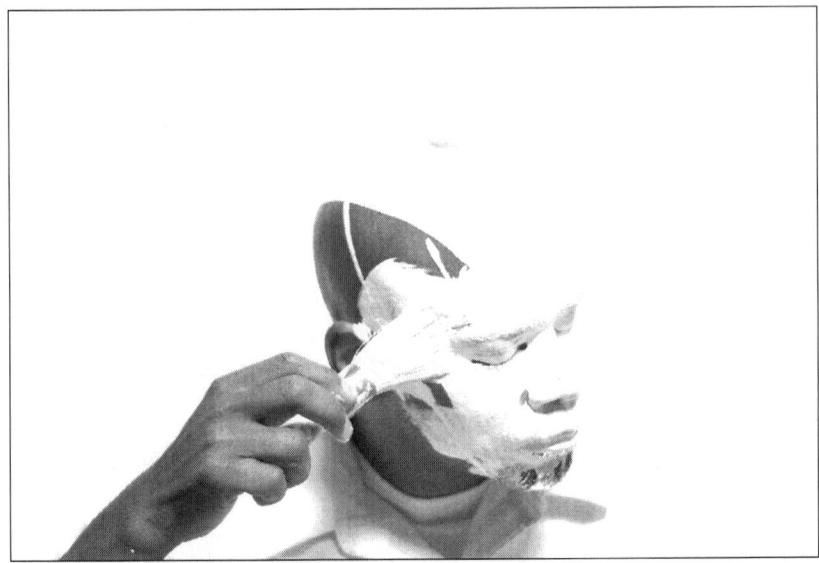

Jefferson Pinder, *White Noise #9*, 2008. (Courtesy of Jefferson Pinder.)

trapped, by whiteness? And, if so, what of the fact that he is the imprisoning agent, that the liquid mask was applied by his very own hands? Notably, after covering his face completely, Pinder raises both the front and back of his unpainted hands to the camera. The gesture is a layered one: now void of tools and instruments, he establishes the conclusion of his whitening process. In doing so, however, he also reminds the audience of the persistent blackness that lies beneath the white paint that camouflages his form.

This pointed acknowledgment of Pinder's persistent blackness—the blackness that lies beneath the paint—revisits a common dramaturgical strategy. Once again the exercise of whiting up is done with an explicit and purposeful incompleteness. Recalling the intentional disclosure evidenced in other whiteface performances, Pinder's *White Noise* also brings to life a visual articulation of optic whiteface—the brilliance of the "pure white" paint against Pinder's brown skin makes it truly appear (in the words of Ralph Ellison's character Kimbro) "as white as George Washington's Sunday-go-to-meetin' wig and as sound as the all-mighty dollar."[2]

Once the whiting-up process is complete, the screen begins to explode with a deluge of still and moving images, all of which are cast on Pinder's canvaslike visage. The spectacles that dance across his face include National Aeronautics and Space Administration (NASA) footage from the 1960s; film clips from Nicolas Roeg's *The Man Who Fell to Earth* (1976), Stanley Kubrick's *2001: A Space Odyssey* (1968), Philip Kaufman's *The Right Stuff* (1983), and Ron Howard's *Apollo 13*; and images of civil rights activists and everyday citizens. All the while the video is accompanied by an array of sound bites and audio clips from Gil Scott Heron's *Whitey on the Moon* and Martin Luther King Jr.'s "I've Been to the Mountaintop" speech—both of which overlay the continuous *pipa* music that hauntingly plays in the background.[3]

Suturing this quilt of pictures and sounds together is the central image of a rocket launch. The rocket explodes into the cosmos, vertically aligned with Pinder's equally erect form. We follow the rocket's journey as the video cuts back and forth between fictional and real-life images related to both space travel and earthly, civic concerns. The rocket's trajectory becomes more uneven as Pinder's form becomes increasingly unsteady. The tone and tenor of the unfolding imagery are accentuated by lyrical fragments from Gil Scott Heron.

> A rat done bit my sister Nell.
> (with Whitey on the moon)
> Her face and arms began to swell.
> (and Whitey's on the moon)
> I can't pay no doctor bills.
> (but Whitey's on the moon)
> Ten years from now I'll be payin' still
> While Whitey's on the moon ...[4]

Heron's poetry swells and falls throughout the piece, juxtaposed against bits and pieces of Dr. King's hopeful yet haunting premonitions.

> We've got some difficult days ahead. But it doesn't matter with me now. Because I've been to the mountaintop.... Like anybody ... long life. Longevity has its place ... And He's allowed me to go up to the mountain.

And then, on cue, the rocket rips apart, its shuttle falling with a fiery trail as we witness what looks like its impending, catastrophic return to earth.

Appearing as a ball of flame, the shuttle rapidly descends in a full blaze. As if magnetically attracted to Pinder's form, the fiery orb seems determined

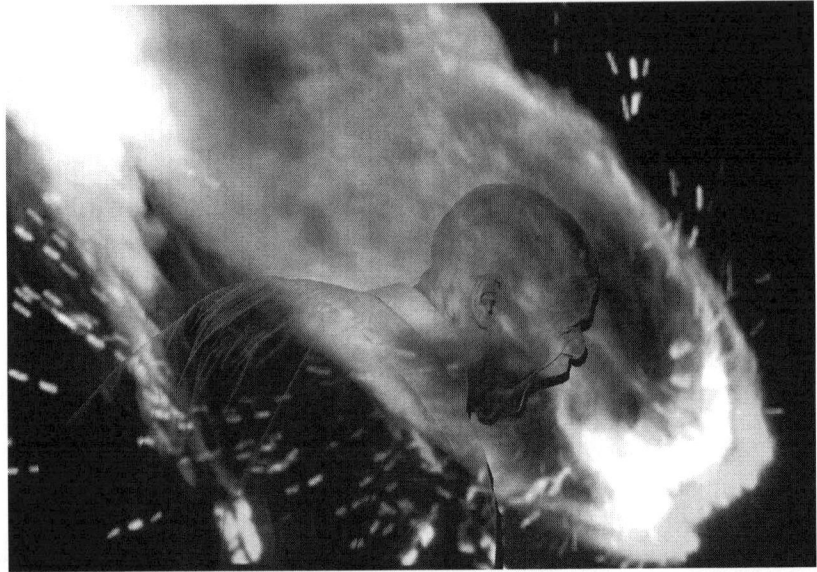

Jefferson Pinder, *Afro-Cosmonaut/Alien #4*, 2008. (Courtesy of Jefferson Pinder.)

to devour his whitefaced protagonist. An unwavering, destructive mass of orange, yellow, and red flames oscillates between crowning his skull and consuming it, and all the while Pinder repeatedly contorts his body as if in excruciating pain. With clenched eyes he expels silent screams, giving the impression of an intense and tortuous experience—one that extends beyond the physicality of the attack. After all, the whitefaced figure is not only pummeled by fire, but he is assaulted with a cacophony of sounds and images that invade his space and forcibly inscribe themselves on his flesh. Finally, there comes a brief moment in which Pinder's body is absent from the screen and we witness what looks like an atomic explosion hitting the earth. Pinder's pallid and still form quietly returns to the screen, eyes cast downward, as the monitor returns to an obliterating whiteness.

PINDER'S POSTBLACK EXPRESSIONS: USING WHITEFACE TO CRITIQUE POSTRACE

Similar to the whitefaced Selma marcher, Pinder's use of whiteness can be read as highly utilitarian, as well as a symbolic call for humanity, equity, and justice. The practical aspect of Pinder's optic whiteface is the way in which it enables the actor's body to serve as a dynamic canvas for the kinetic essay that plays across his features. The use of the white paint, as well as the way Pinder's body integrates narratives concerning America's struggles, past and present, speaks to the successes and shortcomings of the Civil Rights Movement. Furthermore, it is the knowledge of Pinder's blackness, in relief against the video's references to the public strife of the 1960s, that ignites the impulse to determine how *White Noise* serves to comment on racialized conditions and circumstances.

Like other whiteface performances, Pinder's white mask successfully satisfies a common goal: his optic whiteface makes whiteness appear strange, otherworldly, and "alien"—a point underscored by the piece's full title, *Afro-Cosmonaut/Alien (White Noise)*. Not only does Pinder's performance defamiliarize whiteness, but it opens up questions about representations of blackness. Pinder situates his own body in his video's stream-of-conscious narrative and, by painting himself white, appears to disrupt the stories of technology, exploration, and nationhood that have historically denied the presence of black humanity. In so doing, he personifies the "blank page" of history books, becoming that on which new memories and perspectives could be cast.

However, the inscriptions of these visible narratives on Pinder's whitened form also beg the question. Is his whiting up a requirement for entry and inclusion?[5] Is it a symbol of assimilation, suggesting to audiences a way to claim space in our nation's cultural narratives? Or does it simply provide a way to refute black absence and assert a consistent presence that must be fully acknowledged? Through Pinder's body, the vastness of space (often signified by blackness) is colonized by whiteness, yet blackness also invariably claims ownership by inhabiting what was historically considered "white territory." Thus, at once colonized and colonizer, Pinder's painted form could suggest that donning whiteness is required if black people are to "be seen" as a part of the American fabric, its history and heritage. On the other hand, Pinder's blackness, revealed and clearly identified from the very beginning, is presented in such a way as to help us reenvision how we read the annals of our history and imagine our future.

The layered, capacious, and even contradictory ways audiences may interpret *Afro-Cosmonaut/Alien (White Noise)* reveals how Pinder's artwork resists a unilateral, didactic message and denies black-white binarism. Like many of the enactments of whiteness discussed in this book, *White Noise* is not a reductive condemnation of white people, nor is it a reactive response to the use of blackface minstrelsy. Rather, the visual potency of Pinder's process of whiting up, in tandem with syncretic riffs on American history and culture, prompt his spectators to consider the fullness of his work as an individual artist, as well as reconsider any impulse they may have to read *White Noise* strictly through the confines of a single, racialized lens.

Aiding audiences to read beyond the surface interpretations of his work, Pinder offers explicit guidance for those who may be tempted to dismiss the complexity of his artistic ruminations. One way he does this is by clearly indicating that his use of whiteface is inspired by the Butoh dance form. Butoh, a slow-moving, controlled dance that is traditionally performed in full-body white makeup, originated in 1950s Japan. While many cite Butoh's initial development as a response to the atrocities of World War II, it is now commonly characterized as an art form that wrestles with politically subversive or taboo issues. For Pinder, a multidisciplinary artist who continually exposes himself to different genres, the inspiration to use Butohesque whiteface was equally multifaceted. First and foremost, he was intrigued with the ideological roots of Butoh: "I was drawn to its protest sensibilities and how it emerged out of post–World War II, postatomic rebels to create these ghosts, these people that have these amazing physical qualities that almost seemed outside the body."[6] Moreover, Pinder was fascinated by (1) Butoh's relative lack of a clear-cut, defining description; (2) the widely held belief that there are no self-proclaimed "masters" of Butoh; and (3) the knowledge that there were no well-known Butoh artists of African descent at the time of his own critical inquiry. Taking these understandings together, Pinder felt compelled to reference the dance form within his work—a motivation that not only led him to acquaint himself with texts and videos on the topic, but also led him to participate in a Butoh workshop.[7]

Perhaps even more revealing in relation to how *White Noise* resists cursory readings is the fact that Pinder readily acknowledges that the featured process of whiting up—an exercise that seems to burst with racially poignant subtexts—was not, initially, part of his artistic vision for the piece.

> I was doing it for almost purely formal reasons. I mean, as strange as it might sound, I knew I wanted to do projections and I also knew that the best way this projection's going to be seen is if everything's white. And so, I mean, that's the process. I'm letting you into the process because, to be honest, I was thinking about the images of propulsion, of violence and intensity, and I wasn't aware—I wasn't looking at myself putting on "whiteface."[8]

However, as Pinder started working on his preproduction preparation, it immediately became evident to his lone audience member—his cameraman—that the preparation process could also powerfully inform the content of his work: "I have to give credit to a good friend, Curtis Stoltzfus, who happened to be operating the camera for me. I was putting on the whiteface and he was like, 'Oh my god, that's so god damn powerful. There's just something about that this should be the start of the piece.'"[9]

Though grateful for the layered metaphors that came from this added prologue, Pinder is also quick to emphasize that *White Noise* was not created to convey the story of a particular character or even a specific racial or cultural community. Rather, what initially propelled his artistic vision was the desire to produce a piece about "breaking free of the gravitational pull."

> I see the protagonist as having almost a utopian narrative, an idealized perspective in some regard, like a voice. The essence of this spirit is representative of something else, something greater—like a feeling or a consciousness of an experience, more or less. . . . In some way this character is representative of me transforming myself, allowing me to take this journey. . . . I'm thinking of breaking free of the gravitational pull. I mean I'm thinking of a story in which it defies this understanding that's grounded with all of the things that we associate with it—maybe "tradition." It's the idea of leaving the weight of the world. It's like a spiritual state that is expressed in physical terms. So I guess the character that you see is more of a symbol of a particular kind of creative communication rather than actually a person who is in a literal story.[10]

And while Pinder acknowledges that the issue of race is among the threads traced through *White Noise*, "As much as this is about blackness it's about breaking away from blackness or being allowed to step outside of it and do something that's more formal. There's formal exploration and allowing all these different ideas to come in, too."[11]

In strengthening the expansiveness of this idea, Pinder also turned to another inspirational text: Ilya Kabakov's installation art piece *The Man Who Flew into Space from His Apartment* (1985). Originally created in Moscow in 1985, *The Man Who Flew into Space* tells the story of a Russian citizen, a self-appointed cosmonaut, who creates an oversized slingshot in order to catapult himself into outer space. The man believes that his pursuit of space travel, fueled by the indoctrination of Soviet nationalism, will be rewarded with a utopic existence. The installation piece is the room in which the man planned and executed his phenomenal escape from Earth; it is what remains for spectators to see of the already-transpired event. The walls of the room are fittingly plastered with Soviet propaganda, pictures, and diagrams, and in the middle of the room are the central objects of interest: a gigantic slingshot made of bedsprings and a cavernous hole where the ceiling had once been intact.

The art theorist Boris Groys brings the story of Kabakov's protagonist to life in his book *Illya Kabakov: The Man Who Flew into Space from His Apartment*.[12] Writing with whimsical depth, Groys chronicles how Kabakov's cosmonaut was, indeed, seeking to rid himself of the limitations of human existence in order to experience both physical and metaphysical transcendence.

> Utopia will be a long time coming, as we all know, for the construction of the ultimate utopia is a slow historical process that requires the collective effort of generation upon generation. But not everyone can live with that. And one who couldn't was the hero of Ilya Kabakov's installation *The Man Who Flew into Space from His Apartment*. He didn't want to wait until the whole rest of society was ready for utopia; he wanted to head off for utopia there and then—flying out into cosmic space where he would no longer be tied to a particular place, a particular topos, but would be in an *ou-topos*, a "not-place," weightless, floating free in the cosmic infinitude.[13]

These are, indeed, among the same sentiments that Pinder expresses when he discusses his own artistic aims, and it is the interest in their exploration that served as a springboard for his creation of *White Noise*.

What is equally intriguing to me, however, is that Groys's meditations on utopia—that it "will be a long time coming" and will demand "the collective effort of generation upon generation"—are also profoundly resonant when one thinks of the way "utopia" was often framed in national discourses at the time of *White Noise*'s creation. Not only was *White Noise* a response to the High Museum's prompt about the artistic aftereffects of the Civil Rights Movement, but it was created in 2008, a year that seemed to finally answer the fervent calls of the civil rights era. While the 1965 whiteface photographs of the Selma march captured blacks' struggle to obtain equitable representation at the polls, 2008 was a time in which black folks went to the polls in unprecedented numbers; a year in which a black man was elected president of the United States. The tremendous social and political progress marked by President Barack Obama's election inspired many to claim that we were finally entering a utopic, "postracial era."

Postracial, in this sense, suggests that we are beyond distinct—and often socially debilitating—racial demarcations, that our knowledge of the frailties and fallacies of racial differences have propelled us into an era that is no longer negatively impacted by racist tenets. It was this simplistic incarnation of *postrace* that became common parlance during Barack Obama's 2008 presidential campaign—a time in which optimism regarding social change was at an all-time high. Judiciously used by mainstream media outlets (newspapers, magazines, television, the Internet, etc.), *postrace* and *postracial* quickly became conventional shorthand for ideologies and social structures in which race is increasingly depoliticized, carrying with it the promise of racism's rapid and certain demise.

This, of course, is the unstudied interpretation of postraciality, repeatedly espoused and accepted at face value. While the basic promise of postraciality seemed to dominate the American imagination during—and certainly following—Obama's election, critical race theorists, sociologists, legal scholars, and like-minded cultural philosophers dutifully interrogated the postrace premise. Among their critical observations was postraciality's overreliance on examples of exceptionalism, as well as its failure to recognize the way surrogate forms of racism proliferate under the seemingly innocuous guise of neoconservative policies.[14] There is also the concern that postraciality denies us the opportunity to champion cultural differences, that "color-evasive" expressions will subsequently result in *culture*-evasive representations. If actualized, postracial sentiments and strategies either result in less-detectable discriminatory practices or they diminish celebratory distinctions and offer, in their stead, banal sameness.

And so, while elements of Pinder's *Afro-Cosmonaut/Alien (White Noise)* can, arguably, speak to the reimagining of racial dynamics and suggest a progressive postraciality (its devising, visual articulations, and potential interpretations extend far beyond the specific issue of racial differences), its unavoidable portrayal of our still racialized present and its intimations of our socioeconomic realities disqualify it from fully inhabiting a utopic, postracial vision. In fact I would argue that Pinder's *White Noise* serves as a resplendent refutation of postracial sentiments. Using his unique whiteface performance to stage a visual dialectic about Americans' progress and preventions in the realm of civil rights, *White Noise* animates the *hope* of humanistic transcendence, yet its symbolic spectacles ultimately synthesize to suggest the impossibility of transcendence at this cultural juncture. In the words of Pinder himself, "The final moments of this performance video do not echo the utopian vision of the Civil Rights Movement, but rather the grim reality of smoldering smoke and a figure that is still standing after a turbulent ride."[15]

While decidedly *not* postracial, Pinder's *White Noise* does seem to exude a "postblack" sensibility—one that acknowledges and gives voice to claiming complex cultural and racial positions. It was art critic and curator Thelma Golden who coined the term *postblack* when discussing the featured artists in the *Freestyle* exhibit at the Studio Museum in Harlem in 2001. Golden famously asserted that postblack artists are those who are "adamant about not being labeled 'black' artists, though their work was steeped, in fact deeply interested, in redefining complex notions of blackness."[16] It is this latter defining characteristic that sets postblack apart from seemingly similar, contemporaneous phrases. For example, while some cultural critics have extended the meaning of *postsoul* to signify a contemporary black identity that distances itself from the past,[17] *postblack* is "a critical term that takes exception not to blackness but to the ways it has been framed and limited both by dominant Western culture and sometimes from within black culture as well."[18]

Exhibiting this evenhanded sensibility, Pinder's *White Noise* amply acknowledges the past, yet its thematic trajectory is not strictly shaped by civil rights issues. In utilizing various genres, pieces of media, and sources of inspiration, Pinder's work intentionally explores an expansive terrain of sociopolitical and philosophical quandaries. However, he also readily concedes that his knowledge and experience (embodied and otherwise) in relation to race do, at times, inform his work without intention.

> I think of moments like the Martin Luther King moment [in *White Noise*], which is, quite honestly, something that I feel like I was fighting against—using that kind of imagery . . . [but] that is like the crux of the whole piece. I feel like it was the biggest part of the struggle, and for the piece as well. I'm informed by all this information and it makes me who I am and the information is so rich and abundant. It's like I was trying as hard as I could to stay away, but that one moment was just almost *too* much—and it was like he's in there for maybe, what, five seconds?

And yet, while Pinder resists the label "black artist," he is equally hesitant to assume the label "postblack artist," noting that, despite what has been written, postblack art

> is something that hasn't really clearly been defined, and I think part of the reason is because there's always been postblack artists. I think the terminology begins to frame something that's so much larger and more complex. The only good purpose for the terminology is to get us to really look at things *again* because the problem has always been the same as far as having the freedom to be able to liberate yourself from an identity based on someone else's interpretations.[19]

Certainly, work like *Afro-Cosmonaut/Alien (White Noise)* powerfully demonstrates an artist's endeavor to defy expectations and liberate his work from traditional interpretations. In fact, Pinder's unconventional use of a whiteface aesthetic epitomizes what is evidenced throughout *Coloring Whiteness*: dramaturgies of whiteness in contemporary African American performance have been—and will continue to be—used in myriad ways, contextualized and recontextualized by the circumstances of their creation, intentions of their devisers, and understanding of their audiences.

Like many of the artists discussed in this book, Pinder's use of whiteness aids the effort to create work that addresses social inequities while troubling monolithic assumptions regarding African American identity. Moreover, it is not only the work itself that defies assumptions; the principles and practices of the individual artists featured in this book also help to challenge the highly mediated ways black bodies and cultural producers have been historically perceived. As *White Noise* helps to disclose, we are not yet living in a postracial or nonraced era but in an era that increasingly acknowledges and validates syncretic, multiracial, and hyphenated identities. *Coloring Whiteness* contributes to this recognition, demonstrating how African American artists use whiteness, in both expected and unexpected ways, to complicate readings of both self and other. In doing so, these artists create performance and social texts that evoke a conversation, one that interrogates—rather than simply affirms—the way we interpret and value identity through visual and aural representations.

Notes

Introduction

1. Steven Kasher, *The Civil Rights Movement: A Photographic History, 1954–68* (New York: Abbeville Press, 1996).

2. Notably, the photograph by Moneta Sleet that Cherise Smith comments on in her article features two young men donning the VOTE-encrypted whiteface, one of which is the man featured in the photo reproduced in figure 1. See Cherise Smith, "Moneta Sleet Jr. as Active Participant: The Selma March and the Black Arts Movement," in *New Thoughts on the Black Arts Movement*, ed. Lisa Gail Collins and Margo Natalie Crawford (New Brunswick, NJ: Rutgers University Press, 2006), 215.

3. "A racial project is simultaneously an interpretation, representation, or explanation of racial dynamics, and an effort to recognize and redistribute resources along particular racial lines." Michael Omi and Howard Winant, *Racial Formation in the United States from the 1960s to the 1990s* (New York: Routledge, 2004), 56.

4. E. Patrick Johnson, "Black Performance Studies: Genealogies, Politics, Futures," in *The SAGE Handbook of Performance Studies*, ed. D. Soyini Madison and Judith Hamera (London: SAGE Publications, 2006), 446.

5. E. Patrick Johnson, *Appropriating Blackness: Performance and the Politics of Authenticity* (Durham, NC: Duke University Press, 2003), 2–3.

6. For more on the rhetorical and discursive practice of signifyin(g) in African American culture, see Henry Louis Gates Jr., *The Signifying Monkey: A Theory of Afro-American Literary Criticism* (New York: Oxford University Press, 1998).

7. Johnson, *Appropriating Blackness*, 9.

8. Harvey Young, *Embodying Black Experience: Stillness, Critical Memory, and the Black Body* (Ann Arbor: University of Michigan Press, 2010), 20.

9. Ibid.

10. "Regulated improvisation" is from Pierre Bourdieu, *Outline of Theory of Practice*, trans. Richard Nice (Cambridge: Cambridge University Press, 1977), 22.

11. Brandi Wilkins Catanese, *The Problem of the Color[blind]: Racial Transgression and the Politics of Black Performance* (Ann Arbor: University of Michigan Press, 2011), 21.

12. Johnson, "Black Performance Studies," 447.

13. Ibid., 449.

14. See David R. Roediger, ed., *Black on White: Black Writers on What It Means to Be White* (New York: Schocken Books, 1998); Ruth Frankenberg, "Introduction: Local Whitenesses, Localizing Whiteness," in *Displacing Whiteness: Essays in Social and Cultural Criticism* (Durham, NC: Duke University Press, 1997); Birgit Brander Rasmussen et al., eds., *The Making and Unmaking of Whiteness* (Durham, NC: Duke University Press, 2001); and Steve Garner, *Whiteness: An Introduction* (New York: Routledge, 2007).

15. Ruth Frankenberg, "The Mirage of Unmarked Whiteness," in *The Making and Unmaking of Whiteness*, ed. Birgit Brander Rasmussen et al. (Durham, NC: Duke University Press, 2001), 76.

16. Eric Lott, *Love and Theft: Blackface Minstrelsy and the American Working Class* (New York: Oxford University Press, 1993); Dale Cockrell, *Demons of Disorder: Early Blackface Minstrels and Their World* (New York: Cambridge University Press, 1997); Annemarie Bean, James Hatch, and Brooks McNamara, eds., *Inside the Minstrel Mask: Readings in Nineteenth-Century Blackface Minstrelsy* (Hanover, NH: Wesleyan University Press, 1996); W. T. Lhamon Jr., *Raising Cain: Blackface Performance from Jim Crow to Hip Hop* (Cambridge, MA: Harvard University Press, 1998).

17. Susan Gubar's *Racechanges: White Skin, Black Face in American Culture* (Oxford: Oxford University Press, 1997), for instance, offers a fascinating treatment of transracial mimicry in the twentieth century. While Gubar primarily focuses on how the white imagination has presented visual tropes of blackness, she does mention some instances in which acts of mimicry go from black to white. David Krasner's *Resistance, Parody, and Double Consciousness in African American Theatre, 1895–1910* (New York: St. Martin's Press, 1997) was formative in its discussion of the whiteface performances of Bob Cole and his "hobo" character, Willy Wayside. Similarly, Nadine George-Graves's work on the Whitman Sisters, *The Royalty of Negro Vaudeville* (New York: Palgrave Macmillan, 2000), opened new avenues of discussion by revealing how the Whitmans' vaudevillian acts of the early 1900s not only engaged in strategic acts of "passing" in everyday life but also performed whiteface on the theatrical stage. Helen Gilbert's "Black and White and Re(a)d All Over Again: Indigenous Minstrelsy in Contemporary Canadian and Australian Theatre," *Theatre Journal* 55.4 (December 2003), is also a fascinating read, offering an entrée into the contemporary practice of whiteface and its historic and cultural nuances beyond US borders and American identity politics.

18. Mary F. Brewer, *Staging Whiteness* (Middletown: Wesleyan University Press, 2005).

19. McAllister's first book, *White People Do Not Know How to Behave at Entertainments Designed for Ladies and Gentlemen of Colour: William Brown's African and American Theater* (Chapel Hill: University of North Carolina Press, 2003), introduced his historical and theoretical musings on whiteface minstrelsy and stage Europeans. His second book, *Whiting Up: Whiteface Minstrels and Stage Europeans in African American Performance* (Chapel Hill: University of North Carolina Press, 2011), fortified and expanded on his earlier explorations. Within these works, McAllister expounds on the notion of "whiteface minstrelsy" as coined by performance scholar Joseph Roach. McAllister defines whiteface minstrelsy as the "extratheatrical, social performances in which people of African descent appropriate white-identified gestures, vocabulary, dialects, dress or social entitlements. Attuned to class as much as race, whiteface minstrels often satirize, parody, and interrogate privileged or authoritative representations of whiteness." He also names the phrase "stage Europeans," which refers to the practice of "black actors appropriating white dramatic characters crafted initially by white dramatists and, later, by black playwrights." See McAllister, *Whiting Up*, 1.

20. It may also be helpful to note that what I refer to as theatrical whiteface lives under the rubric of McAllister's definition of the *stage European*. I find the nomenclature of the stage European to be very useful in terms of citing formal staged presentations that animate white characterizations through the bodies of black actors, especially when referencing performances that are not scripted with the intention of interrogating whiteness. However, the satirical quality of the theatrical whiteface acts discussed in *Coloring Whiteness* are too different in intent and design for me to comfortably pair them with more serious-minded white characterizations performed by black actors (for me, the latter, not the former, are what I would address as a "stage Europeans").

21. McAllister, *Whiting Up*, 9.

22. I am also hesitant to uniformly use the term *minstrelsy* in relation to acts of racial passing, transraciality, or class-based expressions in the everyday life performances of African Americans. I am guarded when it comes to using language that may suggest that the stylings of a black-identified individual's dress, behavior, linguistic expressions, or corporeal features in everyday life are necessarily affectations of a racial identity that is contrary to that individual's understanding of his or her own blackness. These issues and concerns are especially poignant in relation to chapters 4 and 5, in which I consider the aural performances of African American voice-over artists and the physical machinations of the late, great pop star, Michael Jackson.

23. A concise example of this undertheorizing of transracial performance is what

occurred when the African American model, talk show host, and television producer Tyra Banks made viral headlines in 2009. Many criticized the use of "blackface" in her show *America's Next Top Model*. The episode in question used extensive makeup and ethnic dress to cast aspiring models as "biracial" within a thematic photo shoot. Despite heated popular discussion, these supposed blackface performances received little critical attention. For instance, commentators failed to fully speculate on the theme of "mixedness" presented by the photo shoot. Rather, "blackface"—with all its assumed connotations—was deployed as a catchall category for all these transracial performances. America's complex and highly contested history with blackface minstrelsy makes this relegation understandable. However, the lack of specificity and contextualization in terms of the historic moment, content, intent, and audience reception also reveals an adherence to a way of thinking about race (and transracial performances) that is rigid, unilateral, and dependent on binary constructs of white *over* black. The media reactions to Banks's visual stunt clearly disclosed the persistent anxieties and uncertainties Americans feel when confronted with transracial performance. But when taking the nature of the performance itself into account—its dramaturgical framing, if you will—one must consider how the episode placed an uncommon emphasis on "biraciality" beyond the paradigm of black and white (models were made up to appear "Malagasy and Japanese," "Mexican and Greek," or "Tibetan and Egyptian"). To be sure, the attempt to make the models appear "mixed" still adheres to other faulty essentialisms, yet it simultaneously denies the assumption of discrete and fixed identities and champions aesthetics beyond the standards of Eurocentric beauty. Furthermore, the very fact that visual impressions of race and culture could be cultivated before the audience's eyes eloquently illustrated the constructed nature of racialized appearances.

24. I am deeply indebted to those who have offered me the time and space to learn and grow as a dramaturg, among them Arena Stage, Crossroads Theatre Company, TheatreWorks, Center Stage, the John F. Kennedy Center for the Performing Arts, Young Playwrights Theatre, Black Women's Playwright Group, and Theater J.

25. I glean these words and considerations from Geoffrey S. Proehl's *Toward a Dramaturgical Sensibility: Landscape and Journey* (Madison, NJ: Fairleigh Dickinson University Press, 2008), 19.

26. With the noted goals in mind, a production dramaturg may take on a number of complementary and definable tasks, including researching the social, historical, and literary elements of the play; creating "resource packets" for the actors and ensemble; writing program articles and/or educational materials for theatre audiences; offering artistic feedback and informed responses to the playwright and/or director; serving as a featured speaker at group events and facilitating production-related panels and pre- and postshow discussions; and responding to the press regarding production matters. But again, this is a sampling of what dramaturgs may do—it is all contingent on the particulars of a given project.

27. Certainly, these considerations and concerns are not unique to the process and practice of professional dramaturgy. On the contrary, scholars and artists from countless fields routinely use any combination of these approaches and endeavors in their effort to assess performance texts. What is distinctly dramaturgical about my approach, however, is my conscious and deliberate intention to raise questions in service of creative praxis.

28. Proehl, *Toward a Dramaturgical Sensibility*, 16–18.

29. Ibid., 17.

30. Faedra Chatard Carpenter, "Addressing 'The Complex'-ities of Skin Color: Intra-racism and the Plays of Hurston, Kennedy, and Orlandersmith," *Theatre Topics* 19.1 (March 2009).

31. *New York Times*, "Theatre 1964 presents Adrienne Kennedy's *Funnyhouse of a Negro*," theatre advertisement section, January 17, 1964, 24.

32. Howard Taubman, review of *Funnyhouse of a Negro*, by Adrienne Kennedy, *New York Times*, January 17, 1964.

33. Penny Mickelbury, "BIBR Spotlight: Saluting an Innovative Dramatist," *Black Issues Book Review* 5.5 (2003): 34–35.

34. Robert Scanlan, "Surrealism as Mimesis: A Director's Guide to Adrienne Kennedy's *Funnyhouse of a Negro*," in *Intersecting Boundaries: The Theatre of Adrienne Kennedy*, ed. Paul K. Bryant-Jackson and Lois More Overbeck (Minneapolis: University of Minnesota Press, 1992), 108.

35. Ibid.

36. Harry J. Elam Jr. writes of this tactic in his discussion of August Wilson's play, *King Hedley*: "At times people suffering from various forms of psychosis imagine themselves to be kings, queens, or figures of royal standing, power, and privilege in order to combat their fragmented sense of self." Harry J. Elam Jr., "August Wilson, Doubling, Madness, and Modern African American Drama," *Modern Drama* 43.4 (2000): 618. Whether Wilson was consciously paying homage to Kennedy in his crafting of *King Hedley* is uncertain, but the parallel is noteworthy.

37. Lotta M. Löfgren, "Clay and Clara: Baraka's *Dutchman*, Kennedy's *The Owl Answers*, and the Black Arts Movement," *Modern Drama* 46 (Fall 2003); LeRoi Jones, "The Revolutionary Theatre," in *Home: Social Essays* (New York: William Morrow, 1966); Larry Neal, "The Black Arts Movement," *Drama Review* 12 (Summer 1968).

38. Neal, "Black Arts Movement."

39. Homi Bhabha, "Of Mimicry and Man: The Ambivalence of Colonial Discourse," in *The Location of Culture* (New York: Routledge, 1994).

40. Adrienne Kennedy, *Funnyhouse of a Negro* (New York: Samuel French, 1969), 5–6.

41. The character Sarah verifies this notion when she informs the audience that Victoria asks *her* (Sarah) to tell the Queen Victoria about whiteness. This suggests

that the queen does not actually understand whiteness. She, too, must be indoctrinated, thereby reinforcing the notion that white identity is constructed and defined in relation to blackness. Ibid., 14.

42. Deborah Thompson, "Reversing Blackface Minstrelsy, Improvising Racial Identity: Adrienne Kennedy's *Funnyhouse of a Negro*," *Post Identity* 1.1 (Fall 1997): 14. See also Gates, *The Signifying Monkey*.

43. Richard Dyer, *White* (New York: Routledge, 1997), 11.

44. Jacqueline Wood, "Weight of the Mask: Parody and the Heritage of Minstrelsy in Adrienne Kennedy's *Funnyhouse of a Negro*," *Journal of Dramatic Theory and Criticism* (Spring 2003), 17. Wood also provides a detailed discussion of *Funnyhouse* as a Bakhtinian reversal and parody of blackface minstrelsy.

45. "Victoria," in *Collier's Encyclopedia*, vol. 23 (New York: Macmillan Educational Company, 1990), 121–22.

46. This reading of the events spawned by Napoleon III is informed by Richard O'Connor's *The Cactus Throne: The Tragedy of Maximilian and Carlotta* (New York: G. P. Putnam's Sons, 1971).

47. Ibid., 264–65.

48. Strikingly, Carlotta's banishment, as described by O'Connor, is reminiscent of the maddening, museumlike milieu of Adrienne Kennedy's protagonist, Sarah. Of Carlotta's family castle, O'Connor writes: "There Carlotta was incarcerated at the age of twenty-six in a setting that might have been chosen by Edgar Allen Poe for one of his hapless heroines, surrounded by sculptured knights, ancestral portraits of titled thugs, regiments of armor, acres of canvas and tapestry depicting scenes of conquest, walls bracketed with halberds, swords, battle axes, arquebuses and other souvenirs of a bloody past. . . . Ultimately Carlotta, too, became a museum piece." Ibid., 276.

49. Kennedy, *Funnyhouse of a Negro*, 9.

50. As Linda Kintz asserts, Kennedy's work suggests "another way of living as subjects, one not caught up in the phobic insistence of purity and its cleanly separated categories, unities, and singular identity." Linda Kintz, *The Subject's Tragedy: Political Poetics, Feminist Theory, and Home* (Ann Arbor: University of Michigan Press, 1992), 144.

51. For another discussion of the play's varied use of masks, particularly the African-influenced masks specified in the play, see Thompson, "Reversing Blackface Minstrelsy," 13–38.

52. Kennedy, *Funnyhouse of a Negro*, 12.

53. Claudia Barnett, "The Fundamental Challenge to Identity: Reproduction and Representation in the Drama of Adrienne Kennedy," *Theatre Journal* 48.2 (1996): 150.

54. In using the term *deprivileges*, I am paying homage to Helene Keyssar's reference to the "de-privileging of absolute, authoritarian discourses" in Bakhtinian the-

ory. See Helene Keyssar, *Feminist Theatre and Theory* (New York: St. Martin's Press, 1996), 110.

55. Kennedy, *Funnyhouse of a Negro*, 14.

56. Ibid.

57. Dyer, *White*, 3.

58. Dyer credits David Lloyd's study of Immanuel Kant and his *Critique of Judgment* with informing his discussion of how "whiteness aspired to *dis*-embodiedness" (ibid., 38–39).

Chapter 1

1. George Gent, "29 of 119 Stations Drop First TV Laboratory Show," *New York Times*, November 6, 1967, 95.

2. For further discussion of the works of Adrienne Kennedy in relation to those of LeRoi Jones, see "Introduction" in this volume.

3. Nat Hentoff, "You're Hot, You're Poor, You're Nothing . . . ," *New York Times*, November 14, 1965, X5.

4. Ibid.

5. Douglas Turner Ward, telephone interview with the author, August 6, 2013.

6. Howard Taubman, "Theater: Satiric Twin Bill," *New York Times*, November 16, 1965, 56.

7. Even the Negro Ensemble Company's remount of *Day of Absence* deemphasized the pairing of the two plays by coupling the former piece with another Ward one-act, *Brotherhood*, instead of *Happy Ending* during its 1969–70 season. Relatively few scholars have examined *Happy Ending*, the notable exceptions being C. W. E. Bigsby, who briefly discusses both plays in "Three Black Playwrights: Loften Mitchell, Ossie Davis, Douglas Turner Ward" in *The Theatre of Black Americans: A Collection of Critical Essays*, ed. Errol Hill (New York: Applause Books, 2000); and Trudier Harris, who focuses on *Happy Ending* in her critical work *Mammies to Militants: Domestics in Black American Literature* (Philadelphia: Temple University Books, 1982).

8. Douglas Turner Ward, telephone interview with the author, January 27, 2012.

9. W. E. B. DuBois, *Darkwater: Voices from within the Veil* (New York: Harcourt, Brace and Howe, 1920), 29.

10. Hentoff, "You're Hot, You're Poor, You're Nothing," X5.

11. Clinton F. Oliver and Stephanie Sills, *Contemporary Black Drama: From A Raisin in the Sun to No Place To Be Somebody* (New York: Scribner, 1971), 321.

12. Douglas Turner Ward, telephone interview with the author, January 27, 2012.

13. José Esteban Muñoz argues that acts of disidentification work "on and against dominant ideology" in order to "transform a cultural logic from within." For more on "disidentificatory" practices, see José Esteban Muñoz, *Disidentifications: Queers of*

Color and the Performance of Politics (Minneapolis: University of Minnesota Press, 1999), quoted at 11.

14. Douglas Turner Ward, telephone interview with the author, January 27, 2012.

15. Among the relatively recent and highly illuminating analyses of *Day of Absence* are those offered by Daniel Banks in "Unperforming the Minstrel Mask: Black-face and the Technology of Representation" (PhD diss., New York University, 2005); and Marvin McAllister in *Whiting Up: Whiteface Minstrels and Stage Europeans in African American Performance* (Chapel Hill: University of North Carolina Press, 2011). For an interesting discussion regarding white actors performing *Day of Absence* in whiteface, see Brandi Wilkins Catanese, "Teaching A *Day of Absence* 'at [Your] Own Risk,'" *Theatre Topics* 19.1 (2009).

16. Banks, "Unperforming the Minstrel Mask," 254–55.

17. In detailing the defamiliarizing and alienating aspects of whiteface in *Day of Absence*, Marvin McAllister applies Daphne Brooks's ideas of "afro-alienation" to Ward's play. See chapter Five in McAllister, *Whiting Up*, 158.

18. Douglas Turner Ward, Happy Ending *and* Day of Absence: *Two Plays* (New York: Dramatists Play Service, 1966), 33.

19. Ibid., 34.

20. Ibid., 36.

21. Ibid., 37–38.

22. Ibid., 41.

23. Ibid., 36.

24. Ibid., 41.

25. Ibid., 45 (emphasis mine).

26. Ibid., 38.

27. Ibid., 44.

28. McAllister, *Whiting Up*, 179.

29. Ward, Happy Ending *and* Day of Absence, 47.

30. McAllister, *Whiting Up*, 184.

31. Ibid.

32. Ward, Happy Ending *and* Day of Absence, 45.

33. Ibid., 56.

34. As mentioned in the introduction to this volume, Adrienne Kennedy's Obie Award–winning play *Funnyhouse of a Negro* also used whiteface in 1964, making it a very recent, and critically acclaimed, whitefaced production.

35. Ward, Happy Ending *and* Day of Absence, 29. Although Ward conceived this play as one in which the majority of the actors would be of African descent, he does open up the possibility of deviating from this concept in his stage directions. It is this prospect that is addressed by Catanese in "Teaching A *Day of Absence* 'at [Your] Own Risk."

36. Michael Smith, "Theatre Journal," *Village Voice*, November 18, 1965, 11.

37. Taubman, "Theater: Satiric Twin Bill," 56.
38. Ibid.
39. Herbert Kupferberg, "Negro Plays: Sparks, but No Real Fire," *New York Herald Tribune*, November 16, 1965, 18.
40. Tom Prideaux, "A Long Leap for the Short Play: Four New Ones Off Broadway," *Life*, January 28, 1966, 10.
41. Lee Ivory, "'Day of Absence' Powerful Story but Offends No One," *Baltimore Afro-American*, December 11, 1965, 11.
42. John McCarten, "Burdensome Baggage," *New Yorker*, December 25, 1965, 50.
43. This, of course, was a major point of concern for many artists and proponents of the Black Arts Movement as epitomized in Larry Neal's formative essay "The Black Arts Movement," *Drama Review* 12 (Summer 1968).
44. James V. Hatch and Ted Shine, "Introduction: *Day of Absence*," in *Black Theatre USA: The Recent Period, 1935–Today* (New York: Free Press, 1996), 264–65.
45. Douglas Turner Ward, telephone interview with the author, January 27, 2012.
46. Ibid.
47. Douglas Turner Ward, interview with Daniel Banks, in Banks, "Unperforming the Minstrel Mask," 243–44.
48. Catanese, "Teaching *A Day of Absence*," 31.
49. Ibid.
50. My reading of the makeup design in *Day of Absence* is based on Ward's stage directions, detailed photographs of the original production, my viewing of the 1967 PBL televised version of the play, and photographs of the Signature Theatre Company's 2009 staged reading directed by the playwright.
51. While this choice seems to parallel the traditional, unnatural color used for blackface minstrelsy (a concoction that was, traditionally, created out of burnt cork), both white and black audiences easily recognize that the white makeup used in *Day of Absence* is not a realistic skin color. This same awareness was not always present when it came to white audiences being able to recognize that the skin color of "blackened-up" minstrels was not real. The racism and ignorance of white audiences did not always equip them to discern "fact" from "fiction," especially when the fiction fulfilled racist fantasies.
52. Ralph Ellison, *Invisible Man* (New York: Vintage, 1980), 201–2.
53. Harryette Mullen, "Optic White: Blackness and the Production of Whiteness," *Diacritics* 24.2–3 (1994): 74.
54. Ward also envisioned the important role of lighting within the play, noting forthrightly that the lighting design should also have a red, white, and blue theme. The playwright also suggested that the costuming of characters should follow suit (e.g., he notes that the mayor might wear a "Seersucker white ensemble, ten-gallon hat, red string-tie and blue belt"). Ward, *Happy Ending and Day of Absence*, 29–30.
55. The significance of making the whitefaced characters in *Day of Absence* highly

stylized and "doll-like" was not lost on theatre scholar, playwright, and director Molette when he directed these productions. Confronted with the fact that modern advances in costuming had made synthetic wigs "so natural looking that they would give an unwanted aspect of reality to the stage production," Molette opted to have all the whitefaced characters (men and women) wear yarn wigs, thereby giving the entire ensemble a striking "rag doll" aspect. See Bettie Seeman, "Yarn Wigs: Design, Construction, and Styling," *Theatre Crafts*, May–June 1976.

56. The PBS version of *Day of Absence* explored the "dollish" aspect of the play's whiteface even further by including a brief but affective visual gag: among the protesters there is a mother carrying her child—a brown-skinned doll painted in whiteface.

57. Ellison, *Invisible Man*, 19.

58. Allen S. Weiss, "Desublimation and Morbidity," *TDR: The Drama Review* 43.1 (1999): 149.

59. Banks, "Unperforming the Minstrel Mask," 258.

60. Hentoff, "You're Hot, You're Poor, You're Nothing," X5.

61. Douglas Turner Ward, "American Theater: For Whites Only?," *New York Times*, August 14, 1966, 93.

62. I find the omission of Adrienne Kennedy's name to be a striking one. As discussed in the introduction to this volume, Kennedy's play *Funnyhouse of a Negro* was a critical success, and, despite the fact that the debut production had a limited run of only thirty-four performances, its significance is marked by the fact that it earned Kennedy a 1964 Obie Award for Distinguished Play. I suspect that the omission of Kennedy's name at the time of the article's inception reflects the political intracultural tensions around her work.

63. Ibid.

64. W. E. B. Dubois, "Criteria of Negro Art," *Double Take: A Revisionist Harlem Renaissance Anthology*, ed. Venetria K. Patton and Maureen Honey (New Brunswick: Rutgers University Press, 2001), 134.

65. Ibid.

66. Ibid.

67. August Wilson, "The Ground on Which I Stand," *American Theatre* 13.7 (1996).

68. I refer here to the response August Wilson's speech yielded from Robert Brustein, then artistic director of the American Repertory Theatre and theatre critic for the *New Republic*. Brustein penned a cutting rebuttal to Wilson's "The Ground on Which I Stand," accusing the celebrated playwright of championing "subsidized separatism." The Wilson-Brustein debate, as it became popularly known, was a well-documented exchange in the pages of *American Theatre* magazine, and it culminated in a mediated meeting at Town Hall in New York in January 1997 titled "On Cultural Power: The August Wilson/Robert Brustein Discussion." See Robert Brustein, "Subsidized Separatism." *American Theatre* 13.8 (1996): 26–27.

69. Ward, "American Theater: For Whites Only?," 93.

70. By the time the Negro Ensemble Company was formed in 1967, the efforts of the Group Theatre Workshop had clearly been rewarded: fifteen of the original seventy students in the workshop had become Equity members while others were continuing their acting training with the aid of scholarships. See William Glover, "Two Negro Actors Start Drama Group with Ford Backing," *Washington Post, Times Herald*, August 6, 1967, E29.

71. Originally known as the Educational Television and Radio Center, National Educational Television was founded in November 1952 with a grant from the Ford Foundation's Fund for Adult Education. See http://www.lib.umd.edu/NPBA/subinfo/ford.html. To this end, it should also be noted that not only did the foundation help to fund the NEC, but PBL was fully financed using a $7.92 million Ford Foundation grant. The foundation also awarded a $175,000 grant to the Congress of Racial Equality to support the organization's efforts to bolster Negro voter registration for mayoral elections in Cleveland, Ohio.

72. Jack Gould, "Georgia U. Will Not Carry TV Lab's First Show," *New York Times*, November 5, 1967, 84.

73. "Save Sunday Night!," *Washington Post, Times Herald*, November 5, 1967, B10.

74. Ibid.

75. Jack Gould, "News Laboratory Experiences Some Birth Pains," *New York Times*, November 3, 1967, 60.

76. Jack Gould, "Georgia U. Will Not Carry TV Lab's First Show," 84.

77. It should be noted that Hale's critique regarding the short notice given his station seems to be justified. According to Hale, the PBL did not inform the University of Georgia station of its plans to air *Day of Absence* until Friday, November 3, only two days before the program aired. See Gould, "Georgia U. Will Not Carry TV Lab's First Show," 84.

78. Ibid. As noted in Ward's "Notes on Production," the playwright specifies that the play is set in an "unnamed Southern town" on a "somnolent cracker morning—meaning no matter the early temperature, it's gonna get hot." Of course, Ward's glib, tongue-in-cheek descriptions mean even more than that. In using the term *cracker*, he implores his audience to make some overriding assumptions about the townspeople in his unnamed southern city. As "crackers," these characters are to be understood as a particular *type* of white person: white, but also socially unprogressive, poor, and intellectually deficient, all of which inevitably (or, perhaps, purposefully) could be interpreted as general descriptions of *any/every* southern resident, a sentiment that could have distanced potential southern viewers had they been aware of it.

79. "PBL Debut Wins Praise, Cancellations," *Washington Post, Times Herald*, November 7, 1967, D11. Later newspaper articles insist that a total of six (rather than five) South Carolina stations dropped the PBL broadcast from their slates.

See George Gent, "29 of 119 Stations Drop First TV Laboratory Show," *New York Times*, November 6, 1967, 95.

80. Gould, "News Laboratory Experiences Some Birth Pains," 60. In Gould's follow-up article, "Georgia U. Will Not Carry TV Lab's First Show," Ward is characterized as being "shocked" over the question of his play's quality, interpreting such a consideration as "an insult to the acting company of the Negro ensemble theater."

81. Ibid., 60.

82. The following observations and quotations come from my viewing of the tapes of the PBL broadcast at the Library of Congress. Douglas Turner Ward, *Day of Absence*, Public Broadcasting Library, episode 101, November 5, 1967, Library of Congress, Washington, DC (video).

83. Ibid.

84. Ward, Happy Ending *and* Day of Absence, 50.

85. As previously mentioned, the reality of racial riots is addressed directly in *Day of Absence* through the Announcer's final report: "A pitiful sight, ladies and gentlemen. Soon after his unsuccessful appeal, Mayor Lee suffered a vicious pummeling from the mob and barely escaped with his life. National Guardsmen and State Militia were impotent in quelling the fury of a town venting its frustration in an orgy of destruction—a frenzy of rioting, looting and all other aberrations of a town gone berserk." Ibid., 56.

86. Ibid., 53–54.

87. Ibid., 48–49.

88. This moment brings to mind *The Autobiography of Malcolm X*, in which Malcolm X shares his deep-felt regrets when he reflects on the time a white, female college student sought advice on how to help improve race relations, asking him, "What can I *do?*" The pre-Mecca Malcolm X responded, "Nothing." Malcolm X, with Alex Haley, *The Autobiography of Malcolm X* (New York: Ballantine Books, 1992), 312.

89. Ward, Happy Ending *and* Day of Absence, 47.

90. Ibid., 48.

91. According to Daniel Banks, in "Unperforming the Minstrel Mask," the set design for the original November 1965 stage version of the play consisted of furniture on platforms. The elaborate background flats were introduced later and featured in both the PBL taping of the play, done in 1967, and its later airing in the early 1970s for the *Hollywood Television Theatre* series. My analysis of the play is based on the script and the 1967 PBL version of *Day of Absence*.

92. Franklin's reference to Dr. C. K. Marshall was echoed in a 1962 *Ebony* magazine article on the Reconstruction era: "For the freedmen, emancipation was a catastrophic social crisis. Tens of thousands died of privation, disease and want. In some communities, one out of every four Negroes died. 'The child is already born,' crowed

the *Natchez Democrat*, 'who will behold the last Negro in the state of Mississippi.' Dr. C. K. Marshall, a learned and wealthy minister, was more precise: 'In all probability,' he said, 'New Year's Day, on the morning of the first of January, 1920, the colored population in the South will scarcely be counted.'" Lerone Bennett, "Black Power in Dixie," *Ebony* 17.9 (1962): 86.

93. Jack Gould, "TV: An Experiment That Aims to Rock Status Quo," *New York Times*, November 6, 1967, 94.

94. George Gent, "TV Laboratory's First Venture Gets Largely Adverse Reaction," *New York Times*, November 7, 1967, 86.

95. "Reality without Illusion," *Washington Post*, November 7, 1967, A16.

96. Gent, "TV Laboratory's First Venture Gets Largely Adverse Reaction," 86.

97. Gould, "TV," 94.

98. "PBL Debut Wins Praise, Cancellations," D11.

99. Gent, "TV Laboratory's First Venture Gets Largely Adverse Reaction," 86.

100. Gould, "TV," 94.

101. Jack Gould, "A Noble Experiment: Nowhere to Go but Up," *New York Times*, November 12, 1967, 155.

102. Douglas Turner Ward, telephone interview with the author, January 27, 2012.

103. Carlos Russell, telephone interview with the author, March 24, 2011.

104. Carlos Russell, e-mail interview with the author, July 22, 2013.

105. According to a brief *New York Times* article dated November 1, 1969 (p. 20), the New York mayor reported that the city's municipal employees "may participate in 'Black Solidarity Day' work stoppage as on any ethnic observance but without pay as on other occasions."

106. Carlos Russell, e-mail interview with the author, July 22, 2013.

107. In 2011 Yale University convened its sixteenth annual Black Solidarity Conference, featuring Dr. Cornell West. On the conference home page, the organizers drew a direct line between the annual event and its theatrical past, noting, "The Black Solidarity Conference was founded in 1994 around the concept of Black Solidarity Day, an event inspired by Douglas Turner Ward's play *Day of Absence*. The conference serves as a forum for students of color to exchange ideas and opinions about pressing issues while providing an avenue to network with peers." http://www.yale.edu/bsc/. Accessed February 4, 2011.

108. See Jihan Headlam, "Black Solidarity Day Develops Community," *New Paltz Oracle*, November 7, 2002; Alexis Marion, "Black Solidarity Day," *Tufts Daily*, November 5, 2007; and "What the Heck Is Day of Absence and Day of Presence?," *Cooper Point Journal: Student Newspaper of the Evergreen State College*, April 5, 2010. Of particular interest is the absence/presence programming at Evergreen: "On the Day of Absence, while students and staff of color are away, white students and staff typically plan educational workshops and invite guest speakers to campus to work on

issues of community and multiculturalism from an ally perspective. In later years, the Day of Presence was added by students and staff of color in order to reunite the college community and honor diversity and unity as a whole campus."

109. Haki R. Madhubuti and Maulana Karenga, "The March, the Day of Absence, and the Movement," in Maulana Karenga, *Million Man March/Day of Absence, a Commemorative Anthology: Speeches, Commentary, Photography, Poetry, Illustrations, Documents*, ed. Haki R. Madhubuti and Maulana Karenga (Chicago: Third World Press, 1996), 5.

110. Reflecting on the Million Man March, Carlos Russell expressed that he was pleased that Farrakhan's vision supported his own, but he also expressed disappointment that organizers did not take the opportunity to execute the march on Black Solidarity Day: "If that had happened, I believe that the concept of Black Solidarity Day and Doug's *Day of Absence* would have had a greater socio-political impact on the nation." Carlos Russell, e-mail interview with the author, July 22, 2013.

111. Jacqueline Trescott, "A 'Day' That's Come to Pass? Million Man March Harks Back to a Landmark '65 Play," *Washington Post*, October 16, 1995.

112. *Day of Absence* program booklet, Center Stage, October 1995.

113. Trescott, "A 'Day' That's Come to Pass?."

114. Of particular note was Demetria McCain's article, "A 'Day without a Mexican' Déjà Vu: Douglas Turner Ward's Black Theatre Unforgotten," which was originally published in the June 4, 2004, issue of the *Portland Medium*. See http://kathmanduk2.wordpress.com/2008/03/09/from-the-archives-a-disappearance-a-day-of-absence-and-a-day-without-a-mexican/, accessed January 4, 2011. Again, however, the makers of *Day without a Mexican* staunchly deny previous knowledge of *Day of Absence*. When asked his opinion on the matter, Ward simply replied, "I am skeptical about the claim of their ignorance and naïveté." Douglas Turner Ward, telephone interview with the author, August 6, 2013.

115. According to Arizmendi, she and her husband (the film's director, Sergio Arau) initially created a short version of the film in 1997, inspired by California governor Pete Wilson's reelection campaign based on Proposition 187. Public reception of this early film inspired them to create the full-length feature in 2004. See "Film Examines 'A Day without a Mexican,'" *News and Notes*, May 1, 2006, National Public Radio transcript, accessed December 6, 2011, http://www.npr.org/templates/story/story.php?storyId=5372878.

Chapter 2

1. J. L. Austin, *How to Do Things with Words* (Cambridge, MA: Harvard University Press, 1962).

2. Lydia R. Diamond, *Toni Morrison's The Bluest Eye* (Woodstock, IL: Dramatic Publishing, 2007), 10.

3. Richard Dyer, *White* (New York: Routledge, 1997), 39–40.

4. For a critical examination of this trope, see various essays in Birgit Brander Rasmussen et al., eds., *The Making and Unmaking of Whiteness* (Durham, NC: Duke University Press, 2001), especially Ruth Frankenberg's "The Mirage of Unmarked Whiteness" (72–96).

5. Dyer, *White*, 45.

6. Certainly, those who can relate to the reflections of bell hooks (who wrote powerfully on the experience of "whiteness as terror") would not frame whiteness as some invisible specter. See bell hooks, "Representing Whiteness in the Black Imagination," in *Displacing Whiteness: Essays in Social and Cultural Criticism*, ed. Ruth Frankenberg (Durham, NC: Duke University Press, 1997), 165–79.

7. Diamond, *Toni Morrison's The Bluest Eye*, 9.

8. Ibid., 15–16.

9. Ibid., 16–17.

10. Ibid., 17.

11. Ibid., 17–18.

12. Debra T. Werrlein, "Not So Fast, Dick and Jane: Reimagining Childhood and Nation in *The Bluest Eye*," *MELUS* 30.4 (Winter 2005): 64.

13. Diamond, *Toni Morrison's The Bluest Eye*, 51.

14. Sandra L. Richards, "Writing the Absent Potential: Drama, Performance, and the Canon of African-American Literature," in *Performativity and Performance*," ed. Andrew Parker and Eve Kosofsky Sedgwick (New York: Routledge, 1995), 83.

15. Ibid., 65.

16. See Patricia Hill Collins, *Black Feminist Thought: Knowledge, Consciousness, and the Politics of Empowerment* (New York: Routledge, 2009).

17. Diamond, *Toni Morrison's The Bluest Eye*, 18–19.

18. Louis Althusser, "Ideology and Ideological State Apparatuses (Notes towards an Investigation)," in *Lenin and Philosophy and Other Essays*, trans. Ben Brewster (New York: Monthly Review Press, 1971).

19. Frantz Fanon, *Black Skin, White Masks*, trans. Charles Lam Markmann (New York: Grove Press, 1967), 113–14.

20. Judith Butler, "Performative Acts and Gender Constitution: An Essay in Phenomenology and Feminist Theory," *Theatre Journal* 40.4 (1988).

21. Toni Morrison, *The Bluest Eye* (New York: Washington Square Press, 1970), 34.

22. Ibid., 40.

23. Diamond, *Toni Morrison's The Bluest Eye*, 7–9.

24. Ibid., 8.

25. See Michael Omi and Howard Winant, *Racial Formation in the United States: From the 1960s to the 1990s* (New York: Routledge, 1994), 22.

26. Lydia Diamond, telephone interview with the author, May 27, 2011.

27. Werrlein, "Not So Fast, Dick and Jane," 58.

28. Ibid., 56.

29. Diamond, *Toni Morrison's The Bluest Eye*, 9.
30. Ibid., 9–10.
31. Diamond, *Toni Morrison's The Bluest Eye*, 21.
32. Ibid., 30.
33. Ibid., 30–31.
34. Ibid., 31.
35. This reading is inspired by the observations of Susan Willis, who writes, "Claudia's intractable hostility towards Shirley Temple originates in her realization that in our society, she, like all racial 'others,' participates in the dominant culture as a consumer, but not as a producer." Susan Willis, "I Want the Black One: Is There a Place for Afro-American Culture in Commodity Culture?," *New Formations* 10 (Spring 1990): 77.
36. Lydia Diamond, telephone interview with the author, May 27, 2011.
37. Diamond, *Toni Morrison's The Bluest Eye*, 30.
38. Morrison, *The Bluest Eye*, 40 (emphasis mine).
39. Diamond, *Toni Morrison's The Bluest Eye*, 25.
40. Ibid., 26.
41. Ibid.
42. Morrison, *The Bluest Eye*, 20.
43. Diamond, *Toni Morrison's The Bluest Eye*, 27.
44. Ibid., 56.
45. bell hooks, "Eating the Other: Desire and Resistance," in *Black Looks: Race and Representation* (Boston: South End Press), 1992.
46. Kyla Tompkins, *Racial Indigestion: Eating Bodies in the Nineteenth Century* (New York: New York University Press, 2012), 171.
47. Diamond, *Toni Morrison's The Bluest Eye*, 17.
48. Diamond carries over Pecola's misguided vision of Mary Jane from the original novel. Within Morrison's text, Pecola admires the picture of the Mary Jane girl on her candy wrapper before consuming the sweets: "A picture of little Mary Jane, for whom the candy is named. Smiling white face. Blond hair in gentle disarray, blue eyes looking at her out of a world of clean comfort." Morrison, *The Bluest Eye*, 43.
49. It should be duly noted that blue eyes and blackness are not inherently incompatible. Albeit a less common coupling, there are, of course, brown-skinned people with blue eyes.
50. Diamond, *Toni Morrison's The Bluest Eye*, 60.
51. Ibid.
52. One of the most striking, analogous uses of a white doll is in George C. Wolfe's 1996 *Bring in 'da Noise, Bring 'da Funk*. Among the episodes in Wolfe's award-winning music and dance extravaganza is the memorable "Uncle Huck-a-Buck" and "Lil' Dahlin" scene in which a life-sized doll (reminiscent of Shirley Temple) is at-

tached to tap dancer Savion Glover, granting the illusion of animation to the mute, lifeless doll.

53. Diamond, *Toni Morrison's The Bluest Eye*, 27.
54. Morrison, *The Bluest Eye*, 101.
55. Walter Dallas, interview with the author, November 21, 2011.
56. Morrison, *The Bluest Eye*, 12.
57. Diamond, *Toni Morrison's The Bluest Eye*, 60.
58. Ibid., 27.
59. Ibid., 54.
60. Ibid., 55.
61. Ibid., 54.
62. Ibid.
63. Ibid., 66.
64. Ibid., ,65.
65. Ibid., 5.
66. Lydia Diamond, telephone interview with the author, May 27, 2011.
67. Harvey Young and Jocelyn Prince, "Adapting *The Bluest Eye* for the Stage," *African American Review* 45.1–2 (Spring/Summer 2012): 150.
68. Ibid.
69. Ibid., 151.
70. Ibid., 148.
71. Ibid., 149.
72. Diamond revealed that the adaptation of *The Bluest Eye* was originally "only intended for this one venue [Steppenwolf] at this one time, and then [Toni Morrison] was pleased with its reception, and I think she was pleased enough with the play that she gave it permission to exist in the world, which was really a big deal." Lydia Diamond, telephone interview with the author, May 27, 2011.
73. Steppenwolf Arts Exchange, The Bluest Eye *Study Guide*, accessed June 19, 2011, http://www.steppenwolf.org/_pdf/studyguides/bluest_eye_studyguide.pdf (emphasis mine).
74. The attention this chapter gives to Walter Dallas's University of Maryland production of *The Bluest Eye* is grounded in my interest in how this specific production eloquently emphasized the play's themes of absence, presence, and (in)visibility. As an audience member, I can attest to the impressive beauty of this production; however, I am in no way trying to suggest that Dallas's directorial choices were more appropriate or exemplary than other manifestations of Diamond's adaptation. In fact, in my interview with Diamond, the playwright addressed this issue directly when she expressed her appreciation of two very different approaches to the play, one directed by Walter Dallas for the Plowshares Theatre in Detroit and the other directed by Eric Ting for Long Warf and Hartford Stage. Of Dallas's production,

she said, "I do think Walter's interpretation is perhaps the most pared down that I've had the pleasure of seeing—and that actually worked very well with my aesthetic, because I do think that the piece is about the language, [the] story, the simplicity of the storytelling, and the power of ensemble. . . . Walter absolutely understands the world of the play. I think that the way he's done it, it sets up beautifully." That being said, however, Diamond also affirmed that more elaborate productions of the play could be equally powerful: "Eric Ting directed a really beautiful production of the play at Hartford Stage and Long Wharf, which was a joint production. I would say that of the successful productions that I've seen it was the most highly produced. [It was a] very successful production, and it was just really, really elegant, and things flew in and flew out, but it was very much in keeping with the flavor of what you appreciated about Walter Dallas's. And then a moment I found most exciting was that, during the rape, it actually rained on Pecola and on Cholly in two different places on the stage. It was breathtaking. It rained for a full forty-five, fifty seconds, which is enough time to drive a truck through. You never think you could pull that off. It was horrifyingly beautiful." Lydia Diamond, telephone interview with the author, May 27, 2011.

75. Walter Dallas, e-mail interview with the author, November 20, 2011.

76. Lydia Diamond, telephone interview with the author, May 27, 2011.

77. Prince and Young, "Politics of Lydia Diamond's Adaptation," 147 (emphasis mine).

78. Ibid., 152–53.

79. Diamond, *Toni Morrison's* The Bluest Eye, 51.

80. Ibid., 56.

81. Ibid., 80.

82. Morrison, *The Bluest Eye*, 32–33.

83. Ibid., 92–93.

84. See Faedra Chatard Carpenter, "Reading between the Lines: Intertextuality and the Documentation of African American Theatre History," *Blackstream III* (August 2006).

85. Morrison, *The Bluest Eye*, 40.

86. For more on "racial madness," see Harry J. Elam Jr., "August Wilson, Doubling, Madness, and Modern African-American Drama," *Modern Drama* 43.4 (2000).

Chapter 3

1. For further details regarding Daniel Tisdale's biography and artistic work, see the Radical Presence: Black Performance in Contemporary Art website, at http://radicalpresenceny.org/?page_id=377, accessed April 20, 2014.

2. http://radicalpresenceny.org/?page_id=377, accessed April 20, 2014.

3. Kobena Mercer, "Engendered Species: Danny Tisdale and Keith Piper," *Artforum* (Summer 1992).

4. Shearer West, *Portraiture* (Oxford: Oxford University Press, 2004), 208.

5. Ibid., 210.

6. Ibid.

7. Among the more readily recognized visages featured in *Sign of the Times* are before and after portraits of the Mexican revolutionary Emiliano Zapata (1879–1919) and the popular actress of 1980s and 1990s films (such as *Weird Science*), Kelly LeBrock.

8. The *Post Plantation Pop* series also includes a treatment of Sojourner Truth. For a focused, in-depth discussion of Tisdale's "Truth," see Faedra Chatard Carpenter, "Embodying Anxieties: Race, Culture, and Identity in Contemporary American Performance" (PhD diss., Stanford University, 2005).

9. Richard Dyer, *Heavenly Bodies: Film Stars and Society* (New York: St. Martin's Press), 1986.

10. Ibid., 69–102.

11. Ossie Davis, "Remembering Paul Robeson," an interview with Phil Ponce and Martin Duberman, *Online NewsHour, a NewsHour with Jim Lehrer Transcript*, 1998, accessed August 1, 2005, http://www.pbs.org/newshour/bb/remember/1998/robeson_4-9.html.

12. Rob Nagel, "Biography: Paul Robeson," *Contemporary Musicians* 8 (1992), accessed August 1, 2005, http://homepage.sunrise.ch/homepage/comtex/rob3.htm. It must be noted that the celebrated status of both Paul Robeson and Malcolm X has also been secured by time. During their lives—and in the midst of their greatest controversial moments—neither figure enjoyed the unmitigated acceptance and veneration of the African American community (Robeson, in fact, was denounced by the NAACP and Malcolm X, as a member of the Nation of Islam, was viewed by conservative blacks as a disruptive force in the struggle for civil rights). While there can never be a singular sentiment within "the" African American community (for, of course, the community is far too complex), both Robeson and Malcolm X are now considered to be iconic figures by blacks and whites alike.

13. Ossie Davis, "Malcolm X's Eulogy," Official Web Site of Malcolm X, accessed August 1, 2005, http://www.cmgww.com/historic/malcolm/index.htm. Thirty-three years later, in a PBS interview, Davis addressed the symbolic importance of Paul Robeson for the black community: "Well, for me, Paul was a mountain of joy, an explosive personality that always made me feel greater in his presence than I felt before. You notice, he mentions dignity a great deal. That was a key part of who he was and what he meant to us, we, youngsters, following in his path, you know, and looking upon him as a giant and as an example. We blacks need so much to be reminded of something great. We have heroes that we worshipped and they made a

great difference, like Joe Lewis, for example, or Marion Anderson, and to top it all, Paul Robeson, just to look at him, to be in love with him was to be alive in a different kind of way" (Davis, "Remembering Paul Robeson").

14. David Marriot, *On Black Men* (New York: Columbia University Press, 2000), 44.

15. Dyer, *Heavenly Bodies*, 69. Dyer's assessment of Harold Cruse's evaluation of Robeson is based on two works by Cruse: *The Crisis of the Negro Intellectual* (London: W. H. Allen, 1969); and "The Creative and Performing Arts and the Struggle for Identity and Credibility," in *Negotiating the Mainstream*, ed. Harry A. Johnson (Chicago: American Library Association, 1978).

16. Alex Gillespie, "Autobiography and Identity: Malcolm X as Author and Hero," in *The Cambridge Companion to Malcolm X*, ed. Robert E. Terrill (New York: Cambridge University Press, 2010), 27.

17. Ibid., 26.

18. It is interesting to note, however, that when Malcolm was known as Detroit Red he took up the practice of relaxing his natural hair in order to cultivate the popular "conk" hairstyle of the time. In his *Autobiography* Malcolm reflects on this styling process, writing, "This was my first really big step toward self-degradation: when I endured all that pain, literally burning my flesh with lye, in order to cook my natural hair until it was limp, to have it look like a white man's hair. I had joined that multitude of Negro men and women in America who are brainwashed into believing that the black people are 'inferior'—and white people 'superior'—that they will even violate and mutilate their God-created bodies to try to look 'pretty' by white standards." Malcolm X, with Alex Haley, *The Autobiography of Malcolm X* (New York: Ballantine Books, 1992), 61–62.

19. Daniel Tisdale, telephone interview with the author, December 15, 2003.

20. Daniel Tisdale, interview with the author, May 11, 2002.

21. A visit to the Official Web Site of Malcolm X underscores this premise of commodification. Run by CMG Worldwide, "the exclusive business representative for [sic] Estate of Malcolm X," the official website offers Malcolm-related material for the commercial use: "We work with companies around the world who wish to use the name or likeness of Malcolm X in any commercial fashion. The words and the signature 'Malcolm X' are trademarks owned and protected by Estate of Malcolm X. In addition, the image, name, and voice of Malcolm X is a protectable property right owned by Estate of Malcolm X. Any use of the above, without the express written consent of the estate is strictly prohibited." Official Web Site of Malcolm X, accessed August 1, 2005, http://www.cmgww.com/historic/malcolm/index.htm. I suspect CMG Worldwide is not familiar with the work of Daniel Tisdale.

22. Marianna Jenkins, *The State Portrait, Its Origin and Evolution* (New York: College Art Association of America in conjunction with *Art Bulletin*, 1947), 1.

23. Peggy Phelan, *Unmarked: The Politics of Performance* (New York: Routledge, 1999), 2.

24. Daniel Tisdale, interview with the author, May 11, 2002.

25. Transitions, Inc., flyer obtained from Daniel Tisdale, May 11, 2002.

26. K. Sue Jewell, *From Mammy to Miss America and Beyond: Cultural Images and the Shaping of U.S. Policy* (New York: Routledge, 1993), 6.

27. Kobena Mercer, "Black Hair/Style Politics," *New Formations* 3 (Winter 1987): 36.

28. Daniel Tisdale, interview with the author, May 11, 2002.

29. Lynell George, "Brave New World: Gray Boys, Funky Aztecs, and Honorary Homegirls," *Los Angeles Times Magazine*, January 17, 1993, 14.

30. The commodification of racial identity exemplified by *Transitions, Inc.* is a theme that pervades much of Tisdale's work, past and present. *The Black Museum* (1991), for example, is a multifaceted installation piece that uses the voyeuristic dynamic of a museum display to highlight society's material associations with "blackness." Echoing both George C. Wolfe's *The Colored Museum* (and having a particular kinship with the vignette *Symbiosis*), as well as Suzan-Lori Parks's play *The Death of the Last Black Man*, Tisdale's *The Black Museum* highlights some of the everyday material articles that have come to signify "blackness" such as tendrils of tightly curled hair, a black leather jacket (reminiscent of those worn by Black Power activists), a dashiki, malt liquor, cigarettes, hot combs, and NuNile pomade. Yet another exhibit in *The Black Museum*, entitled "The Last African American," features Tisdale's own live, leather-clad body posed on an elevated pedestal. While Tisdale's mannequinesque form readily conjures up images of an enslaved African on the auction block, it also makes explicit the implicit exoticism that still propels white American fascination with the African American body. Remarking on *The Black Museum*, David Pagel of *Art Issues* wrote that Tisdale's installation piece offered "a superficially humorous and profoundly disturbing glimpse into capitalism's capacity to package and profit from simplistic visions of African American identity." David Pagel, "New York Fax," *Art Issues* 24 (1992): 31. Tisdale continues to work along this conceptual trajectory, commenting on society's appetite for racially charged images. His interest in America's consumptive practices is particularly well served by yet another project: a manipulation of the "black-faced" logos that continue to grace the boxes of such products as Argo Corn Starch, Uncle Ben's rice, and Aunt Jemima breakfast items. While Tisdale is certainly not the first artist to interrogate the legacy of these images and their various machinations through the years, his treatment of them is distinctively "Tisdalian" with its emphasis on portraiture and transformation.

31. Daniel Tisdale, telephone interview with the author, December 15, 2003.

32. Daniel Tisdale, interview with the author, May 11, 2002.

33. The fact that Tisdale's "after" images favor each other is strikingly reminiscent of the "sameness" evident in Warhol's portraits. See "Facing Both Ways: Some Thoughts on Portraiture Today," in *Face Value: American Portraits*, ed. Donna De Salvo and Maurice Berger (New York: Flammarion, 1995).

34. Daniel Tisdale, telephone interview with the author, December 15, 2003.

35. Elizabeth Haiken, *Venus Envy: A History of Cosmetic Surgery* (Baltimore: Johns Hopkins University Press, 1997), 177.

36. David Brackett, "The Politics and Practice of 'Cross-Over' in American Popular Music, 1963 to 1965," *Musical Quarterly* 78.4 (Winter 1994): 777.

37. For more on the use of media to promote Motown's crossover acts, see Phillip Brian Harper's "Synesthesia, 'Crossover,' and Blacks in Popular Music," *Social Text* 23 (Autumn–Winter 1989).

38. See MTV.com, accessed September 27, 2009, http://www.mtv.com/news/articles/1614815/20090626/jackson_michael.jhtml.

39. Harper, "Synesthesia, 'Crossover,' and Blacks in Popular Music," 110.

40. In utilizing the concept of the identity theme as posited by reader-response theorist Norman N. Holland, I am arguing that Jackson created performances that ultimately reflected—and consistently reiterated—his own desires, fears, and coping strategies. See Norman N. Holland, "Unity Identity Text Self," in *Reader-Response Criticism: From Formalism to Post-Structuralism*, ed. Jane P. Tomkins (Baltimore: Johns Hopkins University Press, 1980), 120.

41. Michael Goldberg and David Handelman, "Is Michael Jackson For Real?," *Rolling Stone*, September 24, 1987, 57.

42. Haiken, *Venus Envy*, 216.

43. Susan Willis, "I Want the Black One: Is There a Place for Afro-American Culture in Commodity Culture?" *New Formations* 10 (Spring 1990): 89.

44. The question of whether Jackson really suffered from vitiligo was answered by his friends and family members following his death. The truth of his condition was also confirmed by Jackson's Los Angeles autopsy report, which lists vitiligo in the examiner's "Anatomical Summary." The examiner also describes "focal depigmentation of the skin, particularly over the anterior chest and abdomen, face and arms." "Michael Jackson Autopsy Report," The Smoking Gun, accessed December 15, 2012, http://www.thesmokinggun.com/documents/crime/michael-jackson-autopsy-report.

45. In using the term *racechange* I am referencing it as coined by Susan Gubar in *Racechanges: White Skin, Black Face in American Culture* (New York: Oxford University Press, 1997).

46. Marjorie Garber. "Fetish Envy," *October* 54 (Autumn 1990): 55. In terms of Jackson's "long lustrous hair," the "Investigator's Narrative" of the Los Angeles Department of Coroner reveals that the singer's hair was not simply straightened, but he—in later years at least—actually wore a wig: "The decedent's head hair is sparse

and is connected to a wig." The 2009 autopsy report also specifies that Jackson's "head is normocephalic and is partly covered by black hair. There is frontal balding and the hair can be described as short and tightly curled." "Michael Jackson Autopsy Report," The Smoking Gun, accessed December 15, 2012, http://www.thesmokinggun.com/documents/crime/michael-jackson-autopsy-report.

47. Cynthia J. Fuchs, "Michael Jackson's Penis," in *Cruising the Performative: Interventions into the Representation of Ethnicity, Nationality, and Sexuality*, ed. Sue-Ellen Case, Philip Brett, and Susan Leigh Foster (Bloomington: Indiana University Press, 1995), 15.

48. Ibid., 16.

49. Kobena Mercer, "Monster Metaphors: Notes on Michael Jackson's *Thriller*," in *Reading Images*, ed. Julia Thomas (New York: Palgrave Macmillan, 2000), 19.

50. Michael Awkward, "A Slave to the Rhythm: Essential(ist) Transmutations; or, the Curious Case of Michael Jackson," in *Negotiating Difference: Race, Gender, and the Politics of Positionality* (Chicago: University of Chicago Press, 1995), 175.

51. Ibid., 178.

52. Ibid., 184.

53. Eric Lott, "The Aesthetic Ante: Pleasure, Pop Culture, and the Middle Passage," *Callaloo* 17.2 (1994): 551.

54. Amy Robinson, "Forms of Appearance of Value: Homer Plessy and the Politics of Privacy," in *Performance and Cultural Politics*, ed. Elin Diamond (New York: Routledge, 1996), 237.

55. Mercer, "Monster Metaphors," 30 (emphasis in the original).

56. Ibid.

57. Ibid., 21.

58. Willis discusses several of these videos (*Moonwalker, Speed Demon*, and *Smooth Criminal*) and their shared morphing themes in "I Want the Black One."

59. *Michael Jackson–Video Greatest Hits–HIStory*, NTSX, 2001, DVD special edition.

60. For more on the ways aural cues are used to construct and deconstruct racial difference, see chapter 5.

61. Ron Alcalay, "Morphing Out of Identity Politics: *Black or White* and *Terminator 2*," *Bad Subjects: Political Education for Everyday Life* 19 (1995): 2, accessed August 5, 2005, http://bad.eserver.org/issues/1995/19/alcalay.html.

62. Anthony Synnot, *The Body Social: Symbolism, Self, and Society* (New York: Routledge, 1993), 73.

63. Lott, "Aesthetic Ante," 552–53.

64. Vivian Patraka, "Binary Terror and Feminist Performance: Reading Both Ways," *Discourse* 4.2 (Spring 1992): 176.

65. Rebecca Schneider, *The Explicit Body in Performance* (London: Routledge, 1997), 13.

66. Randy Lewis, "Winless Jackson Scores in Speech," *Los Angeles Times*, February 25, 1993, accessed September 10, 2009, http://articles.latimes.com/1993-02-25/entertainment/ca-727_1_michael-jackson.

67. Goldberg and Handelman, "Is Michael Jackson for Real?," 56.

68. Despite Jackson's later efforts to dismiss such rumors, he and his associates may have actually done more to propel than quell this alien refrain. As early as 1987 Michael's own manager described him as "a cross between E.T. and Howard Hughes." Jackson himself took the comparison to E.T. even further when he compared himself to the fictional extraterrestrial in an interview: "'His story is the story of my life in many ways,' Michael said. 'He's in a strange place and wants to be accepted.... He's most comfortable with children.... He gives loves and wants love in return, which is me. *And he has that super power which lets him lift off and fly whenever he wants to get away from things on earth, and I can identify with that.*'" Ibid., 140 (emphasis mine).

69. The notion of escaping the social strictures of an Earthbound existence is also addressed in my analysis of Jefferson Pinder's video art piece *Afro-Cosmonaut/Alien [White Noise]*. See "Coda" in this volume.

70. In retrospect, one can't help but make the correlation between "induced sleep" and the assertion that the abuse of the "sleep-inducing" sedative, Propofol, is believed to have contributed to Michael Jackson's untimely death.

71. A notable exception is Jim Farber of the *Daily News*, who dismisses the sequence as incongruent, claiming that it is "a mystery why Michael at one point examines art by Magritte and Warhol." Jim Farber, "That 'Scream' You Hear Is Jackson's," *New York Daily News*, June 14, 1995, 3, accessed September 14, 2009http://www.nydailynews.com/archives/news/scream-hear-jackson-article-1.688008.

72. Harper, "Synesthesia, 'Crossover,' and Blacks in Popular Music," 103.

73. While I have not verified whether or not Jackson was familiar with Munch's *The Scream*, its relative ubiquitous presence in pop culture grants this assumption considerable validity. Furthermore, it's been noted that Jackson was deeply interested in art history. In fact, La Toya Jackson makes this point in her own autobiography: "Michael's bedroom walls were filled with hundreds of books on different subjects, but especially philosophy and biography. He's probably read about every great artist, businessman, and inventor that ever was, posing questions afterward." Seth Clark Silberman. "Presenting Michael Jackson™," *Social Semiotics* 17.4 (2007): 426, quoting from La Toya Jackson, with Patricia Romanowski, *La Toya: Growing Up in the Jackson Family* (New York: Dutton, 1991).

74. As an intriguing side note, there has been some speculation that Andy Warhol's serial portraiture can be perceived as an "autobiographical invocation of Munch's *The Scream*." While the film historian David E. James offers this as a possible reading, he cautiously acknowledges that it "would be going too far." He imme-

diately follows this caveat with the acknowledgment that Warhol sketched his own version of Munch's masterpiece, entitled *The Scream (After Munch)*, in 1983. David E. James, "The Unsecret Life: A Warhol Advertisement," *October* 56 (Spring 1991): 35.

75. "The Masterworks of Edvard Munch," *MoMA* 10 (Spring 1979): 6.

76. Jackson's video offers a powerful visual referent to Munch's painting, one that seems even more transparent when you reflect on Munch's black and white lithograph *The Shriek* (1896), which he created for the purposes of mass production. In the spirit of acknowledging "iconic status," not only does the Munch lithograph speak to the popularity of *The Scream* during the era of its inception, but I would be remiss not to acknowledge the proliferation of Munch's images in contemporary popular culture. The central figure has been reproduced and mimicked in various guises and can be regularly seen on everyday items (such as t-shirts and coffee mugs), as well as in the form of Halloween decorations. Perhaps one of the best-known "visual riffs" is the likeness of the murderous, masked figure in the *Scream* series of popular horror films.

77. Malcolm Brown and Trey Carpenter, interview with the author, September 23, 2009.

78. "Michael Jackson Memorial Service—Rev. Al Sharpton," YouTube.com, accessed July 7, 2009, http://www.youtube.com/watch?v=_MAKLq865bk.

79. "Michael Jackson Memorial: Paris Jackson Speaks, Says Goodbye to Father Michael," YouTube.com, accessed July 7, 2009, http://www.youtube.com/watch?v=PzP0HcftrVY.

80. Hillary Crossley and Gil Kaufman, "Madonna Pays Tearful Tribute to Michael Jackson at 2009 VMAs," MTV.com News, September 13, 2009, accessed December 12, 2012, http://www.mtv.com/news/articles/1621390/madonna-pays-tearful-tribute-michael-jackson-at-2009-vmas.jhtml.

81. Striking, also, is the way in which Madonna uses this forum to revise and reinvent her own relationship with Jackson and, therefore, her own image. While her MTV presentation offers the impression of a mutual admiration and fondness, taped interviews of Michael Jackson (speaking to Rabbi Shmuley Boteach) reveal that he did not always reflect so fondly on Madonna. See "Michael Jackson Tapes: Madonna 'Is Not a Nice Person,'" CNN.com/entertainment, September 30, 2009, http://www.cnn.com/2009/SHOWBIZ/Music/09/30/lkl.michael.jackson.tapes/, accessed October 13, 2009.

82. Crossley and Kaufman, "Madonna Pays Tearful Tribute to Michael Jackson."

83. Ibid.

84. "About the Film," Michael Jackson's THIS IS IT Official Movie Site and Trailer, http://www.thisisit-movie.com/?hs308=MJ031&kw={}, accessed September 25, 2009.

Chapter 4

1. Lawrence E. Mintz, "Standup Comedy as Social and Cultural Mediation," *American Quarterly* 37.1 (Spring 1985): 71.

2. Alan H. Goodman, "Biological Diversity and Cultural Diversity: From Race to Radical Bioculturalism," in *Cultural Diversity in the United States: A Critical Reader*, ed. Ida Susser and Thomas C. Patterson (Malden, MA: Blackwell Publishers, Inc., 2001), 34.

3. Michael Omi and Howard Winant, *Racial Formation in the United States: From the 1960s to the 1990s* (New York: Routledge, 2004), 55.

4. Ibid., 56.

5. Elizabeth M. Grieco and Rachel C. Cassidy, "Overview of Race and Hispanic Origin, 2000," in *Census 2000 Brief* (Washington, DC: US Department of Commerce, Economics and Statistics Administration, issued March 2001).

6. Ibid., 3.

7. Ibid., 1.

8. Of those "singular raced" people, a total of 75.1 percent claimed "White *alone*" and 12.3 percent claimed "Black *alone*" (other respondents claimed to be "pure" America Indian and Alaska Native, Asian, Native Hawaiian and Other Pacific Islander or Some other Race). Ibid., 3.

9. See Nicholas A. Jones and Jungmiwha Bullock, "The Two or More Races Population: 2010," in *2010 Census Briefs* (Washington, DC: US Department of Commerce, Economics and Statistics Administration, issued September 2012). Also of interest is the fact that the percentage of "all white" folk is the *only* racial group whose numbers decreased (from 75.1 to 72.4 percent). See Lindsay Hixson, Bradford B. Hepler, and Myoung Ouk Kim, "The White Population: 2010," in *2010 Census Briefs* (Washington, DC: US Department of Commerce, Economics and Statistics Administration, issued September 2011).

10. Judith Butler, "Performative Acts and Gender Constitution: An Essay in Phenomenology and Feminist Theory," *Theatre Journal* 40.4 (Dec. 1988): 519–31.

11. *Chappelle's Show: Season One, Uncensored* (Paramount, 2004), DVD.

12. *Frontline*, PBS's documentary series, has been on the air since 1983 and, according to its website, "Since its inception, FRONTLINE has never shied away from tough, controversial issues or complex stories. In an age of anchor celebrities and snappy sound bites, FRONTLINE remains committed to providing a prime-time venue for engaging reports that fully explore and illuminate the critical issues of our times," PBS.org, http://www.pbs.org/wgbh/pages/frontline/about-us/, accessed February 14, 2012.

13. Randall Kennedy, *Nigger: The Strange Career of a Troublesome Word* (New York: Vintage, 2003).

14. In the DVD commentary for *Chappelle's Show*, Chappelle shares a story about

his grandfather—an anecdote that helped inspire the "Clayton Bigsby" piece. The comedian's grandfather was, apparently, a very light-skinned black man who was "born in a white hospital in Washington, DC, in 1911, so one of his parents had to have been white." Chappelle's grandfather, like the character Clayton Bigsby, was also born blind, and although he knew the truth of his racial identity, he "passed" while matriculating at an "all-white" school for the visually impaired. Chappelle tells of his grandfather riding a bus in a black neighborhood after the assassination of Martin Luther King Jr. His grandfather overheard black passengers verbally accosting a white man on the bus—and then realized that it was *his* presence that was causing the uproar.

15. Elaine Frantz Parsons, "Midnight Rangers: Costume and Performance in the Reconstruction-Era Ku Klux Klan," *Journal of American History* 92.3 (2005): 811–12.

16. Ibid., 814.

17. The connection between the enactments of blackface minstrelsy and the performative roots of the KKK have been underscored by many scholars. See Andrew Silver, *Minstrelsy and Murder: The Crisis of Southern Humor, 1835–1925* (Baton Rouge: Louisiana State University Press, 2006), 55; Gladys-Marie Fry, *Night Riders in Black Folk History* (Knoxville: University of Tennessee Press, 1975; Parsons, "Midnight Rangers"; and Joseph Roach, *Cities of the Dead: Circum-Atlantic Performance* (New York: Columbia University Press, 1996).

18. Testimony of Joe Brown, in *Report of the Joint Select Committee to Inquire into the Condition of Affairs in the Late Insurrectionary States* (1872), pt. 6: Georgia, vol. 1, 502–3.

19. This is not to say, however, that there was a complete absence of "Ku-Kluxing" among blacks. On the contrary, it has been reported that there were some freedmen who—due to their criminality or psychopathology—served their own agendas by associating themselves with KKK-related activities. Though not a common occurrence, such incidents and individuals disclose the *possibility* of such scenarios, and it is this potential that Klansmen exploited with the practice of blacking up. Parsons, "Midnight Rangers," 816.

20. Ibid., 828.

21. Ibid., 818.

22. Mikhail Bakhtin, *Rabelais and His World*, trans. Hélène Iswolsky (Bloomington: Indiana University Press, 1984), 122.

23. Ibid., 123.

24. In practice, these types of inversions and conversions can be identified through the very way Klan activities originated as "amusement, based on the laws of carnival" and "enacted fantasy," which "quickly metamorphos[ed] into an actual site of torture." Silver, *Minstrelsy and Murder*, 54–55.

25. Simon Dentith, *Bakhtinian Thought: An Introductory Reader* (New York: Routledge, 1995), 227.

26. The premise that a black body has disguised itself and infiltrated the meeting is an intriguing reversal of real-life Klan infiltrations of all-black meetings. To this end, one of the earliest organized activities of Klan members was their disruption of freedmen's gatherings (such as those of the Loyal League). Fearful of the sociopolitical momentum these night meetings might foster, Klansmen began regularly targeting them. See Silver, *Minstrelsy and Murder,* 61–62.

27. See Bakhtin, *Rabelais and His World.* Certainly, if the tape kept rolling, the audience would have seen Clayton Bigsby's destiny following that of the debased king. Stripped of his previous social and political positions, shorn of his KKK gown and accoutrements, one can only guess that Bigsby would be "abused and beaten when the time of his reign is over . . . Abuse reveals the other, true face of the abused, it tears off his disguise and mask. It is the king's uncrowning" (197).

28. Richard J. Gray II and Michael Putnam, "Exploring Niggerdom: Racial Inversion in Language Taboos," in *The Comedy of Dave Chappelle: Critical Essays,* ed. K. A. Wisniewski (Jefferson: McFarland, 2009), 16.

29. *United States of America v. Leo V. Felton and Erica Chase,* Criminal no. 1:01CR 10198-NG., General Allegations, 1.

30. The "one-drop rule," also known as the rule of hypo-descent, is the colloquial term applied to the historic designation of "black" to anyone who has any traceable black ancestry regardless of how distanced.

31. Paul Tough, "The Black Supremacist," *New York Times Magazine,* May 25, 2003, accessed February 3, 2012.

32. *United States of America v. Leo V. Felton and Erica Chase,* 1 (emphasis mine).

33. Bob Moser, "From the Belly of the Beast: A White-Supremacist Prison Plot Hits the Streets—with an Unusual 'Aryan' at the Helm," *Southern Poverty Law Center Intelligence Report* 108 (Winter 2002).

34. John L. Jackson Jr. *Real Black: Adventures in Racial Sincerity* (Chicago: University of Chicago Press, 2005), 19.

35. Tough, "Black Supremacist."

36. Jackson, *Real Black,* 19–21.

37. Tough, "Black Supremacist."

38. Ibid. Tough describes how Felton has "the words 'skin' and 'head' tattooed on either side of his skull."

39. Ibid.

40. Not only did the Felton case hit the newsstands and Internet prior to the airing of the "Clayton Bigsby" sketch, but Chappelle and Felton share roots in Silver Spring, Maryland, making it quite likely that the Felton case inspired Chappelle's creation of Clayton Bigsby.

41. Michele Elam, *The Souls of Mixed Folk: Race, Politics, and Aesthetics in the New Millennium* (Stanford, CA: Stanford University Press, 2011), 161.

42. "The Racial Draft," *Chappelle's Show: Season Two, Uncensored* (2004).

43. Mintz, "Standup Comedy as Social and Cultural Mediation," 71.

44. Elam makes a particularly astute observation when she comments on the white-black ratio of the commentators in "The Racial Draft": "The panel suggests that for the most part whites are the experts, blacks and people of color the object of their expertise. People of color play the game, but white people putatively understand it: they are the connoisseurs, the evaluators, the arbiters of race." Michele Elam, "They's Mo' to Bein' Black Than Meets the Eye!," in *The Souls of Mixed Folk: Race, Politics, and Aesthetics in the New Millennium* (Stanford, CA: Stanford University Press, 2011), 165.

45. Urban slang for "for sure."

46. S. W. Pope asserts that Tiger Woods "became the defunct 'pioneer' for integrating the long-standing white-dominated sport of golf," but he also readily notes that "with even a cursory survey of the longer history of African American achievements in professional golf, one finds other, 'forgotten' pioneers in this sport." Speckled through the golf history books are a number of athletes who challenged and crossed the color line—often in the face of great resistance. While Tiger Woods may not have been the first black golfer of merit, his rise to stardom occurred "at a fortuitous historical moment, as sportswriter John Feinstein notes, during which time 'no sport needed a black superstar more than golf . . . because no sport has had more of a racist image than golf.'" S. W. Pope, "'Race,' Family, and Nation: The Significance of Tiger Woods in American Culture," in *Out of the Shadows: A Biographical History of African American Athletes*, ed. David K. Wiggins (Fayetteville: University of Arkansas Press, 2006), 327–29.

47. The same, of course, can be said of other sports (e.g., tennis and skiing) that demand accessibility to the appropriate venue, equipment, and lessons if one is to become truly competitive.

48. For additional treatments addressing Chappelle's theatrical whiteface and its visual dissonance (what Elam refers to as a "*dissemblance*" versus a "*resemblance*" to real-life white-identified bodies), see Elam, "They's Mo' to Bein' Black Than Meets the Eye!," 168; and Marvin McAllister, "Dave Chappelle, Whiteface Minstrelsy, and 'Irresponsible' Satire," in *African American Humor, Irony, and Satire: Ishmael Reed, Satirically Speaking*, ed. Dana A. Williams (Newcastle: Cambridge Scholars Publishing), 123.

49. Richard Dyer, *White: Essays on Race and Culture* (New York: Routledge, 1997), 6, 23.

50. Of course, it should also be acknowledged that *ungawa* was adopted in the 1960s and 1970s by the Black Power Movement, as well as in childhood chants and rhymes, yet another example of "revising and revamping" in popular culture.

51. W. T. Lhamon Jr., *Raising Cain: Blackface Performance from Jim Crow to Hip Hop* (Cambridge, MA: Harvard University Press, 1998), 42.

52. "White Like Me," *Saturday Night Live: The Best of Eddie Murphy* (Lions Gate, 2010), DVD.

53. Naomi Pabst, "Blackness/Mixedness: Contestations over Crossing Signs," *Cultural Critique* 54 (Spring 2003): 179–80.

54. Trey Ellis, "The New Black Aesthetic," *Callaloo* 12.1 (1989): 234–35.

55. Ibid. 235.

56. Ibid.

57. Ibid.

58. Tania Branigan, "Colin Powell Claims Scottish Coat of Arms," *Guardian*, May 11, 2004, accessed February 10, 2012, http://www.guardian.co.uk/uk/2004/may/12/usa.world.

59. However, it must be noted that Powell's "Republicanness," perceived whiteness, and, subsequently, perceived blackness, came under renewed scrutiny during the Democratic presidential campaign of Barack Obama in 2008. On announcing his intention to support Obama rather than the white Republican John McCain, Powell faced a cascade of criticism from cynics who argued that his support of Obama was racially, rather than politically, motivated. Among the most vocal of these critics was the always acerbic, right-wing Republican personality Rush Limbaugh, who pontificated on radio, television, and even his personal website, "If Powell had endorsed McCain, you know what would have happened? Donna Brazile and the other black elites in the Democrat Party would never have forgiven him. This was all about Powell and race. It was nothing about the nation and its welfare." Rush Limbaugh, "Powell Endorsement of Obama Has Everything to Do with Race, Elitism," *Rush Limbaugh Show*, October 20, 2008, accessed January 10, 2013, http://www.rushlimbaugh.com/daily/2008/10/20/powell_endorsement_of_obama_has_everything_to_do_with_race_elitism. The passage of time did not assuage some critics from crediting Powell's endorsement of Obama to racial politics. When Powell repeated his endorsement of Obama during the 2012 election campaign, John Sununu, one of Republican candidate Mitt Romney's top advisers, kept the race-based critique alive: "When you take a look at Colin Powell, you have to look at whether that's an endorsement based on issues or he's got a slightly different reason for endorsing President Obama." Lucy Madison, "Sununu Suggests Colin Powell's Obama Endorsement Racially Driven," CBS News.com, October 26, 2012, accessed April 28, 2014, http://www.cbsnews.com/news/sununu-suggests-colin-powells-obama-endorsement-racially-driven/.

60. Eugene Robinson, "What Rice Can't See," *Washington Post*, October 25, 2005, accessed February 10, 2012, http://www.washingtonpost.com/wp-dyn/content/article/2005/10/24/AR2005102401370.html.

61. "Condoleezza's Crimes." *Black Commentator*, April 1, 2004, accessed February 19, 2012, http://www.blackcommentator.com/84/84_cover_condi.html.

62. Ironically, like the reference to Tiger Woods, the Powell reference once again reveals the temporal significance of "The Racial Draft" and further underscores the subjectivity of these interpretations of race. Four years later, when Powell endorsed

Barack Obama rather than John McCain, this seemingly unorthodox shift—by one of the highest ranking Republicans in the nation—spoke profoundly to many as evidence that Powell was not as "whitewashed" as many had previously perceived. Understanding the frailty and instability of public perception, one can certainly speculate on how the comedic power of Powell's conjuring in "The Racial Draft" was contingent on public perceptions of his 2004 political persona. In other words, I doubt this joke would have worked in 2008.

63. William Jelani Cobb, *The Devil and Dave Chappelle and Other Essays* (New York: Thunder's Mouth Press, 2007), 250–51.

64. E. Patrick Johnson, *Appropriating Blackness: Performance and the Politics of Authenticity* (Durham, NC: Duke University Press, 2003), 3.

65. Pabst, "Blackness/Mixedness," 208.

66. Audre Lorde, "The Master's Tools Will Never Dismantle the Master's House," in *Sister Outsider: Essays and Speeches* (New York: Crossing Press, 2007), 110–13.

67. Harriet Margolis, "Stereotypical Strategies: Black Film Aesthetics, Spectator Positioning, and Self-Directed Stereotypes in 'Hollywood Shuffle' and 'I'm Gonna Git You Sucka,'" *Cinema Journal* 38.3 (Spring 1999): 53.

68. For more on "disidentificatory" practices, see José Esteban Muñoz, *Disidentifications: Queers of Color and the Performance of Politics* (Minneapolis: University of Minnesota Press, 1999), 11.

69. As defined by Lois Tyson, an "interpretive community" is comprised of "those who share the interpreting strategies we bring to texts when we read." Lois Tyson, "Reader-Response Criticism," in *Critical Theory Today: A User-Friendly Guide* (New York: Routledge, 1999), 171.

70. Norman N. Holland, "Unity Identity Text Self," in *Reader-Response Criticism: From Formalism to Post-Structuralism*, ed. Jane P. Tomkins (Baltimore: Johns Hopkins University Press, 1980), 21.

71. Cobb, *The Devil and Dave Chappelle and Other Essays*, 248.

72. Mintz, "Standup Comedy as Social and Cultural Mediation," 73.

73. I refer to ideas regarding "the performative" as detailed in J. L. Austin, *How to Do Things with Words* (Cambridge, MA: Harvard University Press, 1962).

74. "Introduction," 3, Chappelletheory.com, accessed October 5, 2007, www.chappelletheory.com.

75. "The Theory, April 20, 2003," Chappelletheory.com, accessed October 5, 2007, www.chappelletheory.com.

76. "Introduction," 2.

Chapter 5

1. I do not mean to suggest that we do not acknowledge or interpret the sound of ethnic differences, but rather I am asserting that we often conflate or supplant

these differences in favor of a more binary, stratified racial context. For example, an English-speaking American might easily detect the difference between a British and Scottish accent, but it would not be unlikely for someone with a similar background to refer to both as "English sounding." Moreover, if either of these accents were heard over the phone by this same American, he or she might automatically assume that the speakers were white, giving little thought to the racial diversity that exists outside the United States. This chapter is particularly interested in the latter scenario—our tendency to *racialize* sound despite the multiple factors (among them ethnicity, geography, class, and education) that shape our speech and its reception.

2. As mentioned in the introduction, Brandi Wilkins Catanese nuances the idea of nontraditional casting through the nomenclature of nonconforming casting. Brandi Wilkins Catanese, *The Problem of the Color[blind]: Racial Transgression and the Politics of Black Performance* (Ann Arbor: University of Michigan Press, 2011), 18.

3. David Wright. "'First Lady Michelle Obama Reflects on Talking 'Like a White Girl': Michelle Obama Tells D.C. Students That Stereotypes Get in the Way," ABC News, March 20, 2009, accessed January 5, 2010, http://abcnews.go.com/GMA/Story?id=7130988&page=1. It should be noted that Ms. Obama's response is not one of naïveté, but rather it outwardly rejects the logic of the children's taunts.

4. By *dialect* I mean the differences in pronunciation, grammar, and vocabulary found within and between languages (thus, distinguishing dialect from the related linguistic term *accent*, which strictly refers to the phonology of a dialect—that is, the sound or pronunciation of words in a given language). It is also important to note that everyone speaks with a particular dialect. See Peter Trudgill, *Sociolinguistics: An Introduction to Language and Society* (New York: Penguin Books, 2000), 5.

5. Like SAE, AAVE is complex and fluid (and similarly shaped by additional factors such as time, geography, socioeconomics, and age), yet it possesses a number of consistent, distinctive grammatical features. Sociolinguist John R. Rickford is among the leading scholars of African American vernacular speech and Ebonics. For a detailed historical, theoretical, and analytic account of AAVE and Ebonics, see John R. Rickford, *African American Vernacular English: Features and Use, Evolution, and Educational Implications* (Malden, MA: Wiley-Blackwell, 1999); and John Russell Rickford and Russell John Rickford, *Spoken Soul: The Story of Black English* (New York: John Wiley and Sons, 2000).

6. Trudgill, *Sociolinguistics*, 42.

7. Ibid., 43.

8. I would be remiss to not acknowledge that accusations of sounding black are equally loaded with judgment and racial bias; however, for the purpose of this study, I am focusing on perceptions of whiteness.

9. Leon F. Litwack, *Trouble in Mind: Black Southerners in the Age of Jim Crow*

(New York: Knopf, 1998), 154, quoted in Stuart Buck, *Acting White: The Ironic Legacy of Desegregation* (New Haven, CT: Yale University Press, 2010), 2–3.

10. Buck, *Acting White*, 3.

11. Nancy Giles, telephone interview with the author, June 30, 2011.

12. I am playfully, yet pointedly, referencing Larry Neal's seminal article "The Black Arts Movement," in which he argues for "the destruction of the white thing." See Larry Neal, "The Black Arts Movement," *Drama Review* 12 (Summer 1968).

13. Timothy Douglas, telephone interview with the author, February 20, 2011.

14. Nancy Giles, telephone interview with the author, June 30, 2011.

15. Peggy Phelan, *Unmarked: The Politics of Performance* (New York: Routledge, 1993), 5.

16. Pierre Bourdieu, "The Form of Capital," in *Handbook of Theory of Research for the Sociology of Education*, trans. Richard Nice (Westport, CT: Greenwood Press, 1986), 241–58.

17. It should also be noted that one's domestic milieu can also inform one's speech in a less expected way; one may consciously work *against* these external factors, intentionally speaking in a manner that deviates from one's domestic sphere as a mode of disassociation and resistance.

18. Wright, "'First Lady Michelle Obama Reflects on Talking 'Like a White Girl.'"

19. M. E. Sprengelmeyer, "Nader: Obama Trying to 'Talk White,'" *Rocky Mountain News*, updated June 25, 2008, accessed January 6, 2010, http://www.rockymountainnews.com/news/2008/jun/25/nader-critical-of-obama-for-trying-to-talk-white/.

20. Notably, this is the same type of critique mentioned in chapter 1 in regards to Carl Stokes's "two-pronged" 1967 mayoral campaign.

21. Ibid.

22. Homi Bhabha, "Of Mimicry and Man: The Ambivalence of Colonial Discourse," in *The Location of Culture* (New York: Routledge, 1994).

23. Nia-Malika Henderson, "Blacks, Whites Hear Obama Differently," *Politico*, March 3, 2009, accessed January 6, 2010, http://www.politico.com/news/stories/0309/19538.html. While I agree with Henderson, I think it is also necessary to characterize Obama's "dog-whistle politics" as speech that is geared to a *younger* audience rather than a primarily black one. Obama's instantaneous ability to oscillate between SAE and AAVE reflects his own socialization within a middle-class black community, but it is also a reflection of his audience: a nation that has been shaped by post-civil-rights realities (from legislation to the influence of hip-hop) and, subsequently, one that has experienced an unparalleled sense of cultural fusion and mixture within the last fifty years.

24. Mark Anthony Neal, "Left of Black: Saggy Pants, Talking White, and the Obama Bully Pulpit," NewBlackMan, blog, March 30, 2009, accessed January 6, 2010, http://newblackman.blogspot.com/2009_03_01_archive.html.

25. Timothy Douglas, telephone interview with the author, February 20, 2011.

26. Erving Goffman, *The Presentation of Self in Everyday Life* (New York: Doubleday Books, 1959), 59.

27. Ibid., 70–71.

28. Jackson also acknowledges that the notions of authenticity and sincerity have changed with the passage of time, noting that their meanings have actually reversed since sincerity used to be "about things" and authenticity used to be "about relations between people." John L. Jackson Jr., *Real Black: Adventures in Racial Sincerity* (Chicago: University of Chicago Press, 2005), 15.

29. Ibid.

30. Carmen Fought, "What Speech Do We Like Best? Watch Your Language," *Do You Speak American?*, PBS.org, accessed January 15, 2010, http://www.pbs.org/speak/speech/reveal/.

31. Mark M. Smith, *How Race Is Made: Slavery, Segregation, and the Senses* (Chapel Hill: University of North Carolina Press, 2006), 2.

32. Ibid., 10.

33. Ibid., 2.

34. Ibid., 7.

35. Ibid., 34, 192.

36. John McWhorter, "The Color of His Skin," *New York Sun*, September 21, 2006, accessed January 6, 2010, http://www.nysun.com/opinion/color-of-his-skin/40050/.

37. As quoted in Henderson, "Blacks, Whites Hear Obama Differently."

38. Cornelia Fales, "The Paradox of Timbre," *Ethnomusicology* 46.1 (Winter 2002): 58.

39. Ibid., 57.

40. Ibid., 58 (emphasis mine).

41. John Putenbaugh, quoted in Nina Sun Eidsheim, "Voice as a Technology of Selfhood: Towards an Analysis of Racialized Timbre and Vocal Performance" (PhD diss., University of San Diego, 2008), 172 (emphasis mine).

42. There are, however, a number of non-racially-specific corporeal aspects that affect timbral quality. Among these are (1) the length, thickness, or viscosity of one's vocal folds; (2) differences between a subject's pharynges and mouth cavities; and (3) the way in which one's voice is trained. Eidsheim also explains that there are additional factors that affect one's timbre such as the lungs and diaphragm (the "breathing apparatus"), the vocal folds, and the vocal and nasal tracts. See ibid., 31.

43. Ibid., 33.

44. Timothy Douglas, telephone interview with the author, February 20, 2011.

45. Eidsheim, "Voice as a Technology of Selfhood," 34.

46. At the time of this writing, I had the great benefit of reading Eidsheim's "Voice as a Technology of Selfhood." Since I first penned this chapter, Eidsheim has produced a number of articles and essays that take to task the erroneous correlations made be-

tween voice and race. Among these pieces are "Voice as Action: Towards a Model for Analyzing the Dynamic Construction of Racialized Voice," *Current Musicology* 93.1 (2012), 7–31; and "Racial Normalization and the Aesthetics of Vocal Timbre" in the forthcoming volume *Rethinking Difference in Musical Scholarship*, ed. Olivia Bloechl, Jeffrey Kallberg, and Melanie Lowe (New York: Cambridge University Press). It should also be noted that Eidsheim is furthering her research through two book manuscripts, tentatively titled *Sensing Sound: Singing and Listening as Vibrational Practice* (under contract with Duke University Press) and *Measuring Race: Listening to Vocal Timbre and Vocality in African-American Popular Music*. I look forward to familiarizing myself with these forthcoming works as they will certainly offer additional insight that will complement and/or challenge my own analysis and explorations. In the meantime, I would like to thank Nina Eidsheim for the generous collegiality she has shown by sharing her work with me and by offering me useful feedback on this chapter.

47. Focusing on the historical and pedagogical machinations of operatic performance and theory, Eidsheim's "Voice as a Technology of Selfhood" examines "the production, reception, and naming of vocal timbre" in an attempt to "denaturalize the devices used in the construction and maintenance of race" (2). I hope to support this effort within the realm of theatrically based performance, but I am also suggesting that the conscious casting of diverse and unexpected vocal qualities may bear efficacious results in terms of democratizing the economic playing field in the performing arts. To strip away notions of black or white voices within the theatre, film, and television industries could not only create greater casting opportunities for actors but also ostensibly aid in the reimagining of embodied characters and characteristics.

48. Ibid.

49. J. Ward and J. B. Mattingley quoted in Cretien van Campen, "The Hidden Sense: On Becoming Aware of Synesthesia," *Revista Digital de Tecnologias Cognitivas* 1 (2009): 1, http://www.pucsp.br/pos/tidd/teccogs/artigos/pdf/teccogs_edicao1_2009_artigo_CAMPEN.pdf, accessed January 10, 2010.

50. van Campen, "The Hidden Sense," 2.

51. Ibid., 6.

52. Eidsheim's term, *performative articulation*, addresses how racialized imagery and vocalizations are cognitively paired and processed in the public imagination. It is similar to my idea of racial synesthesia: "I coin the term *performative articulation* to address the cognitive processes by which audiences connect specific vocal sounds with particular ideas such as race and gender; these categories are consequently reified" ("Voice as a Technology of Selfhood," 26–27). Explaining the cyclical nature of this reification process, she writes, "[A]udiences join sound with concepts; (live or digital) performers respond to these sound/concept compounds, and in turn confirm the listener's linkages" (27). However, my trajectory of inquiry explores the *experienced absence* of performers' physical presence; thus, a confirmation of the "listeners' linkages" does not necessarily occur. In fact the listener may well imagine

a very different embodiment—one that, if revealed, would challenge rather than confirm the listener's racial synesthesia.

53. Alice Maurice, "'Cinema at Its Source': Synchronizing Race and Sound in the Early Talkies," *Cinema Obscura* 49.17 (2002).

54. While Maurice is primarily concerned with how the synchronicity of visible black bodies and audible black voices reinforced traditional expectations regarding black representation (and, simultaneously, helped to propel the popularity of talkies by offering amazingly "authentic" representations), I am also interested in how synesthetic impulses are at play when there is a *lack of synchronicity* between a performer's voice and its assumed body of origin due to a lack of embodied representation. Although Maurice's subject of inquiry deviates from my own, her thoughtful observations regarding the audience's auditory experience are equally valid when applied to the disembodied voices of black actors. Acknowledging that "the black of *black voices* signifies much more than color," Maurice aptly writes that "the action is reciprocal: color/race promises a particular kind of sound, and that sound, once heard, is supposed to refer back to the color/race that produced it." Ibid., 33.

55. Eidsheim, "Voice as a Technology of Selfhood," 45.

56. Ibid., 211–12.

57. Fales, "Paradox of Timbre," 61–63.

58. Ibid., 63.

59. Ibid., 58.

60. Michel Chion, *The Voice in Cinema*, trans. Claudia Gorbman (New York: Columbia University Press, 1993), 21. Chion goes on to explain that once the voice has been identified with a body, they can still be considered an "*acousmetre*" when off the screen, but should be referred to as a "visualized *acousmetre*" versus a "complete *acousmetre*."

61. Nancy Giles, telephone interview with the author, June 30, 2011.

62. Ibid.

63. After becoming a young television star in the 1960s, Sally Field has enjoyed a successful acting career, garnering a number of accolades, including two Academy Awards and three Emmy Awards (she earned the most recent Emmy in 2007 for her leading role in the ABC drama *Brothers and Sisters*).

64. Rayme Cornell, telephone interview with the author, May 28, 2009.

65. Ibid. It should be pointed out that Cornell's experience challenges Chion's assertion that that the visualized *acousmetre* is not only familiar but "reassuring." In film and television (unlike radio), the *acousmetre* is unique in that there not only exists the possibility that a a character's identity will be revealed, but also lurking in the wings is the possibility of exposing the listeners' prejudgments and expectations if, once revealed, the character does *not* look like what the listener previously imagined. See Chion, *The Voice in Cinema*, 22.

66. Chion, *The Voice in Cinema*, 3.

67. Joe Morgenstern, "Our Inner Child Meets Young Darth," *Wall Street Journal*, May 19, 1999. Stepin Fetchit, the stage name of Lincoln Theodore Monroe Andrew Perry, was the first African American actor to become a millionaire, but he did so by contested means. A comedic performer, Perry cultivated a character known as the "Laziest Man in the World." This character (or, rather, *caricature*) went by a number of names in innumerable films from the 1920s to the 1940s, thereby helping to popularize the cinematic stereotype of the bumbling, illiterate, buffoonish black fool. Unsurprisingly, the characters played by the actor were nothing like the real life Perry. A highly articulate and intellectual man, Perry was also a journalist who frequently contributed to the African American newspaper the *Chicago Defender*. For more on Perry, see Mel Watkins, *Stepin Fetchit: The Life and Times of Lincoln Perry* (New York: Vintage, 2006). Likewise, Morgenstern's citing of the actress Butterfly McQueen, undoubtedly alludes to the fact that McQueen often starred in mammy roles, most notably the character of Prissy in *Gone with the Wind* who famously discloses her ignorance and futility when she declares with exasperation, "I don't know nothin' 'bout birthin' babies!" *Gone with the Wind*, dir. Victor Fleming, Selznick International in association with Metro-Goldwyn-Mayer, 1999.

68. See Brent Staples, "Editorial Observer: Shuffling through the Star Wars," *New York Times*, June 20, 1999, accessed January 6, 2010, http://www.nytimes.com/1999/06/20/opinion/editorial-observer-shuffling-through-the-star-wars.html?sec=&spon=&partner=permalink&exprod=permalink.

69. Patricia J. Williams, "Racial Ventriloquism," *Nation*, July 5, 1999, accessed June 15, 2009, http://www.thenation.com/doc/19990705/williams.

70. As Angela Pao rightly notes, "[T]he visual and behavioral aspects of racial and ethnic impersonations have received far greater critical attention than the vocal or auditory aspects." Angela Pao, "False Accents: Embodied Dialects and the Characterization of Ethnicity and Nationality," *Theatre Topics* 14.1 (2004): 355.

71. Ibid., 353. While a critical consideration of ethnicity is important and necessary to further our understanding of how racial and cultural identities are performed, such an investigative thread is beyond the scope of this chapter. Rather, I am intentionally focusing on the consciously reductive question of what the sonic performance and/or interpretation of whiteness (as opposed to blackness) sounds like in the American imaginary.

72. Williams, "Racial Ventriloquism."

73. Harry Newman, "Holding Back: The Theatre's Resistance to Non-traditional Casting," *TDR: The Drama Review* 33.3 (1989): 24.

74. Rayme Cornell, telephone interview with the author, May 28, 2009.

75. Timothy Douglas, telephone interview with the author, February 20, 2011.

76. Ibid.

77. Nancy Giles, telephone interview with the author, June 30, 2011.

78. Phelan, *Unmarked*, 13.

Coda

1. Jefferson Pinder, *Afro-Cosmonaut/Alien (White Noise)*, jeffersonpinder.com, accessed February 15, 2010, http://www.jeffersonpinder.com/newsite/work/afro-cosmonautalien-white-noise/, high-definition video.

2. Ralph Ellison, *Invisible Man* (New York: Vintage), 1980, 201–2.

3. A *pipa* is an ancient four-string Chinese instrument. The musical piece that plays in *Afro-Cosmonaut/Alien (White Noise)*, titled "The Ambush," is performed by Liu Fang.

4. Gil Scott-Heron, "Whitey on the Moon" in "Gil Scott-Heron's Poem, 'Whitey on the Moon,'" by Alexis C. Madrigal, *The Atlantic*, May 28, 2011, accessed July 1, 2012. http://www.theatlantic.com/technology/archive/2011/05/gil-scott-herons-poem-whitey-on-the-moon/239622/.

5. Michael T. Martin with David C. Wall, "'Where Are You From?' Performing Race in the Art of Jefferson Pinder," *Black Camera: An International Film Journal* 2.1 (Winter 2010): 74–75.

6. Jefferson Pinder, telephone interview with the author, July 16, 2012.

7. Ibid.

8. Ibid.

9. Ibid.

10. Ibid.

11. Ibid.

12. Produced as part of the One Work series published to Afterall Books, Groys's unique book-length essay merges art criticism, philosophy, and fiction in order to provide audiences with a nuanced understanding of Kabakov's art and the period in which it was produced. Boris Groys, *Ilya Kabakov: The Man Who Flew into Space from His Apartment* (London: Afterall Books, 2006).

13. Ibid., 1.

14. See Barnor Hesse, "Self-Fulfilling Prophecy: The Postracial Horizon," *South Atlantic Quarterly* 110.1 (Winter 2001).

15. Patricia Sweetow Gallery, *Afro-Cosmonaut/Alien (White Noise)* press release, accessed February 15, 2010, http://www.patriciasweetowgallery.com/exhibition_links/HuffPind.pdf.

16. Thelma Golden, *Freestyle* (New York: Studio Museum in Harlem, 2001), 14 (exhibition catalog).

17. In discussing the proliferation of the term *postsoul*, Marvin McAllister notes that some scholars and cultural critics characterize postsoul artists as those who "tend to be disconnected from a black cultural past, especially the Black Arts Movement, and choose to explore multiple significations of blackness. . . . [T]his generation of artists tends to be unconcerned with overt forms of racism." *Whiting Up:*

Whiteface Minstrels and Stage Europeans in African American Performance (Chapel Hill: University of North Carolina Press, 2011), 237.

18. Brandi Wilkins Catanese, *The Problem of the Color[blind]: Racial Transgression and the Politics of Black Performance* (Ann Arbor: University of Michigan Press, 2011), 145.

19. Jefferson Pinder, telephone interview with the author, July 16, 2012.

Bibliography

Alcalay, Ron. "Morphing Out of Identity Politics: *Black or White* and *Terminator 2*." *Bad Subjects: Political Education for Everyday Life* 19 (March 1995). Accessed August 5, 2005. http://bad.eserver.org/issues/1995/19/alcalay.html.

Althusser, Louis. "Ideology and Ideological State Apparatuses (Notes towards an Investigation)." In *Lenin and Philosophy and Other Essays*. Translated by Ben Brewster, 127–86. New York: Monthly Review Press, 1971.

Austin, J. L. *How to Do Things with Words*. Cambridge, MA: Harvard University Press, 1962.

Awkward, Michael. "A Slave to the Rhythm: Essential(ist) Transmutations; or, the Curious Case of Michael Jackson." In *Negotiating Difference: Race, Gender, and the Politics of Positionality*, 175–219. Chicago: University of Chicago Press, 1995.

Baker, Elizabeth. "Danny Tisdale at Lombard-Freid." *Art in America*, December 1996, 97.

Bakhtin, Mikhail. *Rabelais and His World*. Translated by Hélène Iswolsky. Bloomington: Indiana University Press, 1984.

Banks, Daniel. "Unperforming the Minstrel Mask: Black-Face and the Technology of Representation." PhD diss., New York University, 2005.

Barnett, Claudia. "The Fundamental Challenge to Identity: Reproduction and Representation in the Drama of Adrienne Kennedy." *Theatre Journal* 48.2 (1996): 141–55.

Bean, Annemarie, James Hatch, and Brooks McNamara, eds. *Inside the Minstrel Mask: Readings in Nineteenth-Century Blackface Minstrelsy*. Hanover, NH: Wesleyan University Press, 1996.

Bennett, Lerone. "Black Power in Dixie." *Ebony* 17.9 (1962): 84–90.

Bhabha, Homi. "Of Mimicry and Man: The Ambivalence of Colonial Discourse." In *The Location of Culture*, 85–92. New York: Routledge, 1994.

Bigsby, C. W. E. "Three Black Playwrights: Loften Mitchell, Ossie Davis, Douglas

Turner Ward." In *The Theatre of Black Americans: A Collection of Critical Essays*, edited by Errol Hill, 148–67. New York: Applause Books, 2000.

Bourdieu, Pierre. *Outline of Theory of Practice*. Translated by Richard Nice. Cambridge: Cambridge University Press, 1977.

Bourdieu, Pierre. "The Form of Capital," in *Handbook of Theory of Research for the Sociology of Education*, trans. Richard Nice. Westport, CT: Greenwood Press, 1986.

Brackett, David. "The Politics and Practice of 'Cross-Over' in American Popular Music, 1963 to 1965." *Musical Quarterly* 78.4 (Winter 1994): 774–97.

Branigan, Tania. "Colin Powell Claims Scottish Coat of Arms." *Guardian*, May 11, 2004. Accessed February 10, 2012. http://www.guardian.co.uk/uk/2004/may/12/usa.world.

Brewer, Mary F. *Staging Whiteness*. Middletown: Wesleyan University Press, 2005.

Brown, Malcolm, and Trey Carpenter. Interview with the author, September 23, 2009.

Brustein, Robert. "Subsidized Separatism." *American Theatre* 13.8 (1996): 26–27, 100–101.

Buck, Stuart. *Acting White: The Ironic Legacy of Desegregation*. New Haven, CT: Yale University Press, 2010.

Butler, Judith. *Gender Trouble*. New York: Routledge, 1999.

Butler, Judith. "Performative Acts and Gender Constitution: An Essay in Phenomenology and Feminist Theory." *Theatre Journal* 40.4 (1988): 519–31.

Cabrera, David. "Transitions Inc.: Creative Time Citywide." *Flash Art: The Leading European Art Magazine* 25.166 (1992).

Carpenter, Faedra Chatard. "Addressing 'The Complex'-ities of Skin Color: Intraracism and the Plays of Hurston, Kennedy, and Orlandersmith.'" *Theatre Topics* 19.1 (March 2009): 15–27.

Carpenter, Faedra Chatard. "Embodying Anxieties: Race, Culture, and Identity in Contemporary American Performance." PhD diss., Stanford University, 2005.

Carpenter, Faedra Chatard. "Reading between the Lines: Intertextuality and the Documentation of African American Theatre History." *Blackstream III* (August 2006): 55–59.

Carpenter, Faedra Chatard. "Spectacles of Whiteness from Adrienne Kennedy to Suzan-Lori Parks." In *The Cambridge Companion to African American Theatre*, edited by Harvey Young, 174–95. Cambridge: Cambridge University Press, 2012.

Catanese, Brandi Wilkins. *The Problem of the Color[blind]: Racial Transgression and the Politics of Black Performance*. Ann Arbor: University of Michigan Press, 2011.

Catanese, Brandi Wilkins. "Teaching *A Day of Absence* 'at [Your] Own Risk.'" *Theatre Topics* 19.1 (2009): 29–38.

Chappelle's Show: Season One, Uncensored. Paramount, 2004. DVD.

Chion, Michel. *The Voice in Cinema*. Translated by Claudia Gorbman. New York: Columbia University Press, 1993.

Cobb, William Jelani. *The Devil and Dave Chappelle and Other Essays*. New York: Thunder's Mouth Press, 2007.

Cockrell, Dale. *Demons of Disorder: Early Blackface Minstrels and Their World*. New York: Cambridge University Press, 1997.

Collins, Patricia Hill. *Black Feminist Thought: Knowledge, Consciousness, and the Politics of Empowerment*. New York: Routledge, 2009.

"Condoleezza's Crimes." *Black Commentator*, April 1, 2004. Accessed February 19, 2012. http://www.blackcommentator.com/84/84_cover_condi.html.

Cornell, Rayme. Telephone interview with the author, May 28, 2009.

Crossley, Hillary, and Gil Kaufman. "Madonna Pays Tearful Tribute to Michael Jackson at 2009 VMAs." MTV.com News, September 13, 2009. Accessed December 12, 2012. http://www.mtv.com/news/articles/1621390/madonna-pays-tearfultribute-michael-jackson-at-2009-vmas.jhtml.

Cruse, Harold. "The Creative and Performing Arts and the Struggle for Identity and Credibility." In *Negotiating the Mainstream*, edited by Harry A. Johnson, 47–102. Chicago: American Library Association, 1978.

Cruse, Harold. *The Crisis of the Negro Intellectual*. London: W. H. Allen, 1969.

Dallas, Walter. Interview with the author, November 21, 2011.

Davis, Ossie. "Malcolm X's Eulogy." Official Web Site of Malcolm X. Accessed August 1, 2005. http://www.cmgww.com/historic/malcolm/index.html.

Davis, Ossie. "Remembering Paul Robeson," an interview with Phil Ponce and Martin Duberman. *Online NewsHour, a NewsHour with Jim Lehrer Transcript*, 1998. Accessed August 1, 2005. http://www.pbs.org/newshour/bb/remember/1998/robeson_4–9.html.

Day of Absence program booklet, Center Stage, October 1995.

Dentith, Simon. *Bakhtinian Thought: An Introductory Reader*. New York: Routledge, 1995.

De Salvo, Donna, and Maurice Berger, eds. *Face Value: American Portraits*. New York: Flammarion, 1995.

Diamond, Lydia. Telephone interview with the author, May 27, 2011.

Diamond, Lydia R. *Toni Morrison's* The Bluest Eye. Woodstock, IL: Dramatic Publishing, 2007.

Ditzian, Eric. "Michael Jackson's Groundbreaking Career, by the Numbers." MTV.com Top Stories. Accessed September 27, 2009. http://www.mtv.com/news/articles/1614815/20090626/jackson_michael.jhtml.

Douglas, Timothy. Telephone interview with the author, February 20, 2011.

W. E. B. Dubois. "Criteria of Negro Art." *Double Take: A Revisionist Harlem Renaissance Anthology*. Ed. Venetria K. Patton and Maureen Honey. New Brunswick: Rutgers University Press, 2001.

DuBois, W. E. B. *Darkwater: Voices from within the Veil*. New York: Harcourt, Brace and Howe, 1920.
DuBois, W. E. B. "Krigwa Players Little Negro Theatre: The Story of a Little Theatre Movement." *Crisis* 32.3 (1926): 134–36.
DuBois, W. E. B. *The Souls of Black Folk*. New York: Dover Publications, 1994.
Dyer, Richard. *Heavenly Bodies: Film Stars and Society*. New York: St. Martin's Press, 1986.
Dyer, Richard. *White: Essays on Race and Culture*. New York: Routledge, 1997.
Eidsheim, Nina Sun. "Voice as a Technology of Selfhood: Towards an Analysis of Racialized Timbre and Vocal Performance." PhD diss., University of San Diego, 2008.
Elam, Harry J., Jr. "August Wilson, Doubling, Madness, and Modern African American Drama." *Modern Drama* 43.4 (2000): 611–32.
Elam, Michele. "They's Mo' to Bein' Black Than Meets the Eye!" In *The Souls of Mixed Folk: Race, Politics, and Aesthetics in the New Millennium*, 160–204. Stanford, CA: Stanford University Press, 2011.
Ellis, Trey. "The New Black Aesthetic." *Callaloo* 12.1 (1989): 233–43.
Ellison, Ralph. *Invisible Man*. New York: Vintage, 1980.
Emami, Gazelle. "'America's Next Top Model' Puts Models in Blackface." *Huffington Post*, October 29, 2009. Accessed November 5, 2009. http://www.huffingtonpost.com/2009/10/29/americas-next-top-model-p_n_338741.html.
Fales, Cornelia. "The Paradox of Timbre." *Ethnomusicology* 46.1 (Winter 2002): 56–95.
Fanon, Frantz. *Black Skin, White Masks*. Translated by Charles Lam Markmann. New York: Grove Press, 1967.
Farber, Jim. "That 'Scream' You Hear Is Jackson's." *New York Daily News*, June 14, 1995, 3. Accessed September 14, 2009. http://www.nydailynews.com/archives/news/scream-hear-jackson-article-1.688008.
"Film Examines 'A Day without a Mexican.'" *News and Notes*, May 1, 2006. National Public Radio transcript. Accessed December 6, 2011. http://www.npr.org/templates/story/story.php?storyId=5372878.
Fought, Carmen. "What Speech Do We Like Best? Watch Your Language." *Do You Speak American?* PBS.org. Accessed January 15, 2010. http://www.pbs.org/speak/speech/reveal/.
Frankenberg, Ruth. "Introduction: Local Whitenesses, Localizing Whiteness." In *Displacing Whiteness: Essays in Social and Cultural Criticism*, edited by Ruth Frankenberg, 1–33. Durham, NC: Duke University Press, 1997.
Frankenberg, Ruth. "The Mirage of Unmarked Whiteness." In *The Making and Unmaking of Whiteness*, edited by Birgit Brander Rasmussen, Erick Klinenberg, Irene J. Nexica, and Matt Wray, 72–96. Durham, NC: Duke University Press, 2001.

Frontline. PBS.org. Accessed February 14, 2012. http://www.pbs.org/wgbh/pages/frontline/about-us/.

Fry, Gladys-Marie. *Night Riders in Black Folk History*. Knoxville: University of Tennessee Press, 1975.

Fuchs, Cynthia J. "Michael Jackson's Penis." In *Cruising the Performative: Interventions into the Representation of Ethnicity, Nationality, and Sexuality*, edited by Sue-Ellen Case, Philip Brett, and Susan Leigh Foster, 13–33. Bloomington: Indiana University Press, 1995.

Garber, Marjorie. "Fetish Envy." *October* 54 (Autumn 1990): 45–56.

Garner, Steve. *Whiteness: An Introduction*. New York: Routledge, 2007.

Gates, Henry Louis, Jr. *The Signifying Monkey: A Theory of Afro-American Literary Criticism*. New York: Oxford University Press, 1998.

Gent, George. "29 of 119 Stations Drop First TV Laboratory Show." *New York Times*, November 6, 1967.

Gent, George. "TV Laboratory's First Venture Gets Largely Adverse Reaction." *New York Times*, November 7, 1967.

George, Lynell. "Brave New World: Gray Boys, Funky Aztecs, and Honorary Homegirls." *Los Angeles Times Magazine*, January 17, 1993.

George-Graves, Nadine. *The Royalty of Negro Vaudeville*. New York: Palgrave Macmillan, 2000.

Gilbert, Helen. "Black and White and Re(a)d All Over Again: Indigenous Minstrelsy in Contemporary Canadian and Australian Theatre." *Theatre Journal* 55.4 (December 2003): 679–98.

Giles, Nancy. Telephone interview with the author, June 30, 2011.

Gillespie, Alex. "Autobiography and Identity: Malcolm X as Author and Hero." In *The Cambridge Companion to Malcolm X*, edited by Robert E. Terrill, 26–38. New York: Cambridge University Press, 2010.

Glover, William. "Two Negro Actors Start Drama Group with Ford Backing." *Washington Post, Times Herald*, August 6, 1967.

Goffman, Erving. *The Presentation of Self in Everyday Life*. New York: Doubleday Books, 1959.

Goldberg, Michael, and David Handelman. "Is Michael Jackson for Real?" *Rolling Stone*, September 24, 1987, 53–57, 138, 140, 142.

Golden, Thelma. *Freestyle*. New York: Studio Museum in Harlem, 2001. Exhibition catalog.

Gone with the Wind. Directed by Victor Fleming. Selznick International in association with Metro-Goldwyn-Mayer, 1999. DVD.

Goodman, Alan H. "Biological Diversity and Cultural Diversity: From Race to Radical Bioculturalism." In *Cultural Diversity in the United States: A Critical Reader*, edited by Ida Susser and Thomas C. Patterson, 29–45. Malden, MA: Blackwell Publishers, Inc., 2001.

Gould, Jack. "Georgia U. Will Not Carry TV Lab's First Show." *New York Times*, November 5, 1967.

Gould, Jack. "News Laboratory Experiences Some Birth Pains." *New York Times*, November 3, 1967.

Gould, Jack. "A Noble Experiment: Nowhere to Go but Up." *New York Times*, November 12, 1967.

Gould, Jack. "TV: An Experiment That Aims to Rock Status Quo." *New York Times*, November 6, 1967.

Graves, Nadine George. *The Royalty of Negro Vaudeville: The Whitman Sisters and the Negotiation of Race, Gender and Class in African American Theater 1900–1940*. New York: Palgrave Macmillan, 2000.

Gray, Richard J., II, and Michael Putnam. "Exploring Niggerdom: Racial Inversion in Language Taboos." In *The Comedy of Dave Chappelle: Critical Essays*, edited by K. A. Wisniewski, 15–30. Jefferson, NC: McFarland, 2009.

Grieco, Elizabeth M., and Rachel C. Cassidy. "Overview of Race and Hispanic Origin, 2000," 1–11. In *Census 2000 Brief*. Washington, DC: US Department of Commerce, Economics and Statistics Administration, issued March 2001.

Groys, Boris. *Ilya Kabakov: The Man Who Flew into Space from His Apartment*. London: Afterall Books, 2006.

Gubar, Susan. *Racechanges: White Skin, Black Face in American Culture*. Oxford: Oxford University Press, 1997.

Haiken, Elizabeth. *Venus Envy: A History of Cosmetic Surgery*. Baltimore: Johns Hopkins University Press, 1997.

Harper, Phillip Brian. "Synesthesia, 'Crossover,' and Blacks in Popular Music." *Social Text* 23 (Autumn–Winter 1989): 102–21.

Harris, Cheryl. "Whiteness as Property." *Harvard Law Review* 106.98 (June 1993): 1709–95.

Harris, Trudier. *Mammies to Militants: Domestics in Black American Literature*. Philadelphia: Temple University Books, 1982.

Hatch, James V., and Ted Shine. *Black Theatre USA: The Recent Period, 1935–Today*. New York: Free Press, 1996.

Headlam, Jihan. "Black Solidarity Day Develops Community." *New Paltz Oracle*, November, 7, 2002.

Henderson, Nia-Malika. "Blacks, Whites Hear Obama Differently." *Politico*, March 3, 2009. Accessed January 6, 2010. http://www.politico.com/news/stories/0309/19538.html.

Hentoff, Nat. "You're Hot, You're Poor, You're Nothing . . ." *New York Times*, November 14, 1965.

Hesse, Barnor. "Self-Fulfilling Prophecy: The Postracial Horizon." *South Atlantic Quarterly* 110.1 (Winter 2001): 155–78.

Hixson, Lindsay, Bradford B. Hepler, and Myoung Ouk Kim. "The White Population:, 2010," 1–18. In *2010 Census Briefs*. Washington, DC: US Department of Commerce, Economics and Statistics Administration, Issued September 2011.

Holland, Norman H. "Unity Identity Text Self." In *Reader-Response Criticism: From Formalism to Post-Structuralism*, edited by Jane P. Tomkins, 118–33. Baltimore: Johns Hopkins University Press, 1980.

hooks, bell. *Black Looks: Race and Representation*. Boston: South End Press, 1992.

hooks, bell. "Representing Whiteness in the Black Imagination." In *Displacing Whiteness: Essays in Social and Cultural Criticism*, ed. Ruth Frankenberg, 165–79. Durham, NC: Duke University Press, 1997.

"Introduction." Chapelletheory.com. Accessed October 5, 2007. www.chappelletheory.com.

Ivory, Lee. "'Day of Absence' Powerful Story but Offends No One." *Baltimore Afro-American*, December 11, 1965.

Jackson, John L., Jr. *Real Black: Adventures in Racial Sincerity*. Chicago: University of Chicago Press, 2005.

Jackson, La Toya, with Patricia Romanowski. *La Toya: Growing Up in the Jackson Family*. New York: Dutton, 1991.

James, David E. "The Unsecret Life: A Warhol Advertisement." *October* 56 (Spring 1991): 21–41.

Jenkins, Marianna. *The State Portrait, Its Origin and Evolution*. New York: College Art Association of America in conjunction with *Art Bulletin*, 1947.

Jewell, K. Sue. *From Mammy to Miss America and Beyond: Cultural Images and the Shaping of U.S. Policy*. New York: Routledge, 1993.

Johnson, E. Patrick. *Appropriating Blackness: Performance and the Politics of Authenticity*. Durham. NC: Duke University Press, 2003.

Johnson, E. Patrick. "Black Performance Studies: Genealogies, Politics, Futures." In *The SAGE Handbook of Performance Studies*, edited by D. Soyini Madison and Judith Hamera, 446–63. London: SAGE Publications, 2006.

Jones, LeRoi. "The Revolutionary Theatre." In *Home: Social Essays*, 210–15. New York: William Morrow, 1966.

Jones, Nicholas A., and Jungmiwha Bullock. "The Two or More Races Population: 2010," 1–23. In *2010 Census Briefs*. Washington, DC: US Department of Commerce, Economics and Statistics Administration, Issued September 2012.

Kasher, Steven. *The Civil Rights Movement: A Photographic History, 1954–68*. New York: Abbeville Press, 1996.

Kennedy, Adrienne. *Funnyhouse of a Negro*. New York: Samuel French, 1969.

Kennedy, Randall. *Nigger: The Strange Career of a Troublesome Word*. New York: Vintage, 2003.

Keyssar, Helene. *Feminist Theatre and Theory*. New York: St. Martin's Press, 1996.
Kintz, Linda. *The Subject's Tragedy: Political Poetics, Feminist Theory, and Home*. Ann Arbor: University of Michigan Press, 1992.
Krasner, David. *Resistance, Parody, and Double Consciousness in African American Theatre, 1895–1910*. New York: St. Martin's Press, 1997.
Kupferberg, Herbert. "Negro Plays: Sparks, but No Real Fire." *New York Herald Tribune*, November 16, 1965.
Lewis, Randy. "Winless Jackson Scores in Speech." *Los Angeles Times*, February 25, 1993. Accessed September 10, 2009. http://articles.latimes.com/1993-02-25/entertainment/ca-727_1_michael-jackson.
Lhamon, W. T., Jr. *Raising Cain: Blackface Performance from Jim Crow to Hip Hop*. Cambridge, MA: Harvard University Press, 1998.
Limbaugh, Rush. "Powell Endorsement of Obama Has Everything to Do with Race, Elitism." *Rush Limbaugh Show*, October 20, 2008. Accessed January 10, 2013. http://www.rushlimbaugh.com/daily/2008/10/20/powell_endorsement_of_obama_has_everything_to_do_with_race_elitism.
Litwack, Leon F. *Trouble in Mind: Black Southerners in the Age of Jim Crow*. New York: Knopf, 1998.
Löfgren, Lotta M. "Clay and Clara: Baraka's *Dutchman*, Kennedy's *The Owl Answers*, and the Black Arts Movement." *Modern Drama* 46 (Fall 2003): 424–49.
Lorde, Audre. "The Master's Tools Will Never Dismantle the Master's House." In *Sister Outsider: Essays and Speeches*, 110–13. New York: Crossing Press, 2007.
Lott, Eric. "The Aesthetic Ante: Pleasure, Pop Culture, and the Middle Passage." *Callaloo* 17.2 (1994): 545–55.
Lott, Eric. *Love and Theft: Blackface Minstrelsy and the American Working Class*. New York: Oxford University Press, 1993.
Madhubuti, Haki R., and Maulana Karenga. "The March, the Day of Absence, and the Movement." In *Million Man March/Day of Absence, a Commemorative Anthology: Speeches, Commentary, Photography, Poetry, Illustrations, Documents*, edited by Haki R. Madhubuti and Maulana Karenga. Chicago: Third World Press, 1996.
Madison, Lucy. "Sununu Suggests Colin Powell's Obama Endorsement Racially Driven." CBS News.com, October 26, 2012. Accessed April 28, 2014. http://www.cbsnews.com/8301-34222_162-57541013/sununu-suggests-colin-powells-obama-endorsement-racially-driven/.
Madrigal, Alexis C., "Gil Scott-Heron's Poem, 'Whitey on the Moon,'" *The Atlantic*, May 28, 2011. Accessed July 1, 2012. http://www.theatlantic.com/technology/archive/2011/05/gil-scott-herons-poem-whitey-%09on-the-moon/239622/.
Margolis, Harriet. "Stereotypical Strategies: Black Film Aesthetics, Spectator Positioning, and Self-Directed Stereotypes in 'Hollywood Shuffle' and 'I'm Gonna Git You Sucka.'" *Cinema Journal* 38.3 (Spring 1999): 50–66.

Marion, Alexis. "Black Solidarity Day." *Tufts Daily*, November 5, 2007.
Marriot, David. *On Black Men*. New York: Columbia University Press, 2000.
Martin, Michael T., with David C. Wall. "'Where Are You From?' Performing Race in the Art of Jefferson Pinder." *Black Camera: An International Film Journal* 2.1 (Winter 2010): 72–105.
The Masterworks of Edvard Munch. Introduction by John Ederfield. Commentary by Arne Eggum. New York: *MoMA* 10 (Spring 1979).
Maurice, Alice. "'Cinema at Its Source': Synchronizing Race and Sound in the Early Talkies." *Camera Obscura* 49.17 (2002): 1–71.
McAllister, Marvin. "Dave Chappelle, Whiteface Minstrelsy, and 'Irresponsible' Satire." In *African American Humor, Irony, and Satire: Ishmael Reed, Satirically Speaking*, edited by Dana A. Williams. 118–30. Newcastle: Cambridge Scholars Publishing, 2007.
McAllister, Marvin. *White People Do Not Know How to Behave at Entertainments Designed for Ladies and Gentlemen of Colour: William Brown's African and American Theater*. Chapel Hill: University of North Carolina Press, 2003.
McAllister, Marvin. *Whiting Up: Whiteface Minstrels and Stage Europeans in African American Performance*. Chapel Hill: University of North Carolina Press, 2011.
McCain, Demetria. "A 'Day without a Mexican' Déjà vu: Douglas Turner Ward's Black Theatre Unforgotten." Originally published in the *Portland Medium*, June 4, 2004. Accessed December 6, 2011. http://kathmanduk2.wordpress.com/2008/03/09/from-the-archives-a-disappearance-a-day-of-absence-and-a-day-without-a-mexican/.
McCarten, John. "Burdensome Baggage." *New Yorker*, December 25, 1965.
McWhorter, John. "The Color of His Skin." *New York Sun*, September 21, 2006. Accessed January 6, 2010. http://www.nysun.com/opinion/color-of-his-skin/40050/.
Mercer, Kobena. "Black Hair/Style Politics." *New Formations* 3 (Winter 1987): 33–54.
Mercer, Kobena. "Engendered Species: Danny Tisdale and Keith Piper." *Artforum*, Summer 1992.
Mercer, Kobena. "Monster Metaphors: Notes on Michael Jackson's *Thriller*." In *Reading Images*, edited by Julia Thomas, 17–32. New York: Palgrave Macmillan, 2000.
"Michael Jackson Autopsy Report." The Smoking Gun. Accessed December 15, 2012. http://www.thesmokinggun.com/documents/crime/michael-jackson-autopsy-report.
"Michael Jackson Memorial: Paris Jackson Speaks, Says Goodbye to Father Michael." YouTube.com. Accessed July 7, 2009. http://www.youtube.com/watch?v=PzP0HcftrVY.
"Michael Jackson Memorial Service—Rev. Al Sharpton." YouTube.com. Accessed July 7, 2009. http://www.youtube.com/watch?v=_MAKLq865bk.

"Michael Jackson Tapes: Madonna 'Is Not a Nice Person.'" CNN.com/entertainment, September 30, 2009. Accessed October 13, 2009. http://www.cnn.com/2009/SHOWBIZ/Music/09/30/lkl.michael.jackson.tapes/.

Michael Jackson–Video Greatest Hits–HIStory. NTSX, 2001. DVD special edition.

Mickelbury, Penny. "BIBR Spotlight: Saluting an Innovative Dramatist." *Black Issues Book Review* 5.5 (2003): 34–35.

Mintz, Lawrence E. "Standup Comedy as Social and Cultural Mediation." *American Quarterly* 37.1 (Spring 1985): 71–80.

Morgenstern, Joe. "Our Inner Child Meets Young Darth." *Wall Street Journal*, May 19, 1999.

Morrison, Toni. *The Bluest Eye.* New York: Washington Square Press, 1970.

Moser, Bob. "From the Belly of the Beast: A White-Supremacist Prison Plot Hits the Streets—with an Unusual 'Aryan' at the Helm." *Southern Poverty Law Center Intelligence Report* 108 (Winter 2002): 8–17.

Mullen, Harryette. "Optic White: Blackness and the Production of Whiteness." *Diacritics* 24.2–3 (1994): 71–89.

Muñoz, José Esteban. *Disidentifications: Queers of Color and the Performance of Politics.* Minneapolis: University of Minnesota Press, 1999.

Muratore, M. J. "Review Commentary: Framing Violence—Censorship and Race in American Culture." *Journal of American Culture* 19.4 (1996): 93–95.

Nagel, Rob. "Biography: Paul Robeson." *Contemporary Musicians* 8 (1992). Accessed August 1, 2005. http://homepage.sunrise.ch/homepage/comtex/rob3.htm.

Neal, Larry. "The Black Arts Movement." *Drama Review* 12 (Summer 1968): 28–39.

Neal, Mark Anthony. "Left of Black: Saggy Pants, Talking White, and the Obama Bully Pulpit." NewBlackMan, blog, March 30, 2009. Accessed January 6, 2010. http://newblackman.blogspot.com/2009_03_01_archive.html.

Newman, Harry. "Holding Back: The Theatre's Resistance to Non-traditional Casting." *TDR: The Drama Review* 33.3 (1989): 22–36.

New York Times. "Theatre 1964 presents Adrienne Kennedy's *Funnyhouse of a Negro*," theatre advertisement section, January 17, 1964, 24.

O'Connor, Richard. *The Cactus Throne: The Tragedy of Maximilian and Carlotta.* New York: G. P. Putnam's Sons, 1971.

Oliver, Clinton F., and Stephanie Sills. *Contemporary Black Drama: From A Raisin in the Sun to No Place To Be Somebody.* New York: Scribner, 1971.

Omi, Michael, and Howard Winant. *Racial Formation in the United States from the 1960s to the 1990s.* New York: Routledge, 2004.

Pabst, Naomi. "Blackness/Mixedness: Contestations over Crossing Signs." *Cultural Critique* 54 (Spring 2003): 178–212.

Pagel, David. "New York Fax." *Art Issues* 24 (1992): 31.

Pao, Angela. "False Accents: Embodied Dialects and the Characterization of Ethnicity and Nationality." *Theatre Topics* 14.1 (2004): 353–72.

Parks, Suzan-Lori. *The Death of the Last Black Man in the Whole Entire World.* In *The America Play and Other Works,* 99–132. New York: Theatre Communications Group, 1995.

Parsons, Elaine Frantz. "Midnight Rangers: Costume and Performance in the Reconstruction-Era Ku Klux Klan." *Journal of American History* 92.3 (2005): 811–36.

Patraka, Vivian. "Binary Terror and Feminist Performance: Reading Both Ways." *Discourse* 4.2 (Spring 1992): 163–85.

Patricia Sweetow Gallery. *Afro-Cosmonaut/Alien (White Noise)* press release. Accessed February 15, 2010. http://www.patriciasweetowgallery.com/exhibition_links/HuffPind.pdf.

"PBL Debut Wins Praise, Cancellations." *Washington Post, Times Herald,* November 7, 1979.

Phelan, Peggy. *Unmarked: The Politics of Performance.* New York: Routledge, 1993.

Pinder, Jefferson. *Afro-Cosmonaut/Alien (White Noise).* jeffersonpinder.com. Accessed February 15, 2010. http://www.jeffersonpinder.com/newsite/work/afro-cosmonautalien-white-noise/. High-definition video.

Pinder, Jefferson. Telephone interview with the author, July 16, 2012.

Pope, S. W. "'Race,' Family, and Nation: The Significance of Tiger Woods in American Culture." In *Out of the Shadows: A Biographical History of African American Athletes,* edited by David K. Wiggins, 325–52. Fayetteville: University of Arkansas Press, 2006.

Prideaux, Tom. "A Long Leap for the Short Play: Four New Ones Off Broadway." *Life,* January 28, 1966.

Proehl, Geoffrey S. *Toward a Dramaturgical Sensibility: Landscape and Journey.* Madison, NJ: Fairleigh Dickinson University Press, 2008.

"The Racial Draft." *Chappelle's Show: Season Two, Uncensored.* Paramount, 2004.

Rasmussen, Birgit Brander, Erick Klinenberg, Irene J. Nexica, and Matt Wray, eds. *The Making and Unmaking of Whiteness.* Durham, NC: Duke University Press, 2001.

"Reality without Illusion." *Washington Post,* November 7, 1967.

Richards, Sandra L. "Writing the Absent Potential: Drama, Performance, and the Canon of African-American Literature." In *Performativity and Performance,* edited by Andrew Parker and Eve Kosofsky Sedgwick, 64–88. New York: Routledge, 1995.

Rickford, John R. *African American Vernacular English: Features and Use, Evolution, and Educational Implications.* Malden, MA: Wiley-Blackwell, 1999.

Rickford, John Russell, and Russell John Rickford. *Spoken Soul: The Story of Black English.* New York: John Wiley and Sons, 2000.

Roach, Joseph. *Cities of the Dead: Circum-Atlantic Performance.* New York: Columbia University Press, 1996.

Robinson, Amy. "Forms of Appearance of Value: Homer Plessy and the Politics of

Privacy." In *Performance and Cultural Politics*, edited by Elin Diamond, 237–61. New York: Routledge, 1996.

Robinson, Eugene. "What Rice Can't See." *Washington Post*, October 25, 2005. Accessed February 10, 2012. http://www.washingtonpost.com/wp-dyn/content/article/2005/10/24/AR2005102401370.html.

Roediger, David R., ed. *Black on White: Black Writers on What It Means to Be White*. New York: Schocken Books, 1998.

Russell, Carlos. E-mail interview with the author, July 22, 2013.

Russell, Carlos. Telephone interview with the author, March 24, 2011.

"Save Sunday Night!" *Washington Post, Times Herald*, November 5, 1967.

Scanlan, Robert. "Surrealism as Mimesis: A Director's Guide to Adrienne Kennedy's *Funnyhouse of a Negro*." In *Intersecting Boundaries: The Theatre of Adrienne Kennedy*, edited by Paul K. Bryant-Jackson and Lois More Overbeck, 93–109. Minneapolis: University of Minnesota Press, 1992.

Schneider, Rebecca. *The Explicit Body in Performance*. London: Routledge, 1997.

Schuyler, George S. *Black No More*. New York: Dover Publications, 2011.

Seeman, Bettie. "Yarn Wigs: Design, Construction, and Styling." *Theatre Crafts*, May–June 1976, 19–21.

Silberman, Seth Clark. "Presenting Michael Jackson™." *Social Semiotics* 17.4 (2007): 417–40.

Silver, Andrew. *Minstrelsy and Murder: The Crisis of Southern Humor, 1835–1925*. Baton Rouge: Louisiana State University Press, 2006.

"16th Annual "Black Solidarity Conference." Yale Black Solidarity Conference. Accessed February 4, 2011. http://www.yale.edu/bsc/.

Smith, Cherise. "Moneta Sleet Jr. as Active Participant: The Selma March and the Black Arts Movement." In *New Thoughts on the Black Arts Movement*, edited by Lisa Gail Collins and Margo Natalie Crawford, 210–26. New Brunswick, NJ: Rutgers University Press, 2006.

Smith, Mark M. *How Race Is Made: Slavery, Segregation, and the Senses*. Chapel Hill: University of North Carolina Press, 2006.

Smith, Michael. "Theatre Journal." *Village Voice*, November 18, 1965.

Sprengelmeyer, M. E. "Nader: Obama Trying to 'Talk White.'" *Rocky Mountain News*, updated June 25, 2008. Accessed January 6, 2010. http://www.rockymountainnews.com/news/2008/jun/25/nader-critical-of-obama-for-trying-to-talk-white/.

Staples, Brent. "Editorial Observer: Shuffling through the Star Wars." *New York Times*, June 20, 1999. Accessed January 6, 2010. http://www.nytimes.com/1999/06/20/opinion/editorial-observer-shuffling-through-the-star-wars.html?sec=&spon=&partner=permalink&exprod=permalink.

Steppenwolf Arts Exchange. "*The Bluest Eye* Study Guide." Accessed June 19, 2011. http://www.steppenwolf.org/_pdf/studyguides/bluest_eye_studyguide.pdf.

Synnot, Anthony. *The Body Social: Symbolism, Self, and Society*. New York: Routledge, 1993.
Taubman, Howard. Review of *Funnyhouse of a Negro*, by Adrienne Kennedy. *New York Times*, January 17, 1964.
Taubman, Howard. "Theater: Satiric Twin Bill." *New York Times*, November 16, 1965.
"Testimony of Joe Brown." In *Report of the Joint Select Committee to Inquire into the Condition of Affairs in the Late Insurrectionary States* (1872), part 6: Georgia, vol. 1 501–3.
"The Theory, April 20, 2003." Accessed October 5, 2007. www.chappelletheory.com.
Thompson, Deborah. "Reversing Blackface Minstrelsy, Improvising Racial Identity: Adrienne Kennedy's *Funnyhouse of a Negro*." *Post Identity* 1.1 (Fall 1997): 13–38.
Tisdale, Daniel. Interview with the author, May 11, 2002.
Tisdale, Daniel. Telephone interview with the author, December 15, 2003.
Tompkins, Kyla. *Racial Indigestion: Eating Bodies in the Nineteenth Century*. New York: New York University Press, 2012.
Tough, Paul. "The Black Supremacist." *New York Times Magazine*, May 25, 2003. Accessed February 3, 2012. http://www.nytimes.com/2003/05/25/magazine/the-black-supremacist.html?pagewanted=all&src=pm.
Trescot, Jacqueline. "A 'Day' That's Come to Pass? Million Man March Harks Back to a Landmark '65 Play." *Washington Post*, October 16, 1995.
Trudgill, Peter. *Sociolinguistics: An Introduction to Language and Society*. New York: Penguin Books, 2000.
Tucker, Terence T. "Furiously Funny: Comic Rage in Late Twentieth Century African-American Literature." PhD diss., University of Kentucky, 2006.
Tyson, Lois. "Reader-Response Criticism." In *Critical Theory Today: A User-Friendly Guide*, 153–96. New York: Routledge, 1999.
Untitled Abstract on Black Solidarity Day. *New York Times*, November 1, 1969.
US Department of Commerce. United States Census Bureau. Accessed June 1, 2004, and February 4, 2012. http://www.census.gov/.
United States of America v. Leo V. Felton and Erica Chase. Criminal no. 1:01CR 10198-NG., General Allegations.
van Campen, Cretien. "The Hidden Sense: On Becoming Aware of Synesthesia." *Revista Digital de Tecnologias Cognitivas* 1 (2009): 1–13. Accessed January 10, 2010. http://www.pucsp.br/pos/tidd/teccogs/artigos/pdf/teccogs_edicao1_2009_artigo_CAMPEN.pdf.
"Victoria." In *Collier's Encyclopedia*, vol. 23, 121–22. New York: Macmillan Educational Company, 1990.
Ward, Douglas Turner. "American Theater: For Whites Only?" *New York Times*, August 14, 1966.

Ward, Douglas Turner. *Day of Absence*. Public Broadcasting Library, episode 101, November 5, 1967, Library of Congress, Washington, DC. Video.

Ward, Douglas Turner. Happy Ending *and* Day of Absence: *Two Plays*. New York: Dramatists Play Service, 1966.

Ward, Douglas Turner. Telephone interview with the author, January 27, 2012.

Ward, Douglas Turner. Telephone interview with the author, August 6, 2013.

Ward, J. and J. B. Mattingley. "Synaesthesia: An Overview of Contemporary Findings and Controversies." *Cortex* 42.2 (2006): 129–36.

Watkins, Mel. *Stepin Fetchit: The Life and Times of Lincoln Perry*. New York: Vintage, 2006.

Weiss, Allen S. "Desublimation and Morbidity." *TDR: The Drama Review* 43.1 (1999): 145–51.

Werrlein, Debra T. "Not So Fast, Dick and Jane: Reimagining Childhood and Nation in *The Bluest Eye*." *MELUS* 30.4 (Winter 2005): 53–72.

West, Shearer. *Portraiture*. Oxford: Oxford University Press, 2004.

"What the Heck Is Day of Absence and Day of Presence?" *Cooper Point Journal: Student Newspaper of the Evergreen State College*, April 5, 2010.

"White Like Me." *Saturday Night Live: The Best of Eddie Murphy*. Lions Gate, 2010. DVD.

Williams, Patricia J. "Racial Ventriloquism." *Nation*, July 5, 1999. Accessed June 15, 2009. http://www.thenation.com/doc/19990705/williams.

Willis, Susan. "I Want the Black One: Is There a Place for Afro-American Culture in Commodity Culture?" *New Formations* 10 (Spring 1990): 77–97.

Wilson, August. "The Ground on Which I Stand." *American Theatre* 13.7 (1996): 14–16, 71–74.

Wolfe, George. *The Colored Museum*. New York: Grove Press, 1988.

Wood, Jacqueline. "Weight of the Mask: Parody and the Heritage of Minstrelsy in Adrienne Kennedy's *Funnyhouse of a Negro*." *Journal of Dramatic Theory and Criticism* 17.2 (Spring 2003): 5–24.

Wright, David. "'First Lady Michelle Obama Reflects on Talking 'Like a White Girl': Michelle Obama Tells D.C. Students That Stereotypes Get in the Way.'" ABC News, March 20, 2009. Accessed January 5, 2010. http://abcnews.go.com/GMA/Story?id=7130988&page=1.

X, Malcolm, with Alex Haley. *The Autobiography of Malcolm X*. New York: Ballantine Books, 1992.

Young, Harvey. *Embodying Black Experience: Stillness, Critical Memory, and the Black Body*. Ann Arbor: University of Michigan Press, 2010.

Young, Harvey, and Jocelyn Prince. "Adapting *The Bluest Eye for the Stage*," *African American Review* 45.1–2 (Spring/Summer 2012).

Index

AAVE. *See* African American Vernacular English
African American Vernacular English (AAVE), 197, 199–200, 205, 220, 270n5, 271n22
afro-alienation, 246n17
Ali, Muhammad, 158, 159
Althusser, Louis, 88, 89
American Theatre, 248n68
America's Next Top Model, 241n23
Arau, Sergio: *A Day without a Mexican*, 79, 252n115
Arena Stage, 242n24
Arizmendi, Yareli: *A Day without a Mexican*, 78–79, 252n115
Art in America, 226
Art Issues, 259n30
Asolo Theatre Conservatory, 225
Astaire, Fred, 158, 159
Atlanta-Constitution Journal, 226
Awkward, Michael, 140–41

Baldwin, James, 8, 54
Baltimore Afro-American, 44
Banks, Daniel, 38; "Unperforming the Minstrel Mask," 246n15, 250n91
Banks, Tyra, 241n23
Barnett, Claudia, 21–22
Barrett, Edward W., 57
becoming white, 117–60. *See also* Jackson, Michael; Tisdale, Daniel
Berry, Halle, 181, 183, 187
Best, Ahmed, 220

Bhabha, Homi, 18, 140
bidialectism, 202, 205–6, 223
Bigsby, C. W. E.: "Three Black Playwrights," 245n7
Black Arts Movement, 4, 15, 17, 18, 186, 247n43, 276n17
Black Camera: An International Film Journal, 226
blackface minstrelsy, 3, 10, 11, 12, 19, 28, 46, 72, 172, 184, 185, 231, 241n23, 244n44, 247n51, 265n17
blacking up, 172, 173, 265n19
Black Power, 4, 17, 259n30, 267n50
Black Solidarity Conference, 251n107
Black Solidarity Day, 74, 75–76, 79, 251n105, 251n107, 252n110
Black Women Playwrights Group, 242n24
Boniva, 215, 217–18
Boteach, Shmuley, 263n81
Bourdieu, Pierre, 6, 7, 200, 239n10
Brewer, Mary: *Staging Whiteness*, 10
Bronx Museum, 226
Brooks, Daphne, 246n17
Brown, H. R., 60
Brown, Joe, 172, 173
Brustein, Robert, 248n68
Buck, Stuart, 198
Butler, Judith, 89, 139

Carmichael, Stokely, 60, 63
Catanese, Brandi Wilkins, 7, 46, 246n35; *The Problem of the Color[blind]*, 270n2
CBS News Sunday Morning, 215

Center Stage, 76, 242n24
Chappelle, Dave, 14, 28; "Clayton Bigsby," 162, 166, 167–71, 173, 174–76, 179, 180, 181, 185, 189, 192, 193, 194, 264n14, 266n27, 266n40; drafting whiteness, 185–89; enacting whiteness, 161–93, 214, 267n48; KKK theatrics as whiteface performance, 171–76; policing race, policing Chappelle, 190–93; "The Racial Draft," 162, 163, 166, 174, 176, 181–85, 186, 187–88, 189, 193, 194, 267n44, 268n62; reading race, culture, and the US Census, 163–67
Chappelle's Show, 28, 162, 163, 165, 166, 188, 190, 191–92, 264n14
Chicago Defender, 275n66
Chion, Michel, 215, 219, 274n59, 274n64
Civil Rights Act of 1964, 4
Civil Rights Movement, 3, 4, 5, 15, 26, 226, 231, 234, 236
Cole, Bob, 240n17
Coles, Robert, 67–68
Comedy Central, 192
Congress of Racial Equality, 249n71
constituting acts, 89, 166
Cornell, Rayme, 218–20, 222, 223, 224, 274n64
Crossroads Theatre Company, 242n24
Cruse, Harold, 126; "The Creative and Performing Arts and the Struggle for Identity and Credibility," 258n15; *The Crisis of the Negro Intellectual*, 258n15
Culkin, Macaulay: *Home Alone*, 143, 144, 145
cultural capital, 11, 24, 33, 41, 153, 200, 223; presumed aural whiteness, 196–206

Dallas, Walter: *The Bluest Eye*, 102–3, 109–10, 255n74
Davis, Ossie, 54, 123–24, 257n13
deprivileges, 22, 244n54
Detroit riots, 60
DeWindt, Hal, 32
dialect, 44, 197, 199–200, 270n4; bidialectism, 202, 205–6, 223
Diamond, Lydia: *The Bluest Eye*, 26, 80–106, 157, 254n48, 255n72, 255n74; adaption of *The Bluest Eye*, 107–16
disidentification, 36, 190, 214, 245n13, 269n68
Dolan, Jill, 147

Douglas, Timothy, 199, 203, 204, 208, 209, 222, 223, 224
dramaturg, production, 12–14, 242n26
DuBois, W. E. B., 8, 35, 54
DuBoisian doubleness, 7
Dugan, Dave, 66
Dyer, Richard, 19, 22, 126, 184, 245n58, 258n15; *Heavenly Bodies*, 122; *White*, 82–83

Educational Television and Radio Center, 249n71
Eidsheim, Nina Sun, 209–10, 211, 272n41; *Measuring Race*, 272n45; performative articulation, 273n51; "Racial Normalization and the Aesthetics of Vocal Timbre," 272n45; racialized timbre, 208; *Sensing Sound*, 272n45; "Voice as a Technology of Selfhood," 272n45, 273n46
Elam, Harry J., 243n36
Elam, Michele, 181, 267n44, 267n48
Elder, Lonne, 32
Ellis, Trey: "The New Black Aesthetic," 186
Ellison, Ralph: *Invisible Man*, 24, 47–48, 52, 228
Elson, William, 92–95
English sounding, 269n1

Fales, Cornelia, 208, 212
Farber, Jim, 262n71
Felton, Leo V., 176–81, 266n38, 266n40
Feminist Movement, 4
Fetchit, Stepin, 275n66
Field, Sally, 217, 218, 274n62
Flint Institute of Art, 226
Folgers Coffee, 215
Ford Foundation, 30, 55, 71; Fund for Adult Education, 249n71
Foster, Frances, 32
Frankenberg, Ruth, 8, 9, 253n4
Franklin, John Hope, 69–70, 250n92
French, Arthur, 32
Frontline, 167–68, 169, 175, 264n12
Fuchs, Cynthia J. 140

Garber, Marjorie, 140
Gayle, Addison: *The New Black Aesthetic*, 86
Gay Liberation Movement, 4
Genet, Jean, 46; *The Blacks*, 45

INDEX

George-Graves, Nadine, 10; *The Royalty of Negro Vaudeville*, 240n17
G-Fine Art Gallery, 226
Gilbert, Helene, 10; "Black and White and Re(a)d All Over Again," 240n17
Giles, Nancy, 198–99, 215–16, 217–18, 219, 220, 223, 224
Gillespie, Alex, 126
GlaxoSmithKine, 215; "Consequences," commercial, 217
Glover, Savion: *Bring in 'da Noise, Bring 'da funk*, 254n52
Goffman, Erving, 204, 205
Goldberg, David Theo, 164
Goldberg, Whoopi, 192, 214
Goodman, Alan H., 164
Gordy, Berry, 138
Gottfried, Martin, 45, 47, 72
Gould, Jack, 70, 72; "Georgia U. Will Not Carry TV Lab's First Show," 250n80
Gray, William, 92–95
Group Theatre Workshop, 31, 32, 53, 55, 249n70
Groys, Boris, 276n12; *Illya Kabakov*, 234
Gubar, Susan, 10; *Racechanges*, 240n17, 260n45
Gunn, Moses, 32

Haiken, Elizabeth, 137
Hale, William H., Jr., 56–57, 249n77
Haley, Alex: *The Autobiography of Malcolm X*, 250n88, 258n18
Hansberry, Lorraine, 54, 109; *A Raisin in the Sun*, 31
Harlow, Jean, 94, 96, 97
Hartford Stage, 255n74
Hatcher, Richard Gordon, 60, 62
Henderson, Nia-Malika, 202–3, 204, 271n22
Heron, Gil Scott: *Whitey on the Moon*, 229
Hicks, Louise Day, 61–62
High Museum of Art, 226, 234
Hilton, Nicky, 214
Hilton, Paris, 214
Holland, Norman N., 190, 260n40
Hollywood Television Theatre, 250n91
hooks, bell, 8, 98, 253n6
Hooks, Robert: *Day of Absence*, 31–32, 53–55; *Happy Ending*, 31–32, 35, 53–55
Howard, Ron: *Apollo 13*, 229

Hoyt, Austin, 61
Hughes, Howard, 262n68

Institute of Contemporary Art, 119
institutional dramaturgy, 31, 33, 58, 73, 80
interpretive communities, 190, 269n69
invisibility black, 39, 40; *The Bluest Eye*, 82, 84, 86, 105, 116; whiteness, 22, 81, 83, 105, 227

Jackson, Blanket, 157
Jackson, Janet, 148, 149, 150, 151, 152
Jackson, Jesse, 192, 201, 202
Jackson, John L., Jr., 178, 204–5, 272n27
Jackson, La Toya, 262n73
Jackson, Michael, 27, 118, 119, 161, 162, 241n22, 260n40, 262n73, 263n76; alien, 262n68; autopsy, 260n44; *Black or White*, 141; corporeal performativity, 136–48; death, 262n70; hair, 260n46; HIStory, 153; *HIStory II*, 153; *Men in Black II*, 150; *Moonwalker*, 261n58; reiterations of the makeover, 148–54; relationship with Madonna, 263n81; *Remember the Time*, 143; *Smooth Criminal*, 143, 154; *Speed Demon*, 143; *Thriller*, 140, 142–43; ultimate makeover, 154–60; vitiligo, 260n44
Jackson, Paris, 156, 157–58
Jackson, Prince, 157
James, David E., 262n74
John F. Kennedy Center for the Performing Arts, 242n24
Johnson, E. Patrick, 5–6, 8, 189; *Appropriating Blackness*, 6
Johnson, Robert L., 192
Jones, LeRoi, 54, 245n2; *Dutchman*, 17, 31; "The Revolutionary Theatre," 18
Juarez, 20

Kabakov, Ilya: *The Man Who Flew into Space from His Apartment*, 233, 234, 276n12
Kahn, Michael, 17
Kant, Immanuel: *Critique of Judgment*, 245n58
Kasher, Steven: *The Civil Rights Movement*, 1
Kaufman, Philip: *The Right Stuff*, 229
Kennedy, Adrienne, 245n2; *Funnyhouse of a Negro*, 4, 31, 104, 116, 244n44, 244n48, 244n50, 246n34, 248n62; enacting

Kennedy, Adrienne (continued)
   whiteness in *Funnyhouse of a Negro*, 15–24, 25, 27, 47, 183, 185; *The Owl Answers*, 17–18
Kennedy, John F., 60–61, 243n36. See also John F. Kennedy Center for the Performing Arts
Kennedy, Randall, 168
Keyssar, Helene, 244n54
King, Martin Luther, Jr. 60, 64, 66, 236; assassination, 264n14; "I've Been to the Mountaintop" speech, 229
King, Rodney, 119
Kintz, Linda, 244n50
KKK. See Ku Klux Klan
Krasner, David, 10; *Resistance, Parody, and Double Consciousness in African American Theatre*, 240n17
Kravitz, Lenny, 183
Krone, Gerald S., 55
Krupa, John J., 60
Kubrick, Stanley: *2001*, 229
Ku Klux Klan, 265n19, 266n26; theatrics as whiteface performance 42, 167, 171–76, 179, 192, 265n17, 265n24, 266n27
Kupferberg, Herbert, 44

LeBrock, Kelly, 257n7
Lee, Spike: *This Is It*, 160
Lhamon, W. T., Jr., 12, 28, 184
Life, 44
linguistic whiteface, 24, 28; versus presumed aural whiteness, 213–15
Litwack, Leon F., 198
Lloyd, David, 245n58
Löfgren, Lotta M., 17
Long Warf (Theatre), 255n74
Lott, Eric, 12, 141, 147

Mack, Ron, 32
Madonna, 158–60, 263n81
Magritte, René, 153, 262n71; *The Son of Man*, 152
Malcolm X, 123, 124, 126, 129, 250n88, 257n12, 258n21; *The Autobiography of Malcolm X*, 250n88, 258n18
Marshall, C. K., 69, 250n92
Maurice, Alice, 211, 274n53

McAllister, Marvin: *Day of Absence*, 42, 246n17; postsoul, 276n17; stage European, 241n20; *White People Do Not Know How to Behave at Entertainments Designed for Ladies and Gentlemen of Colour*, 241n19; *Whiting Up*, 10, 11, 241n19
McCain, Demetria: "A 'Day without a Mexican' Déjà Vu," 252n114
McCain, John, 268n59, 268n62
McClinton, Marion, 76–77
McQueen, Butterfly, 220; *Gone with the Wind*, 275n66
McWhorter, John, 207–8
Meek, Russell, 63–67
Mercer, Kobena, 120, 132, 140, 142–43
Million Man March, 76, 77, 252n110
mimicry, 101, 240n17. See also racial mimicry; transracial mimicry
minstrelsy, 10–11, 19, 241n22. See also blackface minstrelsy; whiteface minstrelsy
Molette, Carlton: *Day of Absence*, 50, 247n55
Morgan, Edward P., 55, 58, 59, 68, 69–70
Morgenstern, Joe, 220, 275n66
Morrison, Toni, 8; *The Bluest Eye*, 26–27, 80–115, 117, 162, 254n48, 255n72, 255n74; adaption of *The Bluest Eye*, 107–16
Morsell, John, 71
Motorola, 215
Motown, 138, 260n37
Munch, Edvard: *The Scream*, 153, 262nn73–74, 263n76; *The Shriek*, 263n76
Muñoz, José Esteban: *Disidentifications*, 245n13, 269n68

NAACP. See National Association for the Advancement of Colored People
Nader, Ralph, 201–3
National Association for the Advancement of Colored People (NAACP), 71, 119, 257n12
National Civil Rights Museum, 119
National Educational Television, 55, 249n71
National Visual Artists Guild, 119
naturalized whiteface, 24, 27, 125, 136, 137, 139, 141, 148, 150, 157, 161
Neal, Larry: "The Black Arts Movement," 18, 247n50, 271n12

Neal, Mark Anthony, 203
NEC. *See* Negro Ensemble Company
Negro Ensemble Company (NEC), 55, 73, 74, 245n7, 249nn70–71
Negro Ensemble Theater, 72, 250n80
Neighborhood Health Plan, 215
New Museum of Contemporary Art, 119
New Republic, 248n68
The New Yorker, 44
New York Herald Tribune, 44
New York Times, 16, 32, 43, 44, 53, 54, 56, 70, 71, 215, 220, 226, 251n105
New York Times Magazine, 178
nonconforming whiteface, 7, 24, 28, 100, 101, 104, 157, 162, 171, 173, 179

Obama, Barack, 5, 26, 200, 201, 202–3, 205, 268n59, 268n62
Obama, Michelle, 197
Obie Award, 15, 31, 73, 246n34, 248n62
O'Connor, Richard: *The Cactus Throne*, 244n46, 244n48
Office Depot, 215
Omi, Michael, 164
one-drop rule, 177, 178, 185, 189, 256n30
optic whiteface, 24, 26, 48, 52, 53, 72, 185, 228, 231

Pabst, Naomi, 189
Pagel, David, 259n30
Pao, Angela, 221, 275n69
Parks, Suzan-Lori: *The Death of the Last Black Man*, 259n30
Parsons, Elaine Frantz, 171, 172
Patraka, Vivian: "Binary Terror and Feminist Performance," 147
PBL. *See* Public Broadcast Laboratory
PBS. *See* Public Broadcasting System
performative articulation, 273n51
Perry, Lincoln Theodore Monroe, 275n66
Peterson, Louis, 54
Pettit, Tom, 59, 60
The Phantom Menace, 220–1
Phelan, Peggy, 129, 200, 224
Philip Morris USA, 215
Pinder, Jefferson, 26; *Afro-Cosmonaut/Alien (White Noise)*, 29, 225–37, 262n69; postblack expressions, 230–37

Pius Ix (pope), 20
Plowshares Theatre, 109, 255n74
Poe, Edgar Allen, 244n48
Pollock, Jackson, 152, 153
Pope, S. W., 267n46
postraciality, 5, 26, 29, 235–36
postsoul, 236, 276n17
Powell, Colin, 187–88, 268n59, 268n62
presumed aural whiteness, 24–25, 28, 83, 196–206, 222; versus linguistic whiteface, 213–15
Prideaux, Tom, 44
Prince, Jocelyn: "The Politics of Lydia Diamond's Adaptation of Toni Morrison's *The Bluest Eye*," 111
production dramaturg, 12–14, 242n26
Proehl, Geoffrey S., 14; *Toward a Dramaturgical Sensibility*, 242n25
Public Broadcasting System (PBS), 30, 248n56, 257n13; *Frontline*, 167, 264n12
Public Broadcast Laboratory (PBL), 26, 30, 53, 55–63, 66, 67, 68, 69, 70–71, 72, 73, 74, 247n50, 249n71, 249n77, 249n79, 250n82, 250n91

racechange, 140, 260n45
racial absolutes, 19, 21, 163
racialized timbre, 208, 209
racial madness, 116, 256n86
racial mimicry, 25, 173
racial projects, 5, 164–65, 239n3
Radigan, Joseph, 60
Rasmussen, Birgit Brander, 253n4
regulated improvisation, 7, 239n10
Rice, Condoleezza, 187–88
Richards, Sandra L., 87
Rickford, John R., 270n5
Roach, Joseph, 241n19
Robeson, Paul, 121–23, 124, 125–26, 129, 257nn12–13, 258n15
Robinson, Bill "Bojangles": *Just Around the Corner*, 96; *The Little Colonel*, 96; *The Littlest Rebel*, 96; *Rebecca of Sunnybrook Farm*, 96
Robinson, Eugene, 188
Roediger, David R., 8
Roeg, Nicolas: *The Man Who Fell to Earth*, 229

INDEX

Rolle, Esther, 32
Russell, Carlos, 74, 75, 252n110

SAE. *See* Standard American English
Scanlan, Robert, 17
Schneider, Rebecca, 147
Schuyler, George, 130
Sharpton, Al, Jr., 156, 157, 159, 192
Showroom Mama Gallery, 226
Shuker, Greg, 61
signifyin(g), 6, 12, 19, 93, 119, 214, 239n6
Sleet, Moneta, 239n2
Smith, Bailey, 172
Smith, Cherise, 1–2, 239n2
Smith, Mark M.: *How Race Is Made*, 206, 207
Smith, Michael, 43, 44
Smithsonian Institution, 119
Smithsonian National Portrait Gallery, 226
sounding black, 270n8
sounding white, 25, 194–224
sound of ethnic differences, 269n1. *See also* English sounding; sounding black; sounding white
stage Europeans, 10, 241nn19–20
Standard American English (SAE), 197, 199–200, 203, 205, 206, 270n5, 271n22
Steppenwolf Theatre Company: *The Bluest Eye*, 106, 107, 111, 255n72
Stokes, Carl, 61, 62, 271n19
Stoltzfus, Curtis, 233
Studio Museum, 119, 226, 236

Taft, Seth, 61, 62
Taft, William Howard, 61
Taubman, Howard, 16, 43, 44
Teer, Barbara Ann, 32
Temple, Shirley, 86, 97, 98, 99–100, 103, 254n35, 254n52; *Just Around the Corner*, 96; *The Little Colonel*, 96; *The Littlest Rebel*, 96; *Rebecca of Sunnybrook Farm*, 96
Theater J, 242n24
Theatre Communications Group, 55
TheatreWorks, 242n24
theatrical whiteface, 9, 12, 23, 34, 39, 43, 162, 241n20; Chappelle, 183, 267n48
Thompson, Deborah, 19
timbre 206–12, 272n41, 273n46; racialized, 208, 209

Ting, Eric: *The Bluest Eye*, 255n74
tinted whiteface, 18, 19, 21, 24, 28, 163, 183, 184, 185
Tisdale, Daniel, 27, 139, 143, 145–46, 147–48, 157, 161, 256n1, 258n21, 259n30; "after" images, 128, 260n33; *The Black Museum*, 119, 259n30; "The Last African American," 259n30; *Malcolm X*, 121, 123, 126, 128, 135; performative palimpsests, 119–30; *Post Plantation Pop*, 120–21, 145, 257n8; *Robeson*, 121, 124, 128; *Sign of the Times*, 120–21, 257n7; *Transitions, Inc.* 27, 118, 120, 130–37, 141, 162, 259n30
Tough, Paul, 178, 179, 266n38
transracial mimicry, 11, 19, 240n17
Trilling, Lionel, 204
True Value, 215
Tyson, Lois, 269n69

University of Maryland, 102, 225, 255n74

van Campen, Cretien, 210–11
Village Voice, 43, 44

Wadsworth Athenaeum Museum, 226
Walker, Kara, 110
Walker, Kent, 167, 169, 170, 175, 179, 180
Ward, Douglas Turner
  "American Theater," 54
  Brotherhood, 245n7
  Day of Absence, 26, 30–79, 80, 245n7, 246n35, 247n50, 250n80, 251n107, 252n114
    Chicagoans speak (a black-white dialogue), 63–68
    doll-like imagery, 100
    Florida A&M University, 50
    lighting, 247n54
    mayoral campaigns of 1967, 58–63
    "Notes on Production," 249n78
    persistent presence, 74–79
    Public Broadcast Laboratory, 53–58
    televising, 68–74
    thematic riffs on whiteness, 38–53
    University of Michigan, 50
    whiteface, 185, 246n17, 247n55
  Happy Ending, 31, 32, 33, 34, 35, 36, 37–38, 53, 58, 73, 245n7, 246n35

Warhol, Andy, 119, 127, 152, 153, 260n33, 262n71, 262n74
Washington Post, 55, 70, 76, 77, 188, 226
Wayans brothers: *White Chicks*, 214
Wendt, George: *Cheers*, 143, 144
West, Cornell, 251n107
West, Shearer, 120
Westin, Av, 57, 71
Wexler, Bridget, 180
Wexler Home for the Blind, 180
WGHB-TV, 56
whiteface, 1, 3, 4, 5, 9–11. *See also* linguistic whiteface; naturalized whiteface; nonconforming whiteface; optic whiteface; theatrical whiteface; tinted whiteface
whiteface minstrelsy, 10, 11, 213, 241n19
Whitman Sisters, 240n17
Whitney Museum of American Art, 119
Williams, Patricia J., 220, 221
Willis, Susan, 139, 141, 254n35, 261n58
Wilson, August: "The Ground on Which I Stand," 54–55, 248n68; *King Hedley*, 241n36
Wilson, Pete, 252n115
Wilson-Brustein debate, 248n68

Winant, Howard, 164
Wise, Tim, 8
Wolfe, George C.: *Bring in 'da Noise, Bring 'da Funk*, 254n52; *The Colored Museum*, 259n30
Women's Wear Daily, 45
Wood, Jacqueline, 19, 244n44
Woods, Tiger, 181, 182–83, 189, 267n46, 268n62
Wray, Matthew, 8
WVIZ-TV, 56

Yale Drama School, 222
Yale University, 75, 251n107
Yockey, Francis Parker: *Imperium*, 178
Yoplait, 215
Young, Harvey: *Embodying Black Experience*, 6–7; "The Politics of Lydia Diamond's Adaptation of Toni Morrison's *The Bluest Eye*," 111
Young Playwrights Theatre, 242n24

Zacheta National Gallery, 226
Zapata, Emiliano, 257n7